THE
BREEDING

Avily Jerome

THE BREEDING
Published by Dragontail Press
P. O. Box 54550
Phoenix, AZ 85078

ISBN 978-1-7321879-1-7
Copyright © 2015 by Avily Jerome
Cover design by Kirk DouPonce, Dog Eared Design

Available in print from your local bookstore, online, or from the author.
For more information on this book and the author visit:
www.avilyjerome.com

Brought to you by Avily Jerome

Library of Congress Cataloging-in-Publication Data
Jerome, Avily
The Breeding/Avily Jerome 1st ed.

Printed in the United States of America.

For my family, the reason I do all I do.

ONE

The Eyes were back.

Watching. Mocking.

I thought I could escape the creatures, that here I'd be safe.

Yeah, that didn't work out so well. It was as if knowing I could sense their presence attracted them to me.

I pulled my knees to my chest, watching the slow, drug-induced shuffle of the other patients as they milled around the common room.

The air around me grew cold as one of the entities drew closer—the same one that had been torturing me since the accident. Sometimes there were others, but this one harassed me almost constantly.

Its presence prickled the back of my neck, making the hair stand on end, and sent a shiver down my spine. The bottom fell away from my stomach like when I'm on a roller coaster, plummeting down the steepest hill. The smell of sulfur burned my nose, and my tongue felt as if a layer of foul slime coated it.

The harsh glare of the fluorescent lights overhead seemed to dim, as though clouded over by a swarm of locusts, except they didn't exist. The darkness was only perceptible to me, as the Eyes drew closer. I'd learned not to turn and look. I couldn't see it anyway, and looking only amused the thing—I could feel its mirth echoing in my head—and made me look crazy.

Well, crazier.

I wished I were crazy. Being crazy would've been better than... whatever I was.

The Eyes loomed right behind me. This close, I could sense some of its emotions. Curious, on the surface, at least. But underneath, a sense of seething hatred always lingered.

4

No, not hatred.

Malice. From the depths of its soul—if it had one—burned a need to hurt me. Not for any personal vendetta, but just for the sake of hurting me.

Something tickled the back of my neck, like it was breathing on me.

I cringed.

It laughed.

I'm not sure how I knew it was laughing, but I did.

Goosebumps raised on my arms.

Its nearness smothered me with irrational dread. My fingers dug into the orange plastic that covered the thinly padded chair I sat in. I gulped back my fear, trying desperately to keep it from drowning me.

"Here you are, Jacqueline."

I jumped and looked up.

A rotund nurse hovered over me. Her starched white uniform, reminiscent of the stark, bleached walls, pulled across her ample bosom and gaped just enough for me to catch an unwelcome glimpse of her peach-colored grandma-bra.

"It's just Jack," I said.

The nurse, Gretchen, handed me a little plastic cup with my medication and a paper cup half-filled with tepid water. A patronizing smile stretched across her broad face. "Just take your pills, Jacqueline."

"It's still Jack."

Gretchen gave me her best patronizing smile. Apparently checking myself into this place meant I must have forgotten my own name preferences.

I returned her condescending smirk and sniffed the water. It smelled of chemicals, like this room. Antiseptics and medications and people with no personal hygiene, with a layer of Gretchen's knock-off-designer perfume permeating everything. I grimaced and downed the cocktail of pills.

The thing behind me, the Eyes, whatever it was, cackled. I could hear what it said as clearly as if it had spoken aloud, its voice like fingernails on a chalkboard. *Do you really think that's going to help? I'm not a hallucination. Trying to block me with pills is even more absurd than checking yourself into a mental institution to escape. You were a respected detective once. Look at you now. Pathetic.*

"Gretchen," I said.

Her white tennis shoes squeaked against the linoleum as she turned to face me.

"I'd like to make another appointment with Dr. Campbell. I don't think this medication is helping."

Gretchen gave a curt nod before marching to her next patient.

The hair on the back of my neck stood on end as the Eyes, emanating loathing, whispered in my ear.

You'll never get away from me.

TWO

Dr. Campbell gazed at me over wire-rimmed glasses. "Tell me about what you're seeing."

I shook my head. "I'm not seeing anything."

"What you're hearing, then."

I gritted my teeth. Had he listened to a word I'd said over the last month? "I'm not really hearing. It's more like… sensing. There are these, I don't know, creatures of some sort. They—they smell. Like rotten eggs and burning hair."

"You can smell them?"

I curled my feet under me on the faded blue, plush chair and stared at the numerous framed degrees Dr. Campbell displayed on the wall behind his desk. I wondered if he'd gotten them off the internet, for all the good he was doing.

That wasn't really fair, though. I just didn't know how to describe the sensations.

"No, not exactly. If I breathe, I can smell the pine cleaner they use on the floor, the disinfectant that they use to wipe the tables, medications, body odor. But the creatures—it's like I'm smelling them, but not with my nose. Like, I know the smell is there, but I'm smelling it with my mind, not my physical body."

He jotted something on his notepad without even looking up at me. "Uh-huh. What else?"

"I can feel them watching me. They want to hurt me."

"How do you know they want to hurt you? Is it because you want to hurt yourself?"

Was he kidding? For crying out loud, I *wasn't* suicidal! "I don't know. I can just feel it when they glare at me. And when they talk to me."

"They talk to you? And you can hear them."

I paused, not sure if he believed any of this or if he was just humoring me. "It's like when I smell them. I know I'm not hearing them with my physical ears, but I understand what they're saying in my mind perfectly clearly."

"I see."

"Look, Doc, I know how this works. I'm a cop. I've dealt with my share of crazy. And I know about schizophrenia. I know the symptoms include seeing and hearing and smelling things that no one else does, and hanging on to delusions even when people can prove they're false. I get it."

I pulled at a thread on the couch. "But it doesn't make these… creatures feel less real. Anyway, I don't think I'm explaining it well. I just know the sensations are completely real to me."

"And the medication isn't helping?"

"No. If anything, it's getting worse. Not to mention the side effects make me feel like I'm going crazy in all new ways."

"Okay. I'm going to add another anti-psychotic, and we'll add something to help counter the side effects. Sound good?"

I clenched my teeth. Great. More meds.

I considered diving across the desk and shoving my meds down his stupid throat, but instead I shrugged. "You're the expert."

"Great. Let's check back in a day or two and see how you're doing then, shall we?" He smiled. The same patronizing smile Gretchen used. It was beginning to piss me off.

I nodded. What choice did I have? I had to get rid of the Eyes, and if more meds were what it took, then I'd try every medication in the book.

I left his office and wandered back to the common area.

My hair stood on end and a chill popped the goosebumps on my arm into existence.

The Eyes laughed. *How did it go?*

Clenching my hands to keep them from shaking, I marched toward my favorite table.

"Jacqueline, you have a visitor," Gretchen announced.

Nice. Something to distract me.

I followed Gretchen's rolling hips toward the visitors' lounge, safely away from the rec room at the end of a long hall. They don't like to let the normal people too close to the crazies.

9

Gretchen held the heavy door for me to walk through into the bright lemon-colored room.

I thought there was some theory that yellow was supposed to be sunshiny and refreshing, but that much yellow made my head hurt. The smell of medication and antiseptics paled slightly beneath the overpowering stench of an artificially flavored cherry blossom air freshener.

My headache dissipated somewhat at the sight of the tall blonde woman standing in the lounge fidgeting with her purse. "Bridge!"

Bridget engulfed me in a rib-crushing hug. "It's great to see you, Jack."

I motioned toward one of the seventies-reject couches—olive colored diamonds against a burnt orange background. "Have a seat."

Flopping down across from her, I grinned again. "How are things on the outside?"

"They're good. Captain says hi. He says to hurry up and get sane 'cause we need you back on the force."

I laughed. It felt good. Refreshing. When was the last time I'd laughed?

The air grew cold, and the familiar tingling of my flesh and nausea that accompanied the presence of the Eyes hit me.

My teeth ground against each other as I struggled to keep the grin on my face, to listen to whatever it was that Bridget was saying.

"...really interesting, because he leaves a calling card, like something out of a bad movie, you know? That only makes him easier to find. Anyway, Captain's got just about everyone available working on it. Like we don't have anything better to do than chase a cat burglar, right?"

"Seriously," I agreed.

The Eyes hissed in my ear. *She is something special. Look at those legs!*

What the... was it talking about *Bridget?*

"So then Eric says to me, 'the only reason you're still in this department is because the captain likes watching you.' Can you believe it?"

"What a jerk," I murmured.

The creature snickered at my discomfort. *You thought you'd be safe here, but you're not. And now you've led us right to her. He'll be so pleased with the treasure I found him.*

"I know, right?" Bridget yammered on as if I were actually involved in the conversation, but I couldn't hear anything she said with that thing hissing in my ear.

Oh, yes, he has big plans. Wait until you see what's in store for her.

I clenched my fists, trying to block out the grating, scraping sound of the voice that echoed in my head.

"Jack, are you okay?"

I managed a smile. "Yeah. They're changing my medication. The side effects are brutal."

Bridget nodded, as if that explanation made perfect sense. "So when are they going to let you out of here? I hate coming in here."

"Well, I checked myself in, so technically I can check out any time I want, but until I get my meds figured out..."

"Jack."

"I know what you're going to say."

She said it anyway. "You're hiding again. You always do this. You wouldn't even have made detective if Trent hadn't sent in the application for you. And it took him putting a down payment on the venue for you to even set a date. But you can't hide in here forever."

"I'm not hiding." I scowled at her.

"Right. Of course." She sighed. "Jack... I'm not supposed to tell you anything, but... I think you should know. They found a body."

My heart dropped through the floor. "A body?"

Bridget nodded. "Positively identified through dental records. One of the ones from the list."

"Where? How did she..." I couldn't finish.

"In the desert west of town. Forensics is still working on it. It was bad... decayed way more than it should've been in that amount of time. And they have all your notes, but there's a lot that makes no sense."

My throat tightened. I blinked my eyes against the tears that tried to escape.

"We need you. This was your case. You know all the things that are between the lines of the reports."

"I can't." My voice came out in a hoarse whisper.

She nodded, but didn't say anything more. She always seemed to know just how far to push and exactly when to back off. Ever since the academy, she could read me like no one else. I appreciated that about her. "Just get better soon, 'kay?"

"I'm working on it."

"Great. Well, I gotta run. Great to see you, Jack." She stood, unfolding legs that stretched on to forever before being topped by a tiny skirt.

Shoving down a twinge of jealousy—I'd never be able to get away with an outfit like that—I stood and hugged her. "Thanks for coming, Bridge. Give my love to everyone at work."

"Will do," Bridget promised as she left.

A gloating hiss followed her out. *Yes, he'll have great fun with that one.*

"Don't you dare touch her," I said aloud.

Or what? It cackled.

"I swear, I'll..."

"What's that, Honey?" Nelly, Gretchen's second-in-command, came into the visitor's lounge.

"Nothing."

"Your friend gone?"

I nodded.

"Good. It's just about dinner time. Chicken fried steak tonight!"

Oh, goody. Slabs of rubber, coated with a pasty bread product and covered with a salty gray goo that was supposed to pass for gravy. My favorite.

I followed Nelly to the cafeteria, but I passed on the chicken fried plastic and stuck with something that resembled green beans.

Silly fool.

The hair on my arms raised, the sulfur smell almost made me hurl.

Bridge was right about one thing. This place sucked.

THREE

I sat in the chair in Dr. Campbell's office the next morning, my legs curled underneath me, and plucked at a string coming loose from the upholstery. His cologne was stronger today than usual. Cop senses kicked in, and I wondered whether he was hiding something or whether he was trying to impress someone.

Focus, Jack. He just asked what you want to talk about today. "I don't know where to start," I muttered.

Oh yes, more therapy. Why don't you up your medication again? It worked so well the last time.

I cringed at the metallic scraping sound of the voice. The Eyes were present more often than not now.

Dr. Campbell smiled indulgently. "Why don't you tell me about when you first started hearing the voices?"

I decided not to bother explaining the sensation again. "It was right before... well, kinda during the accident."

He raised an eyebrow. "You were able to discern voices in your head as you were plummeting over the side of a bridge?"

I shook my head. How could I explain? "Not exactly. It was right before the accident. And I saw them then, too. The creatures. Physically, not like now when I only sense them."

"You saw them? What did they look like?"

I wrapped my arms tighter around my chest as the memory washed over me.

Black night. Rain pelted down, making it almost impossible to see the car in front of us.

The red and blue swirling lights overhead reflected against the torrent, giving it an eerie disco feel. I clutched the edge of my seat with one hand and my gun with the other.

The car in front of us fishtailed on the slick road.

Trent grinned. "We're stopping Armageddon."

Taking a deep breath, I pulled myself back to reality and turned to Dr. Campbell. "Trent had been tracking him for months. He was onto something big, but he didn't tell me much about that case. Something about human trafficking and child prostitution."

Dr. Campbell's face blanched. So he did have some feeling, after all.

The Eyes cackled with glee. Its pleasure rolled over me as distinctly as I usually felt its malice. It was all I could do not to vomit all over Dr. Campbell's ugly-ass chair.

I ignored the Eyes and focused on Dr. Campbell. "Yeah, I know. Sick. So we were trying to bring him in for questioning. We'd been on his tail for almost ten minutes, closing in, pushing him toward the roadblock up ahead, when suddenly the sky opens—"

"The sky opened?"

Crap. Now he was really going to think I'd lost it. "Yeah."

"What exactly do you mean by that?"

I sighed. "Have you ever seen, like, a sci-fi movie when they're jumping through a portal of some kind? And there's like this slash of light, then the streak widens and you can see the alternate dimension on the other side?"

Dr. Campbell's eyes grew even wider as he nodded.

"It was pretty much like that, only the only thing I could see on the other side was blackness and the... things."

"What kind of things?"

What kind of things, indeed? I wish I knew. "Monsters. Human in shape—you know, two arms, two legs, and whatever—but huge. And... twisted."

"Twisted?"

"I don't know how to describe it. Their eyes are yellow, but somehow also dark, like hate is their only emotion, and their lips twist in a snarl over gleaming fangs. Their skin is black—charred, not skin tone—and their claws drip with blood. Like gargoyles come to life, only worse."

The Eyes looking over my shoulder erupted in hateful laughter. *He doesn't believe you. He thinks you're crazy.*

Dr. Campbell gave me a reassuring smile. "So the sky opened and these monsters came out. Did Trent see them?"

15

I shook my head. "I don't think so."

He nodded, as if he'd expected that.

Of course. Trent wasn't the insane one.

He pushed his glasses further up his nose. "Okay. What happened next?"

"Out of nowhere, this other car hops the curb and crashes into us. We go spinning out of control, over the embankment, and into the Central Arizona Project river."

"Mm-hmm. Anything else?"

Well, I was in over my head as it was. I might as well tell him everything. "Yeah. The entire time, I could hear the monsters screaming. Really hear them, not just in my head, like now."

"What were they screaming?"

"'Kill the cop.'"

"Jack, may I say something?"

Well, duh! Why the hell else am I telling you all this crap? You're a freaking doctor—yes, tell me something! "Of course."

"It seems to me like you had some sort of dissociative episode. As you were crashing, your mind took a break. It invented this idea of monsters to help you cope with losing Trent."

I rubbed my hands over my arms. It sounded plausible. In fact, it was probably the most reasonable explanation for what I experienced. Nothing else made sense.

Most of our sessions had involved me describing what I was feeling and Dr. Campbell trying to get me to talk about my feelings and how my emotions about what happened were affecting me. The same stupid psychobabble, over and over, like he was trying to get me to diagnose myself and figure out on my own why this was happening. Now, after how many weeks, he piped up with an actual answer? At least it was something.

Dissociative episode. That worked. I could deal with that. At least if I knew what it was, I could figure out how to get past it.

But, even as I turned the idea over in my mind, I couldn't help thinking he was wrong. Maybe I should have been listening to the Eyes all along.

What if I wasn't crazy? What if these things were real?

FOUR

I put on my Thoughtful Face, the one I wear in the interrogation room when I'm playing Good Cop. "I think you're right, Doc."

Dr. Campbell raised an eyebrow. "Jack, I don't want you to agree with me just because I'm a doctor. I want you to really think about what I'm saying."

"I'm a police officer, Dr. Campbell. I'm trained to analyze a situation from every angle in a matter of seconds. Since the medication isn't working, that must mean it's not a chemical imbalance, right?"

He nodded slowly. "Perhaps."

"So, it must be something else. I need to stop hiding in here and face the fact that Trent—" My throat clenched. That, at least, was genuine. "Trent is gone, and he's not coming back."

"Good, Jack, good. I think we're making real progress. What do you say we increase your therapy schedule?"

I gave him a smile. I really didn't think therapy was going to get me very far, but it couldn't hurt. And who knew, it might actually help me face what happened and get rid of these hallucinations or whatever they were. And if they weren't hallucinations, well, I had to find out what they were, and I couldn't do that sitting in the mental ward, and getting Dr. Campbell's okay was the best way to get on with it. "That'd be great. While we're at it, can I get off this medication? It's not helping anyway, and the side effects are killing me."

***

After leaving Dr. Campbell's office, I sauntered down the hall feeling empowered—despite the nauseating presence of the creature hovering over my shoulder—for the first time in I didn't remember how long.

What was that? the Eyes spat.

The emotions I felt from it made me shudder with terror. I pushed the fear aside, burying it beneath growing determination as I made my way to my room.

As in the hallway, plain, bleached floors met stark white walls on every side. The only furnishings were a lumpy-mattressed bed and a rickety metal nightstand. The only decoration was a picture of Trent, sitting by my bed so I could look at him when I went to sleep.

Do you think therapy is going to help you any more than medication did?

"No," I answered aloud.

A flash of shock interrupted the waves of animosity pouring out from the creature. I knew it as clearly as if I could see its contorted features. Why was it surprised? It had been talking to me for ages. It knew I was hearing things. Was it surprised that I finally defied it?

If that was the case, good.

"I know you're real. And I'm done with you, with this place."

It hissed and laughed, but beneath the mocking flowed an undercurrent of fear.

So, then, it could be intimidated.

And if it was afraid, there was probably a reason. It had a weakness, and that meant I could find it.

The air crackled. A sensation like a lightning storm made the air feel alive. My hair stood on end, tingling. The bottom dropped out of my stomach as I watched the air in front of me bend.

A fissure opened, like the one I saw the night Trent died, but more metaphysical than physical, like the Eyes were now. Another presence entered the room. Similar to the one that haunted me, but different. Worse.

The minion—and I suddenly realized it was a minion, next to this commanding presence—hanging around me was a shadow compared to this new one, vapor next to a solid wall.

All the sensations present when the Eyes were near also accompanied the new entity, but multiplied by about seven hundred. Chills made my body spasm, doubling me over. My stomach emptied all over the scuffed linoleum floor in my bedroom, and my muscles tightened into knots that would make a Boy Scout jealous. My legs wouldn't hold me up and I crumpled into the pile of vomit I'd just made.

You are doing as I ordered. Good. Keep her here.

I'm not sure how I knew it was the new one speaking, any more than I knew how to distinguish the Eyes from the other entities bouncing around the hospital. Like the one who haunted Larry, making him sit in the corner with a picture book and drool, or the one that seemed to be a part of Joan, making her scream and become outraged, no matter how many meds they pumped into her, every time someone touched her.

The Eyes—mine, I guess, since apparently I was its assignment—quivered before its superior. *She wants to leave.*

Something happened, something violent. The big one throttled mine, or in some way caused it to howl in pain and rage.

I knelt on the floor, trying to control my spasming body, forcing myself up out of the puddle of sick.

You will keep her here, the big one ordered. *Do whatever you have to do. I will not have her interfering with my plans.*

But, sir, she can hear us. She knows we're here, she knows what we're saying. How can I keep her here if she knows what I'm doing?

What do you mean she can hear us? How is that possible?

I don't know, but she knows. And not just in a schizophrenic way, like before. She's aware.

A streak of heat flamed across my face. My hand slapped involuntarily to my cheek, sending another flash of pain through me.

I pulled my hand away. Blood left a bright splotch on each of my fingertips. That had to be real. I knew delusions were powerful, that if I were schizophrenic I would see and feel things that weren't there, but I wouldn't see real blood, would I? I couldn't possibly be that far gone to think the searing pain in my cheek and the bright red wetness on my fingers was real if it wasn't.

There was no escaping the conclusion. This thing really was real. It was physical, even if I couldn't see it, and it had real claws that could really slice my face open. "I'm not staying here anymore. I'm getting out."

The big one turned to me. *You will do nothing. You will sit in your self-imposed cell and rot, human scum.*

A desire to obey swept over me, encompassing me like a fog. I didn't want to get out of the hospital, didn't want to find out more. What had I been thinking?

Oh, yes. I was sick. I needed to stay here.

The creature sent a wave of satisfaction my direction. He disappeared, sending a shimmer of electric impulses through the air, leaving me and the Eyes huddling away from the spot it vacated.

No one will believe you. You're insane. You'll be here forever, the Eyes smirked.

"No." I pushed through the fog that pressed against me, until I felt my own mind, my own will again. I glared into the air where I felt its presence. Mustering every ounce of will, every drop of fury to fuel a bravery I didn't feel, I spoke aloud to the monster. "I will hunt you down, and I will end you."

FIVE

"I'm good," I smiled at Dr. Campbell. I'd spent three days detoxing, cold turkey, from my meds. Gretchen kept giving me lowered doses, which I pretended to swallow, then flushed. Sitting here, in front of the good ol' doc, it took every ounce of self-control and some serious squeezing of the armrests on the ugly chair to not shake uncontrollably.

Worse, it took everything in me to ignore the hissing in my ear, to not rub the gooseflesh from my arms or shudder at the cold terror that gripped my heart. I focused on the ugly shag carpets, the puke-green walls in dire need of repainting, the chips in the once-fine mahogany desk—anything to keep my mind occupied as I delivered my lies. "It's like, once I realized it was all in my head, I could really start processing it. Then, when the hallucinations came back, I could push them away and stop listening, until they started leaving me alone."

I'd practiced that speech a thousand times, trying to make it sound natural.

Dr. Campbell's face was unreadable. His cheap cologne wafted across to me, increasing the churning in my stomach. I had no idea whether or not he believed me.

"And they're gone now?"

"Not completely. Sometimes, late at night, they come back and I can't get rid of them. And once, I was thinking about Trent, about our wedding… I couldn't get the voices to stop for a long time after that."

Dr. Campbell nodded. "Let's talk about that. How long were the two of you together?"

"Four years. Six months of that, we were engaged."

"When was the wedding going to be?"

"This coming April. We wanted it outdoors, so we planned to have it before it got too hot."

"How were the plans coming?"

I shrugged. "Pretty well."

An invisible claw traced its way down the back of my neck. I winced, biting back the cry that rose in my throat.

I expected blood to rise to the surface, waited for it to trickle down my spine. But the pain was all in my head, like the voice and the smells. Somehow, this one was different from the big one. It could affect me, but not physically. Interesting. And good—I couldn't afford another gaping wound. Dr. Campbell was already pretty suspicious of the cut on my face.

I forced my attention back to what he was asking. "And now that all those plans are cancelled, how do you feel?"

"It's hard," I admitted. "We were a great couple, you know? We hardly ever fought or anything."

He continued to gaze at me, unblinking. I hated when he did that. It was so unnerving.

Whatever. I still had to convince him of my sanity. "We always talked about being one of those couples that still holds hands and kisses when they're sixty."

Finally, a reaction. Just a small smile, but enough to make me think maybe he was buying it.

The secret to a good lie is adding enough truth to make it plausible. I always looked for the part that didn't quite match what I knew to be true when interrogating suspects, then exploited that hole in the narrative. No way was I letting him use the same trick on me. I told him as much of the truth about my feelings that he didn't notice what I omitted—namely, anything that would lead to talking about the creature that still hovered behind me.

Finally, he glanced at the clock. "We're out of time for today. I'll see you next time, Jack."

"Sure. See you next time."

***

"As soon as I'm out of here, I'm coming after you," I threatened the Eyes as it followed me to my room.

The creature's icy laugh in response sent a shudder racing through me. *And just how are you going to do that?*

Good question.

I had no idea.

But I thought I knew where to start. "I know that you're evil. Pure, unadulterated evil. So I'll start by looking for pure good."

Good and evil are social constructs with no real meaning. It tossed my own words back at me with a cackle.

Of course, I didn't really believe that. As a cop, I'd seen evil every day for years. But I did use that line as a convenient excuse to do whatever I wanted.

Still, it wasn't going to do any good to argue philosophy with a monster bent on torturing me. This was war, and right now it had the upper hand.

Time to rethink my strategy. "I'll start by getting out of here, and then... I don't have to tell you my plans, but I know there's a way, and I'm going to find it."

A wave of cold panic rushed out on top of the sense of loathing that the creature always emanated. It disappeared for an instant, its return accompanied by a sense of satisfaction.

The air did that ripple thing again, and the big one returned.

It grabbed my hand and pulled.

"Hey!" I tried to yank away, but the monster was too strong.

Its invisible claw scraped lengthwise against my wrist, opening the vein. Blood gurgled up over my wrist, splattering on the floor.

You'll have a hard time getting out of here if you're on suicide watch, it hissed.

Stupid thing didn't know me very well if it thought threatening me was going to make me back down. It just pissed me off.

And it pretty much just told me I needed to be out of here in order to find the way to kill it.

I grabbed my washcloth and slumped into the corner of my room, holding the cloth to my wrist, whimpering. Let it think it had me beat.

A wave of satisfaction rolled out from the big one and it disappeared. I held my wrist and counted up to one minute. When I was sure the big one wasn't coming back immediately, I jumped up and peered out my door. The hallway was empty.

I trotted down to the nurses' station. Gretchen sat at her computer, staring intently in the way that could only mean she was heavily invested in some game or another. I trotted down the hall, to the room of a paranoid schizophrenic with violent tendencies.

"Cal... They're inside," I said in a harsh whisper.

Cal turned around. I showed him my wrist. "I tried to stop them, but they're coming for you. You'd better hide."

I dashed down the hall and around the corner, and was just out of range of the nurses' station by the time Cal started screeching.

Gretchen scraped her chair along the linoleum and sighed. "What is it now?"

I ducked out of sight and waited for her to waddle out of the station, then tossed my bloody washcloth into the gap so the door didn't click shut.

Cal's screeching was distracting enough that she didn't notice. As soon as she was out of sight, I crept into the station and grabbed a handful of first aid supplies, then grabbed my washcloth, closed the door, and hurried back to my room.

By the time Gretchen got Cal settled down, I had bandaged up my wrist, cleaned the blood spatters from my floor, and tossed all traces of the incident, including the wash cloth, into the locked bio-waste bin outside the nurses' station.

SIX

"I want to go home," I informed Dr. Campbell at out next session, three days later.

I tucked my hands safely under long sleeves, hiding the half-healed scars on my wrists. I knew every trick in the book for hiding cutting.

"Do you really think you're ready for that?" Dr. Campbell asked.

I nodded. "I mean, I still want to come in for therapy and stuff, but I think being in here is making things harder in a way. I think when I'm home and able to focus on work, it will be better."

My hair stood on end as the Eyes screeched at Dr. Campbell. *Look at her wrists! Look at her wrists! She's cutting!*

Dr. Campbell stared at me. "Everything else okay?"

"Sure," I shrugged, hoping to look nonchalant.

"Anything you think I should know?"

My heart thudded against my chest. Blood rushed through my ears, deafening me. "Like what?"

"How are your wrists?"

What the—how did Dr. Campbell know to ask that? Had it heard the Eyes, somehow? Understood what it was saying? But how, without hearing it the way I heard it?

Then again, if he didn't hear it the way I did, maybe he didn't even know he'd heard something. Maybe he just figured that question was out of the blue. Maybe that was how those things worked when they were dealing with normal people.

Play it smooth, Jack.

I raised an eyebrow, like I had no idea what he was talking about. "Fine. Why?"

"Are you hurting yourself at all?"

My jaw fell to the ground. I picked it up, pretending my shock was for a different reason. "Of course not! What kind of question is that?"

Dr. Campbell shrugged. "I just want to make sure before I give my okay for you to leave." He paused. "Technically, you signed yourself in so you can sign yourself out, but—"

"I understand," I assured him. "And I do want your go-ahead. But I really feel like I'm ready."

Dr. Campbell nodded. "Well, as long as you agree to come in for therapy, let's say twice a week? I'll give my stamp of approval."

"Great." I tried to keep my grin from spreading too widely across my face as the Eyes snarled at Dr. Campbell.

That night, just as my eyes began to drift closed on my flat, standard-issue pillow for the last time, the big one came back with six or seven friends. Solid, physical ones, like him. Real monsters with real claws, real slavering jaws filled with vicious fangs.

The minion assigned to me hovered nearby, hollering in glee, as the big one barked orders at the others. One held my arms pinned to the sides of my head while another held my legs, and another clamped his hand over my mouth, claws digging into my flesh. Despite how I thrashed, my range of motion was limited to the few inches I could strain my torso up from the mattress.

The big one stood over me.

An electrical crackling split the dark air above my bed, a lightning storm against the dry, antiseptic atmosphere in the hospital. My breath came in short, quick gasps, my pulse thundering through me.

The air solidified into an unmovable mass of charred, scaly skin, set with glowing yellow eyes and gleaming teeth.

I couldn't breathe. It felt like he was sitting directly on top of my lungs, crushing the life out of me with his heavy, sulfuric presence.

Tears stung my eyes, hopelessness overwhelming me. I clenched my teeth, determined not to cry out, determined not to let them see my fear, determined not to alert the nurse on duty at the desk down the hall as they raked claws over me, digging trenches in my arms, legs, and chest, choking me, pulling my hair.

What seemed like hours later, the leader held up a clawed hand. *That is all we are authorized to do at this time.* He sounded angry at whoever gave the orders that he couldn't continue. The others hissed, malice and frustration rolling out in waves from them.

Don't get comfortable, Worm. I'm not done with you yet. In a flash of shimmering, crackling ions in the air, the monsters disappeared, all except for my assigned minion.

Muscles, bruised and swollen, ached as I pulled myself to the bathroom down the hall to shower away the blood from my torn flesh. How would I explain this one to Dr. Campbell?

I'd figure something out. No matter what, tomorrow I'd be home.

SEVEN

"Thanks for coming to get me, Bridge."

"No prob," Bridget grinned. "Captain pretty much begged me to take the time off. We're all excited for you to come back to work."

I stood at the front desk of the hospital, tapping my fingers on the faux granite, waiting for the head nurse to bring back the final paperwork for me to sign. Behind me, the Eyes seethed, but it was more than anger that pulsed out from it. It was fear.

You don't know what kind of mistake you're making. In here, you're safe. Protected. If you leave, my master will destroy you.

I gripped the edge of the desk. I'd picked a fight with Cal the night before, managing to make it look like I'd been the victim of random rage, in order to explain the extensive bruising. I said I wouldn't press charges if we could expedite the discharge process, but the Eyes was doing its best to keep me here.

Finally, the head nurse came back with a wheelchair. "Looks like you're all set. Have a seat and I'll take you out to your car."

"I don't need a wheelchair."

"Sorry. Regulations."

I rolled my eyes and plopped into the chair. It was better to just comply and get out of there than to argue about it.

When we finally got back to my apartment, Bridget carried the meager box of my stuff from the hospital inside. "Regulations," she grinned.

I glared at her, but couldn't really fault her for the teasing. I'd have done the same thing to her.

30

The elegant feel of my modernly-decorated apartment with its pale gray walls and leather furnishings, accented with wrought iron candle sconces on the walls, washed over me in a flood of nostalgia.

I flopped on my lush sectional couch, almost palatial after the torture devices that passed for furniture at the hospital, glad to be out of the still-hot October sun.

Trent's sock stuck up from between the cushions. He was such a slob!

My throat tightened. What would I do around here without his laundry to pick up?

I glanced up at Bridget, lounging in Trent's recliner. "Stay for dinner?" I begged.

"Of course." She smiled, her eyes sympathetic. She didn't ask. Didn't need to. She glanced at the stupid sock I still clutched and changed the subject to one of her trademark inanities to distract me. "So, I was thinking…"

The grating in my ears as the Eyes hissed threats at me never let up. I don't know why I thought it would give up after I left the hospital. The big one hadn't come back, but with the minion constantly by my side, I didn't doubt he'd return.

Claws traced the back of my neck, up and down my arms, and dug into the small of my back.

Bridget stopped chattering and stared at me.

I realized I was supposed to be responding to something she said. "Seriously?" I asked.

"I'm not even kidding," she gushed. "Tony Mancuso! He's so freaking hot! We're going out on Friday."

Rubbing the goosebumps from my arms, I stood and sauntered to the kitchen. "So, where are you going?"

"I don't know. He said something about the Biltmore."

"Nice!"

Staring up at me from the shelves in the fridge were boxes of moldy, left-over take-out and rotten vegetables. The smell was almost powerful enough to overwhelm the stench of sulfur that wafted from the creature by my side.

Almost.

"How long was I in the hospital, Bridge?"

"A little more than four weeks. Why?"

"My fridge is gross. There's nothing edible in here. Wanna go out?"

"Sure. So, anyway, Tony says…" she rambled on as we walked out to her car.

I slid into the passenger seat, stifling a yelp as the seat burned my leg below my shorts. Sometimes I hated Phoenix weather, but still, it beat shoveling six feet of snow out of a driveway in the winter. "Where do you want to go?"

"You pick," Bridget grinned. "You're the one who just got out of the looney bin."

"You have no idea what that institutional crap tastes like. I could kill for a good steak."

"Bill Johnson's?"

"Totally." For a second there, I'd managed to ignore the Eyes that bored into my skull.

Maybe I should try this conversation thing more often.

***

The Eyes refused to let me sleep that night. It hissed in my ears and clawed at my skin, the sensation no less painful for not leaving any marks. The few times I managed to doze off, I woke to stabbing pains on various parts of my body.

Crawling from bed, I stumbled to the bathroom. I glanced in the mirror at the tired, haggard face reflected there. When did I get so old? Had a month in an institution really made my eyes that baggy? My skin that splotchy?

Some of those weren't splotches—some were welts, still puffy and red from the attack the night before. "What did you do to me?" I asked aloud.

Yellow eyes appeared behind my reflection. Slitted, like cat's eyes, filled with hate and evil. All the air whooshed from my lungs, magnifying the thudding against my chest.

Whirling around, I searched the empty bathroom for any sign of the creature whose presence felt so tangible.

Nothing.

I glanced back in the mirror, but the Eyes were gone.

Tremors, beginning in my hands then spreading through every part of my body, consumed me until I couldn't stand. I collapsed to the floor. "What are you?" I choked.

The only answer was a malicious laugh, echoing in my head.

EIGHT

I went into the precinct, a few miles from my apartment complex in north Phoenix, first thing in the morning. This area was a little more upscale than further south, but still far from the posh areas heading east toward Scottsdale or the newer neighborhoods in the far outlying sections of the Valley.

The heavy aroma of strong coffee permeated the air, punctuated by greasy burgers and fries from a couple of desks. My heeled sandals clacked against the checkerboard floor. Damn, it felt good to be home.

"Jack!" Cheerful greetings rang out around me.

"Man, is it good to see you again! When you coming back to work?"

I smiled at the lanky sergeant who grinned at me beneath large, brown, puppy-dog eyes. "Hey, Lee. Soon, I hope. I'm here to see the captain to talk about it."

A heavy hand clapped against my shoulder. "Good to see you, Jack."

I turned to see a tall, broad-shouldered officer smiling down at me. "Thanks, Ken. It feels good to be here."

Ken took it hard when Trent and I started dating, but his eyes told me he was truly sympathetic about what had happened.

"Okay, guys, give her some room to breathe." Bridget shouldered her way through the mass of uniformed bodies. "Captain's waiting to see you."

She pulled me by the hand.

"You okay?" she asked once we were out of earshot. "You look terrible."

Apparently my meticulous make-up job wasn't as camouflaging as I'd hoped. "Yeah, I didn't sleep well last night."

She eyed me like she wondered if I should've stayed at the hospital. "What happened?"

"Nothing. It was just weird, you know? Being there without Trent."

Her eyes softened. "Yeah."

She rapped at the door to the captain's office.

"Come in."

I never would have believed I could miss that rough voice, but the sound flooded me with warmth. I couldn't wait to get back to work.

Bridget pushed the door open and waited for me to go in.

"Hey, Captain."

"Good to see you, Jack. Have a seat."

I settled into one of the bright red, cushioned chairs positioned across from his desk and folded my hands in my lap.

Captain Holsinger shuffled a couple pages on his cluttered desk. "Bridget tells me you want to come back to work."

"Yes, sir. As soon as possible."

"You sure you're ready?"

I nodded.

Sharp pain pierced my side as the Eyes tried to dissuade me. I stifled a wince.

He raised an eyebrow. "You okay?"

"Fine. Cramp. But I'm totally ready to come back to work."

He looked skeptical, but gave me a quick nod. "I'll have a chat with your doctor, and we'll get the paperwork ironed out. I'll give you a holler when I get you back on the schedule."

"Thanks, Captain."

I rose to leave, Bridget following me out. "You'll be back in no time," she encouraged. "You headed home now?"

"No, I've got some things I have to do first."

"Like what?"

"Well, I need some groceries. I spent half the night cleaning out my fridge since I couldn't sleep anyway. Then I thought I might—" I paused.

"Yeah?" Bridget urged.

"I need to stop by Trent's grave."

Bridget's crystal blue eyes filled with sympathy. "Do you want company?"

I shook my head. "I need to go alone."

She nodded. "I understand. I'll come by after I get off work to check on you, okay?"

"Thanks, Bridge." I didn't tell her that I would also be retracing our steps, going back over everything Trent and I had done the night he died, looking for answers.

I slid into my forest-green Tacoma and eased out onto the street. Almost immediately, sharp claws slashed at my eyes, blinding me. It was trying to get me killed!

Honking horns blared at me as my truck veered between lanes. I blinked, struggling to see, but the attack continued. Panic welled up, sending my heart leaping, as I searched through blurred vision for the nearest parking lot. I swerved into an empty space, shifted into park, and grabbed a napkin from my glove box to dab my running eyes.

The emotions I felt from the Eyes contained a combination of triumph and pure hatred.

"You think this is going to stop me?" I screamed. "I'm not giving up!"

I stepped from the truck and slammed the door.

Too late, I realized I'd locked my keys—and my phone—inside.

Screw it. Bridget had a key to my apartment, and Trent's keys were in the box of his things on the desk in my home office. I needed to find a place with a phone so I could call Bridget to come rescue me.

Sweat soaked every inch of my body as the sun seared my flesh. The smell of the city—asphalt and garbage and emissions from the cars that raced by—seeped through the ever-present rotten-egg, sulfur smell that emanated from the creature by my side.

I scanned the parking lot I'd ended up in. Why was it so empty on a weekday?

I rubbed my eyes and tried to make out the sign. "Saving Grace Fellowship."

A church, then. There ought to be a phone in there somewhere, right? I started toward the cluster of buildings that sat side-by-side at the center of the expansive property.

The Eyes clawed at my ankles now, its claws neither physical nor ethereal, trying to make me fall. I stumbled on, determined, especially since it was pretty obvious just how pissed it made the creature.

I took another step toward the main building of the church, a pristine steeple adorned with a white cross towering above a tan-painted chapel. Two other buildings—offices or classrooms, I assumed—stood to either side of the main building.

I stepped from the parking lot to the sidewalk.

The Eyes screeched, hissed, and cursed, blocking out every other sound. Its flurried attacks, claws and teeth pummeling me, drove me back, away from the church.

The sky opened and the creature's superior emerged. It held me by the neck with its huge fist, claws—physical, penetrating claws—digging into the sides of my throat.

Emotions tumbled out of the minion. Anger and malice, as usual, but threaded with an undercurrent of... was that *fear*? Was it afraid of me? Of its commander? Or of the church?

My apologies, Dionysius, the Eyes groveled.

So the big one had a name. Good to know.

You almost let her in there, Dionysius screamed at the Eyes. *You're lucky I got here in time.*

My eyes traveled to the church. It was as though I saw it through a curtain of flies, like fresh air was just on the other side, and if I could get there, I'd be free, but I couldn't quite reach.

Dionysius's fingers tightened around my throat, crushing the air from me. I gasped, trying desperately to suck life-saving oxygen into my lungs, with no luck.

Darkness clouded my vision. My legs buckled beneath me. As the world around me became fuzzy, then black, Dionysius told his minion not to let me come near the church again.

NINE

I woke in my apartment with Bridget standing over me, dripping cool water on my forehead. "What happened?"

"Heat stroke, best I can tell. You collapsed outside a church, and the pastor found your truck in the parking lot. He unlocked it and found your phone, and since I was the last person you called, he called me."

"How did he unlock it? I accidentally locked the keys in."

Bridget shrugged. "He didn't say. He was just trying to find someone who knew you. He wanted to call 911, but I knew you'd be pissed, so I swore I'd take care of you. Drink some water." She shoved a cup toward my lips.

I gulped it down, though I knew dehydration wasn't my problem.

The Eyes—and Dionysius—really wanted to keep me away from that church. Maybe someone there knew something that could help me.

"So, the captain doesn't want you coming back until you're well. Are you planning to collapse on a regular basis?"

Yes. You'll never be free of me, the Eyes hissed.

I chuckled, trying to lighten the atmosphere. "No. I'm okay. I just haven't had enough to drink today, and going off my medication is dehydrating me. Grab me a vitamin water and I'll be fine. What did he say? Am I good to come back?"

"He hasn't talked to your doctor yet, but assuming that checks out, you can come back this week."

"Excellent. I can't wait to get back to work. I have therapy this afternoon, so I'll ask Dr. Campbell to tell the captain I'm good. I really want to get back on the case Trent and I were working on. I *am* going to figure it out." I directed that last toward the creature, and I think it knew.

With a hiss, it disappeared, returning a moment later accompanied by the convulsing in the air that announced Dionysius's presence. Shivers shot up my spine as the air turned to ice. The stench of putrid flesh and rotten eggs assaulted my nose and mouth. Bile rose up in my throat, choking me.

I sat up, preparing to rush to the bathroom, when Dionysius's voice filled my head, nails on a chalkboard screeching inside my brain.

So, this is her. The assignment's friend. You were right. She is delectable.

A feeling of maggots swarming over my arms and down my back washed over me at his words. My fingers dug into the leather couch.

"Hey, Bridge, can I get that vitamin water?"

"Oh, right, sure. Hang on."

She jumped up, blonde ponytail swinging and hips swaying as she trotted to my kitchen.

"I won't let you touch her," I growled under my breath.

And how will you stop me? She'll be mine, inextricably attached to me before you even know about it. And when she carries my offspring, there will be nothing you can do.

"Your...? That's not possible. You're not even human."

Deep, rumbling laughter, sinister and cold, erupted from Dionysius, echoing through my apartment, discernable only to me.

Pitiful worm, you have no idea what is going on all around you. He addressed the minion. *Do not call on me again. This dirt is no threat. Only continue to keep her away from... bad influences.* He leaned close to me, his foul rasping breath tickling my ear. *Don't worry, Scum. I'll take good care of your friend.*

TEN

The Eyes kept me from sleeping well, so it was late morning by the time I got up and early afternoon by the time I made my way to the precinct.

I couldn't get what Dionysius said out of my mind. I didn't know if what he'd threatened was possible, but I wasn't going to take any chances.

The way I figured it, the only way to keep Bridget safe from monsters was to be constantly by her side. If that meant shadowing her both on and off the clock, so be it. She'd never understand the threat, and she wouldn't recognize it.

I needed to get back to that church at some point, too, but right now, Bridget was my priority.

The only thing standing between her and whatever Dionysius would do to her was a crazy lady who had no idea what she was dealing with or how to counter it.

Sometimes I awed even myself with my optimism. But I didn't have time to think about that now. I needed to find my best friend.

From the outside, the police station looked the same as it always had—concrete walls in need of repainting, flat roof, Phoenix Police Department insignia emblazoned on the glass front doors.

I noticed more, now, though. Strange things I hadn't paid attention to yesterday but now stood out in stark contrast to everything I remembered as "normal." A cloud of... something... hovered in the air. Like smog, but invisible to the human eye, it seemed to coat each building with an oily taint.

"Jack, what are you doing?"

I turned to see the receptionist peering out the door.

"It's beastly out here. Come on inside."

I followed her in, relieved by the wall of cool air that hit me as I walked through the door. The sensation of a putrid blanket covering everything continued inside. Dark, cold presences inhabited the room. The smell of sulfur filled my nose, and goosebumps peppered my arms. Beings, like the minion that dogged my every step, seemed to be everywhere.

As I focused on each one, I became aware of differences between them. Not just between individual beings—I'd always been able to tell them apart from each other—but between types.

Most were the same type as the minion assigned to me. Ethereal, ghost-like presences, but there were a few like Dionysius, strong and... solid. Physical, albeit invisible.

The ghostly beings were by far the more prominent, I noticed as I wandered toward the captain's office. Most hovered over specific people, chattering at them, although a few seemed to be inside people, as much a part of them as their toes. I wasn't sure exactly how that worked, but decided I didn't really want to know.

Oppression pushed down on me the deeper I went into the building, freezing me, choking me. The dervish of minions like mine in every corridor, filling every room, was enough to send my stomach tumbling in an attempt to flee my body.

I heard whispers, both human and otherworldly, as I walked through the office.

She just got out of a mental institution, the minion attached to me announced to the room.

His words were echoed by a human, a young man with a perpetual sneer on his weasely face, as he whispered to the officer next to him.

Fantastic. That confirmed that the Eyes could influence people even though they couldn't hear him.

"Jack! Back already?" Ken's head popped up almost at my elbow.

"Hey, Ken. I was just looking for Bridget. Is she here?"

"Nope. Not sure what time she's coming in. She's on security at the Suns game tonight, so she wasn't going to come in first thing."

Damn. I didn't want to call her—protecting her wouldn't do much good if she realized I was doing it. She'd just find ways to avoid me. "Do you mind if I hang out 'til she gets here?"

"Sure. You can wait at my desk."

Poorly disguised eagerness shone from his eyes, but I didn't have an excuse not to, especially after I just asked if I could.

"Have a seat." Ken pulled out his padded, swiveling office chair and offered it to me, taking the hard plastic one on the other side for himself. He grabbed a file folder and started flipping through it.

I sat and appraised him. He looked tired—bags under his eyes, his too-long hair greasy, and his pointy nose red. "What are you working on?" I asked.

His eyes rolled overly-dramatically. "More UFO sightings. Why this is our job, I have no idea, but the police have to investigate every claim, and I ended up with the short stick on that one."

Knowing that feeling well, I chuckled. "Anything interesting?"

He shrugged. "A couple of them sound like they might not be completely made-up. Could be drones or something. I'm going to talk to a couple more people today. You... um... you want to come along?"

Served me right for being nice. "Thanks, but I need to talk to Bridget."

"It's cool. I don't mind waiting 'til you're done."

Take a hint, Kenny. "Not this time."

His hopeful, puppy-like expression fell momentarily then brightened again. "Well, I've got Sunday off. If you want, I could come over in the morning and help you out."

Help me? What the? "What do you mean?"

"Well, Bridget mentioned you'd probably be wanting to clean out some of Trent's stuff. I just thought you might want a hand."

Thanks a lot, Bridge. "Thanks, but I don't think I'll be doing that any time soon." I probably ought to amend that, since he'd still probably want to hang. "Anyway, I'm busy on Sunday."

"What are you—"

"Bridget!" I tossed Ken an apologetic smile. "See you."

I hurried to her side. "Hey, Bridge, are you okay?"

She raised an eyebrow. "Sure. Why wouldn't I be?"

Because my creepy tormentor told his boss about you and you're being threatened by an other-worldly monster. "Um... no reason. I just had a bad feeling. You mind if I ride along with you today?"

Her normally smooth brow crinkled. "You know that usually I'd love it, but I'm doing security during the basketball game. Opening night and everything. Not really a ride-along sort of gig."

"Oh, right. I knew that. Okay, call me when you're done, okay?"

"Sure." Her crystalline eyes told me she was a little concerned about my sanity.

Whatever. I couldn't really explain the details, but I wouldn't let Dionysius have her. At least at the ball game she'd be surrounded by

42

people, including other cops. I didn't think Dionysius would be able to do anything in that sort of setting.

Well, he'd probably be able to, but I got the impression they liked to keep a low profile, and people would definitely notice a cop getting beat up by invisible monsters.

The minion cackled at me. *You'll never be able to protect her. He'll have her, and you can't do anything.*

My hands clenched. If only they could read my mind, sense my intentions the way I seemed able to sense theirs. If only I could threaten them with something. If only I could bluff my way without actually saying anything.

"If onlys" would get me nowhere. I had to do something.

I'd send Bridget along with my best wishes for her safety. That was the best I could do at the moment. And somehow I'd find a way to throttle that creep.

"You okay?" Bridget asked.

I realized I'd been staring into space for the last couple of seconds. "Fine. Why?"

"No reason. You just seem… distracted."

"Oh. Yeah. Sorry. I was just thinking about something. When do you have to leave for the game?"

"Pretty much now. I just have to check in with the captain."

"Okay, see you tonight, then?"

"Yeah."

She turned away, but her eyes held concern. I'd have to figure out a more subtle way to have conversations with my invisible friends.

I watched Bridget waltz out, my mind churning, searching for some sort of answer to how I could help her.

"Jack, you here again?"

I turned, slapping a smile on my face. "Hey, Captain."

"Listen, as long as you're gonna be haunting this place, you might as well be getting paid."

My grin widened in genuine pleasure. "Really?"

He waved me toward his office with a folder. Once inside, he closed the door behind me. "I talked to your doc and just got the paperwork faxed over. As long as you keep going in for therapy, he's fine with you coming back to work."

"Great. When can I get back on the clock?"

"Tomorrow soon enough for you?"

ELEVEN

It was almost two in the morning when Bridget finally called. "Hey, sorry it's so late, but I knew you'd never forgive me if I didn't keep my promise to call."

"You're right," I said. "I wouldn't have. You okay? No trouble?"

"Of course. Were you expecting me to get in trouble?"

"I just know how traffic at those things can be."

"Well, no worries. Everything's fine. Great, actually."

"You're sure?"

"Seriously, Jack, quit worrying. I just got into my apartment and I'm totally good. I'll see you tomorrow."

She was right. There was nothing more I could do tonight, and she already suspected I wasn't quite as back-to-normal as I pretended. "Okay, thanks for calling, Bridge."

I flopped back against fluffy pillows, doing my best to tune out the grating voice of the minion hovering over my bed.

She didn't tell you everything. She didn't tell you who she met tonight. Dionysius will have his way with her before you know anything about it, let alone do anything to stop it.

I had to come up with a solution. Soon.

I went over and over what I knew about these things. They came through a rip in the air. From where? Another dimension? Space? Texas?

What else?

They were sent to kill Trent. The night he died, the night I first saw them, they were chanting, "Kill the cop." Whatever Trent was working on had something to do with these things.

His case, the child trafficking, was related, but how? Were the monsters protecting the traffickers? Why?

I had no answer, but it was my best lead. When I went into work tomorrow I'd look over Trent's notes. There had to be a clue in there somewhere.

Just before I drifted to sleep, another thought occurred to me. The last time I'd been seriously attacked, it had been outside that church. I vaguely remembered Dionysius ordering the minion to keep me away from there. I couldn't imagine why, but if it pissed him off, I wanted to do it.

"I think I'll go back to that church," I said aloud.

That sent the Eyes into histrionics. I smiled, glad to have found a way to pay it back for some of the mental torture it inflicted on me.

I never thought I'd actually be eager to go to a church. I hadn't even planned to get married in a church, despite Trent's strong Catholic background.

The Eyes still glared hate at me. Hissing curses filled the air around my head. I pretended it was soothing white noise and buried my head under my pillow, willing myself to sleep for a few hours at least.

***

Clocking in the next morning may have been the greatest moment in my life after the day Trent proposed.

I spent a few minutes reorganizing my desk and getting settled, but only a few. Everything was more or less as I'd left it—my files, the picture of Trent and me in L.A., even my desk organizer with my gel pens and paperclips all in their places.

Ken wandered by after a few minutes. "Hey, Jack, you settling in okay?"

"Yep, great. Thanks."

"Do you need anything?"

"Nope, I think I'm good."

"All of Trent's things are in that box." He nodded toward a box on the floor by my feet. "We figured you'd want to keep them. Some of the guys wanted to put your stuff in a box, too, but I knew you'd be back."

"I appreciate that."

"No problem." He smoothed his uniform with his hands. "And Jack?"

"Yeah?"

"It's really great to have you back."

I smiled. "Thanks, Ken. It's good to be here."

The captain saved me from further reply by sticking his head out of his office. "Jack, come in here a minute."

I stepped into his office. "What's up?"

"How are you doing? Getting back in the swing of things?"

"I guess. I just got here."

"Anything on your mind, or anything you want to start with?"

"I was kind of wondering about the case Trent was on when—before the accident."

He nodded. "That's understandable. We closed that case."

"What? You found the guy?"

"His car was recovered at the bottom of the Central Arizona Project. Two bodies inside, one of them identified as a Richard Hunt. We believe he was the one behind the sex trafficking ring. There was no evidence to lead us to his base of operations, but with him dead, and Trent—well, we had no more leads."

"What about the other guy in the car?"

"He could not be identified. He was abnormally large, so we suspect he must've been Hunt's protection. Probably an illegal alien since we couldn't find any dental records or fingerprints or anything else to identify him."

"So that's it, then?"

"Unless something else turns up, yes."

"If you don't mind, I'd like to take a look at his files, just to see if anything stands out to me."

The captain nodded. "Of course. I'll have someone bring them to you later."

"Thanks."

"If there's nothing else, are you ready to get back to work?"

"Beyond ready. I have to go in for therapy this afternoon, but other than that, I'm all yours. What's up?"

He tossed a file at me. "You remember the missing persons thing you were working on?"

"Yeah, of course. Bridget said you found a body. Where are we on that?"

"Not much further than we were before."

"I've been gone over a month! Nothing new?"

"Actually, it's worse. The rate of missing girls has more than doubled in the last month."

My skin rippled with bumps as the ever-present minion by my side cackled with delight. I'd gotten pretty good at ignoring it most of the time, but when it suddenly spoke or laughed, especially in that harsh, metallic way, the symptoms redoubled involuntarily.

"How is this possible? There must be clues somewhere. There's no way for this to keep happening and not have anyone leave any evidence behind."

I flipped through the folder at pictures of teenage girls, all reported missing. Dozens of them, mostly twelve to fifteen years old, although the occasional older or slightly younger face popped out at me.

No pattern that I could discern—race, economic status, school, area of town, place they were last seen—all different, with no way of determining any possible next targets or best places to stake out.

A pretty, freckled face set with soulful hazel eyes and framed by bright red curls stared up at me. Tamara Cohen, thirteen years old. Disappeared somewhere between her school and home. None of her friends had seen anything and no one had come forward with any information, despite a generous reward being offered by her parents.

From the next page, Ariana Valdez, fourteen, grinned. She'd disappeared from a convenience store when she was with her friend Nicole. Nicole stated that she was trying to convince some lady to buy cigarettes for them, and when she turned around, Ariana was gone.

Kelsey Reyes was only twelve. She'd disappeared from her own backyard.

One after another, young women, scarcely more than girls, cried out from the pages of the folder, begging me to find them, to save them from whatever sicko had abducted them.

"I want you to get right back to work on this," the captain's voice broke through my thoughts. "You were as close as we got."

TWELVE

Moments after I returned to my desk, Ken flopped down in the chair beside me. "What does the captain have you working on?"

I stared at the pages of the file, trying to appear completely absorbed. "The same case I was on before."

"How's it coming?"

Weak, Kenny. I expected a little better excuse for coming over to sit by me. "I don't know yet, I only got the file two minutes ago. Just trying to catch up."

"Right. Well, let me know if you need anything."

"I will, thanks."

"Hey, Jack, I was thinking. Maybe after work…"

Damn. He was going to ask me out. Intercept before he can finish. "Listen, Ken, everyone is watching me to see if I'm crazy, or headed that way again. I really need to concentrate on getting some work done, okay?"

"Right. Sorry. I didn't mean to distract you."

I turned back to the file, summarily dismissing him. "No prob."

"Okay… so we'll talk later, then?"

"Sure." I kept my gaze intent on the file until he wandered away.

Finally, peace and relative quiet. Time to get some work done.

A dozen phone calls later, I at least had a place to start.

I tapped at the captain's door before popping in and settling opposite him. "Okay, I think I may have something here. I don't know if this means anything, but more than half the missing girls had split homes, primarily with absent father figures."

A sudden spike of emotion—wariness, it felt like—charged the room, alerting me to a presence. How had I not noticed it before? Was I really so used to the ever-present feel of the monsters all around me that I could miss one until it made itself obvious?

Step it up, Jack. You can't afford to get lazy here.

I jerked my attention back to the captain, but kept a corner of my mind occupied by monitoring the dark presence invading the room. "Several of the others had fathers who were alcoholics or workaholics, or for whatever reason were gone a lot. So, not necessarily absent, but unavailable."

"Hmm." The captain rubbed the stubble on his chin. "Not conclusive, but at least it gives us a better idea of who might be at risk."

"There's more. I got a hold of some of the girls' friends. The ones I talked to each mentioned a boyfriend—somebody the girl met online or something, but they didn't know of any plans to actually meet the guy."

The captain nodded. "So we're looking for an online predator who goes after vulnerable, fatherless girls."

"Right."

"Get on that."

"Will do." I took my findings back to my desk just as Bridget sauntered in.

"Great to have you back," she grinned.

"Thanks. How are you? You okay?"

She raised an eyebrow. "Of course. Are you still weirded out about whatever it was last night?"

I smiled. "No. Just checking."

She must have read something on my face that belied my words, because she gave me an exasperated sigh. "I'm fine, Jack. Seriously, I thought you left your issues at the hospital." She nodded toward my computer screen. "What are you doing?"

"Creating an online profile."

She sat on the edge of my desk, stretching long legs out in front of her. "Is that really the best use of taxpayer dollars?"

I grinned. "I'm a thirteen-year-old girl from a broken home."

Bridget's eyebrows climbed toward her scalp. "Now I *know* that's unethical."

I laughed. It felt good to laugh. I'd missed that. "I'm working on the case I was on before, trying to get a lead on our kidnapper."

"Oh. Right. How's it coming?"

I shrugged. "I guess we'll find out in a little bit."

She ran a manicured hand through her golden curls. Why did she have a fresh manicure? She almost never got her nails done.

"Hey, what are you doing tonight?" Bridget asked. "Want to go to a party with me?"

"I thought you were going out with what's-his-name?"

"Tony? No, that's so not happening. Apparently he's still trying to get back with his ex. So, party, yeah?"

I uploaded a stock photo of a teen girl selfie. "Yeah, maybe. If I don't plan to stay out too late. I'm still trying to play catch-up."

"Deal. I'll pick you up at eight?"

"No, I want my truck in case I want to leave early. I'll meet you there. Where are we going?"

She snatched a piece of paper from my desk and scribbled the address down.

I took the paper from her and glanced at it. "Scottsdale? Who do you know in Scottsdale?"

Color crept into her cheeks. "Derek Thorne."

"Derek Thorne? Isn't he…"

"One of the Suns," she nodded. "I met a couple of them last night at the game."

The pink in her face deepened.

I forced my jaw back into place. "Did you two hook up last night?"

"Me and Derek? No."

I started to breathe a sigh of relief, until I noticed her biting her bottom lip. Sure sign she was hiding something.

"Bridge?" I tried to make my tone as accusatory as I could.

"I may have met one of the others…"

"Who?"

"Bridget, I need you in here right away," the captain hollered from across the room.

She glanced from me to him and back again. "I'll see you tonight."

"Okay. And then you *will* tell me everything."

I turned back to my computer and set to work. By the time I finished my shift, I'd made friends with a dozen pimply-faced little dweebs, but had no idea if any of them might be a link to my kidnapper.

I stretched, reaching my hands back over my head and closing my eyes.

When I opened them, I found Ken perched on my desk. "How's it coming?"

I suppressed a sigh. "I don't know. We'll find out, I guess. I'm going to talk to the friends of some of the missing girls and see if they know of a specific website or anything I can go on. How's your UFO thing?"

His eyes rolled. "The usual. 'I've been abducted.' 'The aliens did experiments on me.' 'I think I've been impregnated.' Yada, yada, yada."

I grinned. "You always get the best gigs."

"Right. Hey, what are you doing tonight? Wanna grab something to eat?"

"I can't, sorry. I'm going to a party with Bridget."

"A party?" Ken's eyes begged pathetically for an invite.

I pretended not to notice. "Yeah. One of her friends. I don't know them. I guess I'll see you later."

As quickly as I could, I grabbed my things and scurried away.

I stopped by my apartment to change before heading toward the address Bridget had given me.

This couldn't be the right address. Tucked back in against a mountain, the palatial home had to be twice the size of the police station.

I glanced down at my dark green sundress and kitten heels, suddenly feeling way underdressed. What did one even wear to a party like this? Maybe this was a bad idea. But I couldn't leave Bridget vulnerable to Dionysius's attack.

Bridget pulled up behind me and hopped out of her car. She sauntered toward me in a tiny skirt and sequined halter top.

As soon as I stepped from my truck I was hit with a wave of nausea. Along with the thumping of loud music and the sounds of revelry from inside came the icy, sickening terror I felt when Dionysius was around, but multiplied by a zillion.

There were monsters in there, dozens of them. Possibly hundreds.

The Eyes, ever-present with me, urged me on. *Go on in. It will be fun.*

Unable to control myself, I crumpled to the ground on my hands and knees and retched. Shudders ripped through me, shaking my whole body, sending torrents of sickness through my body, over and over.

Bridget knelt beside me, pressing her hand against my forehead. "Jack! What's going on? Are you okay?"

"I don't feel good," I muttered.

"No kidding."

"I'll be okay—I just need to go home."

"Your skin's all clammy and you're turning green. Maybe you should go to a hospital."

"No, I'm okay. But I don't think I'm gonna make it to the party."

"You think?" Her sarcasm was as thick as my vomit.

"Sorry." I clutched my stomach again.

"It's cool. Go home and rest. Call me and let me know you made it, okay?"

"Sounds good."

I slipped back into my truck and closed the door. Somehow, the doors insulated me enough from the presence of the monsters that I managed to catch my breath and quell the sick that threatened to erupt again.

Bridget watched me for a few moments until I started my engine and waved her away. I pulled away from the house, each inch taking me away from the unsettling sensations that overwhelmed me. I sped away as quickly as I could without completely mutilating the residential speed laws.

When I could think again, I realized that it was after eight on a Friday night, and I had no plans. Bridget didn't want to leave the party even when she thought I needed a doctor, so the chances of getting her to come away for a quiet cup of coffee or something seemed pretty slim.

I briefly considered hanging out with Ken, but discarded the notion immediately. The last thing I needed was a rebound relationship, and I didn't want to lead him on.

The only other thing I could think of was to try that church again. I didn't know what the chances were of anyone being there at this hour, but it was the only plan I had.

I turned at what I thought was the street I came in on, but something didn't quite seem right. Nothing looked familiar, and the more I tried to find my way back, the more I got lost in the maze of winding residential streets and cul-de-sacs.

The little blue dot on my phone's GPS meandered in and out of the maze, but the app apparently didn't register all the new construction that had gone on in this area.

I glanced down at the directions in Bridget's elegant handwriting, hoping to find a familiar street name.

Stop.

I didn't know if I heard someone say it, or if it was just a sixth sense of some kind, cop reflexes or something, but I slammed the brakes, screeching to a halt in front of a girl standing in the middle of the street, waving her arms.

What the?

I opened my door, ready to give her a stern talking-to about playing in traffic, when she collapsed on the hood of my car.

I rushed to her side and lifted her in my arms.

Bright orange curls dulled by dirt and sweat matted around her face. Wide, hazel eyes blinked up at me, and parched lips moved as if to speak.

No way. I knew that face. Tamara Cohen.

"Help me," she croaked.

"I've got you." Supporting most of her weight, I lifted her to a stand.

It was then that I noticed her stomach.

She was *pregnant?*

THIRTEEN

By the size of her distended abdomen, I guessed she had to be at least seven months along—maybe even eight. She'd only been missing for two months, and nothing in her file said anything about a pregnancy, but there was no mistaking the bulge around her middle. She was definitely pregnant.

A strange sort of vibe emanated from her. Something vaguely reminiscent of the otherworldly sense of evil that overwhelmed me when one of the creatures like my minion or Dionysius came near, but different somehow. Muted. Like a watered-down, made-from-concentrate evil.

What in the world was going on?

The girl moaned, bringing me back to the present. I helped her to the passenger seat of my truck and belted her in. "You're going to be okay. Can you talk?"

She nodded. "Yeah."

"Do you know your name?"

"Tamara. Tamara Cohen."

I was right.

"I'm going to take you to the hospital and get you checked out, okay, Tamara? Is there anyone I should call?"

"My mom. She'll be... so worried." Tamara's eyes rolled back in her head, and she fainted against the truck's window. Shit. This could not be good.

"Now if only I can figure out how to get out of here," I muttered aloud, grabbing my phone again.

I zoomed out on the map until I found a major street, then traced it back with my finger until I found the blue dot that was me.

I saved my location, knowing I'd need to bring the cavalry back here once I announced that I'd found Tamara, and then followed the map out of the residential area. I made about four wrong turns when my phone told me to drive through a mountain or into a dead end, but finally I found the road that led back toward the city.

As soon as I pulled onto a road I recognized, I called the captain. "Captain, it's Jack. I just found one of our missing girls. Tamara Cohen."

"What? How?"

"Blind luck. I'm taking her to the hospital. St. Joes, downtown. Call her parents and have them meet me there."

"What's going on, Jack?" my boss demanded.

"I'll explain when we get there. But Captain, we may be in the maternity ward."

"The maternity—"

"Please, just call the parents. Don't tell them anything except that we found her and we'll meet them at the hospital. Hopefully the doctors will be able to tell us more."

After hanging up, I raced down the freeway toward the hospital.

Not too many minutes later, I pulled up in front of the ER and flashed my badge. An orderly scurried out with a wheelchair and rolled Tamara inside.

I told the doctor who she was and where I'd found her. In short order, they wheeled her upstairs for an exam and an ultrasound while I paced the waiting room.

A little while later, a stout, flame-haired woman burst from the elevator. "Where is she? Where's my baby girl?"

I stood. "Janet Cohen? I'm Detective Davidson. Your daughter is being examined right now."

"How did you find her? Where?"

The how, I had no idea. "In Scottsdale. I was there for—something unrelated, and I happened across her. A lucky coincidence."

Even as I said the words I knew it was more than that. Something led me there at just the right time. But how did I explain that?

Better not to try, I decided.

I led Ms. Cohen to a chair. "I'm hoping when Tamara is feeling a little better she can tell me what happened. And with any luck, she can help me find the others."

"There are others?"

I nodded.

Ms. Cohen opened her mouth again, but before she could speak a doctor pushed through the doors. "Detective Davidson?"

I nodded and gestured toward the woman by my side. "This is the girl's mother."

The doctor nodded. "I'm Dr. Reyes. Come with me, please."

"How is she?" Ms. Cohen babbled, prancing along behind the doctor, almost running him over in her haste.

"Mostly just scared, I think. A little dehydrated and malnourished, but both she and the baby seem to be doing fine."

Janet Cohen's pattering footsteps stopped, and her mouth fell open. "The baby?"

"Yes, ma'am. According to her ultrasound, your daughter is almost eight months pregnant."

Ms. Cohen's jaw snapped shut. She pursed her lips in disbelief. "Well, she can't be. She wasn't pregnant when she disappeared. She'd never even had sex! And that was just two months ago. You must've made a mistake. Or else it isn't Tamara. Oh, if it's not her... where could she be?"

Apparently deciding it wasn't worth arguing over, Dr. Reyes turned and led us to a room about halfway down the hall. "She's awake. Come on in."

He stepped aside so she could enter.

Ms. Cohen hurried into the room and stopped, dead still, just inside the door.

"Mom?"

Tamara's voice seemed to break through her mother's shock.

"I'm here, baby," Ms. Cohen soothed.

"I'm sorry, mom," Tamara wept. "I'm so sorry."

Ms. Cohen seated herself in the chair by the bed, grabbing Tamara's hand as she sat. "It's okay, honey. We'll take care of it. It's going to be okay."

I nodded toward the doctor and led him into the hall. "What can you tell me?"

"At this point, nothing more than I just told her mother. She's healthy, the baby seems fine. Whoever had her didn't mistreat her, although she does need rest and fluids." A hint of a Spanish accent gave his words a soothing cadence.

"I have a lot questions," I said.

"I'm sure you do, but as her doctor, I must insist that they wait. She has clearly been through an incredible trauma."

I nodded. "I'll be back first thing in the morning, then."

He peered at me with intense brown eyes, and I suddenly realized he was about my age, and extremely attractive. How long since I had even noticed a guy?

He smiled, and deep dimples formed at the corners of his mouth. "I look forward to seeing you tomorrow, then."

***

I spent Saturday morning organizing things around my apartment and returned to the hospital that afternoon. Tamara looked a little more rested, and her mom sat by her side, still looking tense and confused.

"Hi, Tamara," I said. "Do you remember me?"

She nodded.

"How are you feeling today?"

"Okay, I guess."

"Do you feel up to answering some questions?"

Before she could answer, I felt a tap on my shoulder.

"Detective," Dr. Reyes whispered from behind me, "may I have a word with you?"

My heart skipped a beat.

Grow up, Jack.

"Sure." I followed him into the hallway.

"What can you tell me about her case?" he asked.

"She was one of a few dozen girls to go missing over the last few months. The best I've been able to surmise so far is that they all met someone—I don't know who yet—online."

His deep brown eyes bored into mine with an intensity that made my stomach churn, but in a good way. I shook myself to put my mind back on track. "I... um... I was working the case before, and we had a lead. But I had an accident."

I squeezed my eyes closed in a vain attempt to shut out the memories that flooded over me. "My partner died. I took a couple of months off."

I felt warm pressure on my shoulder, and opened my eyes to see Dr. Reyes's hand resting there, comfortable and comforting.

I managed a brief smile and collected myself enough to go on. "I'm back on the case now, but all our leads at this point are really slim."

Dr. Reyes rubbed his chin. "I'm worried about her."

Alarm bells chimed in my head, almost a premonition of something dire gnawing at me. "Why? I thought you said she and the baby are fine."

His eyebrows pinched together, and he opened and closed his mouth a couple times before any actual words came out. "They are

57

both… healthy, as far as I can tell. The thing is—you said she'd only been missing a couple of months?"

I nodded.

"And she wasn't pregnant at that time?"

I shrugged. "Not according to her mother, but who knows? It wouldn't be the first time a mom was in denial about her child's sex life. Isn't it possible she didn't know she was pregnant? I've heard of people who didn't know they were expecting until they delivered."

"Possible," Dr. Reyes agreed, "but not really plausible. The way she's carrying, it would've been nearly impossible to miss, even two months ago. She wouldn't have grown that much in that amount of time—her progression should have been much more gradual. And I went over the ultrasound again, and things were—let's just say—a little odd."

"So you're saying this isn't an average pregnancy. Fine. But that doesn't really mean anything. Unless there's something wrong with the baby to make it grow like that?"

He paused, brows furrowed, and tapped his foot against the floor a few times, as if trying to think of what to say.

"What?"

He glanced at me, then looked away. I'd been in enough interrogation rooms to recognize the look in his eye. He didn't think I'd believe his story, even though he truly did.

"What is going on, Doc?" I demanded.

He looked earnestly into my eyes. "I'm not sure it's human."

FOURTEEN

The echo of my gasp bounced off the sterile walls of the hallway.

"Before you think I'm crazy, let me explain."

Before I thought *he* was crazy? I almost laughed at that. "Go on."

He hesitated only slightly. "About six months ago I had a patient, a woman within days of delivering her baby. She wasn't married, wasn't in a relationship. When I asked about the baby's father, she claimed that she'd been abducted by aliens ten weeks before, and they had impregnated her."

"Aliens? Are you kidding me?"

"I didn't believe her, either. I figured she'd been raped or something, and this was a coping mechanism."

I nodded. A reasonable explanation for a woman to give meaning to what would've been an incredibly traumatic experience.

"Anyway, the baby was so big, I decided it would be safer to give the woman C-section than have her try to deliver naturally."

I still didn't see where this was going, but I nodded encouragingly. "Okay. What happened?"

"The baby was… grotesque."

Okay, not exactly what I was expecting a maternity ward doctor to say. "What do you mean?"

"Well, for one thing, it was huge. Seventeen pounds."

"How big is a normal, healthy baby?"

"Average, between seven and nine pounds. Up to eleven isn't uncommon. Beyond twelve is rare. Seventeen is virtually unheard-of. And to be honest, I don't think the mother would have survived natural childbirth."

"Okay, that's weird, I'll admit, but not totally absurd."

"There's more. The child had six fingers on each hand."

"That could just be a defect," I insisted. "Maybe incest? But it doesn't prove anything beyond that you had a patient once whose pregnancy was a little weird, just like Tamara's."

"If that were the only thing, I'd be inclined to agree with you. But the baby developed at an alarming rate. By the time the woman left the hospital three days later, the baby had gained five pounds and eagerly reached toward whatever she was eating. That usually doesn't happen until at least six months. Also, it was cutting teeth and rolling over."

A shiver jolted through me. I knew enough about babies to know that was weird. "Where are they now?"

"The baby disappeared. The mom came in a week after his birth and said his alien father came to collect him. She's being treated for a psychiatric disorder. They're trying to determine whether or not she killed the baby, but there's no evidence. He just... disappeared."

Teenage girls disappearing. Tamara pregnant with what might or might not turn out to be an alien baby. Voices in my head telling me I was crazy when I knew I wasn't. Somehow, it all had to add up, but I had no idea how.

Dr. Reyes was still talking, so I focused my attention back. "I don't know how it would be possible—I don't even believe in aliens—but I can't think of another explanation."

"You can't really believe Tamara's baby is alien spawn."

"I don't know what to believe at this point."

I immediately jumped to Ken's caseload. Maybe I should look deeper into what he was working on. If there was something to all this alien stuff...

My thoughts were interrupted by my police captain strutting around the corner, almost barreling into me. "Jack! Everyone okay?"

"Tamara seems to be fine, sir."

"Good. Can she help us I.D. her kidnapper?"

"I haven't asked her yet. This is her physician, Dr. Reyes."

The captain stuck out a beefy hand, and Dr. Reyes shook it. "Anything you can tell me?"

Dr. Reyes shook his head. "Not much. She appears to have been well cared-for, and healthy enough given her circumstances. Her mother is with her now, but she should be able to talk soon."

"Good enough," the captain nodded.

"I'd like to recommend that a 24-hour guard be put on her," I said.

"Why?" The captain narrowed his eyes at me.

"I'm worried that the kidnapper may try to come back for the baby."

Dr. Reyes's eyes expressed gratitude.

I smiled, trying to convey that I wasn't quite ready to tell the captain about the alien theory just yet, either.

The captain frowned. "What makes you think that?"

"Mostly a hunch, but I think it's a reasonable precaution."

He nodded. "Okay. I trust your judgment, Jack."

"Thank you, sir."

The captain adjusted his belt. "I'd like to have a word with her mother, and then I'll let you handle it. I expect a full report on Monday."

"Done."

He went into the hospital room, and a moment later, a low rumbling indicating his conversation with Janet Cohen drifted out.

I looked up at the doctor. "Listen, Dr. Reyes, don't say anything about our suspicions to Tamara's mother or anyone until we know more, okay?"

He flashed brilliantly white teeth in a grin. "So you don't think I'm insane, then?"

"I wrote the book on insane, Doc. Trust me, this is nothing."

He raised an eyebrow.

"I'll explain another time," I laughed.

The captain came out of the room. "I told Ms. Cohen that you're my best man and you'd do everything to get to the bottom of what happened to her daughter."

"Thanks, Captain. I'm going to go talk to Tamara now and see what I can find out."

Tamara's mom sat by the bedside, stroking Tamara's flaming curls and murmuring softly.

"Hi, Ms. Cohen. I'm sorry to interrupt, but I need to ask Tamara a few questions so we can try to figure out who took her."

Ms. Cohen nodded.

"Hi, Tamara. Do you feel okay to talk?"

Tamara nodded.

"Just tell me whatever you can remember."

"Okay."

"Do you know where you were being held?"

Her brows furrowed. Was she repressing, or did she really not remember much?

"It was a house. A really big one. But it was in a neighborhood where all the houses look the same, you know?"

"How about a street number? Or the name of the street it was on?"

Tears welled up in her eyes. "I don't know. I don't remember anything."

Taking her hand, I gently squeezed, careful not to disturb the IV tubes. "It's okay. You're safe now. Do you know how long you walked before I found you? How many streets you passed?"

"Um... five or six blocks, I guess. I don't really know. I was just trying to get away before he found me."

"He? Who is he?"

She shook her head, tears streaming down her face. "He said his name was Chet when I talked to him online."

Good. Confirmation that my theory was correct. I nodded to encourage Tamara to go on.

"He told me he could help me get away—" Her eyes darted toward her mother. "From stuff."

"What do you mean?" Ms. Cohen wailed. "Don't you know I'm doing the best I can? Don't you realize—"

I held up a hand. "Ms. Cohen, please. It's important that Tamara tells me everything she knows. The more details she can remember, the easier it will be for me to do my job. There are other girls at stake."

Ms. Cohen snapped her mouth shut, but her eyes welled up, her expression a cross between anger, confusion, and guilt.

Dr. Reyes stepped forward. "Come on, Ms. Cohen. Let's go get some coffee."

I shot him a grateful smile as he led Ms. Cohen out of the room.

"I don't want you to be mad at my mom," Tamara sniffed. "She's really okay. I just... she doesn't seem to realize I'm not five, you know? We had a fight, and Chet..."

"Chet understood you. He made you feel grown-up and appreciated. Special."

A relieved smile softened her features. "Yeah."

"Okay. So, you met him online, and he promised to rescue you from your mom. What happened? You met up with him after school?"

She nodded. "He picked me up in a silver Corvette. I'd never been that close to something so awesome before. I was so excited I didn't even notice where we were headed. When we got to the house, I didn't think to figure out where I was."

"Tell me about the house. What did the front yard look like? Anything out of the ordinary that you can remember?"

"No, we went in through the garage, so I didn't really notice the front. Desert landscaping, but nothing interesting."

"Anything else you can think of? What about the neighbors?"

"There was a lot of space between the houses, but I didn't see any neighbors or their cars or anything."

"What about Chet? What can you tell me about him?"

"Chet was—"

Her words cut off with a groan as she clutched her stomach. The monitors next to her bed started a cacophony of warning bells.

FIFTEEN

A nurse hurried into the room, followed closely by Dr. Reyes.

"What happened?" Dr. Reyes asked.

"I don't know. We were talking, and then she started groaning and grabbing her stomach."

Dr. Reyes shouted out a bunch of medical jargon and a team of nurses scurried to obey. I slipped out into the hallway where Ms. Cohen stood wringing her hands.

"What's going on in there?"

"The doctor has it under control. Why don't you go home and get some rest?"

She turned a disdainful glare on me. "You don't have kids, do you?"

I choked back the emotion that shot through me at her words. Trent and I always talked about having a family some day. "No."

"I'm not going home," Ms. Cohen said.

"Then at least go get something to eat. The doctor will call you when you can go back in."

She ignored me and continued to pace the hall.

A few minutes later, Dr. Reyes came out. "She's stable. She started to go into preterm labor, so we gave her something to stop the contractions."

Without waiting for permission, Ms. Cohen shoved open the door and went back to sit by Tamara.

"I'm sorry, Detective, but we had to sedate her," Dr. Reyes said. "She's sleeping now."

I nodded. "I understand. It's okay, I have enough to start with. I'll be back tomorrow to see what else she can tell me."

He smiled. Good night, he had a gorgeous smile. "I look forward to seeing you tomorrow, then."

When I left the hospital, I went back to where I'd found Tamara and drove slowly up and down the blocks, looking for any sign of... anything.

You'll never find him. You got lucky once, but you're done now. The Eyes whispered in my ear, taunting me, declaring my failure over and over as I wove in and out of one dead end after another.

It was like a game of hot and cold. The more he yapped in my ear, the closer I was getting. But apparently not close enough.

I drove around until after dark, finding nothing. I had to try a new tack. At last, I went home and went to bed. I had some things to do in the morning.

The next morning, I arrived at Saving Grace Fellowship a solid two hours before the first service was scheduled to start. I pulled into the parking lot and experienced the same sensations as the time before. The Eyes completely flipped out. It screamed at me, tearing at my mind, shredding my sanity from within me.

I parked at the very edge of the parking lot, close to the street. I didn't trust myself to maneuver even the short distance to the parking spots closest to the main building with my minion scrabbling at me, despite the lack of other cars in the lot.

I stepped from my car and walked toward the building.

Loathing and hatred tried to overwhelm me, slowing my steps.

"Lovely day, isn't it," I panted.

The Eyes clawed at me, screaming into my mind. I couldn't block it out, couldn't push past it.

I took another step.

The walls that kept my brain from turning to mush started to crumble, writhing like a pit of snakes, churning.

Air wheezed in and out of my chest as I struggled to breathe, but I took another step.

The creature haunting me grew more agitated and angry, screaming at me and redoubling its efforts to destroy the last shreds of sanity to which I clung.

Halfway across the parking lot, I collapsed to my knees, the weight of oppression pushing me further into the ground. I sucked in another breath and expelled my breakfast when I exhaled.

Reaching one hand out, I pulled myself another inch, past the puddle of vomit and toward the church. Even this early in the morning, the asphalt burned, searing the palms of my hands and my knees, but I couldn't turn back, especially when the Eyes was so clearly trying to get me to.

A sprawling chapel sat in the center of the property, and next to it stood a two-story building. I guessed that part to be where offices and things would be located, and determined that would be the best place to look for someone at this hour. Inch after painful inch, I crawled toward the building, each moment making the Eyes more furious.

At last, I pulled myself around the corner of the two-story office.

A man stood on a ladder that leaned against the wall, fitting letters into the marquee above the door.

Blond, surfer-like curls stuck to his head with a sheen of sweat, and his delicious physique was accentuated by snug, paint-spattered jeans and a white t-shirt with the sleeves cut off.

"Excuse me," I croaked.

He turned toward me, a smile lighting his features until he saw me crouched on the ground.

Warm, sea foam-hued eyes landed on me and turned cold. "You're not welcome here."

What the? What kind of church was this?

Behind me, the Eyes spat in anger. *She is mine!*

It was then I realized the blond man wasn't looking at me. He looked past me, over my shoulder to where I could feel the Eyes salivating.

She belongs to me! I'm not leaving, it hissed.

The man climbed down from the ladder. Those gorgeous green eyes radiated authority as he continued to concentrate on the monster behind me. "You are on consecrated ground. Leave now, or I will cast you out. And I promise you, it will hurt far more than leaving on your own."

The creature writhed, anger and pain pulsing from it in such strong waves that I felt the urge to throw up again, except there was nothing left inside me. I heaved anyway, retching and gasping for breath.

Quiet words began to pour from the man's lips, murmurs too soft for me to hear, but the Eyes started screeching and sending out waves of burning so intense I thought it was about to spontaneously combust.

I can't!

"Well, you can't come in here, either."

Fine! I'll leave! But I'll be waiting for her. You can't protect her forever.

The man nodded, as if he heard as clearly as I did.

Immediately, the Eyes vanished.

For the first time since Trent's death, I could breathe. I sucked in breath after breath of clean, undefiled air. The gooseflesh disappeared from my arms, and the cold tentacles of fear that I'd grown so used to released my heart.

The ever-present weight that crushed me, the constant nausea and chills that surrounded me lifted, replaced by a calm so enveloping, for a moment I wondered if I'd died. Peace like nothing I'd ever experienced, even before the accident, washed over me.

I sat back on the hot concrete and looked up as the man stepped toward me.

"Are you feeling all right?" The warmth returned to his eyes as he knelt beside me.

"How…" I struggled to speak through the heavy breaths I still heaved in around my thick, dry, swollen tongue. "How did you do that?"

He smiled and extended a hand to help me up. "He that is in me is greater than he that is in the world."

Whatever that meant.

"How did you know it was there?"

He paused, tilting his head to the side and furrowing his brow. "I have developed a certain amount of sensitivity toward these things. How did *you* know it was there? Most people have no idea when they're being oppressed like that."

Oppressed. That was a good word for how I'd felt the past several weeks. "I can feel them. Their eyes watch me all the time. And I can… sense their emotions. Especially that one. It hates me."

He still held my hand, and he squeezed gently. "Don't take it personally. They hate everyone. How long has this been going on?"

"A little over a month."

His brows furrowed and he dropped my hand. "Come inside."

He led me into a blessedly cool foyer lined with glass-paneled offices. "In here."

The office door he opened for me was labeled "Chase Gardener, Associate Pastor."

I gestured toward the sign. "That you?"

"Oh, man, I'm sorry. I'm Pastor Chase." He held out his hand.

I shook it. "Jack Davidson."

I settled into a padded office chair across the desk from him and glanced around the room. The wall with the door was one big window overlooking the foyer, while the opposite wall contained a window that overlooked a manicured lawn. Under the window stood a table with a printer, a copier, and a couple other office necessities.

The other two walls were covered, floor-to-ceiling, with books. On Pastor Chase's tidy desk sat a few stacks of paper, an open Bible, and a laptop. An atmosphere of peace permeated the room.

The ability to breathe freely still shocked me. I hadn't realized just how overwhelming the presence of the Eyes was in my life until I had this respite from it, however brief it might be.

Pastor Chase folded his hands on the desk and regarded me. "First, I want to let you know that everything you say to me is strictly between us, unless you give me permission otherwise. I'm protected by the same confidentiality laws that protect doctors and lawyers."

"Good to know."

He nodded. "Okay, then. Why don't you tell me about what you've experienced, Jack?"

Why was he so much easier to talk to than Dr. Campbell? Maybe because he didn't think I was having a nervous breakdown. Whatever kind of sensitivity he'd developed, he knew I wasn't a raving looney.

I told him the same things I'd told the shrink, about how I could sense the creatures, how I could smell and hear them without the use of my actual nose or ears. The only difference was that I didn't leave out any details.

The evil I felt, the threats it made—I even showed the pastor the scabbed-over slices on my wrists and the back of my neck where Dionysius's claws dug into my flesh. "It was trying to make me look suicidal so they'd keep me at the hospital."

"Hospital?"

"Yeah. I checked myself into a mental home because I thought I was going schizo, you know?"

Pastor Chase furrowed his brows again, deep in thought. "And this started about a month ago?"

I nodded.

"That's weird."

"What is?" I asked.

He didn't answer right away. "Do you mind if I ask about your religious background?"

I shrugged. "I don't really have one. My mom took us to church on Christmas and Easter a couple of times, but that's about it."

"How about the occult? Do you dabble in Wicca or mysticism or any Eastern religions?"

What did that have to do with anything? "I messed around with a Ouija board a couple of times in high school, but that's it. Why?"

70

He shook his head. "It's just strange that you would be suddenly attacked like that, especially since you haven't delved into any of the practices that they're usually associated with."

I didn't really know what to say to that. I didn't have a clue, either, otherwise I wouldn't be there in his office in the first place.

"What's even stranger," Pastor Chase went on, "is that you're so aware of them. Typically, people can't sense them at all, let alone hear them and perceive their emotions the way you do, unless they want us to. More often than not, they disguise themselves as a benefactor or a higher power, but you see them for what they are."

"And what exactly are they?"

"Demons."

SIXTEEN

Something inside me vibrated. How could something so unreasonable sound so plausible? It didn't make sense. Things like that weren't real. "I don't believe in demons."

Pastor Chase's laugh had a deep, musical quality. "Well, you've ruled out schizophrenia. Do you have a better explanation?"

Heat rose to my cheeks. "Aliens?" I felt like an idiot even bringing it up, but after what happened with Tamara yesterday, it didn't seem so off-the-wall. Anyway, it was one step less insane than demons, at least to me.

"For the sake of argument, let's assume I have some idea what I'm talking about."

I tried to scowl at him, but his warm, amused smile was annoyingly contagious. "Okay."

"Great. Now, I want you to tell me, in as much detail as you can remember, about the first time you saw, or heard, the demon that has been haunting you."

I closed my eyes and saw again the flash of light that tore the sky and the endless sea of hideous faces on the other side. Demons.

Eyes still closed, I told Pastor Chase about the accident, about seeing the monsters pour from the sky, and about the one who'd stayed to torment me ever since.

When I finished, I opened my eyes enough to glance at Pastor Chase's face, expecting to see an unbelieving stare, or worse, the same look of abject pity Dr. Campbell always wore when I described my hallucinations.

I was pleasantly disappointed.

Pastor Chase regarded me with a thoughtful stare. "That doesn't really explain *why* they attacked you, or why this one has been clinging to you. But I guess we can figure that out as we go."

His words brought to mind the idea of a long-term partnership. The thought was not at all unwelcome.

"In the meantime," he went on, "we need to make sure you're safe."

Safe.

When was the last time—other than in this office today—that I actually felt safe?

A memory pierced my mind with perfect clarity. A few nights before the accident, Trent took me out to dinner at a little hole-in-the wall place he'd discovered downtown. We were walking back to the car, past a side street where the streetlights were out, when a man jumped out of the shadows and grabbed my wrist, yanking me away from Trent and brandishing a knife.

Stupid thug didn't know he was dealing with two off-duty police officers. He didn't stand a chance.

In a matter of seconds, the perp was lying facedown on the concrete, handcuffed, while we waited for a squad car to come pick him up.

Trent pulled me into his arms and kissed me, murmuring into my hair, "It's over now. You're safe."

"Jack? Are you okay?" Pastor Chase's voice jerked me back to the present.

"Yeah. Sorry. What?"

"I asked if there's anything else you'd like to tell me."

"Oh. Yeah, one thing. I'm not sure if it's connected, but there's this girl. She's pregnant, and her pregnancy is weird."

"Weird how?"

"Well, her mom swears she wasn't pregnant when she disappeared two months ago, but now she's almost ready to deliver."

I told him about Tamara's case and about finding her in the street and taking her to the hospital. "And her doctor said there was another baby a few months ago that might have been an alien. And when I'm near her, I feel... something similar to what I feel around the... the demons or whatever."

"I see. I'd like to look into that more, but for now, do you mind if I pray for you?"

What exactly did he think *that* was going to do?

On the other hand, what could it hurt? "Sure."

He came around from behind the desk and placed his hands on my head.

Okay, this was getting weird. But before I could protest, he began to pray, his voice firm and masterful, full of authority. It was far different from the lofty, liturgical prayers I remembered as a kid. Shorter, for one thing. And somehow powerful.

As soon as he said "amen," he jerked his hands away, almost as though it was painful to touch me.

Pastor Chase glanced at the clock on his wall. "I need to get ready for service, but I do want to discuss this further. Will you come back?"

I followed his gaze. Had I really been in here talking to him for over an hour already? I felt like I'd barely scratched the surface of everything that was going on. I nodded.

"Good. Let's make an appointment so we can try to get deeper into what's going on here. Can you come back tomorrow?"

I didn't expect to be quite so summarily dismissed, but I got what I came for, right? I had someone on my side who believed my story, and who wanted to help me figure out what was going on. And I was free of the Eyes, at least for now. I felt good, at peace. Almost enough for me to stop worrying about what would happen when I left the church grounds.

So why was I so annoyed at being shooed from the office?

He led me out to the manicured lawn.

"Wait here," he said. He took a bag into the men's restroom.

I stood awkwardly outside the bathroom as the parking lot started to fill and people filed inside. A few noticed me and smiled. More than one cast a disdainful glance at my cut-off shorts and tank top.

I was tempted to leave, but there was a demon waiting for me in the parking lot, and Pastor Chase had explicitly asked me to wait. I crossed my arms in front of my chest and tried to shrink into the tree that shaded that part of the lawn.

Pastor Chase emerged a few minutes later wearing paint-free slacks and a button-up shirt. He smiled, but the warmth in his eyes was tainted with a cool sort of distance that hadn't been there before.

What in the world was going on with this guy?

"Will you stay for service?"

I gulped, but nodded. Anything to continue the respite from the Eyes. "Sure."

He led me across the walk to the large chapel in the center of the property. "This way."

We entered through a side door near the back of a large sanctuary.

Friendly chatter bounced off the vaulted ceilings as people found their seats. It was tempting to find a spot near the back of the room, but I forbore and followed Pastor Chase down the aisle.

From a stage at the front of the room, a young man with a guitar welcomed everyone and began to sing. The music had an upbeat pop-feel to it—very different from the liturgical chants I remembered from the few times I'd actually attended church as a child.

I found myself clapping to the beat along with the rest of the throng, enjoying the atmosphere of peace and joy that enveloped the room, despite not knowing any of the words to any of the songs.

My arm brushed Pastor Chase's, sending a sudden tingling through me. I glanced up at him, and he smiled coolly before edging away slightly, making me suddenly very aware of just how close we stood to one another.

Heat flooded my face, but he was looking up toward the guy on stage, not apparently noticing my embarrassment.

Finally, the singing ended, and a man in his mid-fifties or so stood up.

"That's Pastor Floyd Emerson, our senior pastor," Pastor Chase whispered in my ear.

I didn't quite know what to expect, but it turned out it didn't matter. Pastor Floyd's rich voice resonated throughout the room, and I'm sure he said something truly profound, but I had a really hard time concentrating.

Pastor Chase's bicep strained against his shirt, and his woodsy, outdoorsy cologne teased my nostrils. I'd forgotten how good something could smell when not tainted by the stench of sulfur. The rushing of blood pumping wildly through my ears drowned out all other sound.

The next thing I became aware of was everyone standing for one final song before the service ended.

Pastor Chase grinned down at me. "What'd you think?"

"It was good. Different from the last time I was in church."

"How long ago was that?"

The corner of my mouth twisted up in a guilty smile. "A long time ago."

"Hi, Pastor Chase," a musical voice behind me chimed.

I whirled around to see a stunning display of womanhood. Sleek, dark hair fell around the woman's shoulders, and deep brown eyes raked over me, appraising, judging, before turning to gaze soulfully up at Pastor Chase. "Who's your friend?"

SEVENTEEN

"Good morning, Desiree. This is Jack Davidson. Jack, Desiree Escobar."

I extended my hand. "Nice to meet you."

Desiree placed a soft hand in mine and gave me a plastered-on smile. "It's a pleasure. So how do you and Pastor Chase know each other?"

"Oh, I... came into the office this morning for some help with..." I paused, racking my brain for a suitable explanation, "...a project."

A twinkle lit her eyes, the kind a person wears when they know a secret they're not sharing. "I see." She turned a brilliant smile on Pastor Chase. "Are you planning to come to Bible study this week? That is, if you're not too busy with all your counseling sessions."

The slight emphasis on the word "counseling" clued me in. I should've gotten it before. I apparently wasn't a threat, because I was only coming to Pastor Chase for counseling.

Whatever.

Like I needed to compete with someone like Desiree Escobar for male attention. I turned to Pastor Chase. "Thanks for everything. I'll let you know if there are any further developments. See you tomorrow."

I brushed past Desiree and walked down the aisle, trying to block out the sound of Desiree's flirtations with Pastor Chase. Not that I cared.

As soon as I left the church lot, I could feel the Eyes again. It spat and cursed at me, lunging toward me. The hair rose on the back of my neck and gooseflesh dotted my arms despite the warmth of the weather.

The horror of its presence washed over me anew, a hundred times worse for having that brief respite from its torments. The smell of sulfur burned my nose and my stomach wanted to empty itself over and over again.

I waited, cringing, for it to call Dionysius, for it to rain down horrors upon me for defying it and going to the church.

In never happened. The Eyes raged, but other than the overwhelming oily, tainted sensation I always experienced, it didn't attack.

Good. I had things to get done.

I stopped to grab some lunch, then headed for the hospital.

Dr. Reyes saw me coming down the hall on my way to Tamara's room and came to meet me. Lines creased his forehead and the corners of his eyes. "Detective Davidson, I'm glad you're here." He put a hand on my shoulder. "Tamara's pregnancy seems to be progressing exponentially."

"What does that mean?"

"Overnight, the thing inside grew more than a week's worth. It could be born literally any day, possibly at any moment."

I snapped my jaw shut. "Can I see her? I'd like to ask her a few questions, if that's okay."

Dr. Reyes nodded. "Of course, as long as it's okay with her mother." He nodded toward a nurse and led us inside Tamara's room.

Tamara's mother sat on one side of the bed. I seated myself on the other side. "Hi, Tamara. I need to ask you some more questions. Are you feeling up to it?"

"Sure, I guess."

Ms. Cohen wrung her hands.

I smiled at her. "Ms. Cohen, I'm going to do everything in my power to get justice for your daughter, but this might not be something you want to hear."

The nurse extended his arm to her. "You look like you could use a break anyway. Why don't we go get something to eat?"

Ms. Cohen sighed but went with him.

I gave him a grateful smile and waited until he and Ms. Cohen left the room before turning back to Tamara.

"I need you to tell me more about the house where you were kept. Can you tell me what happened there? Were you alone?"

77

Tamara's head shook slowly. "There were four of us in my room. Me, Chelsea, Leila, and Madi."

Leila was a name I definitely recognized. I'd seen her in the files. The others sounded familiar, but they were pretty common names—I couldn't be sure.

"There were others in other rooms, but we never saw them," Tamara continued. "We stayed in our room the whole time. We ate in there and everything, except for like an hour a day when they let us go outside."

"Good. You're doing great. Tell me about the room. What did you do?"

"We had a TV and video games and iPads and books. There was a pool, so we could swim when we were outside."

"You couldn't sneak out the window?"

"There were bars on the windows."

The sinking feeling in the pit of my stomach grew deeper with every word. It was like a very posh prison filled with teenage captives.

And the worst part of her ordeal still needed to be addressed. "Tamara, can you tell me about when you got pregnant?"

EIGHTEEN

Tamara's throat visibly jolted as she gulped.

"Was Chet the one who got you pregnant?" I asked.

She nodded.

I smiled and squeezed her hand, encouraging her to go on.

"When he first brought me home, I stayed with him in his room. He told me he loved me and he wanted to help me, but I had to do something for him." She squeezed her eyes closed. Little streams of moisture trickled down her face. The monitor that graphed her heart rate beeped a little more erratically.

I waited quietly until she was ready.

She took a deep breath and went on. "He said he needed my permission first, but at first I was too happy, and then I was too scared to say no. Every morning and every night for a week, he..."

I braced myself, knowing what was coming.

"He took me into a closet and I passed out. I don't remember anything that happened until I woke up back in my room several hours later."

"You were out the whole time?"

Tamara nodded. "Except one time, I kind of woke up, but I'm not sure if I was dreaming. I was in this weird place that was like a lab of some sort, but there were weird lights on the walls, and some kind of monster was doing tests or something on me. He had a really big needle. But before I could scream or anything, I passed out again."

"So Chet... he never, you know, touched you?"

Tamara hugged herself with her arms. "I thought he was going to. That would've been better, I think. Then at least I could've pretended this was because he loved me." She patted her stomach.

"I don't understand. If he never touched you, how…?"

Tamara hugged herself tighter. "I don't know. In the lab, I guess."

That didn't make sense. What kind of human trafficking ring used young girls for lab experiments?

"Anyway, after that first week, he stopped. He put me in the room with the others."

"Were any of them pregnant, too?"

Tamara nodded. "They all were. Chelsea had been there the longest. When it was time for hers to be born, the doctor came—"

"The doctor?" I interrupted.

"Yeah. There was a doctor who came to check on us once a week to make sure we were healthy and whatever. He came and took Chelsea. She was real scared, like screaming and stuff. She said she wasn't going to go, that she wouldn't give her life for the thing inside her."

Apparently Tamara was aware that the fetus she carried was abnormal. Or, at least, Chelsea had been. I wasn't sure whether that was a good thing or a bad thing. "Go on."

"Madi told me that the girl who was in there before me never came back, and nobody would talk about her. One day when she was going outside, she saw a baby, except it was more like a toddler, only not really. It was… scary."

"Scary how?"

"I don't know. Madi didn't say. She just said it really freaked her out, because it looked like a monster version of the first girl. She could tell, because it had her same frizzy black hair. Anyway, so when they took Chelsea, and Madi told me all that, I decided I wasn't going to stick around for that, no matter what."

"Good for you. That took a lot of bravery. How did you get out?"

Tamara drew in a long, slow breath. "About a week after they took Chelsea, Leila's time came. She started kicking and screaming, and she scratched the doctor's face pretty good. Chet and the lady who brought our food came to help him drag her out, and I stuck my foot in the door so it wouldn't close all the way. They were so busy with Leila, they didn't notice."

Resourceful. Girl after my own heart. "Good. That was a smart thing to do."

She offered me a weak smile. "Madi was too scared to come with me, and I didn't have time to try to convince her. I just had to get out of there."

"You did what you had to."

"Yeah, I guess. Anyway, the front door set off an alarm when I opened it, so I just ran as fast as I could, hoping to find someone—anyone—before they caught up to me. And then I saw your car."

"You did the right thing, Tamara." I patted her arm. "We're going to find the rest of those girls, okay?"

She nodded.

I stood to go and pulled one of my cards from my pocket. "You get some rest. I'm going to see what I can find out about where you were, but I'll be back. If you can think of anything else that might help me, either write it down or call me, okay?"

"Okay."

I went into the hallway and found Ms. Cohen pacing, a cup of coffee gripped in her hands.

"You can go in now, Ms. Cohen."

She still looked frazzled, but she seemed calmer than when she'd left. I stepped into the hallway, followed by Dr. Reyes, who closed the door behind us.

"Did you get anything useful?" Dr. Reyes asked.

"I think so. I at least know the names of some of the other victims, and I have some things I can start narrowing down about the house. I need to figure out who 'Chet' is, though. Whoever—or whatever—he is, he's intentionally breeding these things in these girls. I need to find him and the rest of his spawn."

***

It was late when I finally got home. I settled into the couch and called Bridget.

"Hey, you. How are you feeling?" she asked.

"Better. I think it was just some fluke."

"Weird. So what have you been doing all day?"

"Working."

"On a Sunday?"

"Yeah, caught a random lead. I'll fill you in tomorrow. How was the party?"

"Awesome. It's a good thing I was off-duty."

"Wow, sounds like I missed a great time! What about that guy, the one who invited you?"

"Dion. He was fantastic. We spent the night together."

Something about that made my stomach roil. The Eyes cackled in sadistic glee. Sleeping with a guy on the first date wasn't out of character for Bridget, but something about this hookup seemed wrong somehow. But what could I say? "That was really fast."

"I know, but it felt so right. We connected on a level I never knew was possible. I could totally fall for this guy."

"I can't wait to meet him, then."

"Oh, hey, he's here. I have to run. See you at work tomorrow."

"Okay." I hung up the phone and leaned back against the couch cushions. Who was this Dion guy, and why did it make the Eyes so happy that Bridget slept with him?

NINETEEN

I went in to the precinct first thing in the morning and headed straight to the captain's office.

"What did you get from the girl?" he asked.

I gave him a brief rundown of what Tamara had told me about her experience, then pulled up a city map on the computer and found the area. "This is where I found her. She said she had run five or six blocks from the house where she was being kept captive before she ran into me. The house is in a development where they all look the same and there are bars on the windows. It also has a pool. I drove around the area, but it's been pretty massively built up. I had no way of pinpointing which one it was."

"Good work, Jack. That gives us a lot to go on. Anything else?"

"Yeah, one weird thing. Tamara said he never had sex with her. Now, it could just be her repressing the memories, but she claims she was blacked out the entire time, except once she woke up in a lab, briefly, before passing out again."

"No sign of a lab up in that residential area, I assume."

"None."

The captain tapped his pen against his teeth. "Let's go with the repression theory for now. What else?"

I told him about the other girls, the two disappearing after they gave birth, and how the one had fought back.

"Good lord, what kind of sicko does this? What is he doing this for?"

I decided not to mention the part about the babies possibly being alien spawn just yet. "We need to get some patrols out there. Start checking out houses in a seven- or eight-block radius from where I found her. It shouldn't be too many once we narrow down the ones with pools and bars on the windows."

"I'll send a couple squad cars out there right away."

"Thanks. Let me know what you find. I need do a couple things before I get back to the hospital and check in with Tamara. Oh, and will you send a sketch artist down? I'd like to get a composite of Chet circulating, as well as of the lab doctor. He should be easier to identify, especially with scratches down his face."

I left his office and sat at my desk. I logged into the social networking profile I'd created and started browsing through messages. Mostly boring teen stuff, rife with inane babble and atrocious spelling.

One message stood out, though. More mature sounding, articulate. Someone going by the name Gabe. He still used some popular vernacular and text-spelling, enough to make it look like a teen might have written it, but something I couldn't quite put my finger on about the message made me think there was more to him than the average horny teen boy.

I responded to the message, doing my best to make my spelling poor enough to pass for a needy teen girl. I made up a story about how pissed I was at my mom for treating me like a child since my dad left. That should be enough to intrigue my pedophile alien, if Gabe was him.

I logged out of my profile and gathered my things. I'd head to the hospital as soon as I finished jumping through my therapy hoops. Maybe I'd see if Pastor Chase wanted to come…

Crap.

I checked my watch. I'd totally missed my appointment with him this morning.

I pulled out my phone and called him. "Pastor Chase? It's Jack Davidson. I'm so sorry I missed our appointment. I got busy with work and totally forgot."

"I understand. How's the case coming?"

"I'm not sure yet. We're sending some patrols out to the area where I found Tamara to see if we can get a lead on the house where she was being kept. I'm about to head back to the hospital. Do you maybe want to come?"

"Sure. We can talk in the car on the way, if you want."

"Sounds great. Should I pick you up at the church?"

"Yes, I'm here now."

I hung up and started heading out when I remembered I was going to talk to Ken. I stopped by his desk on my way. "Hey, how's your alien thing coming?"

He smiled when he saw me. A little too excitedly. "About the same. Sifting through reports."

"You had one where the woman said she'd been impregnated, right?"

"Yeah, why?"

"Is she still pregnant?"

"No. She said the aliens came to her house in the middle of the night one night and removed the baby from her. She has a scar from where they stitched her up at the hospital, but the doctors couldn't say for sure how she got the cut. She'd been pregnant at some point, but the doctors weren't sure how recently. One doctor suggested she'd miscarried and cut herself as a form of post-partum depression or something."

"Can I get her contact info from you?"

"Sure, why?"

"Just a hunch so far, but I think it might be connected to my kidnapping case."

His brows lifted. "How so?"

"I'm not sure yet. I just want to follow up. Send me an email with that information, would you? I have to run."

I hurried out before he could ask me any more questions.

"Jack!" Bridget's voice stopped me as I was getting into my truck.

"Hey, Bridge. What's up?"

"Where are you going?"

"I'm picking up Pastor Chase and heading down to the hospital to check in on Tamara."

"Pastor Chase?"

"Yeah, I told you about him, didn't I?"

She shook her head. "No. Where did you meet him? Is he cute?"

I couldn't hide the grin that spread across my face. "Gorgeous. I sort of ran into him while I was working this kidnapping thing."

"Single?"

I nodded.

She punched my arm. "Jack, I can't believe you kept this from me! When do I get to meet him?"

"There's nothing going on to keep from you. I only met him yesterday. He sort of ended up helping me work through some things with my schizophrenia issues."

"I thought you already had a therapist."

"I do, but Pastor Chase is different. He's not a shrink, he just has a lot of knowledge about..." About what? Demons? Aliens? Psychotic

86

breaks? "About stuff. He doesn't see me as anything beyond a counseling patient."

"Well, kick his cute butt into gear! Hey, I know. This weekend we should double. Get your pastor on board, and I'll talk to Dion."

"Okay," I agreed, though I had no idea how Pastor Chase would take me inviting him on a double date.

I slid into my truck and hurried to the church to get Pastor Chase. As soon as I pulled into the parking lot, the Eyes started hissing and writhing. I smiled at its discomfort as I trotted toward Chase's office.

It must've taken Pastor Chase's earlier warning seriously, because it didn't try to follow me in. I had to learn how he did that.

"Good morning, Jack."

"Hi, Pastor Chase. You ready to go?"

He nodded. "I see you're free of your little friend."

"Not really. It's waiting by my truck. It never leaves me alone, but I'm getting pretty good at tuning it out."

When Pastor Chase got in the car, the Eyes began to hiss and spit, like Bridget's cat did the one time one of her friends brought his dog over, throwing a fit and hiding in the corner, even though the dog couldn't have cared less that the cat was there.

"I've been thinking about your situation," Pastor Chase said. "I've been trying to figure out exactly why and how it is you're aware of the demons—"

"I'm not convinced demons are what I'm dealing with. There's a lot of evidence they could be aliens. Or some kind of monster. I haven't decided yet."

Pastor Chase smiled. "Fair enough. Suppose we call them monsters."

"Deal."

"Point being, you know they're real entities. They've affected you physically, and others are aware that they exist. Me, for one. However, most people have no idea they exist or that they can affect this reality."

"Right."

"Yes. Well, I've been doing some research, and I think I have some insight. I believe these monsters are demonic. Previously, I'd always been under the belief that they operate on a strictly spiritual plane, but my research suggests they're much more than that. They're real, and they're powerful."

I'm pretty sure I concluded the same thing more than once. "Mmm-hmm."

"Everything I've read suggests these creatures exist not just on a supernatural plane, but on a physical one that overlaps with ours."

"Meaning?"

"They dwell in another dimension."

My heart sped up, the familiar nausea sending chills through me.

Another dimension.

Like the one behind the rip in the sky the night Trent died.

TWENTY

"Alternate dimensions?" Despite what I'd seen, I couldn't quite get my head around the idea.

He shook his head. "No, not alternate, exactly. More like additional."

I stared at him, trying to wrap my mind around his words. "What do you mean, additional?"

"Let me see if I can explain it. We perceive things in three spatial dimensions, right? Height, depth, and length?"

"Sure."

"Do you have something I can write on?"

"Napkin in the glove box."

He pulled one out and retrieved a pen from his pocket. He drew a stick figure on the napkin. "Okay, this guy lives in a two-dimensional world. He's got height and length, but no depth." His finger traced the paper in the directions he was explaining.

I glanced at him periodically while still trying to keep my eyes on the road. "Okay."

"Now, suppose I could stick my three-dimensional finger through his world." He ran his finger past the side of the napkin as though inserting it through the picture. "He'd see something—an oval floating through space, maybe. He wouldn't know exactly what it was, and he wouldn't be able to see it unless we kept our finger in his world, right?"

Anyone who doesn't think physics is interesting has clearly never had it explained to them by a sexy preacher. "Makes sense."

"And we could affect his dimension, perhaps. He'd see the effects but wouldn't know what caused it."

"Right, I get that."

"Okay, now apply that theory to us. We're in our little three-dimensional world, and the spiritual—or alien or monster, if you prefer—realm exists in a fourth dimension. We may be able to see the effects they have on our reality when they choose to enter, but we don't know what's causing it."

Right, then. Great explanation, but it didn't explain squat about why I could feel them all the time. "So why can I sense them? Why am I aware of their presence here when other people aren't?"

"I'm getting to that. You said you and Trent were on a case, and when the rift opened you heard them saying, 'Kill the cop,' right?"

"Yeah."

"For whatever reason, they didn't want Trent following his lead or capturing the suspect. They entered our dimension at that moment, and somehow you got sucked in."

I had to jerk the truck to stay in my lane. "Excuse me?"

"You got pulled through that vortex or whatever it was, and now part of your mind is still there. You're aware of that dimension that overlaps ours, just enough to sense the beings that reside there, but without really being immersed in it."

"This is all kinds of crazy talk. You can't seriously think my mind is melded with an alternate dimension."

Pastor Chase shrugged. "Like I said, it's just my theory. I've got plenty more research to do, but this is the working theory I'm using as a jumping off point."

We pulled into the hospital parking lot a few minutes later. When we got upstairs, Janet Cohen was pacing the floor in the waiting room.

She stopped when she saw us. "They're doing the C-section now."

"Already?"

Ms. Cohen wrung her hands and nodded. "She went into labor a couple hours ago, and Dr. Reyes didn't want to risk her having the baby naturally because it's so big."

Pastor Chase put a hand on her shoulder. "Hi, there. My name is Pastor Chase. I'm here to help in whatever way I can. She's in good hands. Try not to worry."

Her lips stretched in a tight line that I think was supposed to be a smile. "Thank you, pastor."

His answering smile revealed the cutest dimples.

Get it together, Jack. This is not the time to be drooling over cute guys.

"Can I get you anything?" Pastor Chase asked Ms. Cohen. "Coffee? Something to eat?"

"Coffee."

He nodded and turned to me. "Jack?"

"Coffee would be great, thanks."

He disappeared down the hall.

I sat in one of the vinyl chairs. A memory of the waiting room at the mental hospital washed over me, making me shudder. I was glad when Pastor Chase returned carrying three cups of coffee. He looked so sweet, going out of his way to make us comfortable. I could totally see myself going out with him.

That reminded me of Bridget's proposition.

Pastor Chase handed one cup of coffee to Ms. Cohen and one to me before digging sugar and creamer packets out of his pockets.

Ms. Cohen walked to the other side of the room and gazed through the window down the hall.

I took a deep breath. This was as good a time as any. I ripped open some creamer and sugar, staring hard at them so I wouldn't have to look at him as I asked my question. "My friend Bridget really wants me to come out with her this weekend and meet her new boyfriend. I don't really want to be a third wheel, so do you maybe want to come along?"

I took a sip of coffee to hide my nervousness and burned my tongue. I was still sputtering and trying not to look like an idiot when he answered.

"Sure."

That didn't help my coughing fit. "Really?"

"Yeah, why not?"

"Great. I'll let you know what the plan is whenever I talk to Bridget."

"Sounds good."

I grinned like an idiot child and quickly brought the coffee shield back up to hide my face.

Thankfully, all attention turned away from me as Dr. Reyes came through the door. He smiled at Ms. Cohen. "The surgery went well. Your daughter is doing fine. You may go in and see her now."

"What about the baby?"

"He seems to be healthy."

If Janet Cohen noticed the slight pause, she didn't acknowledge it. She hurried through the doors.

As soon as she was out of sight, I turned to Dr. Reyes. "What's wrong?"

He winced. "There's nothing I can put my finger on. He seems to be a perfectly healthy human child, only big. He's over seventeen pounds, and she's only been pregnant for a couple months, but by all appearances, he's fine."

"Can I see him?"

"You need permission from Tamara or her mother. Hospital policy. Come on, I'll take you to them."

Pastor Chase and I followed him down the hallway and into Tamara's room. I took a seat on the opposite side of the bed from her mother. "Hey, kiddo, how are you doing?"

Tamara shrugged. "It's all still so unreal, you know?" Her speech slurred and her eyes looked groggy, probably from the anesthesia.

"I understand. Do you mind if I see your baby?"

She nodded. "Of course."

I brushed a strand of hair from her face. "Thanks. I'll be back in a little bit. We can talk after you get some rest."

"Okay." Tamara closed her eyes and leaned back against the pillows on her bed.

I glanced at Dr. Reyes. He nodded and led the way to the nursery. As soon as the door opened, I felt a wave of nausea wash over me. I knew immediately which baby was Tamara's. Not just because it was easily twice as big as any of the others, but also because of the waves of evil that pulsed out as steadily as a heartbeat.

How could that thing be human, even partially?

I stood over the crib and looked down. The baby looked up at me. Instead of sweet, cherubic innocence, its eyes conveyed a depth of hostility, as though it wanted out of the tiny body which bound it. There was something else, something I almost didn't catch at first. I glanced again, and it hit me.

The child had six fingers on each hand.

I stepped back, not sure what to do or even think.

Dr. Reyes put a hand on my shoulder. "Any thoughts?"

I blew a heavy breath through pursed lips and raked my hand through my hair. "It's not human, I'm sure of that. Beyond that, though, I don't know. And I'm not sure what, if anything, can be done."

Dr. Reyes frowned. "Let me know if there's anything I can do to help."

"I will. Thanks."

He started to walk away.

"Oh, hey, Doc?"

He turned around, smiling. "You can call me Isaac."

He had a great smile, too. Why was I suddenly surrounded by men who looked hot when they smiled at me?

93

I pushed the thought away. "Isaac. I'm going to need Tamara to help me find the house where she was held, so if you could let me know whenever she's able to be released, even temporarily, I'd appreciate it."

"Of course."

He would make a good ally. That was all. Just like Pastor Chase. A collaborator in this war against inter-dimensional… whatever they were.

The world was on the brink of something. I didn't know what, yet, but I could feel in my gut as surely as I could feel the antagonism of the Eyes hovering just over my shoulder that it would be catastrophic. Whatever was coming, I would need all the allies I could get.

Tamara was sleeping when I returned to her room. I sat down to wait, and Pastor Chase sat beside me. "Do you need me to take you back to the church?"

"No. We can stay as long as you need to."

I smiled at him. "Thanks."

A shout came from down the hall.

I jumped up and rushed toward the nurses' station.

A cacophony of electronic beeping, running feet, and shouted orders echoed down the hallway.

The sounds of panic.

In an instant, my gun was in my hands, and I was racing down the hall toward the source of commotion. Toward the nursery.

An alarm pealed, and two security guards rushed onto the floor.

Dr. Reyes—Isaac—stood next to a white-faced, slack-jawed nurse. I took a step closer and was immediately assaulted by the chill and nausea that accompanied the solid monsters, ones like Dionysius, but I couldn't feel an actual presence in the room. It felt more like a residue left by whatever monster had been here.

I choked back the bile that rose in my throat and looked around the room. A scorched black line stretched across the majority of the linoleum floor. "What's going on?"

Isaac's eyes reflected profound confusion. "Tamara's baby disappeared."

TWENTY-ONE

"What? How?"

"I don't know. Natalie was on duty when it happened." He nodded toward the very freaked-looking nurse.

I flashed my badge toward the group of nurses and gawkers crowding the room. "Please step out. I've got the situation under control." I turned toward Natalie. "What did you see?"

"I... I'm not sure."

"What about that?" I pointed to the black scorch mark on the floor. "How did that get there?"

Her gaze followed my finger, but nothing registered in her eyes. "What about what?"

I blinked. How could she not see it?

It dawned on me that the scorch mark existed in the other dimension. I was the only one who could see it. Great. Just when I thought I was done looking like a crazy person.

I shook my head. "Nothing. Never mind. I thought I saw something." I looked at Isaac. "Can you put someone else on duty in here and find us a quiet place to talk?"

"Sure. Kendra, take over for Natalie, please."

I turned toward the two security guards. "Secure this area. Lock down the exits. Get every available man searching the hospital. When the cops get here, let them know where I am."

I called my captain next. "Tamara had a C-section this morning, and her baby was just kidnapped from the hospital. I have security searching the hospital, but we're going to need backup."

"I'm sending them now."

"Thanks." I hung up and looked at Isaac. "Doctor?"

"This way." He added, "Detective."

I took Natalie gently by the arm and followed Isaac down to his office. He offered me his chair. I scooted it around to the front of the desk so it sat next to the one in which Natalie seated herself. "Dr. Reyes, would you ask someone to get us some coffee, please? Water, too?"

He gave a curt nod and stuck his head out the door, relaying the request.

I looked at Natalie, searching her eyes. "Can you tell me exactly what happened in there?"

She shook her head and ran her tongue over her lips. "I don't know. It's impossible."

"Natalie, listen to me. I don't care how crazy it sounds, just tell me everything you remember."

"I was in the nursery, and there was a flash of light."

The memory of the sky opening the night Trent was killed smacked me with a sharp pang.

A tap sounded at the door and Natalie and I both jumped.

Isaac opened it and took cups from whoever was on the other side. He handed each of us a cup of coffee and one of water.

Natalie gulped down half her water before continuing. "I saw something. It looked human, but... not. I don't know how to describe it."

"It's okay. Go on."

Another sip of water. "It was like I blacked out, but I was still awake. I watched everything happen, but I couldn't move, like time was frozen around me."

Once again I was in the squad car, water splashing around my feet as the river seeped in, Trent bleeding beside me, as time stood still and I watched the creatures march back through the hole they'd ripped between dimensions.

Despite my effort to remain calm for Natalie's sake, my heart raced, and my stomach churned. I took a sip of my coffee. "What happened next?"

"The thing came through the light and picked up the baby. It looked at me, and I felt—"

Her face took on an almost greenish pallor. She opened and closed her mouth a couple times, but no sound came out.

"What did you feel, Natalie?"

Her voice came out in a harsh whisper. "It wanted to kill me."

Goosebumps prickled my flesh at the thought. I knew that feeling all too well.

Natalie dropped her head in her hands. "I know this all sounds insane."

"I believe you, Natalie. You're doing fine. What happened after he took the baby?"

Her head wagged. "I don't know. Everything is blank after that. It felt like hours, but it was only a few seconds before Dr. Reyes came in and found me, and that's when I screamed."

"Okay. Thanks. You can go now." I handed her my card. "Call me if you think of anything else."

I waited until the door closed behind her before turning to Isaac. "Does Tamara know yet?"

He shook his head.

"We need to tell her. Is she recovered enough to come with me? Officers have been combing the area where I found her for potential matches to the house she described, but I really need her to identify it. That's our best chance of finding out who—or what—took her baby. And how."

Isaac and I hurried back toward Tamara's room. "No way. She just got out of surgery. Twenty-four hours, minimum, before we can possibly expect her to move."

Damn. That would make things harder.

We passed Ms. Cohen in the waiting room as we went by.

"Ms. Cohen, can you come with us, please?" I asked.

I sat down by Tamara's bedside. Groggy eyes looked up at me.

"What's going on?" Ms. Cohen demanded.

I took Tamara's hand. "Tamara, I'm sorry to have to tell you this, but someone took your baby. He was kidnapped from the nursery. We're not sure yet how it happened."

Her eyes narrowed. "Good. I hate it. I don't want it."

I glanced at Isaac, then back to Tamara. "It's okay, Tamara. I understand your feelings. And we're going to make sure Chet doesn't do to anyone else what he did to you, and for that I really need your help. I'm going to come back tomorrow after you've had a rest, and if you feel well enough, maybe you could take a ride with me and try to find the house where you were kept?"

All the color drained from her face. "I don't know."

I put my hand on top of hers. "You won't have to do anything but sit in the car and tell me if you recognize anything."

Silence stretched out for several seconds before Tamara finally answered. "Yeah, okay. I'll go."

"Good girl. I'll be back tomorrow, okay? Get some rest."

I left her room. It was only when I saw Pastor Chase sitting in the waiting room that I realized I'd totally forgotten about him. Crap. "I am so sorry. Something came up. Do you want me to take you back to the church?"

"Only if you want to. I'm all yours if you need me." His neck and ears turned the slightest shade of pink. "That is—I'm here to help."

I smiled. He was cute when he was flustered. "I've done about all I can do for tonight. I'm coming back in the morning to take Tamara down to the place where I found her to see if she can help me identify the place she was kept. If you want, you can ride with Tamara's mom. I know she'll want to be close by, but I'd like someone I trust to keep an eye on her."

"It would be my pleasure."

"Thanks. I'll take you back to the church meet you here in the morning?"

"Sounds good."

I dropped him off, and then called my captain. "Security couldn't find any trace of the abductor. I'm not ruling out the possibility that he somehow drugged the nurses in order to get past them," I said, mainly because that was the most plausible explanation I could think of, "but I think my best bet at getting to the bottom of this is to find the house where she was kept and try to find her abductor. Her doctor won't let her move for at least twenty-four hours, so I'm coming back in the morning to take her. I'll need backup when I get there."

"I'll have them meet you there. Just let me know when you're heading over."

"Great, thanks."

I arrived at the hospital twenty-four hours after the C-section almost on the nose.

Isaac wheeled Tamara out and loaded her into my truck. Pastor Chase followed behind with Ms. Cohen in his car, a sensible little Nissan sedan. A short while later, we arrived at the neighborhood where I'd found Tamara. Ken and a few others were already there.

I pulled out my radio. "Follow me." I turned to Tamara. "Okay, this is where I found you. Do you remember what direction you came from?"

Her green eyes flickered up one street and down the next. "I don't know."

It's okay. Take your time. Do you see anything that looks familiar?"

She swung her gaze slowly across the street, and stopped. "That house with the well in front. I'm pretty sure I passed that."

"Good work." I pulled slowly toward the house, pulling out my radio as I did so. "I need the list of possible houses we compiled," I said.

Someone sent it to my phone. I glanced at the addresses as we drove slowly past the house with the well. "Look around some more. Do you recognize anything else?"

A tear trickled down Tamara's face. "I don't know."

I patted her arm. "It's okay. Just relax. I'm going to keep driving. Just let me know if you see anything that stands out, okay?"

She sniffed. "Fine."

We drove up and down several streets before she finally recognized anything. "There!" She pointed to another house with a well out front. "That's the one, not the other one with the well. I remember, because I almost ran into that cactus."

I drove past the house.

Tamara squinted and frowned, finally pointing up the street. "Maybe over there?"

I edged the truck up the street.

"I think I passed that house. I'm not sure, it just looks kinda familiar."

A strange chill crept up my spine. The hair rose on the back of my neck and the bottom dropped out of my stomach.

In an instant, I knew.

TWENTY-TWO

Three houses down on the left, just inside the cul de sac. The house was sprawling, though not as large as the one where Bridget went to the party.

The large front lawn was all rock, with a few scattered shrubs accenting it. The house, like all the others on the street, was painted in a nondescript sand color, and southwestern tiles by the front door announced the street number.

I spoke into my radio. "Ken, any of those addresses in this neighborhood?"

"Yeah, a couple of them on this block."

"Thanks." I knew beyond a doubt which one it was, but I couldn't make a move without Tamara's positive identification. "Tamara, we're in a cul de sac. Do you remember if the house you were in was in one?"

"Um... maybe. Yeah, I think so."

"Do any of these houses look familiar?"

"I'm not sure."

Agitation pricked me. I pushed it down, forcing my voice to remain even for Tamara's sake as I slowly circled the dead-end. "Take your time. Think. Was it one of these? That one has bars on the windows."

I knew I was leading, but I also knew that what I felt couldn't be denied.

"Yeah, maybe."

So close. "I need you to be sure, Tamara. Is that the house where you were being kept?"

"I think so. Yes, that was it."

102

Good enough. I picked up the radio. "We have a positive I.D. Let's go."

I jumped out of the truck and pulled my gun. Ken and the others who came as backup joined me.

Pastor Chase stepped out of his car and stood there, looking awkward.

"Stay here with Tamara. Keep her safe," I ordered.

He nodded. "Of course."

I pointed to Ms. Cohen, still sitting in Pastor Chase's car. "You stay in the car."

She nodded.

I motioned some of the other officers around the back and some to follow me as I marched up to the front door. I pounded on it. "Police, open up!"

From inside, I heard a scream.

Probable cause.

I kicked the door in.

People lined the wall of the entryway, hands in the air. They all wore the same pale blue shirts and navy slacks, and their faces bore the same expressions of terror and submission.

"Find the girls," I ordered my men. A group of officers streamed past me, filing into the house.

I glared at the group in the hall. I did a quick mental assessment, gauging which seemed to be most likely to be cooperative. One man looked at me with pleading eyes. He wore an apron over his uniform. A chef? He'd do.

"Where's Chet?"

The man collapsed in a heap on the floor.

I shifted my gaze to the woman next to him, a stout, Hispanic woman. "Where's Chet?"

"He's... he's gone. About an hour ago, he and all the girls just... disappeared."

"What do you mean 'disappeared'?"

"I don't know. I was in the kitchen, and when I went to serve lunch, they were all just gone."

Ken came out of the back room. "The rooms are all completely empty. There are no teenage girls here."

"Gather everyone. We're taking every person here down to the station." I looked at the woman. "You're going to tell me everything—and I do mean *everything*—that went on in this house."

Her head bobbed. "Yes, ma'am."

Except for the seven people—three men and four women—claiming to be maids, cooks, and midwives, the house was deserted. No inter-dimensional monsters, no pregnant teens, nothing except for empty rooms that looked like they'd been vacated in a hurry. Drawers hung open, rumpled blankets covered the beds, and a few scattered items of clothing were strewn around, but otherwise there was no sign of habitation.

I stood in one of the rooms and closed my eyes. If there was nothing here, how did I feel *it*? How did I know this was the right place?

I touched the wall and a shudder ran through me. Some sort of residual taint covered everything. Like the house was some sort of inter-dimensional hotspot. Which, I guess, it kind of had to be. Chet had gotten in and out without raising the suspicions of his neighbors.

"Jack, you coming?" Ken called from outside.

"Yeah." I joined him in the front yard. "Close this place off. It's officially an active crime scene. I want forensics down here, and I want to know everything there is to know about this place. And talk to the neighbors, see if anyone saw anything. Even the most minute detail."

Ken nodded. "Got it."

A bevy of activity went up with a line of police tape. There was something else happening here, something in the Eyes' dimension, but I couldn't concentrate on it with everyone else here.

I walked back to my truck. "You did great, Tamara. Let's get you back to the hospital now, okay?"

She nodded and I motioned to Chase. "I want to come back here after everyone else is gone. Maybe tomorrow or the next day. Will you come with me?"

"Of course," he said. "Just let me know when."

I dropped Tamara back off at the hospital with her mom. I nodded to Pastor Chase. "You ready to go back to the church?"

"Sure." He stared at me, through me.

"What is it?"

"What happened back there? When you came out of the house, you looked like you were going to be sick."

"I knew that was the place. I had to wait until Tamara identified it before I could make a move, but as soon as we got near the cul de sac, I knew exactly which house it was. I could feel the—I don't know, the residual effects of the other dimension, I guess. But there was nothing there. Chet, or whoever he is, was gone, and the girls with him."

"You felt the same thing at the hospital, after the baby was taken."

"Yeah, how did you know?"

"I could see it in your eyes. You saw something that the rest of us couldn't see."

"There was a mark on the floor, like a scorch mark, at the hospital. I think that was where the dimensional portal or whatever opened up. There's one thing I don't understand, though. How did Chet get away? I mean, I guess I understand with the baby, since it's half-monster, or demon, or whatever, but those girls are bound to this dimension. How did he escape with them?"

"I guess you'll have to ask him that when you find him."

"How am I supposed to find him when he can escape to another dimension?"

"You have access to that dimension. You just have to figure out how to use it."

"I guess. Thanks." I smiled and reached out to squeeze his hand. It was a perfectly innocent, friendly gesture, but he pulled his hand away, his body language getting cold and distant.

Every time I thought we were connecting, every time I thought things were starting to go well, he pulled away and suddenly things were awkward between us. What had I done? How had I managed to alienate him and make things all weird?

A wave of relief washed over me when we finally pulled into the church parking lot. "Listen, I really appreciate you hanging around all day. It really helped having you there."

"It was my pleasure."

I nodded. "So, I guess I'll see you later."

"Yes. Please let me know any further developments you come across in the case."

I smiled, still feeling awkward and not knowing why. "Sure. Later."

I was glad to get to the station and begin the rounds of interviews. Maybe something one of those servants from the monster brothel said would give me a clue as to what the hell was going on.

TWENTY-THREE

I began my series of interviews with the man who'd collapsed when I questioned him at the house.

"Please state your name for the record."

"Ronald Partridge."

"Ronald, what can you tell me about the house where you were picked up?"

"The man who owned the house never told me his name. The girls called him Chet, but I doubt that was his real name."

"How many girls?"

"Sixteen at a time. I only worked there a few months, but in the time I was there I saw about thirty of them cycle through."

"What did you do there?"

"I helped with cleaning and taking the girls out for their exercises."

"Tell me about the girls. Why were they there?"

"Chet was..." His face reddened. "He said they were his soul mates, that he needed them."

"Are you telling me you stood by and knowingly allowed him to rape underage girls?"

His face paled and his Adam's apple bobbed. "I didn't know how old they were, and they came willingly."

"Willingly? Really? You're telling me none of them wanted to leave?"

He stared at the table. "Not exactly. They came on their own."

"But they were kept against their will." It wasn't a question.

"Yes."

"And you still did nothing?"

His eyes widened, and his hand on the table began to tremble. "I couldn't. I was trapped inside the house. I tried to leave once, and there was... some sort of barrier. I couldn't see it, but it kept me from going further than the mailbox. And the day after I tried to leave, my son—" His voice cracked and he swiped a hand across his nose. "Chet gave me a picture of my son in the hospital, bruised and torn up. They told me next time I tried to leave or draw any attention to the house, they'd kill him."

"You lived there?"

He nodded. "We all did. We had two staff bedrooms on the other end of the house from the girls, one for men and one for women. Chet said it was temporary, and we'd get to go home soon if we cooperated."

"Why didn't you call the police?"

"The house didn't have a phone."

"You didn't have a cell?"

His head wagged. "I did, but I couldn't use it. There was some sort of interference. I couldn't get through."

"Okay, you were trapped, no phone, no escape. How did you get there in the first place?"

Color rose in his cheeks and he focused again on the table. "It's a little hard to understand."

I gave him my best glare. "Try me."

"I have some latent psychic abilities. I was communicating with one of my spirit guides, and he offered me a chance to help with a project that would ultimately bring about world peace."

I turned away so he wouldn't see the incredulity on my face and took a deep breath, schooling my features to impassivity. "Go on."

"Naturally, I was flattered to receive such an offer. My spirit guide told me to tell my family I'd be out of town for awhile, then go to an address downtown. Someone would be waiting for me."

"What was the address?"

"I don't remember now, but there was nothing there. It was an empty lot. A car was waiting for me."

"So the car took you straight to the house?"

"I guess so. I fell asleep almost as soon as I got in the car. When I woke up, I was inside the house. Chet told me what my job would be, and that was it."

"What happened if you didn't do your job?"

A shudder wracked his body. "I never wanted to find out. There were rumors about someone who refused to do their job."

I waited with clenched fists, trying to be patient as I waited for him to continue.

"Nothing solid, just a bunch of conflicting stories, but most of them involved a severed hand out back."

I felt bile rise up in my throat. "A what?"

"Somebody found a hand in the back yard that supposedly belonged to the former cook who refused to be a part of what was going on and wouldn't do what she was told."

"A severed hand?"

"Yeah."

I shook my head, as if that would shake the image from my mind. "So you did your job. What next?"

"Then the one girl escaped a few days ago."

"How? If there was a barrier blocking the house, how did she get out?"

"I have no idea. The barrier was still there when I went out yesterday morning."

"Then what?"

"Earlier today, Chet came in and took the bodyguard aside, but I could still hear him. He said he got the baby, but they needed to move now, so gather the girls and meet him in the office. He took them all in, and the next thing I knew, they were gone. All of them just disappeared."

"What do you mean disappeared? Drove away? What kind of car?"

He shook his head. "I mean disappeared. One minute they were there, the next they were gone. The car was still in the garage. We tried to leave, but the barrier was still up. I have no idea how the girl got out or how you guys got in or how we got out after that. Anyway, about an hour after they disappeared, you guys showed up."

"Anything else?"

He shook his head.

"Okay. I may need to talk to you again. Don't leave town."

The rest of the interviews were virtually the same. Lured under false pretenses, threatened if they didn't do what they were ordered, no way to call out, some sort of force field keeping them from leaving. It was like I'd stepped into some B horror movie.

I spent the rest of the week working on the case, nonstop except for a few breaks to go to therapy.

I heard the same things over and over. In the house caring for the girls were a cook, three women to clean and care for the house and the girls, two men, Mr. Partridge and one other, who acted as security and general caretakers, and a midwife who gave the girls prenatal checkups. She was the only one who had any new information for me.

"When the girls went into labor, I delivered their babies and took care of them. I was not permitted to attend to the girls' aftercare, despite that I could tell there was massive hemorrhaging. Chet insisted I focus only on the babies. He claimed he'd take the girls to the ER."

As we'd never gotten any reports of any of those missing girls showing up in any hospital, I had to assume he was lying about that. Big surprise. "Did you believe him when he said that?"

She shook her head. "No. But what could I do?"

It was true. Based on everything I'd heard, there really wasn't much she could've done. But the question remained, what had Chet done with the girls? Were they still alive? Did they die after giving birth? If so, what had he done with the bodies?

Maybe forensics had something, any sort of clue I could use to figure out what had happened. Or if I could find the lab Tamara mentioned—but I had no information that front any more than any other.

Deep down, though, I knew they hadn't escaped. The girls could be buried in some alternate dimension where I'd never find them.

My phone beeped, indicating a voicemail. It was from Isaac, telling me Tamara was being released from the hospital, but that her mother promised to be available if we had any more questions.

This whole case was nightmarish on every level. I got up to refill my coffee, then and pored over the transcripts from the interviews, hoping to catch something I'd missed, anything that would give me a clue that I could follow.

My perusing was interrupted by Bridget's staccato greeting. "Hey, Jack, we still on for tonight?"

What? What was she talking about?

She apparently interpreted my blank stare correctly. "Our double date?"

"Is it Friday already?"

She cocked her head at me.

I ran a hand through my hair. "I mean, yes, as far as I know. I have to check with Chase, but I think we're good."

"Great." She glanced pointedly at the clock on the wall behind my head. "So you're heading home any minute to get ready, then?"

I grinned. "You should talk."

Golden waves bounced as she tossed her head. "I'm leaving right now."

"Me, too. I'll see you there."

I tried to remember if I'd actually called Chase to confirm.

Yes. I'd called him after Bridget told me the plans to go to dinner. I left a message on his voicemail, and he'd texted back. Good.

I picked up my phone and dialed his number. "Hi, Chase, it's Jack."

"Hey there. You're not calling to cancel, are you?"

"Nope, just making sure you're still on. Do you want to meet me there, or do you want me to pick you up?"

"I'm good with carpooling, if that's okay with you. I'm still at church, so if you don't mind swinging by here, I'd appreciate it."

"Sure. I'll see you in about an hour?"

When I got home, I showered and dressed quickly, then stopped by the church to pick Chase up. He smiled warmly when he saw me, but he didn't hug me or even shake my hand or do any of the physical gestures that one might expect on a first date.

Was it a pastor thing?

I had no idea, but at least it wasn't super awkward or tense, like I'd worried it would be.

We arrived at the restaurant and Chase walked by my side, but without any actual physical contact.

He opened the door, and a pervading sense of evil overwhelmed me. Chills shot up my spine. Every hair on the back of my neck stood on end. The bottom fell away from my stomach and was replaced with a vicious churning. The air felt heavy, oppressive, closing in on me from every side.

The feeling was so much worse than anything I'd ever experienced—the same sensations, but stronger. I doubled over.

Pastor Chase's warm hand touched my back, and I heard his voice as if through water. "Jack, are you okay?"

Forcing myself upright, I nodded. "Yeah, I just—"

Another wave of nausea threatened to drown me, and with it came the unmistakable sense of familiarity.

Bridget's voice made its way through the fog. "Hey, Jack."

I glanced at her, but my attention was diverted by the tall, statuesque form behind her.

Bridget's voice sounded distorted, like it was winding its way through a thick soup. "Jack, this is my boyfriend—"

I gagged, the word barely forming on my tongue. "Dionysius."

TWENTY-FOUR

"Did you say something?" Bridget asked.

I shook my head.

"As I was saying, this is my boyfriend, Dion. Do you know him?"

I choked back the bile that rose up at his nearness, never taking my eyes from him. "No, but I know who he is."

Bridget's chatter about how they met faded into the background as Dionysius and I stared each other down. It was as if I could see him with two different sets of eyes.

Physically, he looked human. Tall, ripped muscles, thick, honey-colored hair, hazel eyes. Physically, he was gorgeous, god-like, the epitome of human beauty. No wonder Bridget was head-over-heels.

But the other part of me, the part that, if Pastor Chase were correct, was trapped in the next dimension, saw what he looked like under the mask. Gleaming yellow, feline eyes in a twisted, grotesque, scaly face.

When he smiled in the human realm, a row of perfect white teeth showed instead of the yellowed fangs I saw behind leathery lips.

He extended a hand, seemingly broad and strong, but to me rough and clawed.

"It's a pleasure to finally meet you, Jack. Bridget has told me so much about you." His lips twisted in what could have been a smile, but I saw a victorious sneer. He thought he'd won something.

I stepped back, almost falling into Pastor Chase. His strong hands gripped my shoulders, a solid, comforting presence giving me strength. I smiled and put on my polite voice. "It's nice to meet you, too, Dion." I turned to Bridget. "Let's eat. I'm starving."

She scampered off behind the hostess who led us to our table.

"What do you think you're doing?" I asked Dion in a low voice as we trailed behind Bridget and the hostess.

"I'm on a date, what does it look like?"

"What are you planning to do to her?"

A laugh that sounded more like a cackle escaped from him. "Oh, don't worry, I won't do anything she doesn't want me to do."

What was that supposed to mean?

"If you touch her, I swear, I'll—"

He laughed again. "You can't do a thing to me. Bridget belongs to me, and our son will rule with me after we win the war."

"Your son?"

"Oh, didn't I mention it? Bridget is pregnant. She won't realize it for a few more days, but she's going to have my baby." He hurried after Bridget, but I couldn't move.

I would've fallen if Pastor Chase hadn't been holding me up.

"Jack?" His voice sounded concerned. "What just happened?"

"What do you mean? Weren't you listening?"

"Jack, he didn't say anything. You two just stared at each other for a long time, and then he walked away."

No. Not possible. I didn't make all that up. I'm not crazy.

Chase turned me to face him and pressed his hand against my cheek. "Are you okay, Jack? What's going on?"

"It's him. Bridget's boyfriend is Dionysius, the demon or monster or whatever it is that assigned my minion to stalk me. He's the one in charge."

Pastor Chase's brows furrowed and his eyes darkened. "What do you mean?"

"Dion. He's not human."

"Do you have any idea what you're saying?"

"I'm not hallucinating. I don't know how, but he's the creature that was haunting me. Somehow he made himself look human to everyone else. Like Chet did with those girls. He's a demon."

The implications of that hit me full-force. Tamara, the girls at the house—what had happened to them was happening to Bridget at this very moment, and there was nothing I could do.

"Do you want to leave?" Pastor Chase's voice brought me back to the present.

"No. We need to stay."

Pastor Chase's lips brushed my forehead. He winced, like it hurt him to do so, but he didn't pull away.

Great. The first time he showed any affection or interest in me whatsoever, and I was about to hurl on his shoes.

I gulped back the nausea that churned my insides. "Let's go find them."

Pastor Chase took my hand and squeezed. "Let me know if there's anything I can do, okay?" He drew his hand away quickly, as if he was still uncomfortable getting too close to me.

"There is one thing," I said.

"Yes?"

"Find me a way to kill it."

TWENTY-FIVE

I wound my way through the restaurant and plopped down next to Bridget.

"You okay?" she asked. "You don't look great."

"Yeah, I just had a little bit of nausea, but I'm fine now."

She raised an eyebrow and leaned in to whisper in my ear. "Are you pregnant, Jack?"

Was *I* pregnant? She had to be kidding. I don't think I'd ever appreciated true irony until that moment. "No, Bridge, I'm not pregnant."

She cocked her head and gave me a disbelieving stare. "Okay."

After ordering, I got up to go to the bathroom, mainly just to get a breath of fresh air away from Dion's toxic presence.

Bridget followed me. "Are you sure you're not pregnant?" she asked again, as soon as we were ensconced in the privacy of the ladies room.

"Bridget, I haven't had sex since before Trent died. I'm not pregnant."

"Well, you look terrible."

"I'm probably coming down with something." I doubted that was as convincing as I tried to make it sound, but she didn't contest it.

In typical Bridget fashion, she shifted the conversation to herself. "So, what do you think of Dion?"

Could that be a more loaded question? "I don't know, Bridge. I just met him. I've only said a few words to him." Apparently.

"Jack, I know you well enough to know you're holding out on me. What is it?"

How do you tell someone her boyfriend is a monster whose goal is to impregnate her with his demon spawn? "Okay, um, first impression? He seems like a bit of a player. Like he's never really serious about anyone or anything."

Bridget just laughed. "Well, yeah. He's a professional basketball player. It goes with the territory."

Clearly, not the best warning I could've given her.

She pulled a tube of lip gloss from her purse and smeared it over her lips. "Anyway, that's part of what makes him so hot. Especially since it's different with me. He says he's never met anyone like me."

My jaw dropped. "And you fell for that? Bridge, he probably says that to *everyone* to get them into bed."

She had the grace to blush.

There was a very decent chance she really was pregnant.

"Why would you jump into something physical so soon? You've only known him a week."

"Almost two!"

I rolled my eyes. Her math was faulty, but she didn't give me a chance to argue the point.

"Besides, it's not just that he says it's different for him. It's different for me, too. I think I'm in love with him."

What the hell kind of mind control had he put on her?

"Bridge, I just think… I mean, he's a basketball player. He's going to be gone all the time on the road, surrounded by adoring sluts."

Her lip curled in a sneer. "Right, maybe I should find a preacher like you did."

"I didn't mean that and you know it. I don't want to fight. I just don't want to see you get hurt."

Her face softened a little. "I appreciate your concern, but I'll be fine. I'm really happy with him, and as my best friend, you should be happy for me."

She stalked from the bathroom, leaving me no choice but to follow.

I could barely eat, the nausea and chills were so bad, but I managed to sit there and pretend well enough. We ordered coffee and dessert, making small talk that no one but Bridget really seemed to enjoy. Finally, there was a lull in the conversation.

Dionysius glanced at me and gave me a smile, sinister and sadistic, before turning to Bridget. "Bridget, my love, I don't know where to start. I've never met anyone like you. From the moment I saw you, I knew there was something about you I couldn't live without. I've heard

117

when you find 'the one' you just know, and... well, I guess I just know."

Bridget beamed and kissed him. "I feel the same way."

"I was going to wait until we were alone," Dion continued, "but I can't think of a more fitting time than here with your best friend." He slid from his chair and sank to one knee in front of her, holding her hand. "Bridget, will you marry me?"

I didn't hear her answer. Bile rose in my throat and I escaped to the bathroom. I didn't need to hear it to know her answer, anyway. The look on her face told me without a doubt what she would say. I knew, too, that Dion was anything but in love. The only reason he'd proposed was to torment me.

That sounded totally narcissistic of me, but I knew it was true. That look he gave me, that smile—he wanted me to know that I couldn't stop him.

After emptying my stomach of everything I'd just managed to put in it, I went back to the table, a smile on my face.

"I'm so sorry about that, something seems to not be agreeing with me. Bridget, congratulations," I said with as much sincerity as I could muster. She had no idea what she was getting into, and if I ever wanted to earn her trust or help her at all, I needed to be here for her. I embraced her tightly and whispered in her ear. "All I want is for you to be happy. You know that."

She returned the hug. "I know. Thanks."

I pulled away and smiled. "I'm sure you two want to be alone. Call me later, okay, Bridge?"

I turned to Chase and held out my hand. He squeezed it, but dropped it quickly, turning toward the table. "It was very nice to meet you both."

Dionysius smiled that hateful grin again. "We'll have to do it again sometime."

Chase waited until we were out in the parking lot before speaking. "What's on your mind? I can almost see the wheels turning."

"He doesn't have any intention of marrying her. He just did that to get to me. He's only after one thing, and apparently he already got it."

"What do you mean?"

I turned to look him full in the face. "She's carrying his spawn. Like Tamara, like all those other missing girls, she's pregnant with a half-breed alien monster."

He stopped and stared at me. "What do we do?"

"Like I know? You know more about these things than I do."

"I know their nature, but I don't know their motives, their methods, or their end game."

Something tickled the back of my mind. Something Dion had said, but that hadn't registered at the time. What was it? When we had that silent conversation, he told me something.

"Jack? Are you okay?"

"I know what he's planning. I think. Dion told me, when he told me Bridget was pregnant, he said 'Our son will rule with me after we win the war.' They're planning a war. This breeding program—I think they're building an army."

TWENTY-SIX

Pastor Chase's face went white.

"Pastor Chase? Do you know what he's talking about? Do you know something about the war?"

"You can just call me Chase, you know," he said. "I'm afraid I may have a guess. Do you have time to come by my office?"

"Sure."

He pulled out his phone as he slid into the passenger seat of my truck. "Hi, Floyd, it's Chase. I need your help. Whenever you get this message, will you please meet me at the church?"

I parked at the church and followed Chase to the office building, leaving the Eyes in the parking lot, as had happened last time I came here.

Pastor Floyd arrived as Chase was pounding in the alarm code. "What's going on, Chase? You sounded like something was wrong."

"It might be." Chase disabled the alarm and led Pastor Floyd and me to his office. "Floyd, you remember I told you about Jack Davidson?"

"Of course. It's a pleasure to meet you, Jack." He smiled and extended his hand, but something in his eyes seemed wary. What had Chase told him about me?

I smiled back, gripping his hand in a firm shake. "Nice to meet you, too."

Chase went immediately to the giant Bible that sat on his desk and opened it to a spot near the beginning. He pushed the Bible across toward Pastor Floyd. "What do you know about this passage?"

Pastor Floyd adjusted the bifocals perched on his nose and peered at the page. "Ah, yes. The controversial Nephilim passage. Well, as I understand it, there are two main differing points of view. One, the more popular, of course, and then the more fringe theory."

I raised my hand. "I'm sorry, I have no idea what you're talking about. Can I get some background first?"

Chase took the Bible back and read aloud. "'When human beings began to increase in number on the earth and daughters were born to them, the sons of God saw that the daughters of humans were beautiful, and they married any of them they chose. The Nephilim were on the earth in those days, and also afterward, when the sons of God went to the daughters of humans and had children by them. They were the heroes of old, men of renown.'"

I blinked. I understood all the individual words, but the passage he read made no sense to me.

"What does that mean?"

"As I was saying," Pastor Floyd said, "two schools of thought. One is that the term the 'sons of God' refers to the righteous line of Seth, and the daughters of men refers to the ungodly line of Cain. The Sethites intermarried with the Cainites against God's will, producing a line of people who didn't follow God."

Okay, I was no Bible scholar, but that didn't sound all that interesting, and it didn't help me for crap with the problem I had with Dionysius.

Apparently Chase thought so, too. "That's what I've always heard, too. But what if we're wrong? What if it's the other one?"

Pastor Floyd steepled his fingers. "Hmm."

Chase rambled on without really waiting for an answer. "Until now, I never really saw it as a particularly probable explanation, but after this week it suddenly seems possible. I'd have to look into the theory a little more. Research some of the Hebrew nuances in context. I'd have to see some pretty convincing evidence to make me change my mind, though."

Did Chase even remember I was here, or was he just talking to Pastor Floyd now?

"Um, excuse me? Can someone please explain what's going on? What is the other theory?"

Pastor Floyd removed his glasses and rubbed them clean with the corner of his shirt. "Throughout Scripture, the term the 'Sons of God' is used to refer to angels. In this case, fallen angels. The theory is that the fallen angels, or demons, who were kicked out of heaven for rebelling against God, desired the women of earth and mated with them, creating a race of hybrid creatures, half-human and half-demon."

"You've got to be kidding me." I rubbed my temples with my fingertips.

This whole conversation was insane. A couple months ago I would've recommended *they* be locked up in the looney bin. But after the last few weeks? And especially after seeing Tamara's baby?

"That passage isn't the only one that makes reference to these hybrid creatures." Pastor Floyd took the Bible from Chase and flipped over a bunch of pages. "See here? After the Israelites left Egypt—do you know the story?"

Again, not a Bible-scholar-preacher-guy, but I wasn't completely biblically illiterate. I'd heard Bible stories the few times I'd gone to church, and Trent had made me watch The Ten Commandments. I knew enough about the plagues of Egypt and the parting of the Red Sea to have an idea what he was talking about. "Of course."

"Right," Pastor Floyd said. "So, they got to the Promised Land, but then they were afraid and didn't take the land, because the land was filled with giants. The word 'giant' is the word 'nephilim,' the same word that is used to describe the men of renown referred to in the first passage we read."

"Whoa."

"Quite. The Israelites were terrified of these giant men and refused to take the Promised Land. It was because of this that they wandered in the desert for forty years. Point of interest, though, when they eventually did take the Promised Land, God's instructions were to kill every man, woman, and child of certain tribes. Some people think that was because those tribes weren't fully human. They were made up of these unholy hybrids."

"That's just too weird."

"Exactly. Which is why so few people believe this view," Pastor Floyd said. "There are other references, as well. Do you know the story of David and Goliath?"

Duh. "Yes, I'm familiar with the general idea."

"It specifies that Goliath was from Gath, and there are references to the remnants of these hybrid tribes settling in Gath, so it seems plausible that, if the origin of these creatures is, in fact, fallen angels, that Goliath was a descendant—not entirely human."

The pieces were coming together, but there was something missing. Something I couldn't quite put my finger on.

Of course. One of the three things I looked for in potential suspects.

There was no motive.

"Okay, so these fallen angels impregnate these women and have these freakish half-breed children. Why?"

Pastor Floyd coughed. "Some of the research I've done seems to indicate that it was a plot on the part of Satan to corrupt the human race, thereby thwarting God's plan for a savior—Jesus. That's why God sent the flood. To wipe out the corrupted race and start over."

"Wasn't the Ten Commandments thing after the flood?"

Pastor Floyd nodded. "Yes."

"So, if the flood wiped them out, how did they end up in the Promised Land or whatever? And I'm not saying I totally buy into the Bible story aspect of all this, but suppose your theory is correct and God stopped the plot the first time, why did they try the same thing again?"

Chase and Pastor Floyd looked at each other, mouths open, for a moment.

Finally, Chase looked at me. "I don't know. It says they thought human women were beautiful. Maybe that held true. Or maybe they were still trying to continue with the same plan. Or maybe they had a new plan. Or maybe they were setting a precedent for it to happen again."

"Okay, then, why did they stop? I mean, there's no evidence that they kept on with this throughout history."

"Actually, there may be more than we realize, if we look in the right places." Chase stood, went to his bookshelf, and searched through the titles. "Ah, here it is." He pulled a book from the shelf and handed it to me.

"Unearthing Atlantis, by Dr. M. Ross." I looked at Chase. "I heard about this a few years ago. A bunch of archaeologists uncovered what they thought might be the lost city of Atlantis. Cool stuff, but what does it have to do with demons mating with humans and spawning hybrid monster babies?"

"More than you might think. Dr. Ross believes there is evidence of this phenomenon throughout history. Virtually every culture has some sort of legend about supernatural beings mating with humans to create a race of super-humans. The Greeks, especially, with all their god-myths and half-god heroes, like Hercules, point to the idea that inter-species breeding is a reality not a fantasy."

I tapped the cover of the book. "And that's what Dr. Ross says?"

Chase nodded. "Based on her findings at the dig site she believes may have been Atlantis, she believes these beings invaded Greek culture, portraying themselves as gods. They were revered, and as such had access to the beautiful human women. Half-breed progeny were not uncommon, and these half-humans, with their superior size and strength, were regarded as heroes."

"I always thought all those were just myths."

Pastor Floyd shrugged. "Dr. Ross asserts that all myths are based in historical facts. But her work is not the only evidence. Similar discoveries of unnaturally large human skeletons with six fingers on each hand have been made in South America and even here in the United States, in Wisconsin."

"Okay, but I'm not wrong about it being weird. It's not like this happens all the time."

"True," Chase said. "There are only a few obscure references throughout history to indicate this has been an ongoing phenomenon."

"So why now, then? Why all of a sudden are there hundreds of these things spawning all over?"

Pastor Floyd coughed.

"What is it?" Chase asked.

"I think the answer to that may be in the book of Matthew," Pastor Floyd said. "In chapter twenty-four, Jesus is explaining what the signs are of the end of the world. In verse thirty-seven, He says, 'But as the days of Noah were, so shall also the coming of the Son of man be.' If we take this view of the Nephilim, this verse in Matthew could indicate that the resurgence of Nephilim is a sign of the end of the world."

"Seriously? We're talking Armageddon here?" I'd seen enough movies to know that never ended well. My stomach dropped to the floor beneath my chair. I was a cop. A good one, but still, I was definitely not equipped to handle the end of the world. "I don't suppose Dr. Ross gives any indication on how to fight a half-god, demon, Nephilim thing?"

"No," Chase said. "She's a historian. Documenting facts, not speculating on how to destroy demons in the modern age."

I chuckled. "Sounds like that one guy from TV—you know the one I'm talking about, the guy with the hair?—that talks about aliens all the time."

It hit me like a 9mm slug to the stomach. "The aliens."

"What?" Chase asked.

"It's all connected. The increase in alien sightings, the disappearing girls and their hybrid babies. It's the same thing."

Something Trent said came back to me. In the car, while we were chasing the leader of the sex slave ring. "We're stopping Armageddon."

TWENTY-SEVEN

"What?" Chase and Pastor Floyd asked together.

I hadn't realized I'd said it aloud. "Trent, my fiancé. He knew—something. The case he was working on when he died was connected to all this. Trent knew what was going on. He knew about the war. I need to go."

I didn't really think about the fact that I left the two of them sitting there, staring after me, as I rushed out.

As soon as I got out of the church's parking lot, I felt the presence of the Eyes again, but it didn't attack. It seemed... complacent. Perhaps even bored. Whatever the reason, I sure wasn't going to complain about the brief respite.

The precinct was quiet when I arrived, the night shift busily going about their duties.

"Jack? What are you doing here in the middle of the night?" the overnight receptionist, a portly woman whose name I couldn't remember, asked.

"I just have to look something up really quickly." I made my way to my desk. The captain had sent me the case file on my first day back, but I'd been so absorbed in Tamara's case I hadn't had time to go through it.

Trent's notes were all in order, but it seemed very run-of-the-mill. Interviews with a C.I., but there was a note that the C.I. died of natural causes later. No mention of his name, so that was a dead-end. The C.I. had found a warehouse where the organization had run things from sometime in the past, but it had been totally cleaned out by the time Trent got there.

A restaurant that had been used as a front to launder money made from the prostitution of the sex slaves had since been shut down. Trent couldn't prove their connection to the trafficking ring, but he had managed to shut them down based on health code violations. Even he admitted it was just a stop-gap, though—the ring would find another way to launder the money unless the police found the root of the problem.

Finally, something useful. A name, given to Trent by the C.I.

Richard Hunt.

The captain had mentioned that name—he was the guy they found in the car we were following, the man who died the same night as Trent. He was a stockbroker by day, but according to Trent's notes, no one he worked with knew about his side job—importing sex slaves, housing them in appalling conditions, only to rent them out to the highest bidder.

A few bodies had been found—wait, what was that?

I read the coroner's report on one of the bodies that had been found. The woman, a young Hispanic girl, had a cut along her abdomen. Like a poorly-performed C-section.

I looked through the others. Two more had C-section cuts. Cause of death was blood loss from those incisions. Apparently, no attempt was made to stitch the girls up or save their lives.

And there were two more bodies thought to be related to the trafficking ring. Both had given birth naturally and had suffered traumatic injuries due to the birth. Again, cause of death appeared to be blood loss and lack of post-partum care.

I grabbed my own case file. One of the missing girls from my list, the one whose body had been found in the desert, though her body had been too far deteriorated to get a conclusive cause of death, seemed to have suffered some trauma to the abdomen.

So, much like the girls Tamara was housed with, these women might have been used to incubate unnatural spawn and then discarded.

I looked at the report of the accident, the car that was found at the bottom of the river. Richard Hunt, dead by drowning. And his unnamed companion.

The report seemed incomplete somehow. What was it? The details of the other guy's autopsy were sketchy, as though the coroner didn't have much to say, other than cause of death appeared to be from debris piercing his heart rather than drowning, and the subject was exceptionally tall.

Could it be? No, that didn't make sense.

Did it?

I stared at the report, only half-seeing, as I pieced together a theory in my mind. What if his companion was Chet?

Not *the* Chet, obviously, since Chet was still alive, but someone like him. Abnormally large, extremely powerful, bent on impregnating as many unsuspecting young women as possible, using a sex-trafficking ring to procure victims, whereas Chet used the internet.

And Dion used his influence as a basketball star.

My stomach roiled at the thought. Was this what was in store for Bridget? Bleeding out after a traumatic birth because her demon lover didn't care enough to keep her alive once he got what he wanted?

I finished going through the pile of reports in the file. It helped to paint a comprehensive picture, even if I couldn't prove anything, but it was incomplete. I had no idea who these monsters were. They could be anyone, posing as rich, influential humans, getting away with whatever they wanted, and I had no way of finding them.

There had to be more. Something I was missing.

Whatever it was, it wasn't in this file. With a sigh I leaned back in my chair and closed my eyes, stretching my feet out in front of me.

I kicked something under my desk.

The box of Trent's things. I'd stuck it under there because I hadn't had the heart to go through it yet. The memories were too fresh and painful.

I had no choice, now. I had to find out whether there was anything else he knew. I picked up the box and set it on my desk.

One by one, I pulled the items from his desk out of the box. Trent's name placard, the mug with the picture of his little sister on it that he kept his pens and pencils in, a picture of the two of us at the Grand Canyon. It was all so homey and mundane. Nothing to indicate he was on the verge of uncovering a plot that could bring about the end of life as we knew it.

Behind me, the Eyes cackled in a bored-sounding taunt, looking over my shoulder and hissing at me about the uselessness of my mission. *You'll never find anything. There's nothing to find. You are useless against us. Powerless to stop us.*

On and on, until its words blended together and the icy, nauseating chill of its presence faded to the background of my mind.

At the very bottom of the box, hidden by Trent's Diamondbacks baseball cap, lay a little stuffed toy dog. I hated that thing. Trent found it on the side of the road one time when we were walking, and I protested so much he thought it was funny to keep it.

It was as ugly as I remembered, with its lopsided eyes and patchy, faded fur that made it look diseased. I'd begged Trent to throw it out, but he refused.

I remembered his grin as he held the stupid thing above my head so I couldn't grab it. "No, look, this could be important. There's a hole on the back of its neck, under the collar. Nobody can see it. It would make the perfect place to hide top-secret information."

I asked him what kind of top-secret information he was planning to hide, but he just laughed and promised to keep it at work so I wouldn't have to worry about getting germs from it all over the apartment.

I smiled and started to aim for the trash can, but stopped. Even as much as I despised the stupid toy, I couldn't get rid of that memory. At least not yet.

I held it in my hands and turned it over, touching the lopsided eyes, the patchy fur, the hole under the collar—

What in the world?

Something was in there. I stuck two fingers into the hole and pulled out the little hard plastic thing stuck inside.

A flash drive.

TWENTY-EIGHT

So, Trent really *had* hidden top-secret information. What was on here? My fingers trembled as I turned on my computer and inserted the drive.

On it was a single file labeled "Jack."

My hand trembled as I clicked it open the document.

My dearest Jack, if you're reading this, it means something happened to me. This may be hard for you to hear, but I need you to trust that what I'm about to tell you is completely true.

Reading his words made my eyes sting. I could almost hear his voice reassuring me, feel his hand taking mine and squeezing as he laid out the things he'd uncovered while working on the trafficking case.

At first, it was all stuff I knew. Girls being impregnated, babies that weren't quite human, creatures of unknown origin. Why he didn't tell me all this before, I had no idea. Maybe because he knew I wouldn't have believed him.

Even after seeing things like Tamara's pregnancy with my own eyes, I still would've been skeptical. Experiencing it, though, spending over a month in the looney bin being tortured day and night by the Eyes had opened my mind to the reality that something else was going on, something more than just sex-trafficking or kidnapping.

Jack, I know this all sounds absurd, but I'm just getting started. I found something in my investigation that leads me to believe this is much, much bigger than a sex-trafficking ring, or even more than an isolated monster trying to propagate its spawn. There is a plot underway that will change the course of history.

I continued reading, ignoring the night shift cops and everything and everyone else around me, as Trent unfolded a fantastical theory about how these creatures would bring about the end of the world.

"Jack?"

My head snapped up. "Hi, Ken."

"What are you doing here this early on a Saturday? And what are you wearing?"

I glanced down. I still had on the cute green dress I'd worn on the double date last night, my hair was still up, though tousled, and I still wore heels. I minimized the letter from Trent and smiled at him. "I was following up on a lead and lost track of time. What time is it, anyway?"

"Almost seven."

Had I really been there all night? "Oh. Wow. Okay. Good morning. I'm really busy, though. See you later."

I stared at him until he walked away, then pulled the letter from Trent back up. I'd seen enough movies to know I would need more than one copy of something like this, so I saved a copy to my desktop, a copy to an online backup service, and put a copy on another flash drive. Finally, I printed out a hard copy.

I put the original flash drive back in the hole in the stuffed dog, then carefully set the dog back in the box and placed Trent's baseball cap over it.

I stuck the second flash drive in my purse and pulled the hard copy from the printer. I needed to show this to Chase. I went straight to the church from the precinct.

It was deserted. Where was he?

It took me a minute before it dawned on me that he probably had better things to do than hang out at an empty building at seven o'clock on a Saturday morning, especially after I'd ditched him in the middle of the night.

I called him.

"Jack?" He didn't sound like I'd woken him up. Good.

"Are you okay?" he asked. "Floyd and I were really worried when you ran out last night."

"I'm fine. I found something you're going to want to see."

"I was just getting breakfast. I always go to the bagel place down the street from the church on Saturdays. Want to meet me there?"

"Sure. I'll see you in a few minutes."

I found the bagel shop, a little hole-in-the-wall place called Morning People, and grabbed the printed copy of Trent's letter. I was still way overdressed, but I hadn't had time to go home and change.

I made my way through a handful of bicyclists and other early birds milling around outside the front and was blasted by cool air conditioning when I opened the door. Chase was up at the front, ordering. I made my way toward him, but stopped when he was intercepted by a gorgeous, curvaceous brunette.

Desiree Escobar.

I was close enough to hear her trilling, chirrupy little voice as she feigned surprise at seeing him. "Chase! How funny to bump into you here. Do you come here a lot?"

What a load of crap. She knew exactly what she was doing. Stalker.

"Yes, I'm here most Saturday mornings."

"All alone? You look like you could use some company."

"Actually, I was just about to—"

"I'm actually glad I ran into you. I've been meaning to ask you something. My sister is getting married in a couple weeks, and I was wondering if maybe you'd like to come with me?"

She was inviting him to a wedding? Could she get any more clichéd?

The Eyes cackled in my ear. *Is that any worse than inviting him on a double date?*

Damn it. Little freak had a point.

"I might be able to go," Chase was saying. "When is it?"

Great. So he just accepted dates from everyone. Fantastic.

Desiree placed a hand on his arm and started talking about her dress. Neither of them had even noticed me yet.

As much as I wanted to hear about Desiree's sister's colors and the bouquet that didn't match, I had work to do.

I walked up next to Chase. "Hey."

"Jack! I'm glad you're okay." He leaned over to give me a hug, but immediately stiffened and pulled away.

What was that? Was it because Desiree was standing there? Or did I have massive body odor I couldn't detect on myself? Or was it whatever kept him from touching me before? He didn't seem to mind standing or sitting next to me, but any physical contact and he went all Puritan on me.

"Desiree, you remember Jack?"

Desiree stuck out her soft, limp hand. "Of course. So nice to see you again." Her eyes traveled slowly over my body, from my tousled hair to my classy, albeit rumpled, dress, to my heels. "That's quite the outfit for Saturday morning at the bagel shop."

"I was up all night working."

132

Her perfectly plucked eyebrows rose. "That's what you wear to work?"

"I—" I snapped my mouth shut. It wasn't worth the effort. Instead, I turned to Chase. "I found a letter from Trent."

Just then, the barista handed him two coffees. He handed one to me.

"Thanks." I fought the grin that wanted to spring to my face at the look on Desiree's face.

"My pleasure. You found a letter? From Trent?"

I nodded. "On a flash drive, hidden in his stuff. He knew... everything."

"Who is Trent?" Desiree asked.

I glanced at her. "My fiancé. He's dead."

Her face softened immediately. "Oh, no wonder," she said, almost in a whisper. She took my hand. "I'm so sorry for your loss. How did he die?"

"He was murdered by demon aliens."

TWENTY-NINE

The sympathetic smile froze on Desiree's face. "I see."

"Yeah, I think he was getting too close to unveiling their plans for taking over this reality, and they had to shut him up."

She dropped my hand. "Well, it sounds like the two of you have a lot to talk about. Chase, I'll see you at church tomorrow." She scurried away.

Chase was holding in a grin, not very successfully. "Was that really necessary?"

I shrugged. "What? She asked."

He chuckled. "Come on, let's sit. May I see the letter?"

I sat in the chair he pulled out for me at a table by the window and handed him the printed pages. I sipped my coffee and waited for him to read. The lines on his face grew more and more tense as he went on.

Finally, he set the papers on the table and looked up at me. "Jack, this is huge."

"I know."

"If he's right..."

"I know."

"We have to find Richard Hunt."

"He's dead."

"What?"

"He's the guy Trent and I were chasing the night of the accident. They found his body in the car at the bottom of the river along with that of an unknown companion."

Chase glanced over the letter again. "Where did he get all this information?"

"I don't know. Research. Interviews. The confidential informant he mentioned. Your guess is as good as mine."

"And all the time he was investigating this, you had no idea?"

I shook my head. "He never said anything to me. Not about the case, and definitely not about demons or war. The only reason I was in the car with him at the time of the crash was because we had been out. He got a tip from someone about where the perp was going to be in half an hour. He tried to leave me behind, but I insisted he needed back-up."

"So you found the guy? Richard Hunt?"

"He was in the car that matched the informant's description, leaving the place where the tip said he'd be. We followed him, hoping he'd lead us to wherever he was keeping the girls, but he made us and led us on a chase that ended with him and his companion dead in the river, Trent dead beside me, and me with half my mind trapped in an alternate dimension."

Chase blew out through pursed lips. "You think he's right about all this?"

I shrugged. "I trust him. He wouldn't have told me all this if he wasn't absolutely sure."

"So you believe me, then, that these creatures you're encountering are demons?"

"Trent believed they were, so I guess I do, too."

"And the rest of it?"

"You mean the part where Trent said they were breeding an army of half-human, half-demon soldiers to fight in a coming war and take over the world? I don't have a better explanation for what we've seen. You?"

Chase grinned. "It's as plausible as an alien invasion, in my opinion."

"So, the question of the hour: how do we stop them?"

Chase shuffled through the stack of pages. "We need to find this source Trent talked about, this Mr. E."

"I'm pretty sure that's not his real name."

"Yes, but presumably he is a real person. Is there any way to find out who he is?"

"I could go through Trent's notes again, but I don't know what I'd find. He was always very careful to make sure his confidential informants stayed confidential."

"Well, see what you can find. I'd love to find out how he knows all this. From what Trent says, this guy has a far greater understanding of

135

biblical prophecy than any I can claim. I'd love to know where he gets his insights."

"I'll see what I can do. In the meantime, we need to find out where these little half-breed spawn are being kept. They're half-human, so does that mean they're bound to this reality? Or, since they're half-demon, can they be whisked away to the other dimension? Tamara's baby was taken, so I assume they can be transported, but do they have a place there—wherever *there* actually is—to keep them, or do they have to come out on this side?"

"If I had to guess, I'd say something in between, sort of like what you're experiencing, but more so. You can sense the other side, but can't fully be present in it. I'd speculate that they can be fully aware of it and maybe even affect it and be affected by it, but they're still anchored here."

"Okay, the half-breeds can, but humans can't. But if we can't enter the other dimension, how did Chet get the girls out without anyone seeing him? All the servants said the same thing—they just disappeared."

Chase shrugged. "I don't know. Why don't we go have a look around the house and see what we can find out?"

"Good call. I wanted to do that anyway, but I haven't had time."

Chase followed me out to my truck and we made our way to the house where Tamara had been kept. Police tape still covered the doors and windows, and a cop still guarded the front. Not strictly necessary, but I'd asked for a twenty-four hour guard, just in case Chet or anyone came back for whatever reason.

I flashed him my badge. "He's with me. I need to take a look around."

The cop nodded and let us by.

Room by room, we wandered through the house, looking for any clues. The Crime Scene Unit had already combed the place, but they were looking for evidence of a kidnapper, not an inter-dimensional demon.

I could still feel traces of the other dimension lingering in the house, but dissipating in the atmosphere. The sensation of tingling on my skin, the smell of sulfur in the air spoke of the reality that this place had once housed demons, but that they were gone now.

A few scattered clothes littered the bedroom floors, a half-empty mug of something that had grown a glob of stinky blue fuzz sat on a dresser, a book lay open, face-down on a pillow.

Chase muttered something under his breath.

"What was that?"

136

He shook his head. "Nothing. Just praying."

I continued my search, through bathrooms, an outrageously large formal dining room, and an equally ostentatious kitchen, until I reached a large walk-in pantry.

Here, the feeling of the other dimension was stronger.

"What is it?" Chase asked.

"Shh." I stepped into the pantry and looked around. My arms stretched out in front of me almost involuntarily, the way they would if someone shut off all the lights and I was trying not to run into the wall.

I took a step forward.

The room grew colder, my skin broke out in goosebumps, the hair on my arms stood on end.

I looked around for something, anything that would explain the sensation.

There, along the floor and running up the wall behind an array of canned goods was a black scorch mark, like the one in the hospital when Tamara's baby was taken.

I reached my hand toward it. The tingling increased as my fingers passed over the line, almost like my hand falling asleep.

"Jack, what just happened?"

"What do you mean?"

"Your hand. It's... fading."

I couldn't see anything different, but I had a suspicion. I took a step over the scorched line, and everything changed.

THIRY

"Jack? Jack, what's happening?" Chase's eyes darted back and forth and his fists clenched as he stepped toward me.

"I'm okay," I said.

"Your voice is fading, like your body. I can still see you, but it's like you're half-way to getting beamed up to the mother ship."

"Hold on, let me see if I can figure out where I am."

I examined my surroundings, the space beyond the pantry. It was dark, barren, but thickly hot, like the desert in the dead of summer. I could see the sky, but instead of bright blue, it was a dark red—so dark it was almost black. The sun was a flickering orange flame, a sad, sputtering light that fought to maintain a glow through a thick haze. It reminded me of a movie portrayal of the surface of Mars.

I could still see the things from my reality—Chase, the house, my truck out front—but it was like how I normally perceived the Eyes—phantoms, sensations that didn't really exist. Like I was seeing them through the other side of a two-way mirror.

The smell of sulfur burned my nose. I turned to look, and for the first time, I actually saw it.

The Eyes.

The vicious little imp who'd been haunting me since the accident stood before me.

But it wasn't a vicious little imp. It was huge. It had to be at least eight or nine feet tall. Its feral yellow eyes were wide, fangs bared in what I took to be an expression of shock.

I took in its appearance at a glance, cop-trained attention to detail recording and storing every inch. It was roughly humanoid in form, two arms and two legs, but its skin was a dull, leathery gray and it had no hair anywhere on its body.

Yet I could tell what it looked like. Despite the coloring and the fangs, it was somehow still human, with a squared jaw and full lips and eyes that would've been almost nice if they weren't shadowed by such a heavy brow ridge.

A scar ran down its chest, right over where its heart would be, if it had one. And try as I might, the one thing I couldn't help but notice was that it was distinctively male.

And it had six fingers on each hand. Just like Tamara's baby. Just like—

It—he—recovered from his shock and hissed at me. "You can't be here."

"Well, I am."

He slashed at me with a six-clawed hand.

I stepped back, reeling from the sting, and touched my face. I glanced at my fingers. Blood.

I looked at him. "You're corporeal here."

"Of course," he hissed. "This is *my* world. Here, you're the insignificant worm."

"Good to know." I took another step back, keeping the space between us wide.

"How did you get here? It's impossible without…"

"Without what?"

He hissed and lunged at me. I dodged and landed a blow to his stomach. Good night, he was enormous.

He grunted, but his stomach didn't seem nearly as fazed as my fist.

I aimed a high kick at his groin as he lunged at me again. He howled, but the pain only seemed to enrage him.

I pulled my gun and fired, but nothing happened.

Snarling, fangs dripping saliva, he dove toward me.

I jumped away, toward the spot where I'd entered this realm, and tumbled out, back into my own dimension, straight into Chase. Both of us crashed to the floor of the pantry.

Chase threw his arms around me—he didn't even seem to squirm like he normally did when he touched me—and pressed his lips against my temple in a hard kiss. "What just happened?"

I relaxed against his chest, breathing deeply, unaware until that moment how exhausted I was.

"That spot is a… a portal of some kind. I went through into the other dimension."

The Eyes screeched at me, threatening to kill me if I ever made it back into that dimension.

"The demon that's been haunting me. Over there, he's solid. Strong and powerful. And a giant. He can't affect this reality, but there..." I touched my face.

Blood seeped out from the gashes across my face. A shudder ran through me as I realized how narrowly I had escaped being demon lunch, lost forever in a demon wasteland.

"There was something else," I said. "It had six fingers on each hand, like—"

"Like a Nephilim," Chase finished for me.

I nodded. "But Tamara's baby, it's real. It's physical. They're the same, sort of, so why isn't this one able to be present in this reality?"

Chase tensed. "I don't know. We should ask Floyd."

"I am sure about one thing, though. I'm pretty sure this is how they got the girls out. They took them through that hole and traveled through the other dimension to get to safety."

Chase released me and stood up. He walked toward the portal and stuck his hand through.

Nothing happened.

He took a step, and another until he was on the other side of the scorch mark. "I don't see anything."

"The Eyes—he said something about how I shouldn't be there, that it was impossible without—something. He didn't tell me what. Humans apparently can't cross over without something, which they used to get the girls out without being seen, and which I apparently have but you don't. And I'm guessing I can only go through a hole that has already been made, since I haven't randomly found myself wandering through a demon dimension before this."

"That makes sense. But if that's so, why didn't your demon follow you out?"

"I don't think it can. If it could've, it would've come through at the hospital or some other hole. It's stuck there, for whatever reason. I can go in, but it has to stay there."

Chase frowned. "Unfortunately, there's only one way to test the theory, and I'm not comfortable with that option."

Right. I wasn't terribly eager to jump through the portal and into the Eyes' waiting claws, either. But I had to figure it out. I had to know if I was right.

"The hospital. Chet or whoever took Tamara's baby tore through a hole in reality there, too. I need to at least see if that's a portal, too."

"I really don't think that's a good idea," Chase said.

"Neither do I. But I don't have any other leads." I led the way out of the house.

"Whoa, what happened to your face?" the cop on duty asked.

"Ran into a wall," I said.

I hopped in my truck and Chase climbed in the passenger side and we hurried to the hospital.

Isaac met us in the waiting area. "Jack, Pastor Chase, what brings you here? You know Tamara was released two days ago?"

I had been so obsessed in work, I'd only half paid attention to the message he'd left letting me know they were sending her home. "Yes, I got your message. That's not why we're here. I have a theory about how the kidnapper was able to abduct her baby without anyone seeing him. I'd like to check it out if that's okay."

Isaac nodded and led us back to the nursery. He waved the nurses out and stood by the door. "What are you looking for?"

I could still see the scorch mark on the floor, but it was fading much more quickly than the one at the house.

I stuck my hand over the line, prepared to yank it back if the Eyes attacked, but the Eyes stood several feet away, not too close to me, and didn't seem prepared to pounce. I took a step, gingerly crossing over the line, wary of an attack by the Eyes.

The other dimension was there, but less tangible. Or I was less tangible in it. At any rate, the Eyes didn't attack me, so maybe I wasn't really there. More like I was looking at it through a window rather than actually entering it.

"Anything?" Chase asked. "I can still see you like normal, so it must not be working correctly."

"There was definitely a portal here, but it's almost gone now."

"Portal?" Isaac asked.

"This was only used once. Chet came in to retrieve his spawn, but he was alone and he only came one time. At the house, the neighbors never saw anything out of the ordinary, so I bet he brought the girls in through the pantry. The hole between dimensions there must be... I don't know the word I'm looking for. Wider, maybe? Like the wall separating the two is thinner, the hole is torn open wider due to frequent use."

"The wall between dimensions?" Isaac sounded incredulous. "What are you talking about?"

I faced him. "This is going to sound a little nuts, but we believe that the man who kidnapped and impregnated Tamara and the others may be from another dimension, connected to but outside ours. Chase, do the finger-through-the-paper thing."

141

Chase explained the theory about the nature of the fourth dimension to Isaac as he had to me.

"And you believe somehow this creature transported these girls—and Tamara's baby—through this alternate dimension?"

"Yes," I said.

"And for whatever reason you, and *only* you, can go through the tear in between dimensions and see the other side?"

"Yes."

"Why you?"

THIRTY-ONE

"I have no idea," I said. "Something happened to me. It's a long story, but the night my fiancé died, I saw these creatures rip open the hole and hundreds—no, thousands—of them came through. Ever since then, I've been aware of the other side. I can sense when the creatures are near, hear them when they talk, even sense their emotions. One of them has been haunting me ever since. He's like a spirit on this side, he can't affect me physically, but there, he's a giant."

"Wait." Isaac stepped closer to me. "There's something I don't get. If it's like a spirit here and only solid over there, how did it impregnate Tamara? Did it take her there to do it? But if so, how did it get her there in the first place, if it can't affect her physically here?"

I thought a moment, remembering back to the moment in the hospital when I'd first encountered Dionysius, the difference I'd felt between the two entities.

I pressed my fingers to my temples.

"Jack? You okay?" Chase asked.

"Hold on, I'm thinking." I pieced together the information I'd collected over the last couple weeks. "There are two different kinds. One is solid, physically present in this dimension. That's what I believe Chet is. The other is like a shadow compared to those kind. They still have influence here. I've seen them speak into people's minds, giving them ideas they thought were their own, but they can't touch them physically in this dimension."

"You said one has been haunting you?" Isaac asked. "Is it still?"

I nodded and pointed to the other side of the room where the Eyes stood, anger and malice boiling out toward me. "He's right over there."

144

Isaac's gaze followed my finger. "Jack, I know I said I didn't think Tamara's baby was human, but... well, this has been a very tough experience for you. I think perhaps..."

"I know what you're thinking. There's nothing there. I can't see him, either. But I know he's there. The only time I actually saw him was when I was on the other side, but I've felt him nonstop for the last two months."

"But you can't get there from here?"

I shook my head. "The rift is almost sealed. I need a bigger portal, one where the distance between the two is more open."

"Like at the house?" Chase asked.

I nodded.

"Or..." Isaac began.

I looked at him. "Or what?"

"Or a place where it was ripped wide open. Maybe somewhere that thousands of them came through at once?"

The bottom seemed to drop from my stomach as I realized what he was saying. "The accident."

He nodded.

My knees felt weak, but there was nowhere to sit. I leaned back against the wall between two empty cribs. "I haven't been back there. I don't know if I can."

Isaac reached out and squeezed my hand. "I get off in half an hour. Want me to come with you?"

I smiled. "That would be nice."

Chase stepped closer. "We'll wait downstairs until you're done, then. Come on, Jack, I'll buy you a coffee."

A short while later, Isaac met us in the hospital lobby. I'd never seen him in anything other than scrubs. He looked good in a tight T-shirt and snug jeans.

I caught myself staring and quickly took a sip of my coffee. "We'll have to take two cars, unless you two want to snuggle in the cab of my truck."

Isaac chuckled. "I'll follow you."

I drove slowly, not talking, toward the last place I'd seen Trent alive. Memories flooded over me. I didn't want to go, didn't want to relive that night, but I had to. I owed it to Trent to figure out why he died. To finish what he'd started.

I parked in an empty lot and walked along the sidewalk onto the bridge.

The hole where the car had gone over was surrounded by orange traffic cones and draped with caution tape, but had not yet been repaired.

Someone had put a marker, a little cross covered with silk flowers that were already fading, at the spot. I reached out and tenderly touched the flowers.

My heart stuttered. Someone had cared enough to remember his death. This was the sort of thing I should have done. The sort of thing I would have done if I hadn't hidden in a mental hospital.

Who would've put this here? Probably Cameron, his baby sister. I should call her. I hadn't seen or talked to her since the funeral. She probably felt as weird about getting in touch with me now that Trent was gone as I did about getting in touch with her.

I felt a hand on my shoulder and looked up.

Isaac stood there, smiling sympathetically. I straightened and looked around. A few feet away, was a long, black scorch mark, bigger and darker than either of the others, stretched across the highway. I stepped toward it and felt the pulsing of the other dimension almost tangibly.

"It's here."

The Eyes hissed at me. *Come on through. I can't wait to see you again.*

"He's waiting for me. He'll kill me as soon as I cross over. I'm no match for him there."

"Can you... I don't know, shoot him?" Isaac asked.

"I don't think so. My gun is bound to this dimension. I don't know if it would even work over there, or if that thing is mortal."

I'm not mortal, foolish girl. You can't kill something that is already dead.

"Wait, what?"

"What is it?" Chase asked.

"Shh!" I stepped forward, to the very edge of the portal. "What did you say?"

I am immortal. You cannot kill me. But I can kill you. I'll snap your neck the instant you cross over.

"That's not what you said."

He hissed.

"You can't affect this reality because you don't exist in it. Here, you're just a ghost. What are you the ghost of?" I remembered its grotesque, giant form... and the six fingers on each of its hands. "You're the ghost of a Nephilim!"

The screech he emitted shook my whole body, vibrating my senses that were attuned to the other dimension like a gong. And then he was gone. I could no longer sense his presence at all.

146

Where had he gone?

It didn't matter. I had to take the opportunity offered.

I stepped across the line, through the portal, and found myself fully immersed in the other dimension.

"Jack?" Isaac's voice wafted through, pale and distant, filled with concern.

"She's okay," Chase reassured him.

I walked along the dusty, barren landscape. Even the topography here was different, though similar. The river was just a waterless gorge, the mountains that dotted Phoenix and messed up the near-perfect grid of streets were dusty red hills. There were no buildings or trees, though I could see the ethereal outlines of structures from the other side, like holograms here.

Even the bridge I stood on seemed misty and unreal, but I didn't fall into the gorge, so apparently enough of my essence was still on my side that it kept me anchored. Or enough of the bridge existed here to keep me on it.

As I suspected, I didn't see the Eyes anywhere in sight. He seemed genuinely terrified to know I'd figured out what he was. I wasn't sure why that was such a big deal, though. It didn't change the fact that he could still kill me here, or that he couldn't touch me in the real world.

And it didn't get me any closer to figuring out why any of this was happening.

I kept walking, absorbing the feel of the place, beginning to acclimate to it. The nausea and chills, though ever-present, dwindled to a distant annoyance rather than an immediate focus. As I went, I became aware of the beings.

Beyond me, beyond the bridge, where the ethereal forms of humans carried on their daily lives, the creatures swarmed like flies. They were everywhere. They didn't seem to be aware of me, though, much like most people in my world were oblivious to the presence of these creatures there.

Most of them hovered around people, sometimes several at once, flocking around a particular person. Some even inhabited the same space as a person, as though hitchhiking inside them.

All the ones I saw, though, were like the Eyes. Solid and menacing here, but physically impotent there.

I wondered what Dionysius would be like here. If a ghost could be a horrific beast, how much more so would a creature that was already fearsome and powerful be?

I didn't have to wait long to find out.

I saw a flash of light, several miles away but so bright it was almost blinding. Something flew through the air, racing directly toward me.

I stumbled backward, tripping over my own feet. The thing drew closer by the second, and with it came the overwhelming icy sickness I felt around the creatures. I doubled over in pain, retching, but still trying to get back to the entrance of the portal to my world.

The creature landed in front of me, a monstrous winged beast, leathery skin, razor claws, rippling muscles, like a twelve-foot gargoyle come to life.

My mind flashed back to the night of the accident. Everything from that night clarified for me. The yellow-eyed monsters pouring out of the rip in the sky... *This* was what they were—this snarling, salivating monstrosity in front of me.

"You pathetic fool. Did you really think you would stand a chance against me here when you couldn't on your own side?"

"Dionysius."

THIRTY-TWO

Dionysius's yellow eyes gleamed with cruel amusement. "I am much more impressive here than when I'm trapped in human form, am I not?"

My hand went instinctively to the gun in the thigh holster under my dress.

Dionysius laughed. "Your human weapons are useless here."

I fired anyway.

He was right. Though it fired, the bullet passed through him, not even a fly-twitch of annoyance to him.

He took a step toward me, laughing. "I will enjoy feeling your neck in my hands, the bones snapping under my fingers."

I stumbled back.

He took another slow, menacing step, clearly enjoying cornering me like an animal.

"You'll gasp to breathe, but no air will get through. You'll claw at my arms with your fingers, but they will be no more effective than the buzzing of a gnat."

My heart thudded against my chest, my breath came in short pants. I took another step back.

"I will crush the life from you, just as I did from your boyfriend."

I gasped.

He laughed and lunged toward me.

I dove out of the way, through the hole, back to my own dimension. Dionysius tumbled after me, his form changing as he came through, taking on his human appearance.

I rolled and fired several shots at him.

Most went wide, thunking into the concrete pillars that supported the bridge, but one hit him in the shoulder.

He screamed, a vile howl that set my teeth on edge, and jumped back through the portal, leaving a splash of oozing, black-red blood on the ground where he'd been standing.

In a heartbeat, both Chase and Isaac were on the ground beside me, fussing over me like old women.

"I'm fine," I insisted, pushing them away and standing up.

"You disappeared," Isaac said. "You walked through the air and turned into a ghost. Then something flashed through the sky. A UFO, streaking toward where you were, and then you fell back, firing your gun at nothing, and that... thing... followed you through the hole."

"Wasn't that your friend's boyfriend?" Chase asked.

I nodded. "Dionysius. Over there, he's... he's a monster like nothing I've ever seen. He said he's going to kill me."

Isaac took my hand. "We won't let that happen."

Chase placed a hand on my shoulder, but drew it back immediately, like he'd been burned. "What else did he say?"

"That's about it as far as what he actually said. I mean, there was a supervillain monologue about how he was going to kill me, but that seemed more like he was trying to distract me from what he really wanted to hide."

"Which was what?"

"The Eyes, and the others like him, are ghosts. Specifically the ghosts of dead Nephilim. That's why they can't affect this reality physically. They're not really here. Their spirits are still on that plane, and they're very real there, but the physical form they had is dead."

"What's a Nephilim?" Isaac asked.

"The half-breed offspring of a demon and a human. That's what Tamara's baby is."

He blinked, like he was absorbing that information.

I didn't wait for him to process before moving on. "The ones like Dionysius, while they're unaffected by human weapons on that side, the body they take on when they're here is susceptible to harm." I pointed to the blood that stained the concrete. "I think that form can be killed."

I took a step, and my knees buckled.

Isaac grabbed me, narrowly preventing me from crashing to the ground. He set me down carefully on the sidewalk and began checking my vitals.

"I'm fine, I'm just tired," I said. "I didn't sleep last night, and I haven't really eaten today. I'll be okay."

"Let's get you home and get some food into you, then," Isaac said.

"I can take her," Chase said. "I can walk back to my car from her house."

"Why don't I follow you, and then I'll give you a ride when we get her settled?" Isaac suggested.

Chase nodded. "Good idea."

"Do you mind driving her truck? She looks too tired to drive. I don't want her to risk it."

"Of course," Chase smiled.

If I hadn't been so exhausted, I probably would've protested at the way they were babying me, even though I thought it was sweet how they were trying to outdo each other with politeness and trying to take care of me. As it was, I allowed Isaac to half-carry me to my truck and tuck me into the passenger seat.

I handed Chase my keys and gave him directions to my apartment, then spent the majority of the drive with my head lolling against the window, barely staying awake until we got there.

Isaac hopped out of his car and opened my door, gently lifting me out and helping me up the stairs. Chase carried my purse, and he still had my keys. I pointed out the correct key, and he unlocked my door. Isaac sat next to me on the couch while Chase bustled around in my kitchen making coffee and nuking leftovers he found in my fridge.

"You guys don't have to do this. I'll be fine. I just need some rest."

"It's no trouble." Chase handed me a plate and utensils.

"What kind of doctor would I be if I left without making sure you were okay?" Isaac asked.

"Really, I'm fine." But I was too tired to put much force into my words.

Both men hovered over me until I finished eating. I had to put an end to this.

"I'm going to bed. You guys can go home now."

I stood and teetered a little. The whole room spun, and my head felt like I'd had about three too many shots.

Isaac slipped his arm around my waist. "Are you okay?"

"Just a head rush."

He insisted on walking me to my room anyway, only turning around long enough for me to trade my dress for one of Trent's T-shirts, and then tucking me into bed.

Apparently not to be outdone, Chase appeared a moment later with a big glass of water and my phone, both of which he set on the nightstand.

I smiled, touched and amused by their concern and their high school-level competitive tactics. "Shoo, both of you."

Isaac brushed a strand of hair from my forehead. "Let me get your number and I'll call you tomorrow to check up on you."

Chase brushed my shoulder with his fingertips. He only barely touched me, but still he winced. "Will I see you at church in the morning?"

I nodded. "I'll try."

Finally, they left, and I fell asleep, completely dead to the world for almost twelve hours.

***

I was still groggy the next morning, but I managed to get up, shower, and drag myself to Chase's church. I sat at the back, though, not next to Chase, and I didn't even give Desiree a dirty look when she linked her arm in his and pulled him out the side door before he had a chance to see me. I spent most of the afternoon lounging around at home, not doing much.

True to his word, Isaac called in the afternoon. "How are you feeling?"

"Tired."

"I'm a little worried that you're not back to normal yet. Do you have a regular doctor you can check in with?"

"I'm really okay." How many times had I said that in the last twenty-four hours? "It's just been a stressful week, and I guess I'm too old to pull all-nighters any more."

"Promise me you'll at least talk to your doctor if you aren't completely back to normal by tomorrow."

"I promise."

"Good. And make some time to do something other than work, okay?"

I laughed. "I don't even know what to do other than work."

"You must have some hobbies. What did you for fun before you took on demon hunting?"

I leaned back against my couch. What *had* I done for fun before this? I couldn't even think of anything. Trent and I had always talked about learning ballroom dancing, and we were going to start lessons so we could dance at our wedding, but we'd never actually started.

Before that... "I used to love going rock climbing. I haven't been in years."

"I love rock climbing. It helps me destress when I'm not working. We should go to Sedona one of these weekends and climb."

"I would like that." My phone buzzed, and I checked the caller ID. Bridget. "Hey, I have to go. I've got a call on the other line."

"Okay. See you soon."

I hung up and switched to the other call. "Hey, Bridget."

"Hey, Jack. Are you busy?"

"Not really. What's up?"

"Can you come over? I need to talk to you."

I hated it when people said that. I always worried that I was in trouble, especially so now, since I'd just shot Bridget's demon baby-daddy. "Sure, I'll be over in a few minutes."

I took a quick shower, then drove to Bridget's apartment. Nausea and chills wracked my body as soon as I began ascending the stairs to Bridget's apartment, growing stronger the closer I got.

Dion was with her.

I knocked on her door, and she opened it, beaming. A smile stretched across her face, lighting up her already stunning features. Dion stood behind her, his arms wrapped around her waist. He gave no indication that he had a gunshot wound in his shoulder.

I wanted to throw up.

"Have a seat, Jack."

An overwhelming sense of foreboding washed over me.

"What's going on?"

I glanced at Dion.

The demonic yellow glow behind his perfect-appearing human eyes glinted with perverse triumph.

Damn it. Was this what I thought it was?

Bridget turned her head, golden hair falling over her shoulders, and glanced up at Dion. "Do you want to tell her, babe?"

"No, love, you go ahead. It's your news."

Bridget looked at me, eyes shining. "We're having a baby."

I didn't even realize my legs had buckled until my backside hit the couch. "Wow."

Dion had told me, of course, but hearing it from her own lips, knowing it was real…

Dion smiled at me, sadistic pleasure emanating from his entire being.

Apparently Bridget thought my shock was happy, because her grin widened. "We've decided not to wait to get married. Save the date— the wedding is next month, November sixteenth."

THIRTY-THREE

Dion's pleasure spiked, sending a shockwave of emotion through the room, pulsing through me. The lights seemed to dim—or maybe I was just on the verge of passing out. A thousand tiny worms roiled in my stomach.

I leaned against the back of the couch, breathing deeply, searching for my voice. "Wow, Bridge, that's..." Too soon. I didn't have time to talk her out of it, didn't have time to tell her what was really going on. "That's sudden."

Bridget unpeeled Dion's arms from around her. Already the slight swelling of her abdomen verified she carried the demon's spawn.

"You okay, Jack? You look ill." She sat next to me and pressed a hand against my forehead.

Summoning up a smile, I held her had in a reassuring grip. "I'm fine. I just... it's really quick."

She nodded. "I know. But, when it's right, it's right. I can't explain it. It's fate."

"Bridge, I..." I glanced at Dion then turned back to her. "You know I love you and I support you, but I can't help thinking taking that step is moving too fast."

"I knew you'd say that. But Jack, this is what I want, and if you're really my friend, you'll stick by me."

Holy guilt trip.

My eyes travelled to her stomach. She was already pregnant. It was too late. All I could do was be there for her and help her through it, at the very least making sure she got a C-section at the hospital and didn't end up rotting in a demon dimension somewhere. "You know I will, Bridge."

She grinned. "I knew you would. You're awesome. That's why I want to ask you a very important question. Will you be my maid of honor?"

I could almost hear my jaw hitting the floor. But what could I say? I'd already promised her I'd stick by her.

"Of course. I'm so honored you'd ask." My voice sounded wooden, dead to my own ears, but she didn't seem to notice.

She threw her arms around me and squeezed. "Thanks, Jack. You're the best friend a girl could have."

A surge of irritation flashed out from Dion, but he kept a smile plastered on his face. "Well, love, we should let Jack get back to whatever it is she needs to do, and we should get busy. We have a lot of planning to do before next month."

Bridget gazed up at him, her eyes adoring. Her hand rubbed absently across her waist. "You're right. We'll go shopping for our dresses this week, okay Jack?"

She never even looked at me as she spoke, her puppy-dog eyes focused solely on Dion.

***

I arrived at work the next morning to find the office in turmoil.

Ken ambushed me as soon as I walked in and fell into step beside me. "Jack, the captain wants to see you right away."

"What's going on?"

"Feds. Since you found that home, this has become a kidnapping ring, not a missing persons case."

Crap. Trent had worked with the FBI once, and it was a nightmare. Constant vying for superiority and jurisdiction. My first case after the incident, and now I had to share it with the feds.

My stomach rumbled. I'd skipped breakfast, not feeling like eating after Bridget's revelation last night, but now I wished I had. I pushed into the captain's office, resigned to my fate and willing to do whatever was necessary in order to solve the case.

"Jack." The captain gave me a pained smile. "I'm sure you've already heard that you'll be getting help on your case. Meet your new partner."

A woman stood, luscious curves clad in a business suit, dark waves piled on top of her head in a classy up-do.

The captain motioned toward her. "This is Agent Escobar."

Shit.

It was Chase's little minion from church.

157

So all my bravado about Chase helping me with a case was totally wasted on her. On the plus side, she looked as surprised to see me as I was to see her.

"Officer Davidson." She extended a hand. Her grip was considerably stronger than it had been when we'd met at church.

I returned it with equal pressure. "It's *Detective*, Agent Escobar. Why don't we go find a conference room, and I can fill you in on what I know."

She raised her eyebrows, as if surprised at my cooperation.

I smiled, remembering Chase fighting with Isaac just yesterday to tuck me into bed. Oh, the petty thrill of one-upmanship.

I led her past my desk where I grabbed my files, then down the hall to a quiet room. I sat across the table from her and opened the file.

"Okay, here's all the info I have on the girls that have disappeared in the last six months." I tapped Tamara's page. "This is the young lady I recovered last week. The baby was born via C-section on Monday morning and disappeared from the hospital later that afternoon. The hospital staff are unable to account for what happened. The stories from the nurses on duty are somewhat... hard to believe."

Her dark eyes scanned the pages. "How's that?"

"They claim the kidnapper never entered or left the hospital. He— or it—appeared in the room, took the baby, and disappeared."

Agent Escobar flattened perfectly manicured hands against the table and gave me a stern glare. "Disappeared?"

I wondered how much of the supernatural angle to fill her in on. Despite her connection to Chase, I got the impression she wasn't going to be terribly open-minded about this.

I shrugged, trying to be nonchalant. "That's what the witnesses said. I suppose maybe he had some sort of parlor trick, drugs or some way to make the nurses on duty believe that's what they saw. The only concrete evidence we have is that the girl's baby is gone, and we have no knowledge of how a visitor could've come in and gotten out with the baby unnoticed."

"I see. Anything else?"

"We believe the kidnapper to be the same man who abducted Tamara and the others. The girls knew him by the name Chet, but we have no information on who he really is."

I flipped through the file until I found a printout of my latest activity on the social networking site and explained my attempt at undercover. "I have yet to make any contacts that seem like they might be our perpetrator, though."

I was gratified to note that she looked mildly impressed.

"Okay, um... keep on that. See what you can find out. I'd like to interview the staff from Chet's house."

She paused, then almost grudgingly asked, "Would you like to join me?"

No. I've had about as much time with you as I can stand.

I smiled. "Sure. My notes on the interviews I did are here." I handed her a sheaf of papers. "Where do you want to start?"

THIRTY-FOUR

Driving around with Desiree Escobar proved to be considerably more irritating than sitting in an office with her. She drove a sleek, sexy little two-door Beamer and listened to smooth jazz.

I could almost feel my fingernails curling in agony. It was easily as bad as being in the other dimension with a giant gargoyle demon about to murder me.

We sat in silence until we arrived at the home of our first witness. As we climbed from the car, she gave me a no-nonsense smile. "If you don't mind, I'd like to handle the questions."

"Be my guest." I smiled back.

I managed to stifle my smug smile when Agent Escobar failed to get any more information than I had. The same story, over and over, about how they were coerced into coming to the house and then couldn't leave, how Chet seemed to have supernatural abilities, how after the girls gave birth they completely disappeared.

In short, everything that was already in the file I'd turned over to her.

We climbed back into her car after the last interview and headed back toward the station.

"Well, it seems your file was pretty thorough as far as the witnesses go."

Damn, I'm good.

"But we still have no leads on who this Chet guy is. Any theories?"

I considered telling her, but decided against it. At least for now. "Nothing solid."

"Okay, well, you go ahead and work on that internet thing, and I'll check with my sources and see what I can find out."

Her sources? Wow, she could make anything sound condescending.

Still, I couldn't help but get some amount of glee out of the knowledge that she would have a really hard time finding any information on an other-worldly entity.

The truth was, this was not a matter for the police. Or the feds. The best-case scenario would be for me to find Chet and kick his mortal ass. And maybe take care of Dionysius while I was at it.

At least I knew they could be wounded, and if they could be wounded, maybe they could be killed, at least as far as this dimension went. They'd probably still exist in the other dimension, but maybe they'd be stuck there like the Eyes.

I realized I hadn't actually answered her about doing my internet search.

"I'll get right on that." I don't think I managed the same snarky tone that Desiree had perfected for her regular voice, though, because she just nodded, as though it was no less than she expected.

There were three hits on my online profile when I got back to the station. One of them wanted to meet. He wasn't a guy named Chet, but I had to check them all out anyway. Unfortunately, or maybe fortunately, I looked nothing like a high-school freshman.

However, Trent's sister did. Even now, halfway through college, she could still pass for an eleven-year-old. Trent had used her in undercover work on more than one occasion. It helped him out, and since she was studying criminal justice, it looked good on her résumé.

My heart constricted at the thought of talking to her. She was so much like Trent, despite that they weren't related by blood. But I needed to get back in touch with her anyway, and this was as good an excuse as any.

I dialed her number, and she picked up. "Cameron? It's Jack."

"Hi! I haven't talked to you since…" Cameron stumbled over her words. "I'm sorry, I just didn't know what to say."

"It's okay. Me too."

"Yeah."

Awkward silence stretched between us for a moment before I broke it. "I need a favor."

"Yeah, of course. Anything. What's up?" she said.

I filled Cameron in on my plan to set a trap for the predator, then set the meet with my online boyfriend for later that afternoon. About half an hour beforehand, I met Cameron at the coffee shop a couple blocks from where she'd meet my internet friend.

"Hey, Cam." I suddenly felt shy and awkward.

She smiled, and I could tell she didn't know quite how to act around me, either.

My heart swelled. Even without Trent here to build the bridge, this girl was my sister. I stepped toward her and gave her a big hug.

She leaned into me, quiet sobs shaking her body. "It's really good to see you, Jack."

"You, too."

We stood there for several minutes, just hugging and sniffling, until I finally pulled back. That was enough awkwardness for one meeting. I looked her up and down. Too much makeup and a skirt too short made her petite, athletic form look like a little girl trying too hard. "You look perfect."

I hooked her up with surveillance equipment. "Okay, you're ready. If he invites you to get in the car, go for it. I'll be right behind you. Anything weird, ask him to stop for ice cream, and I'll take care of it. Now, he may or may not be connected to my case, but at least we can get him on intent to have sex with a minor, so make sure you get him to admit what he plans to do with you, and make sure he knows you're underage. Got it?"

Cameron nodded, dark hair bobbing in a ponytail at the back of her head and large hoop earrings swaying. She popped a bubble with her giant wad of gum.

I couldn't help grinning. "You pull that off a little too well."

"I know, right?" she grinned back.

From the coffee shop, she would walk down to the park to meet the suspect. I stayed just far enough back that I could see her without looking obvious, sitting at a gas station. "I'll be here until you get in the car with him, and then I'll follow you. Good?"

"Of course." She grinned. "See you when we nail this bastard."

"Trent's going to come back from the grave to haunt you if you keep up that kind of language."

"Please. Where do you think I learned most of those words?"

"Go on, sis. Get moving."

A wistful smile crossed her face. "I miss hearing you call me that."

My throat tightened. "Shoo. This won't work if he sees you talking to me. I'll buy you dinner later this week and we can catch up."

Half an hour later, I'd arrested a pervert, but was no closer to tracking down Chet than I'd been that morning. My luck, Desiree would have a lead by now.

I called Chase. "Any idea how to track a demon?"

His rich laughter bubbled through the earpiece. "I wish it were that easy. Want to talk about it?"

"Yeah. Coffee?"

"Sure. I'll see you at our place in half an hour."

Our place? We'd met there once, and it was already our place.

Stupid, girlish butterflies attacked one another in my stomach.

Grow up, Jack. "I have to stop by the station first. Forty-five minutes?"

"See you there."

Stupid boy, making me think stupid things. I pulled into the precinct and hurried in to file my report on the operation with Cameron.

Desiree was waiting for me back at the station. "Hey. Any luck?"

"Nope. I managed to nab a run-of-the-mill pedophile, but nothing that pertains to this case. You?"

She shook her head. "Dead end after dead end. Want to go grab coffee and compare notes? Maybe one of us will see something the other missed."

"Sure, but it has to be quick. I have another meeting."

She raised an eyebrow, but didn't ask.

There was a little coffee joint about a block away from the station. Not the same one I went to with Chase, so I directed Desiree there.

I told her about taking Cameron undercover, and she filled me in on the contacts she had that worked on trafficking cases.

"No one seems to know anything about this Chet character," she said. "I can't even get a last name, let alone possible aliases. Even the house he kept the girls in was a bust. He was renting it for way over market value and the landlord had a break-in at his office. A bunch of files were stolen, including the paperwork for Chet's house."

"How convenient."

"Exactly. Whoever is behind this really knows what they're doing."

Well, yeah. No kidding. Almost like they had centuries of experience and literally all the time in the world to plan it out. And could travel between dimensions to get in and out of places like real estate offices undetected.

All I said to Desiree, though, was, "So it would seem."

She toyed with the stir stick in her coffee. "Can I ask you something?"

Uh-oh. That question never boded well. "Sure."

"All that stuff you said the other day, when you met Chase for coffee... what was that all about?"

Oh, good. An easy question. "Um... well, it sort of has to do with this case. I think the case Trent was working on when he died was related to this one."

"Trent was a cop too?"

"Yeah."

"Tell me about his case."

"He was investigating a human trafficking ring. Elements of it were pretty standard, but there were some weird things, too, like bodies turning up of young girls who had been cut open, possibly in a crude sort of C-section, then left to bleed out."

Her face paled and she pursed her lips like she was trying to keep from throwing up. "Who could do something like that? Someone selling infants on the black market?"

Damn it. Why didn't I think of that? I totally could've used that in my reports. That explanation made way more sense than demons spawning an army. "Could be."

"You don't sound convinced."

I shrugged. "It's just that every new lead I find makes me think I'm onto something bigger, that there's more going on here than meets the eye, but I keep hitting one dead end after another."

"I know what you mean. Do you mind if I look into the case Trent was on? See if I can turn up anything new?"

"Go for it. Technically it's closed, though. The guy is dead, and there are no traces of what became of his operation."

"I'd still like to look through the file, if that's okay."

"Sure. I'm going to keep setting up dates with pedophiles. Maybe I'll catch a break. There's one other possible connection I'd like to look into, regarding a case my coworker Ken is on, but it's a long shot. I'll let you know if anything comes of it."

"Sounds good. I'll do the same."

We stood to leave.

"Oh, Jack? One more thing."

"What is it?"

"You may be a shiny, interesting new toy right now, but don't get used to it. Chase is mine."

THIRTY-FIVE

Wow. Just when I thought we were going to get along.

I watched her stalk out, hair swishing, hips swaying.

Well, if that's what Chase wanted, he was welcome to her. I sure wasn't going to turn into some snarky, two-faced troll just to try to snag him.

My phone rang, snapping me out of the trance I was in.

Speak of the devil.

"Hi, Chase. What's up?"

"Are you coming? I thought we were meeting."

"Oh! I'm sorry, I got caught up with work stuff and wasn't paying attention to the time. I'll be there in a minute."

"Good. I found something I think you'll want to see."

"I'll be right there."

I pulled into the other coffee shop a few minutes later. I'd be massively over-caffeinated by the end of the day, but at least I was one up on Desiree at the moment.

Chase was sitting at our table by the window with two cups of coffee and a couple of books.

I sat down across from him. "What is it?"

He looked up from his book and pushed one of the coffees toward me. "I had a thought earlier. I was going through all my Bible study guides and biblical history texts and commentaries, looking for anything that might help us know what we're dealing with, and I couldn't find anything. Very little is said about this phenomenon, and most of what is said is pure speculation. Then it occurred to me—I'm looking in the wrong place."

"How do you mean?"

"The church as a whole has grown increasingly less aware of the supernatural over the centuries. Ever since the middle ages, but especially since the rise of scientific understanding, we've just sort of brushed under the rug the things that are as yet unexplainable."

"Okay, so where do we look, then?"

"Mythology."

"I thought the whole point of mythology was that it was stories—it isn't real."

"That's the commonly held theory," Chase nodded, "but I thought about something Dr. Ross said in that book I loaned you. Did you read it yet?"

"Parts of it."

"Anyway, remember she said that in her research, she has come to believe that everything in mythology has a literal place in history. Even if the stories have been embellished beyond recognition by the time they reach our generation, they had some sort of literal, historical antecedent."

Damn, he was cute when he used big words. Maybe I wasn't as okay with Desiree having dibs as I pretended. "Did you find any answers in mythology, then?"

"Maybe. Dr. Ross talked about the Greek gods and goddesses, so I started there, researching common Greek myths and studying what historians said about Greek culture. Look here."

He pointed to the heading *Tartarus*.

"Tartarus? Isn't that basically like hell?"

"That's what I thought at first, too, but then I discovered some interesting things about the nature of Tartarus. See this description of Tartarus? It's as far below earth as earth is below heaven, it's reserved for punishment for the worst of the worst, and so on. But look at this. The people who were condemned to Tartarus are primarily Greek heroes who offended the gods in some way, or other creatures, for example," his finger pounded the page, "giants."

I gaped at him. "Giants? As in Nephilim?"

He nodded, the grin on his face as eager as a child's. "But not just that. If Dr. Ross is correct, then the Greek gods may have actually been demons, which would make a half-god progeny, like Hercules—"

"A Nephilim."

"Exactly. And those are the creatures who end up in Tartarus."

"So, Tartarus is like hell for half-breed human-demon spawn?"

"In a way, but that's not entirely accurate. The concept we conjure up when we think of the word 'hell' is much closer to the Greek place known as Hades. But Tartarus is much, much different. It's more like a… holding pen for these creatures. They're not human, so they can't make the choice for good or evil and therefore can't go to heaven or hell when they die, so when their mortal bodies die, their immortal spirits have to go somewhere."

"So they go to Tartarus."

"Yes. I found a few passages in Scripture to substantiate my theory, too."

He pulled out his Bible. "Look here. In the book of Jude, verse six, it says, 'And the angels who did not keep their own domain but abandoned their proper abode, He has kept in eternal bonds under darkness for the judgment of the great day.' Now, I read several commentaries, and most agree that the reference to not keeping their own domain could refer to them lusting after and fornicating with human women."

"Okay, but this says they're kept in bonds, waiting for judgment. What does that have to do with Tartarus?"

"I'm getting to that." He flipped a few pages in the Bible. "Look here, Second Peter chapter two, verse four, 'For if God did not spare angels when they sinned, but cast them into hell and committed them to pits of darkness, reserved for judgment.'"

"That just said the same thing."

"Ah, but here's where it gets interesting. In other parts of the Bible, several different words are used that are translated 'hell' in our English Bibles. In the Old Testament, the Hebrew word *sheol*, which means 'the grave' or 'the pit' is used, and its Greek counterpart in the New Testament is Hades."

He flipped a few pages and showed me some of the instances. "The New Testament also uses the term *gehenna*, which means fire. Jesus used this word when talking about judgment. But the word here only occurs in this one passage, not any other place in the Greek manuscripts. The word translated as 'hell' in this verse is actually the Greek word Tartarus."

My mind reeled. "You're suggesting that these angels—"

"Fallen angels. Also known as demons."

"Okay, these demons weren't cast into hell as we think of it, but were cast into Tartarus?"

"Yes. And not just cast there, but *bound* to that place. They no longer have the freedom to move about the cosmos or go to heaven. They're stuck until Judgment Day."

"But they're still here, still present and active here on Earth, in this dimension."

"Yes, that's what I'm getting at. I believe Tartarus is actually the fourth dimension."

I blinked slowly, absorbing that information. "Where the Eyes is, that's…"

"The extra dimension. That's their realm. Our three dimensions are present within that one, which is why they can affect ours, but they're bound to that one. That's why the souls of the dead Nephilim are not only there, but are strong and powerful. It's their natural habitat."

I blew a heavy breath out through my lips and rubbed my temples with my fingertips. "You realize how that sounds?"

Chase grinned and nodded. "A couple of weeks ago, I would've thought I was crazy even entertaining the thought."

"A lot has happened in the last couple weeks," I agreed. "I've seen demons, my best friend got impregnated by one, and I've visited Tartarus. On the plus side, at least I'm now pretty sure I'm not crazy, which I've seriously questioned."

Chase laughed. "And that's saying something." His tone became serious, thoughtful, and just a little tender. "Most people would've long since fallen over the brink into insanity after experiencing the things you have. I'm continually impressed by your strength."

Heat rose to my face. "Thank you. That's sweet of you to say. But I could still go crazy." I waved my hand over the books on his desk. "All this makes my brain hurt."

"I know the perfect cure. There's a great little Thai place in the strip mall up the street. You're not allergic to peanuts, are you? They have the best—"

"Well, fancy meeting the two of you here." Desiree's syrupy voice interrupted him.

THIRTY-SIX

"Hi, Chase," Desiree simpered. "I just popped in at your office to pick up some things for Bible Study, and Pastor Floyd said you were here. I didn't know you'd be here too, though, Jack." Her tone held just a note of warning. "I'm not interrupting anything, am I?"

"Not at all. In fact, we were just wrapping up and heading out to get some dinner," Chase said.

"Oh, good. I'm starving. You don't mind if I come along, do you?"

"Of course," Chase answered before I could deny her.

I was saved from making a snarky reply I'd probably regret by the ringing of my phone. I glanced at the caller ID. "It's Isaac. Dr. Reyes. Mind if I invite him, too?"

Chase's jaw tensed, but he smiled. "Sure. The more the merrier."

I got a little bit of satisfaction from that, and immediately felt guilty for being so petty. But if he could bring a date on our non-date-dinner-together thing, then so could I.

I answered the phone and told Isaac where we were headed. He agreed to meet us there, and a short while later all four of us were seated around a small linen-covered table in a dimly lit Thai restaurant.

Desiree smiled warmly at Isaac. "So, how do you and Jack know each other?"

"He's the doctor who treated Tamara," I said.

Isaac and Chase both looked at me, eyes wide. Chase snapped his mouth shut and swallowed.

"She knows about Tamara?" Isaac asked.

"Yeah. Actually, that reminds me." I turned to Chase. "You didn't tell me she's a fed."

170

Chase stared blankly at me. "Oh. I didn't even think of it. To be fair, though, we haven't actually spent a lot of time chit-chatting about our friends."

Desiree shot me a glare, and I filed away the joy of winning for things to think about when I needed a pick-me-up. "Good point. Anyway, after we found the house where Tamara was being held, the case was officially deemed kidnapping not missing persons, so they called the feds in. Voila, Desiree and I are partners now."

The waiter came and took our orders, then glided away.

Desiree leaned forward and patted my arm. "I wouldn't use the term 'partners,' necessarily." Her voice was so sugary I wanted to gag. "It's a federal case, after all. But my department is very conscientious of involving local law enforcement when possible."

"Of course it is. Even though I already did all the leg work on this case."

"Well, I was only assigned to it this morning."

"I can't believe how hot it is still," Isaac said. "It's practically Halloween and we're still getting cases of heatstroke at the hospital."

I shot him a grateful smile for changing the subject.

He smiled back and reached under the table to squeeze my hand. A small thrill ran through me. At least he didn't get weird on me every time he touched me.

Isaac looked at Chase. "As soon as we both get a break from work, I'm going to take Jack up to Sedona to go rock climbing. Get a break from this heat, at least a little bit."

Chase filled up the gap, fluidly taking the cue from Isaac, and talked about how the church was doing a drive to collect water bottles for the homeless.

Desiree gave me a condescending smile before turning to Chase to simper over his every syllable.

We managed to make it through dinner riding a wave of small talk. Throughout the meal, Desiree inched her chair closer to Chase's and frequently made it a point to stroke his arm or otherwise touch him. Could she be any more obvious?

On the other hand, I couldn't help but notice that he didn't freeze or stiffen or flinch at her touch. So it was definitely me, then, not some weird personal space bubble thing that he had going on.

I was interrupted from further pondering of that singularly frustrating line of thought by the waiter coming with our check.

Isaac insisted on paying the whole thing, claiming it was the least he could do for the public servants of the city.

Desiree linked her arm in Chase's and strode out ahead of us. Isaac offered me his arm, so I took it.

"You really didn't have to get the check," I told him.

"I wanted to."

"Thank you. It was very sweet. Let me know if I can make it up to you."

"There is one thing."

"What's that?"

"Let me take you out alone sometime."

I smiled. "Deal."

He saw me to my truck and kissed me lightly on the cheek before leaving.

Chase and Desiree were still standing by her Beamer as I pulled out.

Chase saw me and waved at me to stop. He came to my window, and I rolled it down. "What's up?"

"Do you mind if I stop by for a minute? There's something I want to look up in that book I loaned you."

"Sure." I couldn't help smirking a little at the way Desiree's teeth clenched.

"Great. I'll see you in a few minutes."

It was closer to half an hour before he finally stopped by my apartment. I suspected Desiree had kept him chatting as long as she possibly could.

"Come on in. Here's the book. Do you want it back?"

"No, I want you to finish it. I just wanted to see if Dr. Ross had anything to say about whether or not these things can be killed. Also, I wanted to talk to you alone." Chase plopped down on my couch.

I sat next to him but left a sizeable gap between us. The last thing I wanted right now was for him to pull away. "Oh? What about?"

"How much did you tell Desiree about the case? I mean, about what's really going on?"

"Nothing. I told her all the facts and details that I'd put in an official report, but none of our suspicions about the nature of these creatures or the possibility of a deeper agenda."

He breathed deeply. "Good." A frown crossed his face. "That came out wrong. It's not that I want to keep secrets from her, I just know she's not ready to hear that part of it. At least not yet."

I nodded. "I'll try not to say anything, as long as it doesn't jeopardize the case."

"That's probably best." He paused in flipping through the book and looked at me. "You two don't like each other much, do you?"

I chuckled. "You could say that."

"Why not?"

I stared at him. "Are you serious right now?"

His brow furrowed, gorgeous green eyes clouded. "Yes. I really don't understand it. You have a ton in common. You ought to get along great."

I tried very hard not to laugh, and mostly succeeded.

"What?"

"Chase, the reason we don't like each other is because we both like *you*."

His head tilted slightly to the side as he absorbed that nugget. "No, Desiree and I are just friends. She doesn't think of me like—wait, you like me?"

This time I did laugh, but mostly to hide my embarrassment. "Yeah, I guess I do."

"What about Isaac?"

I shrugged. "Honestly, I don't know. I think I like him, too. But it's weird, you know? It's only been a couple of months since I lost Trent. Even if I were ready for another relationship, which I'm not and won't be for quite some time, I'm totally out of my element. Trent and I were together for eons. I haven't actually dated in so long, I don't even know how it's done anymore."

He smiled, a wide, genuine smile. "I can live with that." He opened the book again.

We spent the next hour or so researching. The Nephilim seemed like they'd be easy enough to kill—they were big and strong, but mortal, and therefore susceptible to anything that would kill a human. We'd have to keep trying if we wanted to find something that would kill Dionysius and the others, though.

Finally, Chase rose to go. "Keep me posted on what you turn up on the case."

I stared at the door for awhile after he left, not quite sure what to make of our conversation. I decided to conclude that he liked me, too, but wasn't quite to the point that he wanted to pursue a relationship or anything. Plus, there was the fact that he couldn't touch me without cringing. Whatever that was about.

But I didn't have the energy to stress about it tonight. My body craved sleep.

I was just about to crawl into bed when a chill swept over me and a churning swirled in my stomach.

The Eyes were back.

THIRTY-SEVEN

I hadn't even realized the Nephilim spirit wasn't around lately, but now that I thought about it, I hadn't felt his presence since I'd encountered him in Tartarus and figured out what he was.

He didn't say anything, just hovered near my bed.

He seemed... weak, somehow. Like his essence wasn't as strong as it had been before.

"What are you doing here?" I asked aloud.

He didn't answer.

"Dionysius made you come back to haunt me even though you didn't want to?"

No, he spat. *Dionysius gave me leave to abandon you as my target. He'll deal with you himself.*

"What then? Did you miss me?"

The sensible part of my brain told me it was probably a bad idea to taunt a demon monster, but I couldn't help it.

Foolish girl. You know nothing.

"Then clue me in. Why did you come back?"

I had to.

"What do you mean, you had to?"

I was drawn here. I tried to escape, but the further I went, the worse it got. Something is holding me to you, and if I stay away from you, I'll die.

"You're already dead."

He hissed again. *Not a mortal death, stupid. I will cease to exist on this plane. I will go... I don't know where, but I don't want to find out.*

I thought about Hell and Tartarus and all the possible implications. The one thing that stuck with me, though, tickling my mind as I drifted

174

to sleep, was that he could be driven from Tartarus. And if he could be sent away, maybe the demons like Dionysius could, too.

***

When I got into work the next morning, I had two messages on my fake profile from guys wanting to meet. I called Cameron and set up meetings with both of them for later that day.

I settled in at my desk with a cup of coffee to start filling out forms and writing reports about what I'd done and uncovered over the last few days. About half an hour later, Bridget came in and sat down on the edge of my desk.

"When are you taking lunch?" she asked. "Want to go early and look at dresses with me?"

She still retained her amazing figure, but the baby bulge was definitely noticeable. I had to figure out a way to get her out of this mess before it was too late.

"That sounds great." I grinned at her.

The Eyes muttered something about the fruitlessness of my endeavors, but it seemed half-hearted. If I didn't know better, I'd swear he was sulking.

He did seem stronger, somehow, than he had last night. Why would that be? Was he right about being connected to me somehow?

"Jack? Hello?"

"Oh, sorry, Bridge. What did you say?"

"I said I think I found the dress I want, but I want you to see it before I decide for sure."

I smiled. "I can't wait to see it. By the way, is having the bachelorette party after the rehearsal the Friday before the wedding okay?"

"Sure. I can't drink, because of..." She patted her belly.

"I'll figure out something low-key," I promised. I glanced at the clock on my computer screen. "Give me half an hour to wrap up a couple things and then we can go, okay?"

Less than an hour later, we were greeted at the bridal shop by a plump, cheery, matronly woman. "Bridget, welcome back. Did you decide on the dress?"

"This is Jack, my maid of honor. I want her to see it first. And I want her to try on a couple of dresses while we're at it. Jack, come here."

She led me to a rack near the back and pulled off the most vile atrocity I had ever seen in my life. Uglier than Dionysius in the other

175

dimension, it was a pale peach ball of ruffles with a scoop neck and bedazzled with ribbons and bows and gems.

I choked back my reaction. "Okay, if this is what you like, I'll try it on."

"Jack."

I looked at her. "Yeah?"

"I'm totally screwing with you. I wouldn't make you wear that. Here." She handed me an adorable baby-doll dress in a dark, hunter green.

I laughed. "Oh, thank heaven. This is perfect."

The saleslady brought a bag into the dressing room and I helped Bridget get dressed. Her gown was gorgeous. Baby-doll style, like the one she'd picked out for me, with a high waist and flowing skirt that draped over her belly, disguising her abnormal pregnancy. Lightly jeweled embroidery traced its way along the bottom edge, dancing over the trim and across the bodice.

Tears stung my eyes. I wished this were for a real wedding, not a scam perpetrated by a demon to torment me.

"You look beautiful," I said. It was all I could say.

Bridget examined herself critically in the mirror. "You really think so?"

"The dress is perfect. My only concern is that you're rushing into this. You don't have to marry him just because you're pregnant, you know."

She laughed. "I agreed to marry him before I knew I was pregnant. I love him. This is what I want."

Maybe I could find a way to kill Dionysius before this wedding. "Okay, then. Let's buy some dresses."

We made our purchases and headed back to the station. I had to hurry once we got there to get Cameron ready for her undercover date. I dropped her off a block away from the meet. "You know the drill. I'll be right here, so holler if you need me."

Cameron walked toward the park, wringing her hands and twirling her hair in feigned nervousness. Damn, she was good. She'd make an excellent undercover agent some day.

I parked where I could see her, listening on my equipment for anything condemning.

Cameron took a seat on a park bench, swinging her legs and toying with her hair. We didn't have to wait long.

On the other side of the park, nearly hidden by trees and bushes, a light flashed. My heartbeat quickened and I swallowed. That wasn't just a reflection or other natural phenomenon, that was something happening in the other dimension.

I glanced around to see if anyone else sensed anything weird, but of course no one acted differently, since I was the only one who could see it.

With the flash came the familiar chill and nausea, growing stronger as a creature wearing a man's body stepped from the foliage.

Leaving the recording device running, I stepped out of the truck and started walking toward Cameron, but at an angle, so it didn't look like I was walking directly toward her.

The demon walked her direction from the other side of the park. Tall, blond, surfer-like. He matched the description Tamara had given me of Chet.

I radioed it in. There wasn't much the police force could do against a demon, but I figured it was a good idea to be prepared. If anything happened, I'd want backup.

I was close enough now that I could hear them. I kept staring straight ahead so it wouldn't look like I noticed them and bent down to tie my shoe.

"Are you Katie?" The demon smiled at Cameron. "I'm Chet."

Good. He'd fallen for the profile I'd used.

"I thought your name was Mark," Cameron said innocently.

He smiled again. "I use different names online to protect my privacy. You never know what kind of creeper is lurking around the internet."

"Oh. I guess that's smart."

"Do you want to take a walk?"

"Sure."

He held her hand and led her toward the trees. "I was thinking about what you told me when we were chatting, about how your mom drinks and yells all the time. I'm really concerned about you. I care about you, and I don't want you to get hurt."

Smooth.

"I'll be okay," Cameron said. "It'll blow over in a few days."

"If you want, you could come to my house to stay for awhile."

"I don't know. My mom would be pissed. I'm only fourteen."

"I think that's old enough to make your own decisions. Just say the word, and I'll take you to my house where you'll be safe."

"Okay, I guess."

"Is that a yes? Yes, you'll come with me?"

Cameron nodded. "Yes. I'll come with you."

"Come this way." He headed for the trees.

I had enough now to book him on kidnapping. If he were human. But I needed to find his other victims. I followed them to the edge of the trees.

The Eyes started to get restless. I had a feeling he was about to give me away.

I walked on a little bit and turned to look at the space the Eyes occupied. "Listen up. If you make one sound—*one*—I will move into the church basement where you can't get near me and not come out. You'll die, or cease to exist, or whatever it is that will happen to you if I'm not around, got it? You will not do *anything* to let him know I'm following him."

The Eyes hissed, but I could sense from the wave of anger and frustration that wafted out from him that he knew he was trapped.

I quickened my pace toward where Chet and Cameron drew close to the stand of trees.

The moment you cross over, I will kill you, the Eyes said.

"Really? If I'm dead, won't that sever the connection, too? I think it's in your best interest, if you value your existence at all, to keep me safe and sound."

He hissed again, anger, hate, and despair pulsing from him. But he didn't argue.

I jogged to the tree line and glanced around.

The light flashed, and Chet and Cameron disappeared.

THIRTY-EIGHT

I ran to the spot and jumped through the portal after them.

The Eyes clenched his fists. I could tell how badly he wanted to pummel me. Self-preservation won out, though, and he stood quietly while I took stock of my surroundings.

Chet—who looked like a gargoyle in this dimension—carried Cameron, who appeared to be unconscious. Perhaps she couldn't be awake here. Whatever it was that made me aware of this place also allowed me to travel through it while other people were rendered unconscious by the shift through dimensions. That would explain why none of the girls could remember where they were or how they got there.

Chet seemed totally oblivious to my presence.

I followed at a distance, walking over the alien ground, through the walls of buildings as though they weren't there. Which, in this dimension, they weren't.

It also took far less time to get somewhere. A walk that would've taken twenty minutes on regular land, I covered in moments, as though the ground was swallowed up under my feet. It was disorienting and exhilarating all at once.

In a matter of minutes, we were on the other side of town, a distance that even driving would've taken a solid half hour, in an upscale residential community.

One house, at the end of a cul de sac, was surrounded by a six-foot rock wall made with rocks from this dimension. They were solid, not like the walls that bled through from the other side. At one corner was a person-sized hole. Chet ducked to walk through, toward the house.

I took stock of the surrounding area, the name on the ethereal-looking street sign on the corner and the faded house number, then ducked through the hole in the wall.

Chet carried Cameron into the house and up a flight of stairs, into a large closet. It seemed as though he could observe or deny the existence of walls and buildings at will, since he didn't fall through the second-story floor onto the ground. I decided to go on the assumption that I could do the same.

Using his claws, he ripped a hole in the air. Or, rather, reopened a hole that was already there. Wispy tendrils, like frayed edges of a piece of fabric, lined the edges of the hole. He seemed to fade as he went through, and his form changed.

It was weird to see from this side. I could see the human form almost like a costume draping the gargoyle underneath.

I crept toward the house, though my feet didn't seem to make any sound. In fact, almost nothing made any noise. Traffic, people, the wind—I could hear them if I listened, but sound was as muted and ethereal here as the buildings. I followed the convention of using the door even though I didn't really need to, and climbed the stairs to the closet. That was a weird sensation, too, climbing stairs that weren't really there. I could walk through walls, and yet when I wanted them to be, the stairs were as solid as any in the real world.

Almost as though my thoughts made it so.

Chet had carried Cameron down a hallway and into another room. I made a mental note of which direction he'd gone. I wouldn't be able to see through walls once I went back into my dimension.

I stepped through the portal and found myself in the closet in the real world. My knees sagged, my strength completely sapped. I rested against the wall as I quietly called for backup, giving the local dispatcher the address of the house, then opened the door of the closet just a crack and peeked out.

I was in a bathroom at the end of a hallway. The room was empty. I crept out of the closet and looked out the window, which faced the street. I waited until I saw three police cars, sans sirens, pull up and surround the house before creeping out of the room.

I tiptoed down the hall to the room where I'd seen Chet take Cameron. The door wasn't closed all the way, so I pressed myself up against the wall and scooted in for a closer look.

Chet sat on the edge of a bed, Cameron lying beside him, looking groggy.

"You're safe now," he crooned. "I want to be with you. Will you let me show you how much I care about you?"

181

Cameron opened her eyes wide. She scooted back toward the head of the bed, putting more distance between herself and Chet. Her mouth gaped and her eyes were wide orbs.

I had to get her out of there.

I lifted my radio and my gun. "Now!" I shouted into the radio. I aimed my gun at Chet. "Police! Freeze!"

Chet whirled, snarling. He lunged toward me and I fired, hitting him three times in the chest.

He stumbled, but kept coming.

I backed away, leading him toward the stairs.

"Cameron, get everybody out!" I yelled.

I fired again, but Chet kept coming at me.

Cameron seemed to have recovered her wits. She was up, pounding on all the other bedroom doors along the hallway. A flood of teenage girls poured out, most of them noticeably pregnant.

A chorus of screams filled the hallway, punctuated by gasps and sobs. Wide eyes filled with tears followed my progress as I backed down the hallway, leading Chet away.

I paused at the top of the stairs. I couldn't take Chet down the stairs. The girls needed to get out that way.

And where the hell was my backup?

I turned and ran toward the bathroom with the portal in the closet. Chet stalked after me.

Throwing open the closet door, I dove through the portal and jumped to the ground, through the floorboards and walls.

Physics, at least the normal laws, didn't quite work here. In much the same way that I'd walked thirty miles in a matter of minutes, the drop to the ground from the second floor was nothing more than a hop.

Chet leapt through after me. He only took a moment to recover from his shock at seeing me there.

Worse, now that he was here, the bullet wounds that had slowed his human form were mere scratches. No wonder Dion didn't seem any worse for having been shot the other day.

Shit. What had I done?

I looked around. The ghostly forms of Cameron and the girls raced from the house, only to stop at the rock wall. Invisible to their eyes, it was solid and impenetrable to them. On the other side, my backup fought to get in.

Of course. The force field.

The rock wall here was the force field that the servants at Chet's old house had described.

Then how had Tamara gotten out?

My gazed landed on the little hole in the corner. Had Tamara found a similar hole in the wall around the other house? Had she gotten out purely by dumb luck?

Whatever the reason, the girls couldn't get out and the cops couldn't get in with it there. I had to take it down. And not get mauled by Chet in the process.

I ran to the wall and started pulling the rocks down, throwing them at Chet.

He growled as one struck him in the chest.

So, things from this dimension could hurt them. Good to know.

I threw rock after rock, alternating between aiming for his head, his chest, and his groin. It slowed him down a little, but he still stalked toward me.

The Eyes stood by, just watching. I threw a rock at his head. He turned to me, snarling.

"Help me!" I ordered.

He glared at me.

I threw another rock at Chet. "I die, you die," I reminded the Eyes.

Hissing, he began hurling rocks as well.

His throw was stronger, his aim better.

Bonus, Chet didn't know what to make of the fact that one of his own had turned against him.

It seemed to disorient him. He stared, yellow eyes going back and forth between me and the Eyes for a moment.

But just a moment.

I was his primary target, and he charged straight toward me.

Neither the Eyes nor I were a match for him here, and my gun was useless against him. I had to get out of here. But he blocked my path to the portal.

The thoughts rushed through my mind almost faster than I could process them.

This reality was different. Physics didn't work here. *I* was different. I had a certain level of power and control here.

I had seen Chet rip the hole between realities with his fingernails. I had to get this wall down so the girls could be rescued, and I had to get Chet out of there so I could stand a chance against him on my own turf.

All my rock-throwing had created a dent in the rock wall. With a surge of energy, trusting in my control over physics here, I leapt over the wall and started running.

Chet burst right through the wall, shattering a hole in it. Hopefully that would be enough to let people through.

I kept running. The city whooshed by me, the buildings and cacti a blur, like in a superhero movie. I dodged around buildings and leapt over canals, fewer and further between as I neared the edge of the city. After another moment, I was away from the confines of the city, away from civilization, stranded in the desert.

Chet spread his thick, gargoyle wings and flew over my head, landing in front of me, facing me. "You will die now, worm."

Taking a deep breath, I extended my hand in front of me, fingernails first, and tore at the sky. The sky felt thick and viscous, but hot. Like I was running my fingers through a pan of boiling grease.

Light shimmered around the edges of the tiny tear I'd ripped between realities.

Chet lunged.

THIRTY-NINE

I dove through my portal, rolling to my knees on the other side, drawing my gun as I went.

As Chet pushed through, his body transforming to human form, I emptied my clip into his chest. He staggered and fell, his human form twitching as he bled out into the sand.

I dropped the empty clip and shoved a loaded one in. Standing, I walked toward him and stood over him, then fired several shots straight through his head.

His body began to... quiver.

But that's not the right word, because it didn't actually move. It was more like I could sense it moving, in the same way I could sense the Eyes.

What have you done to me?

I recognized the voice as Chet's, but it was different. It was no longer solid, no longer echoing in my physical ears. Now it was... now it was like the Eyes.

"I killed you." The awe in my voice must have been obvious to him, but he began screeching at me. His human form—tall, blond, muscular—lay in the dirt, dead as any human who'd just been shot multiple times, but his spirit...

I could feel him, in the same way I could feel the Eyes. Feel his emotions, his hate, feel where he was in relation to me physically, even though he now only existed in the other dimension.

He lashed out at me, cursing me, slashing at me with impotent claws, but he couldn't affect me here any more than the Eyes.

I took a step away from the body, and my vision grew dark. The effects of all the energy I'd expended must be hitting me, the adrenaline rush starting to fade.

I suddenly felt so exhausted I could barely move.

My knees buckled, and I collapsed to the ground, there in the middle of nowhere, struggling to breathe. My head swam, thick and heavy, and my eyesight blurred. My limbs felt leaden. It was all I could do to pull my phone out of my pocket.

My most recent phone call was to Chase. I tapped his name on my screen, and he picked up.

"I killed Chet," I said.

"What?" Chase asked. "Jack, are you okay? You sound terrible. What do you mean you killed Chet?"

"The physical forms they take on in this dimension can be killed." My words slurred together. I sounded drunk to my own ears—I could only imagine what I sounded like to him. "He's trapped in the other dimension, now."

My eyelids drooped, my words a jumble of syllables mushing together in my mouth. "I saved the girls."

"Jack, where are you? Do you need help?"

"My phone. GPS. Call the cops. Tell them. Come get me."

***

I woke up in the hospital, lying in bed, an IV sticking out of my arm. Bridget sat beside me, thumbing through a bridal magazine. I blinked a couple times. "Bridge?"

My tongue felt thick, dry. It made it hard to talk.

Bridget jerked, her magazine falling to the ground. "Jack! Oh, thank God!"

She pressed the buzzer on the side of my bed then threw her arms around my neck. "We were so worried about you."

"I just got worn out. I'm fine."

"Jack, you've been unconscious for a day and a half. It's Thursday morning."

"No, that's not possible. I was just tired. I fell asleep is all."

The door burst open, and a nurse bustled in. "Hello, there. It's a relief to see you awake. You had lots of people really worried about you."

She quickly and efficiently took my vitals. "The doctor'll be in in just a few minutes." She recorded my stats on her chart. "Is there anything you need, hon?"

I licked my lips, trying to get rid of the dry mouth feeling. "Water."

"You betcha."

She left, and a doctor came in. A second later, Isaac came in, too. He hurried to my side and kissed my forehead. "I'm not your doctor, but I asked to be kept informed of your condition."

Bridget's eyes widened, and she gave me a questioning look.

"Later," I mouthed to her.

She nodded.

The other doctor, a man with graying hair whose nametag read "Richards," pulled one of those rolling stools over and sat by me. "So, you were unconscious for almost forty hours. No sign of concussion, not more than minimal dehydration, no other signs of trauma. Can you tell me what happened right before you lost consciousness?"

"I shot someone."

"You shot someone?"

"He was trying to kill me. He was a kidnapper. Had a house full of underage girls he'd abducted and impregnated."

I could tell by the lack of surprise on his face that he already knew all this. Apparently, he was just trying to see how much I remembered.

"You were about ten miles away from where the police recovered those girls, in the middle of the desert, with the body of the man you shot. Do you know how you got there?"

"I was running. He was chasing me."

"How did you get so far so fast?"

"I can't explain that."

"Hm. Well, other than being unconscious for almost two days, you appear to be in good health. We're going to run some tests, make sure your blood work all comes back normal, do a CT scan for brain injuries, all that. You can plan to be here for at least another day, anyway. Maybe two or three."

Bridget's mouth opened.

I reached toward her and squeezed her hand. "I'm going to be fine. It was just a crash after the adrenaline rush. You wedding isn't for a couple more weeks. I promise to be back to one-hundred percent by then."

"I'm just concerned about you getting better." Her eyes darted toward the bridal magazine as she said it, though.

"Bridge. I'll be there."

She smiled. "I'm really glad you're awake."

"She hasn't left your side since you were brought in," Isaac said.

"Bridge. You can't be doing that. You need to take care of yourselves."

She smiled at my pun. "I—we're—okay."

"Still. You should get some rest. I'll call you when I know anything."

"Okay." She picked up her magazine and headed for the door. "I'll call you tonight."

The other doctor finished examining me and went off to order the tests.

When we were alone, Isaac took my hand. "What really happened?"

"Lots. But Chase should be here for this, too."

"I texted him as soon as I heard you woke up. He should be on his way."

"Thank you."

"Of course." He squeezed my hand. "I have to go check in on my patients, but I will be back."

Twenty minutes later, he returned and sat beside me, interlocking his fingers with mine.

A few minutes later, Chase burst through the door. His gazed landed on our clasped hands, but he didn't say anything. He came to my bedside and gave me a hug. He pulled away quickly, seeming even more uncomfortable than usual about touching me, and sat in the chair Bridget had vacated. "Are you okay?"

"I'll be fine."

"What happened? We heard about your undercover thing, how you found the house where Chet was keeping the girls, but no one would comment to me on an ongoing investigation."

I told them about following Chet as he took Cameron through the portal, how space there was different and we traveled so far, so fast. About the rock wall there that made an invisible barrier here, and about luring Chet away so the girls could escape.

"How did you kill him if your gun doesn't work there?" Chase asked.

"I didn't kill him there, I killed him here."

"He opened a portal and let you escape so you could shoot him?"

"I opened it."

"*What?*" both men asked together.

"Yeah. I opened the portal. Like this." I scratched the air with my fingernails.

Nothing happened.

"Hm. I don't know what's wrong. It worked when I did it before."

Idiot. The Eyes spat from the side of the room.

I hadn't even noticed he was there. I looked toward him. "What?"

Chase and Isaac both looked at me like I was a little nuts, but I ignored them. "Do you know why it isn't working?"

You can't open a portal into there. That would be like... chopping down a tree while it's still an acorn. This world is inferior, less developed. Even we can't do the things here that are possible there. You have to create the portal there for it to be open here.

"Huh. Good to know."

"What is it?" Isaac asked.

"Apparently it only works from the other side. So, anyway, I opened the portal and came through, and when he followed me, I shot him. Now that his physical form is dead, he's like that one." I pointed to the Eyes. "A ghost, trapped in that other dimension, unable to affect this dimension physically, although his essence or spirit or whatever is still able to be here."

"Which means he's unable to impregnate any more girls with his spawn," Chase said.

"Yes."

"So he's dead, and the girls are safe," Isaac said. "Does that mean it's over?"

"Not even close. Chet was just one small chunk of a much larger shish-kebab."

"Meaning?"

"I don't know. Trent said there was a war coming, that this breeding they're doing is to build an army for that war. And Chet wasn't the only one spawning."

"There are more?" Isaac asked.

I nodded. "There was one that was working with a human trafficking ring. The human who was the head of that ring is dead, but we have no idea what happened to that demon or who he was. There have also been increased reports of alien activity and that sort of thing, which I believe may be related. That reminds me, I still need to talk to Ken."

"Who is Ken?" Chase asked.

"A guy I work with. He had the thrilling task of investigating claims of alien encounters, some of which involved abduction and insemination by alien entities. I think that may be related to what we've seen here. It's smart, really, using different types of deceptions so there's never one specific M.O. that can link them all."

"Makes a twisted sort of sense, I guess," Isaac said. "So what about this war?"

"I don't know the details. Trent had a source that told him this stuff, but I have no idea who he is, and Trent's letter didn't give me much to go on. Only that it's coming, and the more of these half-demons that are spawned, the worse it's going to be for us."

"So our job is to stop them from spawning."

"Yes."

"How?"

I shrugged. "One at a time, I guess. Find them, kill them before they can keep spreading, and confine their ghosts to the other dimension."

"How are we supposed to find them?"

"Same way we found Chet. Set them up, I'll follow them through the other dimension to their lairs, lure them out, and kill them."

Isaac shook his head. "No."

I glared at Isaac. "Did you really just say that? You've seen what these guys are doing to these girls. You know the consequences if we don't stop them. Even aside from the demon spawn aspect, they're still evil. They kidnap little girls and perform experiments on them."

Isaac squeezed my hand. "I just meant no, you can't follow them. We have to find another way."

"What are you talking about? There is no other way. Why wouldn't I follow them? I'm the only one who can."

"Because, going to the other dimension is killing you."

FORTY

Chase and I both stared at him.

"What do you mean?" I asked.

"Oh, come on, Jack. You're a detective. It should be obvious. You traveled though that dimension, and when you came out, you were unconscious for almost two days."

"That was just recovering from the adrenaline crash."

"No, it's true," Chase said. "You collapsed after the last time, too, and you were only in there for a couple minutes."

"I hadn't slept the night before. I was tired."

"You're in denial. There is a straightforward cause-and-effect, and you refuse to see it," Isaac said. "The doctors won't find anything when they do the tests, because the cause isn't anything this dimension can test for, but the fact is, every time you go in there, something happens to you. Your body wasn't built for it. If you keep going back, it will kill you."

"He's right," Chase said. "It's too dangerous."

"Guys, I'm really fine."

"This time," Isaac said, "but you can't expect to do things outside the bounds of time and space and not have consequences."

I was saved from further lecturing by the doctor returning with an envoy of minions. One of them took several vials of blood, one did some simple skin and reflex tests, and finally they transferred me to a wheelchair and rolled me downstairs to get the CT scan.

When I got back to my room and hour or so later, Chase was the only one there. "Dr. Reyes got paged. Apparently one of the girls you rescued went into labor."

"They have to put guards in the nursery. Someone is going to come for that baby."

"Chet is dead."

"That doesn't mean there aren't others who will want it. They're building an army. They're going to want their soldiers."

"What do you expect them to do? Put armed guards in a hospital nursery and tell them to fire on anyone who materializes out of thin air?"

"Well, when you put it that way." I scowled at him. "I could go in there. Wait for them to come and follow them back to wherever they're keeping the monster babies."

"Absolutely not. Don't even think about it."

"I really don't appreciate you two treating me like a child."

"Hey, if the shoe fits…" Chase grinned.

I wanted to throw something at him, but the only thing within reach was my pillow, so I settled for smacking him with it.

He laughed. "Case in point."

I frowned. "I'm really going to be okay. So what if I get a little tired after? Isn't that worth it to stop these things?"

"Not if something worse happens to you. We'll find another way."

I sighed and flopped back against my bed. "Fine."

A bone-deep weariness settled over me. As much as I hated to admit it, I wasn't fine. I was still exhausted. And if I ever wanted to get out of this bed, I needed to recover.

"I think I'm going to rest a bit. Thanks so much for being here."

"Of course." Chase patted my shoulder. "Call me when you know anything."

He left, and I dozed until the doctor came in several hours later. All my tests came back normal. He determined I just had an extreme case of exhaustion and I was probably fine, but he wanted to keep me one more night for observation.

At that point I was too tired to argue, so when he left, I went back to sleep.

By the next morning I felt like myself again. My doctor agreed I was good to check out. I called Bridget to come pick me up. I debated between asking Chase or Isaac instead, but I honestly couldn't decide between the two, and I needed to get back to work, anyway.

"You look great," Bridget said when she saw me. "I'll be honest, yesterday I was really worried."

"The doctor said it was just an extreme case of exhaustion. A little R and R was all I needed."

"You have been working crazy since you got back."

"I had a lot of lost time to make up for."

"Yeah, I get that. Could you cool it until after the wedding at least, though?"

"Deal," I laughed.

"Want me to just drop you at home?" Bridget asked.

"Yeah. I need to shower and change, but I'll be in to work in a little bit."

"You probably don't have to come in right away. You'll be lucky if you don't get put on administrative leave. I'm sure the captain will understand if you take a break."

"No, I need to get back. I've missed more this year that I should. I'll talk to him."

"Okay. I'll see you there, then."

I called the captain while I went through my hygiene routine. He agreed to let me come back in as long as I addressed the shooting in therapy. Of course, I agreed, and went into work as soon as I could. Desiree was waiting by my desk when I got there.

Oh, joy.

"Hi. They told me you'd be back today. I heard you took some personal time?"

"You could say that. I was in the hospital. Chase came to see me, didn't he tell you? Or don't you two talk that much?" I knew it was petty, but I couldn't help it.

"He didn't mention you. I guess some people just aren't cut out for field work."

I smiled my best condescending smile. "Well, I did manage to close the case we were working on together, taking down a kidnapper and rescuing more than a dozen of his victims. What did you do?"

She narrowed her eyes but didn't respond.

I decided to consider that a win.

Desiree opened up the file she held. "I think you may have been right about this case being connected to the one your fiancé had been working on."

"Yeah? How do you know?" I leaned in to look at the page she held.

"I was going over the coroner's report for Richard Hunt. It seems like he was actually in the back seat, not the driver as we previously assumed. Someone else was driving, so there's at least one body we haven't recovered. I'm going to order a search of the river. Now, based on the size of the guy with him, we've been going on the assumption he was a bodyguard of some sort, but what if it was the other way around? What if Hunt was protecting *him*?"

194

"Interesting. What evidence do you have?"

"I think this man may have been the father of Tamara's baby."

"That's not possible. I have a positive ID on the man I shot as being the guy who took her. Not to mention he was dead before she got pregnant."

"Tamara already had her baby, and this guy died two months ago. Do the math."

I couldn't really argue the point without explaining the shortened demon gestation, so I changed the subject. "Okay, what makes you think he was the father?"

"He had the same defect."

"What defect?"

Desiree pointed to the place on the report where it had distinctive physical characteristics. "Six fingers on each hand."

FORTY-ONE

I gasped.

The full implications of that fact hit me. No wonder he couldn't be identified. He wasn't human. He was a Nephilim.

No wonder he was helping the trafficker who was dealing in young women—he was one of their progeny.

And no wonder the sky opened up and released a flood of demons when Trent was about to catch him. They couldn't afford for Trent to catch him and find out what was really going on.

"Are you okay?"

I snapped out of my reverie. "Yeah. Fine. Just thinking."

"Well? What about my theory?" she asked.

"I'd say it's safe to assume the man in the car is related to Tamara's baby, in any case. But he's dead, and Tamara's baby is still missing, so we have to assume this is bigger than just the two of them. Someone else wanted that baby enough to break into a hospital to get it."

"It?"

"Him. You know what I mean."

She nodded. "You're right. Someone is still out there. I guess it's possible that the driver of the car may not be dead. He could be the one who kidnapped the baby. That means this case needs to be reopened and the other one not closed. Any suggestions on how to find these guys?"

Yeah. One. But my preacher and my doctor, those boy scouts, wouldn't let me follow it through. "Not really. Every lead up until the other day has been a dead end. One of the girls from the house where Chet was holed up delivered her baby, though. I'd suggest starting by putting a guard on that baby's room, in case whoever kidnapped

Tamara's baby comes back for that one, too. And we could start tracking formula sales. If there are as many of these babies in one spot as I think there are, that's going to be a lot of baby food they're going to need."

"Okay. I'll see about getting the FBI to guard the baby and any others that are born. Why don't you start on that formula purchase thing?"

Damn, I hated that woman.

I started contacting grocery stores as soon as she left me alone to inquire whether they'd had a sudden increase in baby formula or baby food sales recently, but it was almost impossible to tell. Turns out a lot of people buy baby food in large quantities. Yet another dead end.

I breathed deeply and dropped my head to my desk.

"You okay, Jack?"

I looked up. "Ken! You're exactly the person I wanted to see. You busy?"

"Not particularly."

"Mind if I pick your brain about those alien sightings you've been investigating?"

He shrugged. "Sure. I need some coffee. Want to discuss it elsewhere?"

"That sounds fantastic. I need a break, anyway."

"Let me just grab my files. Meet you out front."

I went to the front lobby to wait.

He appeared a moment later. "Do you want me to drive?"

"Sure."

A gust of wind so hot it felt like the breath from a blast furnace rustled the files he carried. He clutched them to his chest. "A nice breeze is supposed to be refreshing," he muttered.

He led me to his little beater car and drove to the coffee shop up the street. We sat at a small table in the corner and Ken ordered us both coffees.

"So, what would you like to know?" he asked.

Where to begin?

I shrugged. "I don't know. I guess, walk me through a typical alien encounter."

He chuckled. "There's nothing typical about an encounter. Everyone seems to have a different story. A lot of these are sightings of lights in the sky or crafts that seem unexplainable. For example, the other day—same day you broke your case, actually, over on the west side, several people saw a light streaking through the sky. Like a shining object traveling at unfathomable speeds."

197

I coughed. I'd seen the same thing when I first encountered Dionysius in the other dimension.

"Lights in the sky like that are weird. One moment they're there, then the next, they're gone. They change direction much too abruptly to be any sort of craft human technology is capable of building, and travel at lighting speeds one moment, only to hover in the same spot for awhile and then dart off in another direction or disappear altogether."

"Sightings like that happen a lot?" I asked.

He nodded. "More than you'd believe. And that's just the sightings that get reported. Most people write it off as a trick of the light or their imaginations. Then there are the actual encounters with an alien entity."

"What are those like?"

"Oh, you know. The same kinds of things you see on TV. Cold. Missing time. The feeling of being watched or waking up in strange places. Unexplained pregnancies that are mysteriously terminated. So far I have a bunch of stories and no substantial claims. No actual evidence of any kind."

"Has anyone ever fought back? Does anyone have any idea how to stop them?"

Ken looked through his notes. "Not that I can tell. Mostly they don't know it's happening until it's over. But I think that has more to do with them than the encounter. This phenomenon, it's all in their heads. Some kind of mass hysteria playing out in the imaginations of the weak-minded."

"Are you sure? Isn't it possible something really is going on?"

Ken raised an eyebrow at me. "What's up with you, Jack? You never used to be the superstitious type."

How much should I tell him? How much could I reveal without him thinking I was crazy? Or, worse, telling the captain I was crazy and have me shipped back to the looney bin? "The case I've been working on—I've come across some similar occurrences that lead me to believe there may be more going on here than mass hysteria or group deception."

"You really think we're being invaded by aliens?"

I shrugged. "I think something."

"Well, I think it's a bunch of crap, but I'm about to head out for an interview. Want to tag along?"

"Sure."

"Great. I just need to take a leak first."

He was gone for longer than I thought it should've taken him, but that wasn't the sort of thing I was about to ask about. When he returned, he smelled faintly of sulfur. I looked around for the source of the other-dimensional cause, but it was impossible to tell.

Demons constantly affected this dimension, both in the flesh and through the dimensional wall, and regular humans rarely had any idea. And again, not something I could really ask. Ken would think I was really insane if I asked whether he'd seen any demons lately. Anyone would.

Except Chase, for some reason. I should really ask him about that.

"Jack? Are you coming?" Ken stood by the door, letting the hot desert air into the coffee shop.

"Oh, yeah. Sorry."

I followed him out to his car, and we drove to one of the addresses in his file.

He gave me a quick rundown of the case. "Nancy Wheaton, forty-two. Began seeing strange lights in her back yard almost every evening. Took some pictures, but they were grainy and blurred. Finally, one evening, she was approached by someone she says was an otherworldly entity."

"What did it want from her?"

"That's what we're about to find out."

He pulled up to the curb in front of the house and led the way to the front door.

A petite woman with wildly curly brown hair opened the door.

"Good morning, Ms. Wheaton. We're here because you called about—"

"The aliens! Yes, of course. Come in." She ushered us inside and brought us each a glass of ice water. "Now, I want to be clear, the only reason I called you is to make sure there won't be any legal problems when I help them. I know Arizona has some pretty strict policies about aliens."

Ken smiled. "Those mostly apply to illegal aliens from other countries. We don't have any strict policies regarding interaction with extraterrestrials."

"Oh, good. I guess I don't need you, then."

"Why don't you go ahead and tell us what happened, anyway? That way we have a clearer idea of what they want and can maybe help them more later."

I eyed Ken, intrigued. He'd always been such a puppy around me, but he read this woman and handled her well.

"Well, it started a few weeks ago. I was in my backyard, weeding my flowerbeds, and I saw these bright lights flashing through the sky. Faster than any airplane or jet that I've ever seen, shooting back and forth, almost like they were dancing."

I thought about chasing Chet through the other dimension, the way he zoomed through the air when he flew, and the way the earth seemed smaller and we covered miles in mere minutes. My theory that their presence in this reality was detectable by others, even if it wasn't quite the same way I sensed it, seemed more and more plausible the longer this woman talked.

If I was right, the demons' movements in the other dimension bled through to here, so a demon flying through an extra-dimensional space could easily appear to be a light or a craft traveling at speeds faster than anything human technology could accomplish.

"Anywho, I saw these lights above my back yard every day for about a week, and then one evening, a man appeared out of thin air, right in front of me."

"Do you mind if we see where?" I asked.

Ken raised an eyebrow at me, but he knew better than to second-guess me in front of someone.

"Sure." Nancy led us out to her spacious backyard, a plot of grass that was unnaturally green for this climate surrounded by large flower beds along the fence on all sides. A large planter sat directly in the middle of the yard with a huge tree growing in it, its large branches shading a good portion of the lawn. Colorful flowers surrounded its base, and hummingbird feeders hung from the lowest branches.

Nancy sat on the brick edge of the tree planter. "I was right here, like this, weeding, and he appeared over there, by the gate."

I walked toward where she pointed. A familiar scorch mark where a demon had created a portal. It was faint—probably old enough that I wouldn't be able to go through, which meant it hadn't been used by many or often.

There was something else, though. It took me a minute to figure out what it was. The grass. The real grass in this dimension, not affected by my awareness of the other dimension, had a faint yellow streak where the scorch mark was.

"You find something?" Ken asked.

"Maybe." I pointed to the grass. "Do you see that?"

Nancy bustled over. "Hm. I don't know how I missed that."

"Did you leave anything there? A garden hose or a rake, maybe, that would've discolored the grass there?" Ken asked.

"Oh, no. I never leave things lying around the yard."

She wouldn't. One didn't get an oasis like this one in the Phoenix desert by neglecting anything, including leaving gardening tools about. Nancy clearly took great pride in her yard. If she hadn't seen the yellow streak until now, it was because the shock of seeing a man materializing in her yard had distracted her.

"What happened next?" I asked.

"Well, like I said, he came into the yard and walked right toward me. Frank's dog, next door, started barking like he was going to have a stroke, but I wasn't afraid. He was so… beautiful."

"Can you describe him?" Ken asked.

Nancy's eyes took on a dreamy cast. "He was tall. Well over six feet, I'd say. His hair was black and shiny, down to his shoulders. His skin was a deep olive color, and his eyes had an exotic slant to them. His neck was thick, like a football player, and he was muscular all over, but I could tell he was gentle. His clothes looked… natural, I guess. All beige and flowing. Loose pants and a loose shirt, like a modern and enlightened hippie."

Ken frantically scribbled notes, while I tried to picture the demon in my mind. Not Chet or Dionysius. How many of those things were there? And if each had spawned, what, a couple dozen half-breed babies, how many Nephilim were already being trained for their army?

FORTY-TWO

"His voice was deep," Nancy went on, "soothing, like a narrator for a life insurance commercial. I knew right away I could trust him."

Was it some sort of spell the demons cast on people? This trance, the blind belief that these creatures were benevolent and magnanimous? Bridget had fallen for it, and apparently Nancy, not to mention countless teenage girls.

"He said he needed my help. They, the aliens, are on a mission to provide enlightenment to our race, but for the sake of the weak minded among us, they're making themselves known slowly, in stages. The first stage is to raise their young among us, so they understand our culture and so we're more able to accept theirs."

"Raise their young?" Ken sounded incredulous.

Nancy nodded. "That's why they need my help. Their transport ship is coming in a couple weeks with a whole crop of their young."

"Crop?" I asked. Weird word, crop. Usually in situations like this, people used words that were common, words they used often. Or words that someone—or in this case, something—planted in their mind. Was that how the demons referred to their own offspring?

Nancy looked at me with poorly disguised derision. "Our notion of a nuclear family is antiquated and ineffective for an enlightened society. Young are produced and raised as part of a global community in more advanced cultures and races. That's one of the many things they're going to teach us when they come."

"What does that have to do with you?" Ken asked.

"I used to run a daycare. With the economy the way it is, I had to shut down, but I still own the property, and it's still furnished. It's perfect for converting into a nursery compound."

"Okay, then," Ken smiled. "Thanks for your cooperation. You don't have anything to fear from the law. Good luck with your... alien nursery compound."

"That's it?" I whispered.

He raised his eyebrows. "You want me to arrest her for taking care of alien babies?"

I clenched my teeth. Sometimes he seemed so bright, but other times I wondered if he even had a brain. How did he not see through this? He was so determined not to believe in aliens he just discounted everything.

"Of course not. But it could be a front for something else. They knew she'd fall for that enlightened crap and used it to gain access to her facility."

"They. You mean the *aliens*."

I glared at him. Please, please, try to understand before one of us dies. "Or criminals who know how to manipulate someone who believes in aliens."

Ken rolled his eyes and turned to Nancy. "Where is your daycare located? Just for our records."

She gave the address, and he smiled.

"Thanks, ma'am. You have a great day."

He led me back to the car and sighed dramatically. "There went a waste of another hour. And this is the kind of crap I've had to deal with for the last six months."

That explained why he was so disconnected and uninvested in his investigation. "I don't think it's all crap."

He arched an eyebrow. "You believe in aliens? By all means, then, let's trade assignments. I'd rather work on a kidnapping partnered with a hot fed any day."

"You think Desiree is hot?" Despite that I already knew she was gorgeous and despite that I had zero interest in Ken, knowing he used to be interested in me but thought Desiree was hot was strangely offensive.

He shrugged nonchalantly, but color suffused his neck. "Well, she's not hideous. What were you saying about it being not a bunch of crap?"

"Oh, I mean, she—Nancy—obviously saw something. And there was something on the grass. Something happened there, enough to make her believe it was aliens who needed her help. I think it warrants looking into the daycare. There's someone who wants it for something. It's not all in her head, even if she's confused about what's really happening."

203

Ken sighed. "I guess it wouldn't hurt to swing by on our way back." He plugged the address into his GPS, and a few minutes later we pulled into the parking lot.

I could feel the otherworldly presences as soon as we got close. The place was teeming with beings, but not quite the solid, nausea-inducing full demons like Dionysius or even the ethereal ones like the Eyes. The feeling was different—solid, but weaker, like Tamara's baby.

Ken looked bored. "This place is deserted."

I could hardly believe he could be so unaware of the activity inside, but that was a common ailment among regular humans. I had a fleeting desire to be that blissfully ignorant, that unaware of the other side, but I quickly shoved it aside. I couldn't go back to not knowing after all I'd seen. "We should at least take a look inside the windows. See if there's anyone lurking in there."

I took a step and smacked face-first into an invisible wall. I stumbled back, my hand going instinctively to my sore nose.

"Are you okay? What happened?" Ken stepped forward, hand outstretched, and came in contact with the wall. "What the—what is that?"

I didn't answer. How could I explain a rock wall in another dimension?

I looked around the property. If this followed the pattern, there should be a hole in it somewhere that they used to get in and out. But I couldn't really go looking for it without explaining how I knew it was there. Neither could I go looking for a portal with him standing there. I would have to come back later.

"That is the weirdest thing." He was still touching the invisible wall. "It's like some kind of—"

"Force field."

He looked at me. "What?"

"The house where my kidnapping victim was found. The servants said they couldn't get out because there was a force field that surrounded the property. It was gone by the time we got there. The house where I eventually found the kidnapper had the same thing."

"Some sort of infrared barrier, maybe?"

"Could be."

"I wonder what it would take to get a warrant to search this place?"

"What good would it do to get a warrant to search a place you can't get into?" I asked.

"We could make them turn it off."

"Who? The aliens? I thought you didn't think anything weird was going on."

"I don't. We could make Nancy do it."

"If she could. I got the impression she knows even less than she thinks she does about what's going on. Whatever this is, whoever put it here—it's bigger than a daycare. Nancy is a pawn."

Ken frowned. "Yeah, okay, you win. There's more here than meets the eye. We have to find out what's in there. We should stake the place out."

"We?"

"I mean, the department."

"Wouldn't hurt to have some idea who's coming and going, I guess." If he was going to stake the place out, I needed to find a portal and do my own recon quickly, or one of them might see me. "We should go back to the station. I've got some things I need to work on."

"Yeah. I need to write up this report," he agreed.

After I wrote my own reports, I went back to the one place I knew I could still get through to the other side. The site of Trent's accident.

I stood and stared at the scorched earth for awhile, working up the fortitude to go in. I needed to get this done, though. It was getting dark, and the other dimension was disorienting enough in the daytime.

I took a deep breath and stepped through the portal.

FORTY-THREE

A wave of nausea washed over me, the stench of sulfur burning my nose and making me gag. It took a few minutes for me to get my bearings, and then I set off at a quick jog in the direction of the daycare.

The Eyes loped along beside me. He still radiated an undercurrent of loathing, but the primary emotion I felt from him at the moment was curiosity.

I ignored him and kept jogging.

It wasn't hard to find the daycare once I got close. It was a huge property surrounded by an enormous rock wall. This was different, though. Two Nephilim ghosts, like the Eyes, guarded the small hole at the corner of the wall. Their forms were human, albeit larger than average, not gargoyle.

I paused, still far enough away that they hadn't noticed me. I skirted around the edge until I reached the other side.

The upside of these rock walls was that they were solid here. The demons couldn't see through them like they could the human buildings, so I was out of sight.

I went to the corner directly opposite the guards and started pulling rocks away from the bottom, careful not to take rocks that seemed to be supporting too many others so it wouldn't cave in on me, creating a tunnel just small enough to crawl through.

The Eyes hissed.

"Go ahead. Give me away," I dared him in a low voice.

He glared at me but did nothing to alert the others to my position.

I got on my stomach, wormed through the hole, stood up on the other side, and brushed the dust from my clothes. The Eyes didn't follow me. He was too big to crawl through the hole I'd made, and these walls were as solid for him as for me.

The inside was as much of a fortress as the wall. The walls were solid, made of some sort of metal that looked like tin foil but heavier. All I'd ever seen of this dimension was dusty, barren landscape, but this structure—it was like nothing I'd ever seen, shining walls and bright lights, like something out of a bad sci-fi flick. A B-movie alien ship.

Realization dawned with a sense of horror. These weren't just gargoyle demon monsters. Much like the aliens they claimed to be, they were an advanced race.

If Chase was correct about their origins, that meant they'd had tens of thousands of years to acquire and share knowledge, to perfect technology, to develop their sciences. If a human saw a glimpse of this or woke up inside, they would surely think they'd been abducted by a superior species.

I crept forward, making my way around the windowless structure in search of a door.

I found one on the other side of the building, located in the same place as the daycare's door, probably so they could get in from either dimension. It was unguarded, as far as I could tell. The demons probably weren't too worried about intruders. I slowly opened the door and pushed inside.

It was like they had rebuilt or reinforced the existing structure within this dimension, so it mirrored the daycare exactly but with materials from this side.

I walked from room to room, examining what appeared to be an ordinary, albeit deserted, daycare.

As I continued on, though, I heard sounds coming from the last room at the end of the hall. I made my way silently down the hall and cracked open the door. The room was filled with creatures, toddler-sized Nephilim, yet not here. They were in the the real world, but their essences bled through, stronger, more palpable than the ghostly forms of humans.

I did a rough estimate in my head. There had to be close to fifty of the things in the room. With them were two human women, apparently charged with caring for them, for they doled out food and cleaned up after the things.

The mini-monsters were grotesque, bizarre looking, despite their distinctly human appearance. Their heads were overly large, misshapen, with eyes that stared out of enormous sockets and looked too old.

Their bodies were thick, solid, like tree trunks, bulging with unnatural musculature.

As I examined the room, I felt a strange sense of... familiarity. My eyes landed on one of the creatures, a boy who looked about four or five, with a mop of curly red hair on top of his head.

I knew that child.

It didn't make sense. He was too old. But I knew without a doubt, that boy was Tamara's baby.

The others ranged in age from infants to what appeared to be boys about ten or twelve years old. Considering how fast Tamara's baby had matured and knowing this had been going on since before Trent's death, I determined that the boys over that age were already being conscripted into the demon army. It was then that I realized they were all boys.

Were the girls kept elsewhere? I hadn't seen anyone in any of the other rooms, although based on the capacity of this one, this facility could easily house several hundred of the things.

Unless there were no girls. I didn't know how or why that would be, but it seemed like the most logical explanation for the lack of Nephilim girl babies in this place.

Maybe, in order to create a stronger army, they'd genetically modified something so when they impregnated the human girls they only got male spawn. Or maybe, like cross-breeding horses and donkeys to get mules, when cross-breeding humans and demons, the result was a sterile male half-breed.

Weariness began to settle over me, and I realized I should probably get out of this dimension soon, especially if Isaac was right about the toll it would take on my body.

I turned around to make my way back out and ran smack into a huge, leathery beast with claws the size of steak knives.

FORTY-FOUR

I stumbled backward. How had I not felt it coming? Was I so focused on Tamara's baby and the others that I hadn't noticed? Was I getting so used to their presence they didn't affect me the same way any more?

The demon laughed. "Well, well. This is a new one for me. I don't know why you're awake, but don't worry. It won't last long." He took a step toward me.

I stepped backward and pressed up against the wall.

A solid, demon wall that I couldn't pass through on either side.

I raised my hand to open a portal, but he grabbed it before I could do anything and wrenched my wrist.

I screamed, my knees buckling from the pain.

The demon reached toward my neck.

"Dionysius!" I shouted.

He paused.

"You can't kill me. Dionysius will want to know I was here."

Interrogation techniques that work on people apparently also work on demons. Throwing out Dionysius's name to evaluate his reaction and gain some leverage worked in my favor.

The demon visibly blanched. He feared Dionysius.

I could use that. I wasn't sure how, yet, but I filed the information away for future reference.

The demon lifted a hand and aimed it at my head.

My neck whipped back at the blow, bright spots spattering across my vision just before everything went black.

I woke in a room reminiscent of a hospital room but made of the same tin-like material as the daycare.

I lay on a metal table, like a gurney or the slab in a coroner's office. Multi-colored lights blinked on the walls and ceiling. Even without the weird technology I would've known I was in the fourth dimension by the feel of the atmosphere, heavy and oppressive, all around me.

I was in a small room, alone, although I could feel presences all around, just outside the door, which was closed.

There was no way I could get out that way. I focused my mind on the presences outside, trying to determine if I recognized any of them. One was distinctly familiar.

Dionysius.

Notably absent was the Eyes.

Was he hiding somewhere? Or maybe being punished for not keeping me under control?

I slid from the table and tried the door, quietly, but it didn't open. Maybe if I could open a portal to my dimension I could get out that way.

I looked around but couldn't see whatever structure might be in the human dimension. No ethereal trees or buildings or people, not even distinguishable space of any kind, just darkness.

Cold tentacles of panic wrapped around my whole being. Where was I, that there was nothing on the other side to see?

I slowly lifted my hand and with my fingernail drew a slight tear in the wall between realities. Searing heat burned my fingers, but I kept on until I could see through the hole.

It took me a moment to realize exactly what I was seeing. It was a rock wall. Not a wall made of rocks, but an entire sheet of rock, like the face of a cliff.

"We're in a cave."

I whirled around, my heart stalling at the voice behind me. "Dionysius."

He smiled, baring long, dripping fangs from his bestial mouth. "You might as well not bother trying to escape. If you get out you'll end up in an underground cavern with no exit. By all means, though, have at it."

Something told me he was telling the truth.

I took a step back.

"What cave?"

"No place you'd be familiar with. The ruler of this province owes me a favor." He looked me over, yellow eyes lingering in discomfiting scrutiny. "You're here. And awake. We've spent no little time discussing how you do that."

"If I knew, I'd clue you in."

His mouth stretched in a feral smile. "I'm sure you would. But now there's the question of what to do with you."

"You could take me home."

"I'm sure you'd like that. I wouldn't get my hopes up on that one if I were you, though. My servants are itching to dissect you."

"Dissect?"

"You're an anomaly, my dear. The occasional subject wakes up for a few moments at a time during our procedures, but their minds can't comprehend the extra mental stimulation, and they shut down. You, though, can enter and function in our world, almost as though you're partly one of us, but more so. Even our offspring have too much human DNA to function here for very long."

I gulped. The longer I could keep him talking, the better chance I had of catching him off-guard. "Really? That's weird, I would've thought... I don't know, I guess because they're so inhuman I thought they'd be more like you."

"On the contrary, they're more like you than us. We've tried any number of experiments, fiddling with your DNA to make a hybrid that is more like us than you while still retaining human physical characteristics, but to no avail. Our current process is the most efficient."

"Yeah? What's that?"

"A nearly equal blend of human DNA with ours, carefully cultivated before being implanted in our gracious hosts. Of course, it helps when the subject is pure and uncontaminated."

"Uncontaminated?"

His yellow eyes gleamed.

"You mean virgin?"

"Previous contamination weakens the specimens. The resulting offspring tends to be smaller, with more human traits."

"That's why all the girls Chet kidnapped were so young. He needed virgins." All the jokes and lore about virgin sacrifices I'd ever heard suddenly took on new and horrifying significances. "What about Bridget, then? She's not a virgin."

He laughed, a sinister cackle that echoed around the small room. "Bridget was special. Aside from being utterly stunning and well worth my time to take, there's the added benefit of knowing it's torturing you."

I gagged. "So you got her pregnant the… um… regular way?"

"Sadly, no. Sometime in history, human physiology changed somewhat, and our kind was no longer able to reproduce with yours. Every so often something would take, but it was the anomaly, not the rule."

"Why would it work sometimes and not all the time?"

"We don't know for sure, but probably because the women were descended from our original offspring and still had traces of our DNA."

Not sterile, then. That was unfortunate. But at least it was a little more complicated for them than just having wanton sex. "So you can't just sleep around and knock up whoever you want."

"No. We've spent thousands of years researching and developing genetic manipulation, and finally over the last few dozen years we've gotten to the point where we can once again cross-breed."

I felt like throwing up, but there was nothing in my stomach. How long had I been here? Hours? Days? Longer?

Space moved differently here, maybe time did, too. For all I knew, I could've been missing for months at home. Or maybe I hadn't been missed at all.

"If I don't show up at work tomorrow, they're going to know something's wrong."

"So what if they do? No one knows where you went, and even if they did, what could they do about it? They couldn't find you here."

He had a point. "So what, then? Are you just going to keep me here until I die?"

"In all probability, yes. I'm not going to kill you just yet, though, so you might as well make yourself comfortable. I would offer you something to eat, but human food doesn't last here. Even if I brought you something, I assure you, it wouldn't be edible. I'll be back later."

Dion started to leave, but then he stopped and turned back. "Oh, and my servants are authorized to kill you if you try anything. That would be quite a pity, though. I'd hate for you to miss my wedding. It's going to be an event to remember."

He left and the door shut with a loud click. I was alone. I sat on the floor for awhile, waiting for I don't know what. My inevitable demise, maybe.

Finally, though, boredom got the better of me, and I stood up and looked around. The lights that blinked all around were imbedded in the walls and the domed ceiling.

I took a closer look at one of the lights. It was white, but up close it looked like something was moving inside. It kind of reminded me of a front-loading washing machine, swirling endlessly.

I had a feeling the lights were performing some function other than providing illumination, but I could barely understand most human technology. Extra-dimensional demon technology went beyond anything I could begin to speculate on.

The only entrance to the room was the one Dionysius came through, and the only items in the room were the gurney-like table I'd woken up on and a counter along one wall. It attached to the wall seamlessly, almost as if it was part of the wall, an extension of it.

It was made of that same weird tin-looking metal that looked fragile, but when I touched it seemed stronger than steel. There was nothing in the room that might pass for a tool or weapon of any sort.

I began systematically ripping holes into the other dimension, wincing every time the heat seared my skin. Just beyond the walls of the room were the walls of the cave, and if there was an exit, it was somewhere beyond the walls of my room.

I opened a portal in the center of the room and walked through into the cave. Fatigue washed over me, but I forced my body to push through. It was too dark to see much, but I felt along the walls looking for an exit but found only stone walls. If only I had a flashlight or anything I could use to search.

I patted my pockets for my cell phone, but couldn't find it.

I still had my gun, though. For whatever reason, they hadn't removed that from me. Probably because it wouldn't do any good, anyway. Still, though, it wasn't exactly useful in finding an escape route.

There must be a tunnel or something somewhere, but it was either small enough or low enough or both that I couldn't detect it.

I stepped back into my prison and sat on the edge of the bed.

It rolled. If I could use that somehow…

I pushed it a little. I could block the door with it, although really I didn't know what that would accomplish.

I pushed it through the portal I'd made.

That was weird.

As it went through the hole, it seemed to bend.

I pushed it the rest of the way through. The metal seemed to warp, waving like a piece of cloth. I pressed down on it. It buckled beneath the pressure, but as soon as I removed my hand it bounced back.

Some element of its composition must be missing in my reality, making it appear the same but not function in the same way.

I took hold of one of the legs and pulled.

It came toward me, bending like a rubber stick, but didn't break. I glanced around at the floor of the cave and found a rock. Using the rock as a club, I banged at the table leg. It dented, but bounced back. I continued smacking it with the rock, and it continued to bounce back to exactly what it looked like before.

Sighing, I pushed it back through the portal. I sat on it, and toppled to the ground as it collapsed beneath my weight, tilting on three legs as the fourth clattered and rolled across the floor.

What the...?

Hitting it with the rock, while seemingly inconsequential in my dimension, must have weakened the integrity of the metal. I picked up the broken leg and stepped into my dimension. It bent, flexing back and forth, until I went back into the demon dimension, where it became hard again, like a steel rod.

Weapons from my dimension were useless here, and structures from here were incomplete there. But, if I had a weapon here, then maybe that would work. I caressed the table leg, examining the jagged edge where it had broken off of the table.

The Nephilim ghosts like the Eyes were about nine feet tall, and I was pretty sure my door was guarded by at least two. There might be some of the twelve-foot gargoyles lurking around, too. I'd have the element of surprise, but that really only went so far when it was one of me against untold hordes of them.

Still, I couldn't stay much longer. I could already feel the drain on my body, despite the unconscious nap I'd taken. My muscles were weak, sapped of strength, and my mind felt clouded. The longer I stayed, the worse it would get.

If I was going to make my move, I needed to do it now.

FORTY-FIVE

I went to the door. Voices filtered through from the other side.

"It's awake?" one of them asked, his voice rough and gravelly.

"Yes, Tsenaha."

"How?"

"We do not know, Master. But she is awake. Dionysius was talking to her."

The master, Tsenaha, growled. "How long did he say she'll be there?"

"He didn't say."

"I hope the Great One burns Dionysius's eyes out of his head. Let me know when he takes her away, and let him know I said our bargain is completed."

Heavy steps echoed down an enclosed area.

I waited until Tsenaha was gone, then pounded on the door. "Hey! I need to go to the bathroom!"

Something moved on the other side, but nobody opened the door.

I banged again. "You guys may not have ordinary bodily functions, but I do, and I need to get out of this room. Hey!"

Something rustled and the door swung outward. A Nephilim spirit stepped through.

I swung the rod as hard as I could toward his head. He staggered backward, more stunned than hurt, but enough for me to shove the bed into him and knock him over.

I bolted for the door, but the other guard grabbed me by the arm. I swung at him with the rod, managing to smack him a couple times, squirming and writhing against him and making a few inches progress down the hallway.

It wouldn't last long. He'd already overcome his shock and was outmaneuvering me as well as overpowering me.

In desperation, I sliced with my nails and made a portal in the hallway. I lunged and fell through it, pulling the creature with me.

He screeched as he saw what was coming, an unearthly howl that made me retch even as I tumbled through the opening.

He fell after me, and as he passed through the portal, disintegrated.

He just ceased to exist.

He didn't follow me through, didn't stay on the other side—he was just gone.

I couldn't even feel traces of his presence, the way I usually did when one of them was near.

I took a deep breath, my strength wavering, and looked around. I stood in a low cave that looked like it had been dug out of the rock by hand, not etched away by time. A few feet ahead, it branched in several directions. I could take any of them and maybe find a way out, or maybe get more lost than before, or even wander endlessly until exhaustion overtook me and I died. I already felt faint, so that was a very real possibility.

Or, I could take my chances in the fourth dimension. I'd probably have a better chance of finding my way out, but then I ran the risk of meeting more demons. I could maybe kill a few with the portal thing, but I couldn't really bank on all of them going through as easily as the last one.

As I stood there debating, I felt a presence draw near. I started to panic until I realized it was the Eyes.

He felt weak. Frail. As though his very being was fading from existence.

He looked at me through the opening of the portal. "Come with me."

I hesitated.

"Now, or it will be too late."

I really didn't have much choice.

I jumped through the portal, back into the demon dimension.

He grabbed my head in his hands and squeezed.

I kicked my feet and squirmed, struggling to get away.

"Hold still!" he snapped.

He wasn't squeezing hard enough to hurt me—only putting a slight amount of pressure on me.

A strange tingling sensation spread through me, and I felt the shroud of exhaustion start to lift from my body and mind.

At the same time, I felt the Eyes start to strengthen. He tilted his head back as he absorbed whatever of my strength he could, then dropped his hands.

"This way." He started down the hall at a quick trot, and I followed.

We covered what seemed to be miles of tunnels, traveling at a slight incline the whole way, turning down twisted passageways, skimming past rooms and even demons, but they weren't paying attention to us. We passed one room where a pregnant woman lay on a table, a demon standing over her with a monster-sized scalpel.

I was fighting the urge to hurl again when a horrifying thought occurred to me. I ran to catch up with the Eyes and touched his arm.

He glanced at me without slowing his pace. "What?"

"Am I... did he get me pregnant?"

"No."

"How can you be sure?"

"He can't. Not without your permission."

Tamara's voice echoed in my head. *He asked every time.*

"If he didn't want me for that, why didn't he just kill me?"

The Eyes kept walking. "He can't."

"Why not?"

"There are rules."

"Rules? What do you mean?"

He growled.

"He said if I tried anything, his servants had orders to kill me."

"He lied."

It hit me like a fist to the gut. Once I thought about it, it didn't really surprise me that Dionysius lied. I mean, he was a demon, hell-bent on spawning a half-breed army, using little girls as incubators. Why wouldn't he lie?

But knowing that he had, that I hadn't known it, hadn't felt it, that I'd blindly believed everything he said—what else had I taken for granted? What other information had I thought I'd gleaned that was totally erroneous?

"We're here. Be careful, it will be guarded." The Eyes stepped forward and opened a large door to the outside. The actual outside—desert landscape stretched ahead for miles.

He was right about the guards. Two Nephilim spirits stood by the door.

"Urgent message from Dionysius," the Eyes said. "I'm to take the prisoner back to Phoenix."

Back to Phoenix? Then where in Tartarus was I?

One of the guards crossed his arms in front of his chest. "I've had no such message. He told me to wait until he comes for her personally. My master will be displeased if I disobey a direct order."

"Dionysius isn't your master, he's mine. What do you think he'll do if I disobey him?"

"That's not my problem."

The Eyes growled and tackled the guard.

The second guard came from the side and lunged toward me. I ripped open a portal just as he dove at me, turning him to dust before my eyes.

The guard fighting with the Eyes stopped and stared.

The Eyes took advantage of the surprise factor and snapped the other demon's neck in one swift motion, then grabbed me by the hand. "*Run.*"

I ran as fast as my human legs would carry me, tearing over desert terrain. Desert in the real world, too, not just the typical demon barrenness.

We passed a city—at least, it would be a city in the real world. Here it was a few demon structures amid a sea of brightly lit ghosts bleeding through from the other side.

There was something familiar about it. I'd been there before.

A shockwave of realization hit me. *Vegas?* I was in Nevada?

We sped past the city and kept running, and in an absurdly short amount of time I saw the lights of Phoenix stretching before me as I descended into the Valley.

The Eyes led me on into the center of the city. Ahead, I saw what appeared to be a bubble, encapsulating a building. As we drew closer, I realized the building was Chase's church.

Palpable relief flooded me, and with it the overwhelming exhaustion that came from running hundreds of miles through a demon dimension after spending who knew how long there. Whatever the Eyes had done to refresh me had been a temporary fix.

We stopped just outside the bubble around the church.

"I can't go any further. You'll be safe in there. If you come back over to this dimension, it will be the breach of a treaty. The rules won't apply, and they'll kill you."

"Treaty? What treaty? And what are the rules everyone keeps talking about?"

The Eyes glanced over his shoulder. "They're coming. Get inside."

He retreated, heading toward the street, leaving me standing there.

Alone.

My knees wobbled. I had to at least get to the other side, where someone would find me.

I opened the hole between dimensions and stepped through. I took a step through where the bubble would be, and a rush like cool air swept over me.

I staggered a few more steps toward the front door. It was night, and there were no lights on, but I was too tired to worry about that. I pushed myself forward, another step, and then one more before I collapsed.

FORTY-SIX

I woke up in the hospital. Again. Chase dozed in a chair by my bed.

I sat up and was hit with the world's worst headache. My worst hangover never felt half this bad.

My groan woke Chase up.

"Jack!" he jumped up from his chair. "Praise God! How do you feel?"

"Migraine," I mumbled around my dried-out tongue. "Other than that, I'm not sure."

He handed me a glass of water from the bedside table. "I need to call Dr. Reyes. You had us really worried."

"I just need to rest." I glanced up at an IV bag that hung from a stand by my bed.

"Yes, you need to rest, because you went into the demon dimension."

"Yeah."

"Without telling anyone."

I gave him a sheepish smile. "I really didn't mean to worry you guys."

"Didn't mean to worry us?" I'd never so much as heard him raise his voice, and now he was yelling at me. He stood up and stalked to the other side of the room. "Jack you were missing—*missing*—for five days!"

"Five days? No, I—"

"I found you on my doorstep, and you've been unconscious for a week. Dr. Reyes, Bridget, and I have been taking shifts by your side, waiting for you to wake up, not sure if you ever would." He raked a

222

hand through his hair. "*Twelve days*, Jack. Twelve days not knowing if I'd ever see you again."

I didn't say anything. What could I say? Thoughts tumbled over one another in my mind.

I'd been unconscious in the demon dimension for five days. They couldn't kill me because of a treaty of some sort, and there were rules that I didn't know about governing a war between demons and humans that only I knew was coming, and I was utterly impotent to stop it. And the creature that had haunted me for months now had been the one to save my life.

I clutched my head in my hands. It was all too much.

Chase sighed deeply. "We've been feeding you with a tube, but if you're up for it, I'll get you something to eat."

Chase stepped out into the hallway. The sounds from the nurses' station wafted in, and then Chase's voice. "She's awake... As good as can be expected, I guess. She complained of a headache. Didn't seem to have any idea how long she'd been gone... Yeah, ordering her some food now... Right. Okay, see you soon."

He came back in a few minutes later.

"Was that Isaac?"

He nodded. "He said you're probably still dehydrated, so drink plenty of fluids."

I obediently took a sip of the water he'd handed me. "How's Bridget?"

"Concerned about you, obviously. Dr. Reyes has been assuring her you'll be okay, and she's been keeping herself distracted by wedding planning. She's taken more than a few shifts sitting by you, too."

"Any new developments on my case?"

He clenched his phone in his hand. "How would I know? People from your work wouldn't talk to me."

"Desiree might."

He considered that a moment. "She hasn't mentioned anything to me."

I groaned. "I need to get back to work."

He didn't answer, but the look he gave me could've melted stone. He reached down to the floor beside the bed and picked up a long rod that looked like metal but behaved like rubber. "You were holding this when I found you. What is it?"

"It's a table leg. From over there."

"They have tables made of this stuff? How would it hold anything up?"

"It's only flexible like that on this side. There, it's stronger than steel."

"How? I thought you said the other side was a barren wasteland?"

"That's what I thought, too, but they have extremely advanced technology. The place I was being held was an elaborate underground bunker."

"Underground?"

I nodded. "They used an existing cave and built inside of it, although I think they dug some of the tunnels themselves. It totally makes sense why people who are abducted believe they're a technologically superior race. That's why I need to get back to work. It all connects and it all adds up to the war—I just have to figure out how. I'm so close I can taste it. I just have to find the missing pieces."

"I have to go. I have a lot of work to catch up on." He tossed me my phone. "We found that in your truck. You should call Bridget and let her know you're awake." He stalked out, the door slamming behind him.

I leaned back against the pillows. Why was he being so twitchy? He knew what was going on. Knew what the demons were doing to those girls.

He knew the stakes.

Not to mention how it was affecting me. He acted like he was interested in me, but he didn't seem to care how the outcome would affect me. Not to mention the fact that it affected my entire life. My fiancé was dead and I'd spent weeks in a mental ward because of this. I had to solve it if I ever had any hope of getting back to normal.

He had to see that. Any sacrifice I had to make to my health was worth it if I could stop these bastards.

A nurse came in a moment later. "Your friend told us you finally woke up. How are you feeling?"

I ran through the various routine questions while she took my stats and unhooked the IV.

"There you are. The doctor will be in soon to check up on you. You should get some rest."

"I will," I said.

I did take Chase's suggestion to call Bridget, though.

"You have no idea how happy I am to hear your voice. I was so worried about you! Did the hospital come back with any results from your blood work yet? Do they know what's causing your episodes? I was reading online about your symptoms and some of the studies I read were about this rare virus…"

224

She prattled on, a thousand words a minute, about all the reading she'd been doing and how I should get tested for this virus and that infection and the other genetic disorder, then segued almost seamlessly into wedding plans and details.

"Oh, I have to show you the flowers. I have a ton of pictures," she said." I'll just come over, okay? I need to see you anyway. Want me to bring you a coffee? I'll be there in like half an hour."

I decided I should probably shower and clean up a bit if I was going to have company. It had apparently been twelve days since I'd engaged in any sort of personal hygiene.

I dragged myself out of bed and hobbled to the bathroom. My whole body ached. I felt like I was ninety years old.

I took my shower and proceeded to try to yank two weeks' worth of tangles out of my hair. I was starting to feel like myself again when I felt the familiar chills and nausea.

Dionysius was approaching.

A moment later, someone knocked at the door to my room. Bridget breezed in without bothering to wait for an invitation, followed by Dion. She set two cups of gourmet coffee on my coffee table and launched herself into me. "It's so good to see you. I was seriously freaking out."

"Yes," Dion echoed, his voice sickeningly sweet. "We were both concerned when we had *no idea* what happened to you. Where were you? And how did you get back?"

I glared at him over Bridget's shoulder as I held her in a tight hug. "I couldn't tell you exactly where I was. I was investigating the case when someone hit me. When I woke up I just started running until I found something familiar, somewhere I knew someone would find me."

"Well, how far did you run?" Bridget asked.

"A long way."

"That's it? You can't tell me anything about where you woke up or how you got from there to here?"

"I was in some sort of lab, no place I'd ever been before. There were guards, but I managed to hit one and get away. I was really out of it, though. I couldn't give you a good description of where I was."

Bridget had cop-face on. "That's going to make it harder."

"I know."

"I'm going to use your bathroom, 'kay? I swear, this baby makes me need to pee every half hour at least."

She disappeared into the other room, and I turned to faced Dion. "So you were *worried* about me? That's sweet. I wonder what Bridget

225

would say if she knew you were the one who was holding me prisoner."

Dion's lip curled. I could almost see the slavering fangs that he'd be baring in the other dimension. "She'd never believe you. What possible motive could I have?"

"I'll tell her what you are."

"Yes, and reinforce her fears that you've had a psychotic break. Brilliant plan."

"I can prove it. I'll take her to a portal and go through to the other dimension. I'll show her the wall around the nursery and show her how fast I can move. I'll——"

"She is expendable." His eyes narrowed, flashing yellow. "If I decide the risk is no longer worth the benefit, I will kill her."

"You'd kill your own baby, too?"

He laughed. "I have hundreds of children and more on the way. I've sacrificed more than one for my goals, you should know that better than anyone. One more or less is meaningless to me."

My stomach churned. I could feel the truth of his words.

"If you say anything to Bridget to turn her against me or make her doubt me, I will kill her. But don't worry." His smile froze me from the inside out. "In a couple more weeks, I'll tell her myself."

The temptation to kill him was overwhelming, but even if I could, I didn't have my gun on me. Chase or Isaac must have put it somewhere. Damn. But I couldn't let him sit in my hospital room and taunt me. "You're not welcome here. Leave, now."

He reeled, as if he'd been punched in the stomach. For a moment, his self-assured swagger faltered, and he stepped back toward the door.

"Bridget?" His voice sounded weak. "I need to make a call. I'll wait for you in the car."

He turned and hurried out, his heavy footfalls thudding on the stairs outside.

I stood there like an idiot, staring after him.

Did that really just happen?

Chase said something similar when I first showed up at the church with the Eyes. I'd have to ask him about that.

Bridget came out of the bathroom. "I don't want him to be out there in this heat for too long. You'd think it would cool off now that we're into November. I'll call you later—there's some wedding stuff I want to do with you. "

I gave her a hug. "Of course. I can't wait to see the progress you made. Thanks for stopping by. It was good to see you. And thanks for the coffee."

"Anytime. I'm glad you're okay. Let me know when they find out what's causing it, okay?"

"I will."

She left, and I immediately called Chase. "Chase, it's me. I have a question. Remember when we first met and the demon was with me and you told him to leave the church and he did?"

"Of course." His voice still sounded cold, distant.

"How did you do that?"

"Demons inhabit this world, but they are subject to its laws, including some laws of personal rights. They can affect places and objects. They can even inhabit people, but only with permission."

"Permission, like you have to say, 'sure, come on in'?"

"No, permission can be much more vague than that. Sometimes it's implied by using things or going to places that are 'theirs,' but any rejection of them or overt denying of permission has to be obeyed."

"Why?"

"Free will. No one can control you unless you let them."

"So that's why he had to leave my room? Because I told him to?"

"I believe so, yes."

"Can I make them do anything I say?"

"No. They are sentient beings, and they have immense power. You can't *make* them do anything."

"How do you know all this? And while we're on the subject, I've been meaning to ask, how did you know the first time we met?"

"What do you mean?"

"You knew he was there. The Eyes. He was haunting me, and you made him leave the church. But how did you know he was there in the first place? I mean, I know you said you've learned to discern their presence over time, but how?"

He paused. "It's like tuning in to a radio. Once I knew they were there, I could focus in on slight changes in the atmosphere."

Even though he was answering my questions, I could still feel the tension in his voice. He definitely had not forgiven me.

"Not the other dimension, just the manifestation of those beings in ours," he said. "There's a sort of aura of oppression, the air feels heavy and cold, and I can sense the spiritual battle. The more I opened myself up to really listening and feeling, the better I got at just knowing when there was a demonic presence nearby."

"How did you learn?"

"Floyd taught me. He has a lot of knowledge about spiritual things. He taught me to quiet my mind and really be aware, so when spiritual forces are at work, I'm not ignorant of them."

"So can you feel Dionysius? Can you tell he's not human?"

"Not in so many words. I can feel that there's something not quite right about him, but it's muted. I might not have noticed at all if I hadn't known to be looking for it. His disguise is very good. I suspect it's actually easier to tell with the other demons, the ones that aren't corporeal here, since they're not adapting to this dimension."

"How does Floyd know all this?"

"I don't really know. He's studied a lot and he's been around awhile."

"I'd like to talk to him. Would he be willing to meet with me?"

"I'm sure he wouldn't mind. I'll ask him to give you a call and set up a meeting."

He hung up without even saying goodbye. He must be really pissed.

I debated with myself about whether to hunt him down and make him talk to me or to give him space and let him come around on his own. I had just about decided to check myself out of the hospital and go after him when another knock sounded at my door.

FORTY-SEVEN

I opened it and Isaac pushed his way in, gathering me in his arms as he came, his chest heaving with emotion.

I caught my breath. The warmth of his hands, his lips on my neck, filled me with a tingling sensation, making my whole body melt against his.

When he finally pulled away long enough to breathe, he held me tightly and whispered against my neck. "Don't ever scare me like that again."

His heart thudded against my chest, his fingers dug into my back. He kissed my neck, the curve of my jaw.

My pulse raced.

His lips traced a line slowly toward my mouth.

I inhaled sharply, anticipating his kiss.

My phone rang.

I groaned. It was the captain.

"I'm so sorry, I have to take this." I pulled away just far enough to answer my phone.

"Jack, I heard you're awake. How are you feeling?"

"Good. I'm with the doctor right now."

Isaac nuzzled my neck. I stifled a giggle.

"Good. Glad to hear it. Any news on what's causing your... erm... condition?"

"Not yet."

"You let me know if you hear anything."

"I will."

"Hey, when are they going to let you out? Do you feel up to coming in? Maybe writing a brief statement about everything you can remember?"

"Sure. After I finish this appointment."

"That's fine. Take your time. But hurry. We may have a lead, but I want to get your statement before jumping to any conclusions."

"I'll be in as soon as I can get everything settled here." I ended the call and looked at Isaac. "Feel like taking a trip to the station with me and sitting around being bored while I make statements and write reports?"

"If it means I get to be with you, then yes, absolutely."

"Good. Can you streamline my discharge?"

Isaac personally saw to the checklist for my release, then pulled his car around to the exit where I sat in the standard wheelchair. Because even though I was being released to go home, they couldn't let me walk outside by myself.

Isaac held my hand the whole way to the station while I filled him in on what had happened in the other dimension.

Ken pounced almost as soon as I walked in the door. "I'm glad you're okay. By the way, I wasn't sure what to put in my report about the, um, force field thing, so I just said we walked the perimeter but couldn't see anything."

"Okay."

That was fairly accurate. I'd fudged details on more than a few reports during the course of this investigation.

Ken stopped staring at me long enough to notice Isaac standing beside me. "Who's that?"

"Dr. Reyes. Doc, this is a coworker of mine, Ken."

Isaac extended a hand.

"Why is he here?" Ken didn't even bother to acknowledge the introduction.

Isaac dropped his hand.

"Because I invited him," I said.

Ken looked a little huffy. "Okay, well, I gotta get back to work. Let me know if you want to go somewhere private to talk about the case."

"Sure." Yeah, like that was going to happen. Ever.

I led Isaac to my desk and indicated a chair for him to sit in. "I'll be right back."

I went to the captain's office. "I don't remember much." I told him basically the same story I'd told Bridget, with the exception of the part about the daycare.

I didn't tell him about the other dimension, of course, but I did tell him I saw people inside and that it appeared to be a functional facility. I also told him my suspicion that this was where Chet and others like him and the head of the trafficking ring were housing the babies they harvested from the kidnapped girls.

"But why? What do they want with a bunch of babies? It doesn't make sense."

I thought of Tamara's baby and how he had aged years in just a few weeks. At that rate it wouldn't take long to develop a whole army of Nephilim. "I wish I had a good answer."

"Okay, tell me what you think of this." He slid a piece of paper across the desk toward me. "We've had virtually identical reports from people all over the city. Not all of them from fruity alien-watchers, either. Ordinary, even prominent people are all saying they've received this same message, some by phone, some in actual letter form, some email. In every case, though, the origin is a mystery. Complete dead end, even on the voice and digital letters."

I scanned the report, reading aloud. "The signs and prophets have revealed that a race of advanced beings will attempt to take over this city. Their technology is superior to ours, and their army is vast. Resistance will be met with annihilation unless you know how to defeat them."

I raised an eyebrow. They were pretty much showing their whole hand here. What was the strategy with that?

I kept reading. "The Prince of the Desert, the rightful ruler of this region, asks that the people of Phoenix acknowledge his leadership. He will take his place as ruler of this region on November sixteenth. If the people accept his leadership, he will save you from the imminent invasion."

I looked at the captain. "Is this for real?"

"That's what we're trying to find out."

I looked at the date again. November sixteenth? Did he do that on purpose?

"Any thoughts?" the captain asked.

I shook my head. "Who is this Prince? Does anybody know?"

"No one has a clue. No one in politics has even heard of him, and no one has seen him. We don't have any confirmation that such a character even exists, but people in city government positions have gotten requests to turn over their power on that date."

"Why that date?"

"No one knows."

"It's a Saturday. The government isn't even doing anything that day."

"How do you know what day it is?"

"It's Bridget's wedding day."

"Oh, right."

"What about this imminent invasion? What is that? A terrorist threat?"

"Not that we can confirm. Even on the federal level there's no substantiated evidence of an attack. Whatever this guy is claiming to save us from is in his head, so far as we can tell."

"Fantastic. We have a guy who may or may not even exist wanting to be our king and save us from an invasion that no one believes is happening. One question. Why do we care? I mean, if it's clearly a nut job making idle threats, then—"

The captain coughed.

"What?" I asked.

"The threats may not be idle."

"What's that supposed to mean?"

"While you were away, the governor suffered from a heart attack. No indication of foul play, but it later turned up she had received one of these letters. And the mayor is… missing."

"Missing?"

"We're still looking for any leads, but there's no forensic evidence, no witnesses, just… nothing. Official story is that he is on vacation in the mountains. But he also received a letter."

Disappearing without a trace. That was a little too familiar.

"What do we do?" I asked.

"Not much. We don't really have anything actionable we *can* do. Just keep our eyes open, look for evidence, see if we can get a lead on who this Prince person is. Anything else not urgent goes on a back burner. Find out who the Prince is and what is plans for this city are."

That's it? Find a phantom?

No problem.

I had an idea who the Prince was. Or what, at least. Chet and Dion and the mysterious trafficking leader Trent was after—they all were minions of the Prince. Of course, I had no proof, and no one would take my word on it that the self-proclaimed Prince of Phoenix was an inter-dimensional demon.

I needed to find some proof. As much as it sickened me, physically and emotionally, I had to get close to Dion. I had to find proof of what he was, and by extension, find out more about the Prince. "I'll get right on it."

I went back to my desk and showed Isaac a copy of the statement.

"Hm. I haven't heard anything about that," he said. "They must be keeping it quiet from the press, at least for now. On the plus side, at least you know what his plan is. The war Trent talked about must be the Prince's plan to take over the city. So now you know what the spawn army is for."

"Right, but I don't know *how* they're planning to do it. And I have no proof."

"But you have a place to start."

I smiled. "Thank you. I needed the glass-half-full perspective. You're right. I know what he is and that he wants to take over the city. Now I need proof. Feel like going on a double date?"

He grinned and took my hand. "Sure."

I called Bridget. "Hey, what are you and Dion doing tonight? I was thinking of hanging out with that doctor friend of mine. Want to double?"

"Sure. I'll let Dion know. Dinner, then drinks at my apartment after?"

"Sounds great." We hammered out a few details, and I spent the rest of the afternoon writing out reports on what I remembered about where I'd disappeared to, minus the part about the alternate dimension cavern fortress.

Isaac sat by my side, keeping me company and playing games on his phone until I finished, and we adjourned to my apartment to freshen up.

We met Dion and Bridget at Bridget's favorite restaurant. Her baby bump looked even more pronounced over her tight, low-rise jeans. She beamed when I walked in and gave me a significant glance when she saw Isaac.

I gave her a hug. "Hey, Bridge. You remember Dr. Reyes, of course."

"Of course. We got to spend some time together while we were waiting for you to wake up."

"Right. Doc, this is Bridget's fiancé, Dion."

Dion smiled his charming smile and shook Isaac's hand. He looked at me. "Another one? You don't waste much time, do you?"

I clenched my fist to keep from making any obscene gestures and smiled at him. "I can't really afford to. You never know when some nut job will declare himself ruler and try to take over the city."

"You heard about that already?" Bridget asked. "It's so weird. We're not supposed to talk about it of course, because they don't want the press getting wind of it, but I told Dion. Openness is very important in our relationship."

"Is it?" I gave Dion a pointed glare.

We ordered our food and continued the discussion.

I turned to Dion. "And what do you think of this insane person—if he exists at all—claiming to be the ruler of our city?"

"I happen to think all threats should be taken seriously."

"So you think we should just roll over and give the city to a psychotic dictator?"

The pulse of irritation from him was worth the jab. He didn't like the inference that his beloved Prince was crazy. Funny, since that's where he tried to drive me.

Dion's eyes flashed yellow. "I think the city would do well to evaluate whether it's worth it to start a war or whether it might actually be better for the city and the people to have new leadership."

"Okay, first of all, we can't just hand over the city to someone. We're part of a larger whole. We don't own the city, so we can't give it away," Bridget said.

Good girl. So she wasn't completely brainwashed.

"Second," she went on, "we don't know anything about this guy, or even if there is a guy or if it's just a big hoax. It's not like we're just going to hand over the keys to the city to someone who may or may not even exist."

Dion's arm slid around her shoulders. "I guess we'll find out, won't we? When is this supposed to happen again?"

"On our wedding day."

Dion smiled at me. He spoke, in that same weird way, through the other dimension, so I was the only one who could hear him. "I told you, you don't want to miss it."

FORTY-EIGHT

Dion kissed Bridget. "Our wedding. That will be an exciting day, won't it?"

Bridget grinned. "I'm much more excited about our wedding than somebody taking over the city."

Dion leaned over to kiss her. "As am I, my love."

The wave of lust that emanated from him made me want to hurl. "So, guys, any theories about this guy? Assuming he's real, what's his motivation?"

Our meal arrived and Dion talked between bites. "Quite clearly, his motivation is to take back what is—that is, what he believes is—rightfully his."

A pulse of satisfaction flared from him. He was subtle, but he was smoothing the way to convincing Bridget of his position.

I narrowed my eyes at him. "Okay, then, why now? Why that date? Why this year, not last year or five years from now?"

"The timing wasn't right," Dion said.

I knew he knew I was fishing, but he was telling me anyway. Much like a narcissistic human who believed he was smarter than the system, his pride demanded credit for his brilliance, an audience to appreciate the details that went into this foolproof plan.

"Timing for what? Does he think the rest of the country will just sit back and let him have Phoenix?"

"The rest of the country will be too busy worrying about itself." Dion's lips didn't move when he said that—he was speaking to me through the other dimension again.

I kept my face passive as well as I could, but I must have revealed some of the emotions roiling inside me, because Isaac squeezed my hand encouragingly.

"My guess," Dion said aloud, "and, of course, this is pure speculation, but my guess is that he has a plan, and the resources to carry it out, to deal with all such contingencies. They must already be in place. That's why he chose this date. He may even have knowledge of similar plans in other cities that will distract those in power from this one."

"Where would he get them?" Bridget asked. "The resources, I mean. How can he prepare for something as huge as taking over an entire major city in a prosperous country with all the necessary manpower and technology and everything else, in total secrecy? I mean, something like that, there would have to be chatter of some kind. Someone would know something."

"Not if he did it right."

"Okay," I said, "let's assume he succeeded at his plan and becomes Prince of the city or whatever. What then? World domination?"

"The world is not his to take. He is merely possessing that which was promised to him." Dion was speaking just to me again, through the other dimension. "He will rule this province and bring it under his control to prepare the way for his king's coming."

His *king*? Who was that? Who else was coming?

"Jack, did the captain put you on this, too?"

I snapped my attention back to Bridget. "Yeah. But with as vague as this is, I don't even know where he thinks we should start."

"Me, neither. On the plus side, it's going to be hard for this guy to win over an entire city when no one knows who he is."

"Perhaps they do know who he is, they just don't realize it," Dion said. "When he reveals himself, they'll follow him naturally because they already trust him."

"I don't see how that does him any good." It was the first time Isaac had weighed in on the conversation. "Even if he were a celebrity or something, that doesn't mean we would trust him to run the city. Besides, the public as yet has no knowledge of his existence. They're not likely to roll over and let themselves be ruled without at least some foreknowledge."

Dion gave a low chuckle. I could hear it echo through the other dimension, a malicious cackle. His voice, only to me, was thick with contempt. "Of course they will. Why wouldn't they? The protection from a bigger threat is worth the inconvenience of the unknown."

I shuddered. I wanted to believe he was wrong, that we as a whole would never just *let* a demon entity dominate us, but a nagging voice in my mind told me I was deluding myself. We'd let him and those like him win because we were too afraid of what would happen if we didn't.

My phone rang, saving me from further ruminations. It wasn't a number I recognized.

"Excuse me." I left the table and walked toward the semi-quiet alcove outside the bathrooms. "Davidson."

"Good evening, Ms. Davidson. This is Pastor Floyd Schneider, of Grace Fellowship Church."

"Oh! Hi. I was hoping to hear from you."

"Yes, I imagined you might be. Chase filled me in on your situation. Would you be available to come to my office tomorrow for a chat? Around noon?"

"Sure, I'd really appreciate that. Thank you. Do you mind if I bring a friend?" I figured if he wasn't working, then Isaac would want to be in on the discussion.

"Actually, if you don't mind, I'd like to talk to you alone. There are some things I think you should know about Trent."

"Trent? You knew Trent? How? What—"

"I really feel this discussion would be better in person. I'll see you tomorrow, Ms. Davidson."

The phone clicked and I was left staring at the screen, wondering what Chase's pastor could possibly know about my dead fiancé.

I was so intent on my thoughts I almost didn't notice footsteps behind me. A hand touched my shoulder and I jumped. I whirled around.

Isaac stood there, looking concerned. "Are you okay?"

"What? Yeah, I'm good. I may have a lead on something Trent was working on."

"That's good, right? Because he knew something about what Dionysius was planning?"

"I think so, yes."

"Good. Then you should go get some sleep. You're still not totally recovered from your last trip to the other side."

I nodded. He was right. We walked back to the table.

"I think I'm going to bail on drinks," I told Bridget. "I need to get some rest."

She stood and hugged me. The monster inside her seemed to taint her with an oily aura that got thicker the longer she was pregnant, sending the familiar nausea, though muted, through me. .

"I'll see you soon," I said.

Isaac drove me back to my apartment. We stood for a moment on my front step. "Do you want to come in?" It felt oddly formal asking

238

him that, given that he'd spent the last week coming and going freely and watching me as I slept.

He smiled. "Yes. But I'm more concerned about you getting some sleep, so I'm going to take a rain check on that one."

He leaned down and gave me a soft kiss on the cheek, then hurried down the stairs.

I fell into bed almost immediately. As I drifted to sleep, I noticed the lack of spiritual presences in my room. I hadn't specifically told the Eyes he couldn't come back, but maybe banning Dionysius banned him, too. It was refreshing to have the peace of silence envelop me for once.

I woke to the sound of my phone ringing.

It was Isaac. "Turn on your TV."

"What's going on?"

"The news. Just watch."

I clicked on my TV and flipped to the local news station. "And you are a spokesperson for the alien race?" a pretty red-headed reporter asked a tall, dark-haired man.

Even though I wasn't in the same room with him, I could tell he was a demon. Moreover, his description matched that of the alien being who had asked Nancy for the use of her daycare facility.

"Yes," the demon replied. "I come on behalf of the race of beings known as the Watchers. They have been monitoring our society for thousands of years, interceding when necessary, to help our evolution and progression. They are dedicated to helping preserve and propel the humans and other races of Earth to a greater knowledge and understanding of the universe."

"What is their purpose? Why are they invading us?" the reporter asked.

"They do not wish to harm us, simply to join us and teach us. Their arrival is imminent. My role is simply to help prepare my people for their coming. They have chosen this city because it most closely resembles their home world, but as they adapt to our environment, they will expand to all cities and countries."

The reporter opened her mouth to ask another question and was interrupted by a shout from the crowd.

"Liar!" a man shouted. He stumbled forward. He, too, was exceptionally tall, and in the glare of the camera I saw the glint of yellow eyes.

Another demon? What was going on?

The second demon lunged forward and wrenched the microphone from the reporter's hand. "He lies!" He turned to look at the one

239

claiming to be the emissary. "I know what you really are. You don't come in peace!" He turned toward the camera. "He speaks in riddles and lies. They do not come in peace. They come to experiment and control. They're *demons*. The only ones who can save us are the angels."

The reporter snatched her mic back as two security guards dragged the man away.

He was letting himself be dragged. Though he made a good show of struggling, I could see the lackluster effort. This was a show, an elaborate performance, but why?

"Don't believe him!" the second demon screamed as he let himself be pulled away. "Only the angels can save us. Call on the Prince of the Angels! Save us!"

So that was it.

The Prince staged a fight to plant the seed of terror about an invasion, to spread propaganda of his role as a savior.

The reporter looked back at the camera, shock still written on her face, but recovered quickly.

"Everyone has a critic," she smiled. She turned back toward the alien emissary. "And what would you say to people like our paranoid friend there, who are more reluctant to trust in the goodwill of our alien brothers?"

He smiled at the camera, and even the people who couldn't see through the outer shell to the gooey demon center couldn't possibly miss the evil glint in his eyes, the cruel curl to his lips, the vicious snarl in his voice. "I would say that anyone who believes in demons and angels clearly has problems and cannot be trusted. We will prove our intentions with our actions, and this city will see the results of our beneficence."

Brilliant. Nice set-up, Prince.

Whoever planned this had a good long-term strategy. Make them believe, then make them fear. By the time the Prince actually took power, they would be begging him to save them.

***

The demons got right to work. When I got to the station the next morning, there were already dozens of reports flying in about alien abductions, experiments, and terror at the hands of alien forces. Over the next few hours, the title "Prince of Phoenix" was a buzzword on social media, and people were sending prayers into the ether for him to come save them from the alien threat.

240

I just hoped Pastor Floyd would have some information I could work with. I wrapped up the lead I was working and headed to my appointment with him.

Chase was in his office when I got to the church. He came out to greet me and walked with me to Pastor Floyd's office. "I'm glad you came in. Floyd is really knowledgeable about these things. More so than even I realized."

"What connection did he have to Trent?"

He stopped and stared at me, one eyebrow raised. "Your fiancé? I have no idea. He hasn't said anything to me about that." He rapped at Pastor Floyd's door.

"Come in." Pastor Floyd stood when we entered and came toward me, hands outstretched. He clasped my hand between both of his. "Jack. I'm glad to see you. Have a seat. Chase, will you excuse us?"

"It's okay. He knows everything. I'd like him to stay."

"Are you certain?"

I nodded.

Chase smiled and sat down next to me.

"I'm sure you have a lot of questions, and I will get to them," Pastor Floyd began. "First, though, I'd like you to just listen."

I nodded.

"This story starts for me more than twenty-five years ago. I was in San Diego, on my honeymoon. My wife and I were walking along the beach and we saw a flash of light streak across the sky and crash into the ground in front of us. The whole beach shook as though there had been an earthquake. When we recovered from our shock, we went to the spot where the thing had landed and found a little boy. He was bruised, and unconscious, wearing only a pair of tattered shorts."

I pictured the little boy, my heart aching for the defenseless child being dragged through dimensions by demons.

"We called an ambulance and escorted him to the hospital where we waited for him to recover. When he woke up he couldn't remember who he was or anything about himself. All he could remember was being in a dark room with weird lights on the ceiling where giants and monsters performed tests on him."

I gagged, fighting to hold back the bile that rose in my throat.

"They never identified the boy, never found his real family. My wife and I were granted temporary custody until a permanent home could be found for him. We named him Trent."

FORTY-NINE

The echo of my choked gasp hung in the air for several moments before Pastor Floyd spoke again.

"Almost a year after Trent came to live with us, we were all out in the back yard grilling hamburgers and corn on the cob. There was another flash of light, and a man stepped into the yard from out of nowhere. Trent immediately started screaming and ran to hide behind my wife."

Pastor Floyd blinked slowly, as though trying to stanch the flow of emotion. "'It's time for you to come home,' the man told Trent. My wife stood between them, yelling at him to get away, threatening to call the police. He laughed and said our human laws have no authority over him."

Tears coursed down my cheeks as I relived with him the horror of that moment.

"The only weapon I had on me was the spatula I was using to grill with. I rushed at him and bashed him with it, but it didn't even seem to bother him. He swung at me and knocked me halfway across the yard. My leg was broken and I couldn't get up. I started crawling toward him, picking up rocks from the yard and throwing them at them, but he didn't even blink. All I could do was watch."

He took a deep breath before going on. "My wife told Trent to go in the house and call the police. He ran in and my wife blocked the way. The man grabbed her by her head and twisted, turning it completely around. I lay there helpless as my bride crumpled to the ground right in front of me." His voice caught.

I reached across the desk and clasped his hand.

242

Pastor Floyd smiled and dabbed at his eyes. "Trent came out of the house carrying my pistol. I kept it in the desk by my bed. He ran to me and handed it to me and I started shooting. I emptied every shell into the beast that was coming straight for us. At last, I hit the creature in the head and it stumbled and collapsed."

I wiped tears from my eyes, thinking of Trent as a boy, being chased by the same beasts that now haunted me. "He never told me any of that."

"As time went on, his memories of the trauma started to fade. We never knew exactly how old he was, but doctors estimated he was no more than seven when we found him."

Seven. What kind of monsters tortured a seven-year-old kid? What could he possibly have done at that age to attract their notice?

"I started researching alien and demon encounters, trying to make sense of what happened, but research is a slow process, and not long after, Trent was permanently adopted. I still got to see him occasionally, sent him Christmas gifts and things, but as he got older he drifted away, and naturally so. He had a wonderful family, and a beautiful baby sister came along a couple years later."

I nodded. Cameron.

"We lost touch completely until two years ago," Pastor Floyd said. "Trent called me one day and asked if I remembered him, and said he needed my help."

"Two years ago? We had just moved in together at that point. How did I not know anything about you?"

"He didn't want to involve you. He wanted you to be safe."

That was so like him. A pang of heartache and nostalgia shot through me. I missed him so much. "What did he need your help with?"

"He said he found out what they wanted with him."

"He found out? How?"

"He was working a case and a woman came in who claimed to be a witness. She said she'd seen the crime. Psychically. He went into the interrogation room, and she started screaming. She told him her spirit guide said he was cursed, and he needed to be healed immediately. She said the spirit world was in flux because he had a purpose but had abandoned it. She told him if he didn't submit to a spiritual cleansing so the gods could do their work in him, the universe would be out of balance."

"Trent was the cause of universal imbalance? That seems like a stretch."

"That's what he thought, too. He thought at first she was crazy, or that it was some kind of set-up to throw him off-balance regarding his case."

"How do you know she wasn't?"

"She started telling him things about his past, triggering memories of his childhood. He was born in captivity, as it were. Specific people from a specific lineage had been kept for generations. They married who they were told, bred, and continued, a very specific, traceable genetic line. He was one of several potential children that were believed to be able to fulfill an ancient prophecy."

"Believed by whom?"

"Demons, and more than one religion."

Wait, what? "Demons believe in prophecies?"

Pastor Floyd nodded. "Oh, yes. Prophecies, true ones, are quite real. Demons know this better than anyone. That is why they are so adamant to see certain ones fulfilled and others thwarted."

"Okay, so what is the prophecy? Who is—was—Trent supposed to be?

"According to everything I've read, there is a recurring figure in the prophecies of multiple religions. This person will come proclaiming peace but will bring about the end of the world. Christianity refers to this person as the Antichrist."

FIFTY

I choked. "You're saying I was engaged to the *antichrist*?"

"No. He was the ideal candidate, the primary one in line to be set-up for that role, but he wasn't the only one. When he was a child, there was a war between various factions of demons. One group, or tribe, if you will, was the primary power, in charge of breeding and grooming Trent for his role. Another faction kidnapped him, hoping to take credit for rearing and training him."

I rubbed my temples. I still couldn't believe Trent had kept all this from me. "Go on," I said.

"When it looked like the original tribe would get him back, they released him on the beach rather than give him back. This set the whole plot behind several years. The original plan was that Trent would've taken some sort of political power by now, paving the way to world domination."

"Shouldn't they all be working together to bring about this prophecy, if that's what they want?"

"In theory, yes. But, like humans, they're all trying to out-do one another, be a step higher on the ladder. As I understand it, they're very territorial. Once upon a time, they ruled as gods, each controlling a specific geographic territory."

"That's what the book said—ancient gods," I said. "Like, Zeus had control of Greece?"

Pastor Floyd nodded. "Exactly. Odin had what is now Scandinavia, and various other demons controlled other parts of the world in greater or larger parcels. Like people, sometimes they betray or kill one another in an effort to gain power among their fellows. They'll even thwart the master plan in order to gain precedence in the eyes of their master when the plan does unfold."

I exhaled. "Okay, so Trent was in line to be this fulfillment of prophecy, but that plan was thwarted when you rescued him. What does that have to do with Dionysius and what's going on now?"

"Everything. He was once a being of great power, referenced in Greek mythology, even, and at some point, he lost his position. I assume this plot is an attempt to regain a stronghold."

"How?" I asked.

"Dionysius was in charge of a faction that was allied with those in power, the ones who were setting Trent up for this role. After his encounter with the psychic, someone claiming to be a prophet approached him, telling him he was destined to be a great leader and fulfill various prophecies. He only needed to submit to his destiny and let higher powers guide him."

"Higher powers being demons?"

"We believed so, yes. Specifically, Dionysius. If Dionysius could return Trent to a position of power, he'd have a stronghold in the coming kingdom."

"I still can't believe Trent never told me any of this."

"As I said, he wanted to protect you. He tried very hard to keep you safe."

"Didn't it occur to him that I might have been able to help?"

"How, exactly?"

I opened my mouth and stopped. Damn it, he had a point. "I don't know. With research or something, I guess."

"Would you have believed him? If he told you a prophet had approached him and said he was destined to be a great leader who would bring peace to the world, what would you have done?"

I didn't have an answer.

"If you hadn't felt the oppression of demonic forces for yourself, would you have trusted he was right about demons?"

I took a deep breath. He was right. "No, I wouldn't have. I would've laughed. Maybe even thought he was crazy."

Pastor Floyd smiled. "He wanted proof, tangible evidence of what was going on, so we started investigating—he through legal, human avenues, and I by reading. What I found was that most religions and belief systems have some sort of prophecy about a coming world leader. Most revere him as a savior of mankind. I believe he will take power with promises of peace only to betray them."

Sounded a lot like this Prince guy.

"Through my research, I determined that a war is coming, a war to end all wars. There will be those loyal to this coming leader, and those who fight against him. So far, the other side is at a distinct advantage, because our side doesn't even know it's coming."

"The war." I squeezed my eyes shut, remembering. "In his letter to me, Trent said—you're his confidential source!"

"Yes."

I looked at Chase. "Why didn't you tell me?"

"I had no idea."

"It's true," Pastor Floyd said. I told Chase nothing of my connection to Trent. This is the first he's heard of it, as well. I didn't know how much to tell you until Chase told me about your experience in the other dimension."

"Okay, so if you're Trent's C.I., you know what he was talking about in the letter. That night, the night he died, he said we were stopping Armageddon. What did he mean by that?"

"I'm getting to that. As I said, my research led me mainly to ancient texts and prophecies. Trent's investigation uncovered layers of political intrigue that encompassed not only this nation, but every facet of world government. The problem was, he had no proof. He found links between ancient religions and modern politics that pointed toward the fact that these politicians are being influenced by demonic forces."

That, at least, I believed. I'd seen people listen to the voices of demons whispering in their ears, even though they couldn't actually hear.

"Trent found additional links between more modern religions that have roots in these older belief systems and national and world governments. Despite how they appear on the surface, most governments have at their core a deeply held religious base."

That made sense, in a way. Trent used to mention how communism was based on the belief that people were ignorant and in need of someone to dictate to them where they could work and live and so on, and how other religions were based on a caste system that created a hierarchy based on status. If those socioeconomic beliefs were religious in origin, it would make sense for them to be at the heart of a nation's politics.

I'd thought I'd known him so well, but underneath all these seemingly unconnected, random bits of information he let slip to me, he'd harbored a whole network of hidden knowledge.

Pastor Floyd coughed. "Trent believed the stage was being set for this leader to take his place with full world support, and part of that process was local governments being under the control of demons, either directly or indirectly."

The connections slipped into place, the jigsaw forming a picture that became clearer every minute. "That's why the Prince wants Phoenix. He said something about the king. The Prince wants to rule this region, like a regent or something, keeping it for the king, whoever he is."

Pastor Floyd nodded. "That's what I believe, yes."

Something still didn't quite make sense. "Why here? Why now? I mean, they've been fighting for thousands of years. What's special about right now?"

"That I don't know for sure. There is evidence that spiritual forces have more power in certain times and at certain places. I don't really understand it all myself, but some areas are more sensitive to spiritual influence—Sedona, for instance, is a hotspot of spiritual activity. And everything from astrology to prophecy to ancient rituals to divination suggest certain times and seasons are better for spiritual rites. I can only assume this time and this place are aligned in such a way as to make this the optimal time for them to implement their plot."

"Okay, but Trent said we were stopping Armageddon. What did he mean? When the Prince takes over the city, is that the beginning of Armageddon? And how was a car chase going to stop it?"

"That I don't know. The last time I talked to him was two days before he died. He must have uncovered something after that but hadn't had time to tell me yet. What do you remember about that night?"

I closed my eyes and took a deep breath, pulling up the memories that tore at my heart. "We were on a date. He got a call. He jumped up and said he had to go, but I insisted on coming with him. He said he had a lead on the head of a human trafficking ring he'd been investigating, so we went to this old warehouse and started following two men in a sedan."

Chase laid a gentle hand on my shoulder. His jaw tightened like it hurt him, but he kept his hand there anyway.

"It started raining and they were going too fast over the bridge," I continued. "That's when… that's when the sky opened. The other car went over the side and we skidded after them, only barely managing not to go in. They were everywhere. The monsters. Demons."

I gulped back the tears. "I could see them through the opening, but then I passed out. I don't know how many came through, but Dionysius told me *he* killed Trent. He didn't die in the accident, Dion cracked his skull. And the two men in the car—at least one was a Nephilim."

"Are you sure?"

I nodded. "I saw the autopsy report. Over eight feet tall, light brown hair, hazel eyes, six fingers on each hand, died from a laceration to his heart."

As I described him aloud, the pieces came together in my mind.

"Holy shit."

I clapped my hand over my mouth, realizing I'd just cursed in a church in front of two pastors.

I jumped up and ran outside just to the edge of where the protective bubble would be and yelled, "Hey! Where are you? Are you here?"

I found the portal where I'd come through the other night. It was almost healed already. I stepped through, only faintly present in the other dimension. "Hello?" My voice echoed off the drab red rocks.

Nothing happened. The other dimension seemed deserted. If there were demon crickets, they'd be chirping.

I walked back through to the other side. Chase and Pastor Floyd were standing there.

"What was that? What happened?" Chase asked.

"The Eyes. I think he was the Nephilim that died in the crash that night. I think something happened when he died, and that's why we're connected."

"Of course," Pastor Floyd said. "I should've guessed. Those demonic sprits are disembodied and are therefore constantly seeking a body to possess. They can only function in this dimension by using a vessel of some sort. They're constantly seeking a host. They have to be invited in, of course, but an invitation is subtle. Implied consent is just as valid as a direct invitation."

He rubbed his chin. "And it doesn't even have to be a human. They've been known to possess animals and even attach themselves to inanimate objects like statues and exert some control over their surroundings that way."

"That doesn't explain how I'm connected to one, though. I'm not possessed, and he's not functional in this dimension. If anything, it's the other way around. If he's not near me, he gets weak."

"Yes, exactly. My theory—and mind you, it's just a theory—is that as he died, his spirit tried to latch onto you. He clawed at anything he could hold on to, like grabbing onto a weed to keep from going over a cliff. He took hold, but of course he couldn't stay here, so he inadvertently took you with him."

"How does that even work?"

"He took a part of your consciousness with him to the other dimension, which is why you are able to function there, why you began to sense the other side in the first place."

"Hm." Chase frowned. "I wonder…"

"What?" I asked.

"Nothing. It's just… I could sense something wasn't right. Whenever I touch you, you feel… empty."

"Empty?"

He nodded. "Cold, like whatever makes you human is missing."

FIFTY-ONE

Was that why he cringed every time he touched me? Why he couldn't so much as pat my shoulder without wincing?

Awkward silence stretched for several seconds before I finally broke it. "Well, that explains that, I guess. But we're still back to square one. We still have to figure out what Trent knew and who the Prince really is. I guess that means I need to get back to work. Dig through his files and see if I can turn anything up. And quickly. We're running out of time."

"What do you mean?" Floyd asked.

"Dionysius is planning something next week. On his and Bridget's wedding day."

"Ah, yes, Chase mentioned that situation," Pastor Floyd said. "Well. I suppose we all have a lot of work to do, then. Chase, come with me. There are some books I'll need your help going through. Chase?"

Chase was staring at me, a smile on his face that seemed almost wistful. "Whatever happens, Jack, I'm glad I got to know you."

I smiled. "Me, too."

"Call me if you find anything."

I made my way back to the station and immediately started going through all of Trent's files again, organizing, categorizing, piecing together as much as I could. I reread his letter a dozen times, filling in the information I had gained, getting a clearer picture of what he'd been trying to tell me.

I went through the box of his things again, searching for anything new, any clues he might have left behind. I sifted through a stack of post-it notes that had been scattered across his desk. He was always doing that, writing random notes to himself.

One said "Pick up Hershey's!" I laughed, tears stinging my eyes, remembering my PMS-induced text to him about a week before he died, "I need chocolate!"

Another said, "Ask Jack about hosting Thanksgiving this year." He'd never gotten around to that one.

Some of the notes were about cases, reminders to add something to a report or update a file or follow up with a phone call to someone. I was most of the way through the stack when a name caught my eye.

Brandon Harding.

Why did that name sound familiar?

I looked up the name online and got several results. One was an author, one was a local contractor... ah ha. There was the one I was looking for. Politician out of Chicago.

I found a picture of him and dropped my coffee in my lap.

He looked so much like Trent, they could've been twins.

I cursed under my breath. *Were* they twins? I studied the man more closely. He looked a few years younger than Trent, but there was no mistaking the resemblance. They could easily be brothers. Was that why Trent was looking into him?

Pastor Floyd said Trent was the top choice for someone to fulfill this prophecy. Maybe, once he was gone, they started grooming his younger brother for the job.

I looked up his contact information and emailed him a brief message saying my fiancé was looking for his biological family before he died, and asking if Trent had contacted him.

I got a brief email back from his secretary saying I must be mistaken, Trent had never contacted Mr. Harding, and Mr. Harding was not missing any relatives.

I called Mr. Harding's office. "I'm Detective Jack Davidson from the Phoenix police department. I need to speak with Mr. Harding about a case. I believe he may be connected in some way."

"I'm sorry, but Mr. Harding is unavailable right now."

"Where is he?"

"He's... taking a leave of absence."

Why did she sound so jumpy? "I really need to get in touch with him immediately. Does he have a cell phone I can try?"

"He didn't take his phone with him. I don't have a way to get in touch with him."

"At all? You don't have any way to get a hold of him? When is he coming back?"

"I'm sorry, detective, I don't have the answer to that."

"Will you have him give me a call whenever you hear from him?"

I left my contact info, hung up the phone, and tapped my fingers on the desk. That was definitely weird.

I called the Chicago PD, and got more or less the same thing. They didn't have a missing persons out on him, but neither did they know anything about where he'd disappeared to.

I stared at the wall. Nothing else in Trent's notes gave me any clues, and none of my investigating turned anything new up. On the plus side, I hadn't had to deal with Desiree except in passing since I got back.

"Jack," the captain's voice from the door of his office jolted me out of my thoughts. "I need you to go downtown and help provide backup. There's rioting and reports of—you're not going to believe this—giants."

If only that was the weirdest thing I'd had to deal with lately. "I'm on my way."

A dozen other officers and I raced downtown to join the forces already there trying to herd the masses of panicked secretaries and government workers that streamed from buildings.

"What's going on?" I asked, jumping from my truck and flashing my badge at one of the officers already on the scene.

"A group of marchers started rioting this morning, insisting that the local government give place to the rightful inhabitants of this earth. Then they were joined by these monstrous men, as tall as giants. For the most part, people ignored them, gawking from afar. When they didn't get the response they wanted, they got violent. Look!"

Around the corner came a mob of people. And not all people, I realized a moment later. Some were demons, and most were Nephilim.

They tore through downtown, destroying everyone and everything in their paths, breaking car windows and building windows, destroying the old granite facades of the historic buildings.

"The first group of officers on the scene was trampled," the officer by my side told me. "At least two are dead, several more wounded, and I don't know how many unaccounted for."

I glanced at the throbbing mass of bodies. We needed to kill the supernatural beings. Unfortunately, I was the only one who could tell the difference between the humans and demons in human skin.

The Nephilim were easy enough. They were even more grotesque as adults than babies, standing eight or nine feet tall, with misshapen heads, overly long limbs, and six fingers on each hand.

"We need to get SWAT in here," I said. "Try to separate the civilians from the giants."

All our attempts to maintain calm fizzled immediately. Barricades were trampled, and at least three more police officers were dead just since I'd arrived.

SWAT arrived but even tear gas and tasers were virtually ineffective against the giants.

The Nephilim marched on, now attacking anyone who wasn't in on their mob. Civilians were dying by the dozens.

Ken dashed toward me, crouching behind his riot shield. "We've gotta do something. They're going to kill everyone."

I took a deep breath. "Kill the giants," I said, as softly as I could while still being heard. "Aim for heads and hearts. It takes several shots to kill one, so make sure you have a clean shot and don't stop until they drop."

He nodded. Downtown Phoenix was a warzone, and we had to protect as many lives as we could. As much as he bugged me on a personal level, Ken was a good cop, and he would do what had to be done.

I left him, and went hunting.

I found the portal where they'd come through behind the courthouse and jumped through to the other side. I followed the mob, waited until they rounded a corner, then jumped from the other dimension and grabbed a straggler, a woman in her mid-thirties. I pulled her away from the group and arrested her, taking her back to the ring of police cars and leaving her in the custody of a rookie who looked like he was going to vomit.

I made my way back to the portal I'd created and did the same thing again.

Even these little hops in and out of the other dimension were wearing me down, but I didn't have time to rest. One by one, Ken and the other officers were taking down the Nephilim, and one by one I was taking out the protesters, but the mob wasn't getting any smaller, and their damage continued to spread. Downtown looked like it had been hit by a bomb, and still the rioters grew more rabid.

We couldn't go on like this. We had to find some way to stop them.

A voice, louder than if it had come from a loudspeaker, thundered over the crowd, echoing off the buildings and making them shake with its intensity. "Peace!"

FIFTY-TWO

A man—demon, actually, though he looked like a man—stepped into the street, hands raised. His voice and presence was powerful enough to get the attention of the mob. "In the name of the Prince of Phoenix, desist. This land is his, and you will not destroy it."

One of the Nephilim lunged toward him. He raised a hand, and the Nephilim fell backward through a small portal, which made him look like he had simply disappeared into thin air.

Clever. The Prince incited riots that he could then quell, pulling inter-dimensional sleight-of-hand to manipulate people into believing in his power. Two more Nephilim rushed toward him and both were repelled the same way.

"Be still. Return to your homes. The Prince will not allow this terrorism to continue in his province."

The mob dispersed, giants and humans alike fading away. Giants through portals, and humans seeming to come out of a trance and look around like they had no idea what they'd just been part of.

"Who are you?" someone asked the demon.

He smiled benevolently at her. "I am known as Kush. I am the emissary of the Prince, here to bring his peace and make way for his coming."

"When will he come?" someone else asked. "When will he save us?"

"Very soon," Kush promised. "I must go. Take heart! Your salvation is at hand!"

He waved his hand at the crowd and disappeared through a portal.

Man, it was going to suck to write this report.

***

Over the next several days, small riots popped up, humans and Nephilim killing and breaking things, and each time, Kush appeared to dispel them, proclaiming the Prince's benevolence and might, until the name the Prince was everywhere and everyone from little old ladies in the supermarket to national talk show hosts were discussing who—and what—the Prince was.

Little by little, the days slipped away. Bridget's wedding drew nearer, and I was no closer to solving this thing than before.

I rubbed my temples.

"You look like you could use this."

I glanced up to see Ken standing by my desk, holding out a cup of coffee.

I took the cup. "You're not wrong. Thank you."

"Any time. What are you working on?"

"The riots, mostly. By the way, what ever came of that report of an alien sighting and the daycare thing?"

He shrugged. "Nothing. We went back and checked it out. Even had uniforms sitting on the place for a couple days, and nothing unusual."

"Nothing at all?"

"I'm not sure what you're after, but it's not there."

Damn. How could they have not noticed swarms of Nephilim babies? Or had the demons moved them after I found them there? Maybe I should go back again and check things out.

But to get inside, I'd need to go through a portal and bypass the human walls. Bridget would never forgive me if I missed her wedding, even if I was in a coma.

That reminded me, I needed to finish planning her bachelorette party. Damn it. There was so much to get done.

I spread the word among our female coworkers about a party for Bridget at my apartment Friday night and made a few phone calls to other friends of ours.

I couldn't really concentrate at work at that point, so I made a trip to the mall for skeezy lingerie and inappropriately sexual party favors, then to the grocery to pick up drinks and snacks.

I spent the next few days doing more of the same and still getting nowhere on the case. Meanwhile, People were crying out in the streets, and local media was oozing with rumors about the Prince of Phoenix.

Who was he? Friend or foe? Savior or dictator? And when would he reveal himself?

Before I realized it, Friday was upon me, and it was time for Bridget's wedding rehearsal.

Bridget had engaged the gazebo and accompanying clubhouse in Dion's gated community for the wedding, so after taking a few minutes to tidy and decorate my apartment for the bachelorette party afterward, I went to the venue to meet her.

I found her directing a handful of clubhouse employees as they draped tulle and flowers over the various pillars, chairs, and other objects in the room.

"Jack, I'm glad you're here." She paused and rubbed her stomach, which now gave her the appearance of being about six months along. "Will you make sure the chairs are in straight lines? I need to go check on the decorations in the reception room."

I spent the next hour and a half running around giving instructions and helping oversee the preparations.

Bridget looked like she was about to have a coronary when I saw her right before the rehearsal was supposed to start.

"Bridget. Everything is fine. It's all taken care of."

"No, because I have to—"

"Bridge. Stop. You should enjoy your wedding day. Everything is taken care of."

"There's just so much."

"You planned this entire wedding in a few weeks, and you did an amazing job. It's going to be fantastic. But right now you need a break. Come here." I took her into the reception room and opened a bottle of non-alcoholic sparkling something.

"That's for tomorrow."

"You have plenty more. You need this more now." I sat her down at the bar and poured her a glass.

"You know this isn't really wine, right?"

"Yes, but it's more about the soothing motion of sitting down to a drink with your BFF than the alcohol content. Drink."

She took a deep breath and closed her eyes, slowly sipping the bubbly beverage. "You're right. This helps. But we should get back in there. It's time to start."

"It can wait. It's not like they can start without you."

"Good point." She took another sip.

I glanced around. "I haven't seen Dion yet. Is he here?"

"He's coming. I'll be glad when the wedding part is over and I'm just married."

I laughed. "Think how I felt. I'd been planning for months."

She sat up straight. "Oh, Jack, I'm so sorry. I've been so wrapped up in my own stuff, I didn't even stop to think about how hard all this must be for you. I'm the worst best friend ever!"

I squeezed her hand. "No, you're not. I'm surprisingly okay with it. I've hardly had time to think about it, actually."

"Still, I'm sorry."

"Bridget, you can't put your own life on hold just because something bad happened to someone else. I want you to be happy."

"Thanks, Jack. And thanks for this." She held up her glass. "You were right. I needed it. Let's go do this thing."

She stood and led me to the other room.

A moment later, chills ran up my spine and my stomach started roiling.

Dion was here.

FIFTY-THREE

Dion sauntered through the door, followed by another exceptionally tall man, although this one was fully human. One of the other basketball players from the team, I presumed. Smart move on his part. It made his cover as a human guy more believable if he had ordinary human friends.

"Honey, you're here." Bridget beamed and went to kiss him.

Dion smiled at me over her shoulder, gloating pleasure pulsing from him as thickly as his trendy cologne.

What had he done to her? How did she not see through him?

I took a deep breath and smiled. "Shall we get started?"

The rehearsal was pretty straightforward, and afterward Dion treated the wedding party and Bridget's family to a fancy dinner at a nearby restaurant.

Conversation was stilted, with Dion and his friend carrying most of the conversation with talk about basketball.

Bridget's mom, sitting next to me, edged her chair a little closer and leaned in, momentarily dropping her usual regal posture. "How are you, dear? Bridget told me you were... ill after your intended passed away."

I smiled at the sensitivity with which she'd asked about my time in the looney bin. "I'm doing much better, thank you. Getting back to work and into a normal routine has helped."

She smiled, her thin lips and normally aloof eyes looking almost warm. "I'm glad to hear that." She nudged Bridget's father. "Jack says she's feeling better."

Bridget's father paused from examining a grease stain under his fingernail and grinned. "Hell yeah. I knew she'd be fine. She's a tough broad."

I'd seen Bridget's mom reduce the most hardened cop to a puddle with a gaze for language like that, but she smiled indulgently at her husband. How a Scottsdale socialite had managed to stay married to a gruff, blue-collar type for all these years, I'd never understand, but they seemed genuinely happy.

She leaned closer and lowered her voice. "Tell me, what do you think of Bridget getting married this quickly?" Her eyes, a moment ago warm and empathetic, narrowed. Her jaw twitched ever so slightly, the same way it did when Bridget told her she'd passed the police academy exams with flying colors.

I paused, considering how best to phrase things. "It's not how I would've done it, but Bridget seems happy."

"And this man? Do you know much about him?"

How did you tell your best friend's mom that her daughter was marrying an evil, inter-dimensional demon whose only interest in her was as an incubator for his spawn, and who was only going through with the wedding to piss you off? "I haven't had a chance to spend a lot of time with him."

She smiled faintly. "It's nice to know I'm not the only one who disapproves."

"I didn't say that."

"I know. And Bridget wouldn't listen if you did. But I'm still glad I'm not alone."

"I'll stick by her even if this ends badly."

She patted my arm. "Bridget is so lucky to have a friend like you."

Dion stood and raised his wineglass. "Thank you all for coming tonight and showing your support by being involved in our wedding. I can't wait to start my life with this stunning woman."

He kissed Bridget, but his eyes were on me.

I'd have the last laugh when I killed him. That thought kept the smile on my face.

After dinner, Bridget and I retreated to my apartment, and a short while later, coworkers and friends started to show up. I didn't plan anything formal, but a few drinks in, nobody minded.

We laughed and chatted and showered Bridget with lingerie until late that night, when Bridget finally begged off to go home and rest.

I was just climbing into bed when the familiar sick feeling of the other dimension washed over me. The air seemed to shimmer and I felt Dionysius's presence just on the other side of the wall, in my neighbor's apartment.

No portal opened, and he didn't appear, he just hovered just outside the bounds of my apartment.

Hello, little one. Tomorrow is the big day. Are you ready?

"Just because you're marrying her doesn't make it that big of a deal. You're already sleeping with her, and she's already pregnant, so—"

His laugh drowned out my words. *Oh, you foolish child. Have you learned nothing? All the clues I left for you, all the progress I've allowed you to make, and you still have no idea.*

"No idea about what?"

I stared at the wall where he wasn't quite coming through from the other side.

You'll find out tomorrow.

His presence faded, disappearing into the other dimension.

"Wait! What do you mean? What are you talking about?"

Like he would tell me.

What clues? What did he mean? And what the hell did he mean he'd let me make progress? I'd figured everything out on my own. He hadn't let me do shit. Why would he? Why give anyone a chance to find out anything that might stop him?

Unless he was just that cocky, so sure he'd succeed that he could drop clues and whatever without any fear of being thwarted.

I thought back over everything he'd told me, especially the parts he'd said only to me, through the other dimension, and put it with what I'd learned from Pastor Floyd.

The Prince wanted control of this region. It was geographically important to him, and he'd laid claim to it however many eons ago. Various demonic factions at war with one another had loosened the Prince's hold on this territory, and now he was getting it back.

The Prince's threats were real—he would stop at nothing to have his territory back. Dionysius made that clear.

For whatever cosmic reason, the time was ripe for the governmental shift. Dionysius knew when it was coming, and planned his wedding for that day. Celebrating the Prince's return to power with a celebration of his own? And the Prince—was he a demon? Or was Trent—or Mr. Harding, now that Trent was gone—the Prince?

The demons' plot was coming together. Everything hinged on what happened the next day, and I still had no idea how to stop it.

Something tickled the back of my mind as I drifted off to sleep. Something Dionysius had said that I couldn't quite remember. Some clue he'd given me that was buried in all the other information, but that drifted away before I could catch it.

I woke to the sound of my phone ringing a little after four in the morning. Who would call me this early? "Hello?"

"Jack? It's Isaac. I need you down at the hospital right away. In an official capacity."

"I'll be right there."

I slipped into jeans and a T-shirt, grabbed my badge and gun, and hurried to the hospital.

The lobby of the maternity ward was in turmoil. Doctors and nurses scurried back and forth shouting orders and calming panicked civilians.

I flashed my badge and pushed through the crowd until I got to the nurses station. "Where's Dr. Reyes?"

By now I was a fairly familiar figure to most of the nursing staff, and the girl on duty led me back toward the nursery. Even as we walked, I felt the chills wracking my body, the nausea threatening to make me hurl all over the pristine white floor. Demonic presences—hundreds, maybe thousands of them—hovered close by.

Isaac was in the nursery when we got there. "Jack, thank God."

"What's going on?"

"I have no idea, but it's big. All of a sudden this morning, all the girls you brought in after that raid went into labor. All of them, at the same time. On top of that, we've had literally hundreds more come in, women who went into labor and came in on their own, and all with those abnormal pregnancies."

"Holy—"

"We're doing what we can, prioritizing C-sections based on the size of the baby and the progression of labor, but we simply don't have the manpower. Half a dozen women have already given birth on their own. Two died during labor and we rushed the others to ICU."

"Can't you send them to another hospital? Or get more doctors on duty?"

He shook his head. "Every hospital in the city is experiencing the same thing. Every doctor on staff has been paged, not just OBs. And it's not just manpower, it's space. We're running out quickly.

"This is a nightmare."

He nodded. "I'm afraid this may be just the beginning. I've gotten calls from birthing centers and cops and concerned citizens—there are thousands of these things about to spawn. Things are about to get much, much worse."

FIFTY-FOUR

I looked around the nursery, felt the pervading sense of evil pulsing from six cribs, saw the too-old eyes staring at me with malice. "What do you need me to do?"

Isaac ran a hand through his dark hair. "Help keep order. The parents of those girls and the loved ones of everyone who has come in with premature labor are out there in total chaos."

"I'll do what I can."

I called the station for backup. By now, they had all heard of the hospital pandemonium.

"You're already there?" the captain asked. "Excellent. Do what you can, I'll send as many officers as I can spare to help out. It's not going to be many, though. There's more rioting, all over the city, and no sign of the Prince or Kush or any of his minions to calm things down. National Guard is already working hard, but they've got their hands full, too, so there's only so many they can spare for delivering babies."

I hurried to the lobby. All hell was breaking loose as panicked family members demanded to know how their loved ones were faring and the stream of laboring women, screaming in pain, grew thicker.

It wasn't hard to spot the families of the two women who had died. One couple was huddled in a corner of the room, weeping softly. I guessed they were one of the girls' parents. Near them stood a man,

264

early twenties, who was raging at the nurse behind the desk, demanding to see the doctor who'd killed his fiancée.

Breathe, Jack.

One thing at a time.

I needed someone I could count on, whose strength I could trust to buoy my own.

I called Chase.

"Hi, Jack. Wow, where are you? It sounds like a circus in the background."

"I'm at the hospital. I need you."

"I'm on my way."

I hung up and approached the shouting man first. "Hello, sir, I'm Detective Davidson. Can I help you with something?"

"They killed my fiancée! Can you arrest the doctor?

"Let's go somewhere a little quieter where we can talk, okay?"

I led him out of the room and downstairs to the cafeteria and bought him a coffee. "Have a seat. I'm so sorry for your loss. Do you want to tell me about it?"

"She was pregnant, but it wasn't mine. We hadn't had sex. She was very religious and wanted to wait until we were married, so… I mean, I respected her. And then she told me God chose her, that an angel came to her and said she would give birth to a great prophet. At first I was so angry, but the pregnancy progressed so fast, I knew it really was a supernatural child."

"I see. As you probably noticed, there's a lot going on here today, but I promise we will get to the bottom of what happened to your fiancée. In the meantime, there's a chapel at the end of this hallway. A pastor is on his way right now. Would you like to wait there until he gets here?"

The man, deflated from his anger for the moment, nodded dumbly. I showed him to the chapel, then hurried back upstairs to the maternity ward. I had much the same conversation with the weeping couple, whose young daughter had apparently been chosen to be the vessel for some Hindu deity. I escorted them to the chapel, as well, assuring them someone would be along to talk to them soon, and returned upstairs.

Every time I left and came back, the crowd seemed to double in size. I had to take control, and now.

I went to the front of the room and leaned over the nurses' desk. "Do you have a microphone or something that can go over the P.A. in this room?"

She nodded and handed me the phone, then pressed a couple buttons. I stood on a chair and yelled into the mouthpiece. "May I have your attention, please!" My voice bounced off the walls, shaking the windowpanes, echoing back to me through the speakers on the walls. The room went silent except for a handful of whimpers and heavy breathing from the expectant mothers.

"If you're not in labor, I need to ask that you make your way downstairs to the cafeteria or go home. The fewer people in here, the easier it will be on the doctors and nurses to give your loved ones the care they deserve."

"What if we don't?" a red-faced woman demanded.

"Then I'll arrest you, and you can wait for news in a jail cell."

She gave a stifled gasp then huffed out of the room.

Apparently the look on my face was enough to convince them I was serious, and a handful of others followed her out. That cut down the crowd by about a fourth. Several people seemed determined enough that they were willing to risk my wrath and stay with the girl they came in with.

I turned around and whispered to the nurse, then spoke to the crowd. "If the person you're with has already been admitted, I need you to follow Natalie here to the conference room down the hall to wait for news."

The young nurse led a flock of them out, away from the maternity ward. It appeared that the only ones left were women in labor and parents or lovers who refused to leave. Even still, the room was packed beyond capacity.

"Only one guest per patient. The rest of you need to go to the conference room. Someone will be there shortly to answer your questions."

Natalie returned and left with the final wave, mainly older men, presumably the fathers of the girls.

With the waiting room cleared somewhat, the nurses had more room to scurry about, admitting patients. For the time being, the laboring girls were forced to remain in the waiting room while they waited for the doctors and nurses to find somewhere to put them.

Beds were brought out of storage and crammed into patient recovery rooms.

Every few minutes a doctor emerged, ready to receive the next patient. Quickly, we established a sort of assembly line, with poor Natalie running back and forth from the maternity ward either escorting a family member to the conference room or retrieving someone to come meet their new family member.

The rest of the nurses monitored labor progressions, determining which woman should go next, while I helped each new patient as they came through the door, panicked and in labor, their frenzied escorts reluctantly agreeing to wait in the conference room upon discovering their refusal would result in an arrest.

The door swung open.

I looked up, expecting to see yet another pregnant woman.

Instead, I was greeted with the most welcome sight I could imagine at that moment.

"Chase."

My relief was tempered a moment later when Desiree walked through behind him.

Shit.

Chase must've noticed the irritation on my face when I saw her. He gave me an apologetic smile and explained, "I ran into Desiree at the coffee shop. She was there when you called. Thought you might need and extra pair of hands."

"Hi, Jack," Desiree simpered.

"Hi, Desiree. I actually could use the help. Thanks. Would you go with Natalie to the conference room and help keep the peace down there?"

I turned to the frazzled nurse. "This is Agent Escobar with the FBI. Will you explain to her what's going on?"

Natalie nodded and led Desiree down the hall. Desiree looked irritated at being shoved off, but she couldn't very well protest and still save face in front of Chase.

When she was gone, Chase turned to me. "What's really happening?"

"They're in labor. Hundreds of them. Thousands, maybe."

"Who?"

"All the women in the city with demonic pregnancies."

Chase made a choking sound. "*Thousands?*"

I nodded. "Every hospital in the city is being overwhelmed. Every doctor on call has been called in, and several who are supposed to be off. Private practice doctors, OBGYNs, midwives with hospital privileges, everyone. Every bed in this ward is filled, and beds in the rest of the hospital are filling up fast. And that doesn't even take into account the ER rooms that are being filled because of the rioting."

"How? Why? How can they all be in labor at once?"

"I have no idea. I haven't had time to try to figure it out. I'm just trying to keep chaos from overwhelming this ward."

"What do you need from me?"

"Two girls have already died today. I'm afraid there will be more, but for now, their families are downstairs in the chapel. One is the fiancé of one of the girls who died, and then there's a couple, the parents of the other. For now, I think they just need someone to talk to."

He nodded. "You got it. I'll check in with you in a little bit." He squeezed my arm, ever so lightly, and hurried away.

I didn't even have time to catch my breath before one of the girls in the room started screaming. Blood pooled between her legs.

FIFTY-FIVE

The girl screamed again, and her mother, by her side, fainted.

Panic spread through the room, causing a palpable wave of fear. I'd seen the havoc that could be caused when a whole group got worked up. These girls were in enough danger as it was. The last thing I needed was a mob of them trampling each other in their desperation.

I beckoned to one of the nurses. "Get her out of here. Into a room, even a storage closet if need be. Anywhere but in front of all these other girls. I'll take care of her mom. And have someone clean up this blood as soon as possible."

I lifted the mother and took her into the hallway. Out in the lobby, where the maternity ward branched off from the other wards, there were a few chairs. I sat her in one and rubbed her wrists until she revived.

"Brittany? Where's my baby?"

"She's with the doctor now."

"Is she going to be okay?"

I wished I could tell her yes, everything was going to be fine, but I couldn't know that for sure. "I'm going to need you to go down this hall here and wait in the conference room. Someone will come get you when they know anything."

Once she was safely tucked away, I went back to the maternity ward. A janitor was wiping away the last traces of blood, and for the moment the room seemed relatively calm.

Isaac emerged a few minutes later. Dark circles shadowed his eyes and the lines in his forehead seemed more pronounced. He walked over to me and enfolded me in his arms. His breath came in shallow hiccups.

I hugged him tightly. "What happened?"

270

"We lost two more. We just couldn't get to them in time, and the births were so... traumatic." He trailed off, his voice breaking.

I just stood and held him until his breathing evened out. At last, he relaxed his grip on me and pulled away so there was a little space between us but his arms still encircled me.

He leaned down and touched his forehead to mine.

Our lips were close, so close. His warm hands moved slowly, caressing my back, his chest expanding and pressing against mine with every breath.

I traced small circles on the muscles of his shoulders with my fingertips, my breath coming in little gasps.

He leaned in closer. Almost automatically, my lips rose to meet his, connecting softly at first, lightly brushing against each other. Warmth spread through me, filling me with a faint tingling.

I pulled him tighter against me, kissing him more deeply.

His mouth opened onto mine, desperate, hungry, needing. I returned the kiss with equal passion, letting the warmth of his touch wash away the tension of the morning.

At last he pulled away and smiled down at me. "A hospital lobby full of unnaturally pregnant women is not exactly how I imagined us having our first kiss."

"You imagined our first kiss?"

He winked. "Among other things." His smile faded quickly, though. "I still need to inform those families."

I reached up and touched his face. "Let me do that. You go get a cup of coffee and take a break."

"I don't have time for a break."

"You should know better than anyone the importance of pacing yourself. You can't afford *not* to take some breaks."

He chuckled. "Using my own logic against me is cheating."

"I'm okay with that. Go take a break, and I'll inform the families."

"Fifteen minutes, that's it."

"Deal."

He leaned in to kiss me once more and I immediately thought of Chase. If I'd thought about it before, I would've said Chase was the one I'd prefer to pursue a relationship with, but after that kiss...

Not to mention, Chase could barely stand to touch me. How could I pursue something with someone who couldn't even give me a hug or hold my hand, let alone anything else?

Empty. Like I wasn't human. That's what he'd said. How was a girl supposed to overcome that?

But that was a problem for another day. I had a job to do.

I got the information about the deceased girls from the nurses and made my way down to the conference room. "Mr. and Mrs. Rodriguez, will you come with me, please?"

I showed them to a small office that Isaac said I could use. "Please have a seat. I'm so sorry to inform you, your daughter had a very complicated labor. I'm afraid she didn't make it."

Mrs. Rodriguez burst into tears and Mr. Rodriguez stood up, stomping around the room. He cursed, alternating between English and Spanish.

I gave them a few moments to absorb their grief before continuing. "There's a chapel downstairs, and a pastor is available if you want to talk to someone. A doctor will be along to explain what happened in a little while."

I repeated the scene with the other set of parents.

Desiree caught me before I could return to the waiting room. "What in the world is happening in there? How is it even possible to have so many people go into labor at once? And the things they're saying in there—most of them have some convoluted story about a god or angel or alien being the father of these children."

"That about sums it up, actually. I don't have much more information than that at this point, but the babies don't seem entirely human."

"How is that even possible?"

I shrugged. "Maybe we can talk after all this is over. I need to get back."

By early afternoon the hospital was jammed with more than four hundred demon-spawn babies. Twenty women had died, some during childbirth and some shortly after, despite being rushed to the ICU. Several more were in critical condition, even some of those who'd had C-sections, simply because their small bodies were not yet mature enough to handle the trauma.

And still they came. As soon as one was admitted, two more came through the doors.

Isaac invited me into the break room. "You look exhausted. Sit."

I sat and he handed me a cup of coffee. He prepared one for himself and sat beside me. Sometime mid-morning my backup had arrived but there was still more than enough work to go around. Many were downstairs helping to maintain order in the ER, which was as packed as we were.

I leaned my head against the wall behind me and closed my eyes. I'd broken up more than one fight today between people lashing out in terror and anger because of their situations. I'd even made a couple of arrests when they couldn't be talked down. And, of course, the media had gotten wind of the situation, and the parking lot was jammed with reporters, accosting anyone coming or going.

I'd set up a perimeter and positioned officers to enforce it, but I couldn't make them go away or keep them from interviewing people who had come out.

Isaac rested his hand on mine and I adjusted mine to interlock our fingers.

"How are you holding up?" he asked.

"I feel like I'm about due for another coma."

He chuckled. "Me, too. How many more, do you think? Women, not comas."

I smiled, despite the situation. "Who knows? There's already more than I could've dreamed. I mean, I knew there were others out there, like Chet and the guy Trent was chasing, who had kidnapped and spawned, but I had no idea there were so many who weren't kidnapped."

I closed my eyes. "All these girls were willing to incubate these creatures. Some are just dumb girls who got sweet-talked into bed, but an overwhelming number have the same story of a divine encounter and a willing choice to be impregnated. And if all these girls are here, how many more are dying in agony in houses around the valley, in the care of demons who are only interested in the spawn and don't care if the girls die in the process?"

Isaac shook his head. "I don't know."

"And what about the ones who were never missed at all? Runaways and others who traded their bodies for a little security and are now dying alone in agony after the babies are torn from them?"

A shudder rippled through him, making my hand tremble with his.

"How is Bridget?" he asked. "Did she go into labor, too?"

"Not that I know of. It's too early for her, anyway."

"That doesn't seem to matter. Even the ones who are coming early still seem to be healthy. Is the wedding still on?"

I nodded. "As of the last time she texted me about an hour ago. I need to go get ready, but I hate to leave when things are still so crazy here."

"You've been here all day. We've got enough other cops around to take care of it. You need to be with your friend."

I squeezed his hand. "Thank you."

I sat with him a few more minutes, until he got up to get back to work, then made my way downstairs.

I stopped in the chapel to see Chase first. Desiree was there, sitting next to and holding the hand of a grieving mother.

I should've known she'd gravitate back toward Chase. At least she looked like she was being helpful. Apparently she was only a bitch to me.

Chase stood when he saw me and came over. "Hey, how's it going up there?"

I shrugged. "Same. They've started sending people home to recover if their surgeries were uncomplicated because they just don't have enough space. I'm leaving, though. I have to go get ready for Bridget's wedding."

Regret washed over his features. "Oh, I'm so sorry. I know I told you I'd come, but with everything going on—"

"It's okay. You're needed more here."

"Are you sure? I hate breaking my word."

I smiled. "Really, it's fine. I release you from your word. No one could've foreseen something like this. I'll call you tomorrow or something."

He smiled and reached out to brush my shoulder with his fingertips. Even that seemed to pain him. The memory of Isaac's hand holding mine, his lips, his arms, every touch that left me tingling but didn't feel quite right because I wanted it to be Chase, washed over me and filled me with frustration with that one pained glance.

I turned away quickly. "See you," I called over my shoulder as I hurried from the chapel.

Reporters mobbed me as soon as I walked out the door. "Excuse me, were you in the maternity ward?"

"Can you tell us what's happening?"

"Is this an alien invasion?"

I shoved past without a word, hurrying across the parking lot to my truck.

How had rumors started already about alien invasion? Somebody made the link between the riots and the births? Or had one of the many demons said something to start the speculation?

The mob of news crews ignored me once I shoved past without a word, looking back toward the door for their next victim.

Except one. One of them was following me.

FIFTY-SIX

I ignored him—I knew it was a him because of the long strides and heavy, non-heeled footfalls—hoping to make it to my truck before he caught up.

It didn't work.

"Excuse me, miss."

I kept walking.

He walked a little faster. "Pardon me, if I could just have a moment of your time?"

Almost there.

But not close enough.

He touched my arm. "I'm so sorry to bother you, I was just hoping I could ask you a few questions."

I turned to face him. "Don't apologize. You're not sorry for bothering me. You're *intentionally* bothering me. You're going out of your way to bother me, in fact."

A wide grin spread over his face revealing perfectly straight, white teeth and deep dimples. His eyes were a bright green, sparkling with mischief.

Wow, he was pretty. I mean, most TV reporters were attractive, but *damn*.

"You got me," he said. "I apologize for my insincere apology. May I ask you some questions anyway?"

He flashed that smile again. I had a feeling he got what he wanted way too often by grinning like that.

I fell for it anyway.

I gave one overly dramatic sigh, though, just so he'd know how much of an inconvenience it was. "Fine."

276

He beckoned to a cameraman who bustled over and aimed his camera at me.

"I'm Scott Teagan, Live at the Site."

"I don't really care." Let his viewers make of that what they would. "What do you want to know? I have places to be."

He glanced down at the badge I had stuck to my hip.

"Could you tell us a little of what is going on inside, officer?"

"It's *detective*. And what's going on is that doctors and nurses are working their asses off caring for patients, just like they do every day."

"Yes, but there seems to be a significantly higher rate of incoming patients, particularly women in their teens, in labor."

"Does there?"

He grinned again, but there was an edge to his smile. "Yes, there does. Were you in the maternity ward?"

"I've been all over that hospital."

"Including the maternity ward?"

"Yes."

"So you saw these patients. Is it abnormal for there to be so many all at once? And is there a possibility these pregnancies are alien in nature?"

"I'm not a doctor, and I've never had a baby, so I'm really not qualified to talk about what's normal."

"Are these women pregnant with alien offspring?"

"I have seen nothing that would make me believe there is extraterrestrial involvement."

Technically that was true. Inter-dimensional was different from extra-terrestrial.

"So if there's nothing abnormal going on, why are you here?"

"I'm just helping out."

"We've seen at least a dozen different officers, and there's a police perimeter set up around the hospital. Are they all just helping out, too?"

"You'd have to ask them."

"What specifically were you doing to help out?"

"I was helping to maintain order."

"So there's disorder?'

"No, Einstein, there's not, because I was maintaining order."

"But there's a worry that there might be disorder, or the cops wouldn't be here to help maintain it."

"There's always the potential for disorder. The world is a chaotic place."

"Is there anything else you can tell me about what's going on in the maternity ward?"

"You mean besides women having babies? That about sums it up."

"Has anyone died?"

"People die every day, especially in hospitals. Beyond that, you'll have to wait for an official statement from the hospital."

"So there have been deaths due to this phenomenon."

"What phenomenon?"

"The women having babies."

"What's phenomenal about women having babies? It happens all the time. Been going on for thousands of years, actually."

"These babies may be extra-terrestrial and the women all going into labor simultaneously is decidedly abnormal."

"Is it? I wouldn't know."

I could see his irritation mounting and smiled slightly. He'd be lucky to get two minutes of quality viewing from this interview. Any second now, he'd realize I was better at this than he was and stop wasting time.

He flashed that gorgeous smile at the camera and then at me. "Thanks so much for your time, Detective."

He turned to the camera. "Once again, this is Scott Teagan, Live at the Site."

He waved the cameraman off and walked with me as I continued toward my truck. "You're good."

"I know."

He laughed. "And spunky. I like that."

Spunky? Really? "Look, Twinkie, I know you're probably used to women telling you anything you ask, but I'm a trained detective. Moreover, I think your flirting is obnoxious, not cute. Please go away."

He stopped and the grin faded. "I'm sorry, Detective. You're a professional. I shouldn't try to ply you with cheap tricks." He stuck out a hand. "Thanks for your time."

I gave him a curt handshake and started to turn away.

He held on. "Oh, Detective?"

I turned back, ready to burn him up with fire from my eyes. "Yes?"

He handed me a business card. "If you do decide to talk to the press, I hope you'll call me first."

I smiled but didn't make any promises.

***

By the time I got home and showered, I only had barely enough time to meet Bridget at the clubhouse. She'd had appointments all day getting her hair and nails done and getting through her other wedding preparations. I was supposed to go with her, but she'd understood why I couldn't make it. I had time to get there for pictures, two hours before the ceremony.

I pulled my hair up into a simple updo and slipped into my dress. It was a little loose—I must've lost some weight while I was catatonic in a demon dimension, but it still looked great. I could kiss Bridget for not making me wear something hideous.

For about the millionth time, my heart tightened as I thought about this farce of a wedding and how there was nothing I could do to stop it. How long would it last before he broke her heart? Until the baby was born? Or would it be worth it to Dion to keep her around after that? Could she bear more than one spawn?

I had no idea what a pregnancy like that did to human bodies. The demons just let the girls die, so I wondered if one pregnancy was all the girls could do.

Whatever happened, I'd be here for her. She wouldn't have to do it alone.

A blast of hot air struck me as I walked out of my apartment. Ridiculous. Even in Phoenix, where it routinely stayed hot well into the fall months, we shouldn't be having this kind of heat wave in the middle of November.

Even running behind schedule as I was, I still beat Bridget to the clubhouse. She breezed into the preparation room a few minutes after I did, panting for breath. "I can't believe how hot it is. I'm melting, here. And I'm late. There's no way we're going to start on time."

"Breathe. It's going to be fine." I handed her a cold bottle of water. "Cool down a little and then we'll get you into your dress."

She breathed deeply and chugged her water.

"Slow down or you're going to need to pee half-way through the ceremony."

She snorted, spewing her water. "Oh, Jack. What would I do without you?"

"Your life would be way more boring, that's for sure."

She smiled. "No doubt. Okay. Let's do this thing."

Bridget stripped out of her oversized T-shirt and leggings, and we went through the process of trying to get her into the various layers necessary to look good in a wedding dress. Especially pregnant.

I helped her touch up her makeup and hair and stood back to take a look. "You look radiant. You're the most gorgeous bride I've ever seen."

"Really? Even with this ginormous baby bump? I can't believe how big he is already."

"He?"

She smiled. "Dion is convinced it's a boy, so that's what I've been going with. I guess we'll find out in a few weeks."

A few weeks? Did she know how soon she'd be giving birth? What had Dion told her?

"When we have the ultrasound. They can tell really early these days."

I smiled. "Technology, huh?"

She nodded. "Crazy, right? You're sure I look okay?"

"Stunning."

She threw her arms around me. "I love you, Jack."

We stood there for several moments before I pulled away. "I'm going to get mascara all over your dress if I'm not careful."

A knock at the door saved us from further sentimentality. I opened it. A petite brunette stood there holding a camera almost as big as she was.

"Come on in," I said.

Bridget beamed as the woman started snapping casual shots.

"Okay, maid of honor, you get in there, too. Help her touch up her mascara. That's perfect. Okay, mime zipping up her dress. Perfect."

After a few dozen shots of Bridget and a few dozen more of the two of us together, we made our way out to the main hall for the formal shots.

Forty-five minutes later, the photographer was done posing Bridget and me and brought out Dion and his best man—another player, a guy named Kirk, and the family. Dion, of course, had no family, but Bridget's parents posed and smiled dutifully.

Finally, we were bustled back to the changing room so the guests could file in and be seated. It was a small wedding, people from work, some old friends that she'd kept in touch with, and local family members, mainly. Therefore, I was shocked when I stepped out of the room to grab a drink and saw press vans and reporters in the lobby.

Including Scott Teagan.

I stalked toward him and grabbed his arm. "What the hell are *you* doing here?"

"My job. Reporting the news."

"It's a wedding. A small, private wedding. What news?"

"Not just any small wedding, Detective." His eyes raked over me. "You clean up nicely."

"Back to the point, Twinkie."

"This is the shotgun wedding of the Phoenix Suns' top player. That's why I'm here. I was invited. One of the very few members of the press to be asked by Dion himself. The thing at the hospital this morning was a bonus. Anyway, what are you doing here?"

"I'm the maid of honor."

"Small world. Hey, maybe after, we—"

"Don't even think about it."

He grinned. "Retracted. See you inside."

I got my drink and went back into the room with Bridget. "Did you know the press is here?"

She gave me a look like I was utterly insane. "Dion is the Suns' top player. We had to invite some press, or we would've been mobbed. Better to invite the few we want and stave off some of the nightmare. Who all is here?"

"You know I don't know the names of newscasters. The only one I know is Scott Teagan, and that only because I met him this morning."

Her grin widened. "He's here? That is so cool. I've had a celebrity crush on him for years. Is he as hot in person as he looks on TV?"

"He's pretty hot."

"Awesome."

A moment later, the wedding coordinator came in. "It's time. Jack, you're up first. Just like we practiced."

She shoved my bouquet at me and escorted me to the back of the hall. I started the long walk down the aisle and took my place at the front, across from Dionysius and his best man, Kirk.

The nearness of Dionysius made me queasy, but I pushed it aside.

The feeling grew worse, though, as several more presences, hovering just out of reach on the other side of the dimensional wall, gathered around him. I'd be lucky to make it through this without throwing up all over the stage.

A thought slammed into my mind like a round from a 9mm.

The thought I'd been trying to catch the night before, the tiny piece of information I hadn't yet put into place.

Dionysius had said his son would rule with him.

He didn't *serve* the Prince. He *was* the Prince.

FIFTY-SEVEN

Bridget appeared, looking radiant, and walked slowly forward to take her place at Dion's side.

I tried to catch her eye, to warn her, but she didn't even see me.

My heart thundered through my dress. He picked this for his wedding day because it was also his coronation. How had I not seen it before? And if he was here, that meant whatever he had planned was unfolding at that very moment.

The minister began to speak. I gulped back my rising terror, frozen.

The ceremony was simple, direct, not too long, and almost before I realized it, Dion pulled Bridget into his arms and kissed her.

Noises outside the building broke the kiss apart. Yelling, shouting, glass breaking. A moment later, rampaging giants broke into the clubhouse.

Bridget turned to stare at them, her fair skin turning red despite the layers of makeup she wore. Her hand clenched her bouquet and she screamed, "You're ruining my wedding, you bastards!"

Immediately they silenced. The whole mass of Nephilim stood still, gazing intently at Bridget, and bowed their knees. One of them said, "I am sorry, my Queen. We only want to protect you."

What the hell?

A man in the audience stood. No, not a man. A demon. He pointed at Bridget. "You're the leader of the giants! You're the one who caused the riots, the one who has been destroying the city!"

Gasps rose up around the room, people staring from Bridget, who they knew and loved, to this man. News cameras zoomed in on both of them.

"What the hell are you talking about?" Bridget demanded.

"They obey you, they call you their Queen. You're responsible for this! The Prince will take care of it. He will save us from your people!"

Dion took a step back so he was behind her and put one hand on her shoulder. He still had the lapel microphone on from when he'd recited his vows, and he spoke loudly enough to be heard over the din. "I should have known. I thought you loved me, but you must have known who I am. I thought today would be the day I got to not only share my life with you, but to announce my true identity. Now only one of those will be true."

Bridget tried to turn to look at him, but he put his hands on either side of her, pinning her against him.

"Dion? What's going on?" she asked.

Dion looked out at the cameras. "Today marks the beginning of a new era in your civilization. At this moment, the children of this succubus are being born all over the city."

A ball of cold fear formed in my stomach.

Bridget squirmed, clearly trying to extricate herself from his grasp, but he was much too strong.

"She intended to use them to destroy and dominate you, but I will use them to bring peace."

Bridget elbowed Dion in the stomach, but he didn't even seem to feel it.

"Why you? And how?" the demon who had denounced Bridget demanded.

"Thousands of years ago this province was given to me to rule, and I have done so faithfully. I am the Prince of Phoenix."

Gasps rose up around the room.

Dion shook Bridget's shoulders.

She whipped her head back, headbutting his chin, but again, he scarcely even moved from the impact.

"This creature thought to usurp my rule," he said, clutching her to him, "but I care too much about the people of this land to allow it. As with many predatory animals, the only way to gain their respect is to take their place as leader."

My hand went to my hip. Of course, I hadn't worn my gun.

"As I said, this is my land. You can join me, serve me as your rightful ruler, or…"

Bridget screamed.

Bright red stained her pristine white dress, under her stomach, spreading in a thick wave down her legs.

FIFTY-EIGHT

"Bridge!" I lunged toward her and was thrown back by an invisible force.

A demon in the other dimension, one I could feel but not see, blocked me from getting to her.

Bridget continued to scream as blood pooled at her feet.

I struggled to get past, but two demons reaching through from the other dimension held me in place.

Dion wrapped one arm around Bridget's waist. His hand no longer looked human—it was the clawed gargoyle hand of his other-dimensional self. At least, that's how it looked to me. I had no idea what anyone else could see.

He drew one finger across Bridget's stomach, slicing through her dress with his claws, tearing a gaping hole in her stomach.

The putrid stench of sulfur and death and vomit permeated the room as the guests reacted in horrified silence to Dion slicing open his bride.

Bridget's terrified, agonized scream was the only sound that could be heard as Dion reached inside her stomach, pulled out his son, and held the freakish, six-fingered monstrosity aloft.

With his other hand, he palmed Bridget's head.

Faster than my eyes could follow, he wrenched it.

The loud snapping of her neck cut off her screaming, and she fell to the floor in a bloody heap.

Kirk, the best man, lunged toward Dion, reaching for the baby. Dion reached out with his free hand and sliced a gash through Kirk's chest. He stumbled backward, blood spurting from the wound, dead before he hit the floor.

Tears streamed down my face as I pushed against the invisible monsters that held me.

"As I was saying," Dion's voice rose above the clamor, "you may obey me as my loyal servants, or, like my lovely bride, suffer my wrath."

The army of Nephilim fell prostrate, all chanting "We serve you, Master!"

The air behind Dion shimmered as one of the demons on the other side ripped open a portal. Dion stepped through, carrying his squalling spawn. A moment later, I was released as the demons followed Dion to wherever he was going.

I rushed to Bridget's side, but it was far too late. She was dead the moment I made Dionysius my enemy. She was right—I always waited too long, doubting myself. The way I'd done with taking the Detective exam. The way I'd done with my own wedding. And now with hers.

My indecision had gotten her killed.

"Somebody call 911," I screamed. The sound of my voice broke the spell over the crowd, and pandemonium broke loose. Guests screamed and trampled over one another to get away, only to be attacked by Dion's Nephilim.

News crews seemed torn between trying to escape and continuing with the coverage of the event. More than one person threw up.

The only one who seemed even remotely composed was the reporter from the hospital, and even he stared around the room with a dazed expression.

I sat holding Bridget's body, screaming for someone to call an ambulance, even though I knew it was too late. Her mother had fainted, and her father knelt over her, trying to revive her.

Half the guests were cops, so they helped corral the guests to one end of the room. Several were carrying guns and opened fire on the Nephilim.

"Hearts and heads," I yelled.

A few went down, and the rest fled, though whether from fear or by prearranged design, I couldn't tell.

"Get everyone out of here," the captain ordered some of the other officers. "Get them to safety." He pushed his way through the crowd and came up to me. "What the hell was that? How did he do that?"

"I can't explain right now. Stay with her."

"Jack, she's gone."

"I know." I stood. "Please, just stay until the ambulance takes her away."

He nodded. "What are you going to do?"

My inaction had killed my best friend. I would not let my own fear and uncertainty be the cause of any more deaths.

I looked at the captain. "Whatever I have to."

I stalked toward the back of the building and stopped in front of the reporter. "Hey, Scott. You awake in there? I need you."

His focus landed on me, his eyes taking in the blood that covered my dress and hands.

"Scott. Are you okay? Can you help me?"

He nodded. "Yeah, I'm good."

"You sure?"

He inhaled and nodded again. "I've seen some pretty weird stuff during my career. I can handle it."

"Good. Is that thing still rolling?" I nodded toward the camera.

"Yes."

I stood in front of it. "My name is Detective Jack Davidson. What you just witnessed was the culmination of a plot by inter-dimensional creatures who have invaded our world. I've been working on uncovering their plan for several weeks now."

I willed my features to remain calm, reassuring.

"What I can tell you is this: these creatures are not to be trusted. They are breeding with human women to create a hybrid race that will serve as their army. You can identify these half-breed creatures by their huge size and by the presence of six fingers on each hand."

I paused to collect my thoughts.

"The man who calls himself Dion, or the Prince, is a creature known as Dionysius. He has laid claim to this city. He is *not* a savior. The army of giants that has been terrorizing this city are not peaceful, nor are they his enemies. They are *his* children and the children of his followers. This scene was an elaborate setup designed to gain your trust. He is the enemy. He is the evil one. He is not your savior. He is a demon who plans to hold this territory and govern it for his master. Don't believe a word he says."

I stalked back toward the front of the room.

Scott Teagan recovered enough of his senses to jog after me. "Detective, wait. Where are you going?"

"I'm going to end this, once and for all."

FIFTY-NINE

"How?" Scott Teagan followed me up the aisle. "How are you going to stop it?"

I paused. "You want an exclusive? Here's a tip." I grabbed a wedding program from one of the abandoned chairs and scribbled down Chase's phone number and the address to Nancy's daycare. "Call this man and tell him I said to meet me at this address. Bring your camera and wait for me. I'll be there as soon as I can."

I turned and walked through the portal Dionysius had used.

I stood on the other side and looked around, getting my bearings.

It was already getting dark in the real world, which meant here it was hard to see anything at all.

Careful examination of the ground confirmed that Dionysius and those with him were headed toward the daycare.

There was no way I could take all of them on by myself. Even if I got lucky and managed to push a few of the Nephilim spirits through portals, that didn't do anything about the Nephilim that were still living or the demons.

I needed a way to attack them.

At least if they were in my dimension, I could shoot them. I'd need way more ammo than I had, though. The rioting had proved that. I needed backup of some kind. I needed... No, that would never work.

Would it?

It was my only shot.

I ran to my apartment and jumped out of the fourth dimension just long enough to retrieve the piece of table leg that I'd pulled off the gurney in the other dimension. This could hurt them, at least in their own dimension. If my other plan didn't work, this would be my only shot.

I strapped on my gun, stuck my backup gun in an ankle holster, and grabbed extra ammo.

Taking a deep breath, I jumped back through the portal.

I had a long way to go, and only my willpower to keep me awake long enough to do it.

I started off at a run, heading north, willing the ground to bend beneath my steps, and in a short while I passed Las Vegas and headed out into the desert.

I had to backtrack a couple times to find where I'd come from before, but I eventually saw what I was looking for.

An alien structure, sticking out of the desert sand.

I ran toward it, and when I got close, started yelling. "Hey! I need to speak to the regent prince of this territory!"

Two Nephilim spirits guarding the door stalked toward me.

I lunged toward one, opening a portal as I went and swinging the table leg at him, knocking him off-balance and sending him tumbling through the portal.

I stepped just inside my dimension so the second Nephilim spirit couldn't touch me. "I need to talk to your prince." My knees wobbled. "Now. Get him."

The Nephilim disappeared into the building. I stayed in my dimension, even though I knew I'd have an easier time staying conscious and strong on the other side, and drew my gun. Just in case the demon didn't want to talk.

He emerged a few minutes later, a gargoyle as big as Dionysius, but gruffer somehow. Less refined. I didn't know how a giant gargoyle demon could be refined, but Dionysius was, more so than this guy, anyway.

"Are you Tsenaha?"

He nodded. "I am. You've got a lot of nerve coming back here."

"I know. I need to talk to you."

"I could just kill you."

"You could try."

He laughed. "I like you, human. You're something else. What do you want?"

"I have a proposition for you."

One brow ridge raised slightly. "Oh? And what could you possibly do for me?"

"I can get rid of Dionysius."

He guffawed loudly. "Do you know how many centuries I've spent trying to rid this plane of him? More than you can fathom, human."

"Yet you allowed him to keep me hostage here, in your territory."

"A strategic alliance. I can't afford to have him angry with me. My hold on this territory is too tenuous. Oh, yes, I have Sin City, as it's so aptly known by your people, but that cesspool is hardly a fortress. Phoenix, though—Dionysius has dug formidable trenches there. The master will be pleased with him."

"You admit your position would be improved if Dionysius were gone."

He narrowed his feral yellow eyes. "I need not discuss my rule with a worm such as you."

"Fine. Whatever. Your issues with him are your own. The point is, I know where his base of operations is. I know what his plan is, and I can keep him from carrying it out, but I need help."

"What kind of help?"

"I need a weapon of some sort. Something that works in your dimension."

"A weapon isn't going to do much against Dionysius's whole army."

"No but it might do something against him. I'm going to kill him."

"You really are a simpleton." His voice held a note of respect despite his words.

"I have a plan."

"I'm sure you do."

"All I need is a weapon."

"I'm sorry, human. I admire your spunk, I do, but it's not worth the risk. Besides, if I did help you, what's to say you wouldn't use it against me once you're done with Dionysius?"

That was the second time I'd been called spunky today. What was with that? "I have no interest in starting a war with the entire supernatural realm. All I want is to save my city and avenge my friend."

"If Dionysius discovers I helped you… well, he banished his own son for helping you escape. You can only imagine what he'd do to me."

"His what?"

"You didn't know? Oh, yes. The creature that helped you get away from here was Dionysius's offspring. One of the first of this generation. That was a failed experiment if I ever saw one. Dionysius thought if he could impregnate a child of the Chosen Line he'd have a

290

more powerful hybrid, but, as you well know, all it took was a piece of glass through the heart to destroy it. Almost as fragile as a human."

The Chosen Line? Like Trent was one of the Chosen Line, set up to fulfill prophecy? Did that mean, in some weird way, Trent was related to the Eyes?

Could this get any weirder?

"Dionysius never has to know you helped me. If I win, he'll be dead and can't hurt you. If he's alive, well, that means I'm dead, and he won't find out from me."

The creature crossed thick arms in front of its chest. "Suppose I do help you. If, in the extremely unlikely event you kill Dionysius, you'll hand control of Phoenix over to me."

"No deal. I'm not saving it from one monster only to give it to another."

"Then what motivation do I have?"

My knees threatened to buckle and my mind felt like I'd had one-too-many drinks. I could not, under any circumstances, allow him to see weakness. I stiffened and slapped one palm with the demon table leg. "It's a sweet deal as-is. Dionysius is out of the way so you can plot whatever schemes you want, and I won't stop you."

"You couldn't stop me anyway."

"I can survive in your dimension without fainting. I've explored this dimension extensively and gained immense control and power here, and I've killed more than one of your minions. You have no idea what else I can do. If you don't help me, I'll still kill Dionysius, and then I *will* come for you."

He blinked.

I figured for a millenniums-old demon, that was a pretty good tell. My existence in the other dimension scared him, and he wasn't sure if I was bluffing.

He growled. "At the very least, I require a truce. If you take Phoenix, we will not be at war with each other. Any plans I make against other demons you'll back up."

I shook my head. "I'll be neutral."

He pondered that for a moment. "Deal."

I nodded. "Good. Now, a weapon."

"Stupid worm. We are immortal. You cannot kill us. There are no weapons that can harm us."

The minion behind him grunted.

"What aren't you telling me?" I asked.

If gargoyles could be constipated, that's how I would've described the look that contorted his features.

291

"So there *is* a weapon?" I insisted.

"There may be a way," the demon grunted. He nodded and beckoned to his Nephilim guard. "Go to the armory and get me the Hamet Sword."

"What's the Hamet Sword? Is that a euphemism for some deadly technology?"

"It's a sword. Spoils of war."

"Which war?"

"The war that has been waged since the beginning of time. I took this sword from my enemy when I fought him for this province. It should help you."

"If it's so powerful, why haven't you used it?"

"I can't."

Before I could inquire further, the minion returned and handed the demon something shrouded in a thick, wool-like cloth.

The demon took it and handed it to me.

I stuck the table leg in my thigh holster and unwrapped the bundle. A leathery scabbard encased it. There was writing on the blade in a language I didn't recognize, but it seemed to almost glow as the lights from the bunker glinted off it.

"A literal sword. You have the advanced technology of thousands of years of demon research and tools and the best you can do is a sword?"

"Idiot human. You asked for a weapon that would work here. Technology means nothing. We designed most of the weapons you have in the first place. But just because it's fancier doesn't mean it's better. The old ways of killing are still the best."

I nodded.

"You must behead him, that is essential. Striking his heart or his brain will only stun him, but perhaps long enough to get the job done."

"Anything else?"

He nodded toward the piece of table leg I held in my hand. "I see you still carry that bit of our technology. Have you noticed how its density and physical makeup change between dimensions?"

"Of course."

"Metal is not the only element to be more solid, more tangible here. You can cause much destruction if you have the right tools."

"Meaning?"

"Fire. A fire on this side will appear as an ordinary fire on your side, but here will become a mass of flames so powerful they will eat through everything in their path, including our walls and buildings. "

"Okay. How do I start a fire?"

"Our buildings harness the world's energy. Earth, fire, water, air. We don't have electricity in the same sense you humans do. Our power comes from channeling the elements. That's how we have light, running water, and so on. The things you take for granted every time you flick on a light switch are things we use, as well, just in a different way."

He paused, as though struggling with how much to reveal to me. "To start a fire, get inside his fortress and destroy the lights. Blue is water, white is air, red is earth, and yellow is fire. Science works the same way here as there. Use fire and a little air to fuel it. Earth or water is likely to put the fire out."

"How do I destroy the lights?"

"With the sword, of course. Now go, before I change my mind."

SIXTY

I strapped the sword to my back and came back through the portal to the demon side, setting off at a run back toward home.

It was fully night by the time I got back, but by this time I had no problem finding my way to the daycare.

It was surrounded. Nephilim and demons on this side of the dimensional wall, and humans, mainly reporters and police, on the other. I got as close as I dared without being seen by the demons and tore a hole between dimensions, climbing through to my own side.

My legs wobbled and my vision clouded, but I didn't have time to faint.

I strode to the parking lot. Chase was there, and so were Isaac, Pastor Floyd, and Desiree. Scott Teagan, along with a handful of other reporters and cameramen, were reporting live, although it didn't appear that they had any idea what they were reporting.

The captain was there with a bunch of other cops from my precinct.

"Jack!" Chase let out a deep breath when he saw me. "Why do you have a sword?"

"I'll explain later."

Isaac ran toward me and gathered me in his arms, planting a kiss on my lips. "I like the sword. It's a good look for you." He kissed me again.

A look of intense frustration crossed Chase's face.

I pulled away from Isaac. "We don't have a lot of time. I have a plan, but it's going to be hard to carry out. Obviously, Dionysius knows we're here, so we don't have the element of surprise. Chase, I'm going to need you, too. There are humans in there. When they come out, I'm going to need you guys to get them to safety, but I'm going to need you to help tell the difference if Nephilim come out with them."

I strode to the captain.

"Jack, what is going on here? Your reporter friend said you'd be at this address, but it's just an abandoned daycare." The captain's gaze landed on the sword hilt sticking up from behind me. "And why do you have a sword?"

I *so* did not have time for this. "Please, Captain. I just need you to trust me on this one. Kill all the Nephilim—the half-breeds—even if they look like children. They're not. They're the beginning of Dionysius's army."

"You want us to do what?" someone asked.

Ken? Where had he come from?

"Kill monsters."

"How do we tell them apart?" the captain asked.

"Look at their hands. Six fingers, abnormal size, misshapen heads, and unbridled rage means they're hybrids."

"We can't kill children," Ken protested.

"They're *not* children. They're monsters. Kill them, or they'll kill all of us."

"What are you going to do?" Chase asked.

I took a deep breath. "I'm going to flush them out."

"How? We can't even get past that force field."

"A hell of a lot of luck."

"Be careful," Ken said. His voice held a note of something. Concern? Yes, and something else, something I couldn't quite put my finger on.

I didn't have time to think about it. "Be ready."

I found the portal I'd made and went through, jogging toward the hole in the corner of the rock wall. Two Nephilim ghosts guarded it. I pulled the sword from its scabbard and crept quietly forward.

The guards looked out over the crowd of humans gathered around with disdain. Clearly, they didn't think we were a threat. And since they weren't worried, they weren't paying much attention. They never even saw me as I slashed. The sword sliced through both of them like an infomercial knife through a tomato.

The sword was heavy, but it seemed to fit perfectly in my hands.

I'd tried fencing once and was totally uncoordinated, the sword unwieldy and my movements awkward. Whether it was the Hamet Sword itself or the difference in the physics of this place I didn't know, but this sword felt fluid, natural, almost like an extension of my body.

I cut through two more guards at the entrance to the building and went inside. The rooms were all filled now, hundreds and hundreds of demon babies jammed into the building.

Each room had two or three humans, running around like frazzled maids, trying to keep up with feeding and caring for the beasts.

Nancy, the owner of the facility, was in one, bustling around, clearly pleased with her role in helping the advanced race fulfill their plans of integration.

I opened a portal and stepped through.

One of the women screamed.

"Calm down. I'm with the police. Come with me now, and you can get out of here before we raid this place."

"We can't get out. We're trapped," she said.

At the same time Nancy said, "Why would you do that? These are peaceful beings. Leave us in peace or suffer Prince Dionysius's wrath."

"How do we get out?" a third woman asked.

"Anyone who wants to escape, gather everyone up and come with me. Quietly."

In a few minutes I had a gaggle of people, both men and women, lined up behind me in the hall. Some of the workers, like Nancy, stayed. She began shouting for Dionysius.

"Let's go," I said to the others, hurrying for the door. I opened it—and ran smack into an invisible barrier.

Damn it.

The door in the other dimension was closed.

One of the women started wailing. "We're trapped."

"Shh!" I ordered. "Wait here." I ran back down the hall to the portal I'd created and jumped through, into the demon dimension, then ran back down the hall to where they waited.

The woman screamed again.

Oh, yeah. She could probably see me, just barely, the way Chase had in the closet at the house where I'd first gone into the other dimension.

I opened a small hole between realities so they could see me clearly through the dimensions, but remained in the demon dimension.

"Are you a g-ghost?" a man asked.

"No. I can't explain now. Just trust me."

I opened the demon door and started ushering them through. "Go to the right. When you get to the force field, follow it all the way to the corner of the lot." I pointed toward the hole. "There's a break in the force field. You can get out there. Police are waiting to help you."

They started running en masse toward the hole in the wall.

Just before the first woman got there, the entrance was blocked by a gargantuan form.

A demon—a real one, not a Nephilim spirit—came through.

He wasn't one I recognized. And he was in the demon dimension, not the human.

Which meant the woman couldn't see him.

"Stop!" I yelled.

She kept running.

"Stop, wait!" Then it hit me. She couldn't hear me, at least not well. I wasn't in her reality. I reached out to create a portal.

It was too late. The demon grabbed her and snapped her neck.

She crumpled to the ground and he stepped over her and reached for the next one.

I ran forward, yelling at the others to stop, even though I knew they couldn't hear me, either. It didn't matter. Seeing two people get their necks snapped by an invisible force was enough to slow them down.

I rushed forward and drew the sword. The demon snarled and raised his hand to block my attack.

The sword sliced a deep gash in his forearm.

The force of the collision sent me stumbling backward, into the rock wall.

He lunged at me, and I swung again, missing him completely.

My shoulder felt like it was burning, but I couldn't pause long enough to check.

The demon lunged again, claws extended, slashing at me. His claws ripped across my forearm.

My grip on the sword wavered. He was so much stronger than the Nephilim spirits.

I swung again. The sword didn't slice through him cleanly. It bounced off, almost like hitting armor.

Before I had time to recover he launched himself at me again and I fell back, landing on my backside, holding the sword in front of me.

The demon had too much momentum. As I fell, so did he, landing on top of me, my sword impaling his chest.

I gasped and tried to push him off me.

He didn't budge.

I pushed again, but he was too heavy. He was quickly crushing my lungs.

I breathed as deeply as I could, focusing on the weird physics of the fourth dimension, and shoved again.

He toppled off as easily as if he were a big feather pillow.

I jumped to my feet.

Cut off his head, Tsenaha had said.

Couldn't be too careful. I sliced through the demon's neck.

In the fourth dimension, his ghost rose up, looking around as though disoriented.

I slashed with the sword, destroying the ghost, then went toward the opening in the wall.

Another demon came through. He wasn't expecting me, and my first swipe of the sword sliced through an arm and into his chest.

Black blood spurted from the wounds.

It wasn't enough to kill him, though.

He struck at me with his remaining hand and knocked the sword to the ground, then came at me.

His giant hand connected with my head, sending me rolling to the ground, crashing against the wall.

I stood just in time to duck away from his fist as it swung toward me again.

I grabbed for the first thing I could get. The demon's severed arm.

I picked it up. The skin was rough and leathery, like a football, and it was heavier than I'd imagined. I gripped it like a baseball bat and swung, smacking him in the head with it.

He stumbled back.

I kept attacking, pushing him back away from the entrance by beating him with the bloody end of his own arm.

He fell backward. I dove for my sword. Snatched it up. Sliced through his neck.

His head rolled along the ground.

I knew what to expect now, and waited for the ghost to emerge from the body. As soon as it did, I destroyed it with the sword.

I ripped open a window into the real world. "Come on!" I yelled at the people who stood like stunned animals. I could only imagine what it must look like from their side of the dimensional wall, watching my almost invisible, ethereal form fighting an unseen foe.

I ran to the hole in the demon rock wall and stepped through. The coast was clear. For now.

"Move!" I yelled.

One of the prisoners stepped toward me hesitantly.

Why did people move like sloths when their lives were in danger?

I ripped open a portal and grabbed him by the hand, dragged him through the hole in the rock wall, and shoved him out toward the captain.

That was all it took to get the others moving. They stumbled through the opening and into the waiting arms of the police and paramedics.

I popped back through to the demon dimension.

Oh, shit.

At least a dozen demons thundered toward me.

SIXTY-ONE

No.

They weren't coming toward me.

They were headed toward the crowd of bystanders littering the parking lot.

Innocents who had no idea what was happening and wouldn't see their deaths coming.

"Hey," I screamed. "I'm right here. Come and get me!"

The whole group of them turned and started toward me.

I ran back toward the daycare, willing my feet over the alien terrain, pausing briefly to make sure the demons were following me and not wantonly murdering civilians. Chase said there were rules, but invading their territory might give them grounds to slaughter.

They were way faster than I was comfortable with.

I ran through the door and into the hall. The screams of unattended demon babies filled the building.

I ignored them and went to the wall that was covered by the eerie, multi-colored lights. Up close, I could see the swirling water, fire, and other things behind the glass.

What had he said? Tsenaha, he told me—yellow was fire. White was air.

I smashed a yellow light with the tip of the sword.

A jet of flame shot out, burning my arm.

I jumped back and a demon grabbed me from behind.

His claws dug into my arms. Talons tore through my flesh and muscles, ripping wider the gashes the other demons had left.

I writhed and swung wildly with my sword. Somehow, I managed to break another yellow light.

I saw it shatter, and I ducked.

The jet of flame passed over my head and scorched the demon.

He screeched, temporarily stunned enough to release his grip on me.

I spun around and lodged the sword in his chest, pulled it out, and swung at his neck.

At first I thought I hadn't succeeded in beheading him—another gargoyle head was in its place.

A second demon had appeared behind the first.

My arm hurt, but not as much as I thought it should have. I glanced down—it was already healing. I had no idea how or why—maybe that was accelerated here, like my strength—but whatever the reason, I'd take it.

I jabbed at the demon with the sword, wounding him, and sent him stumbling into the flame that still poured from the wall.

That bought me a little bit of time.

I ran down the hallway, pausing periodically to smash the yellow and white lights. Bursts of flame filled the hallway behind me, separating me from the demons chasing me.

I opened the doors to the various classrooms and broke lights in each of the rooms. More jets of flame, and a few of air, spurted out of the walls on all sides and devoured the drywall in the real world while melting the metal here.

A demon howled as it charged through the burning hallway.

The jets of flame seemed to have a ripple effect. More lights burst behind me, ones I hadn't smashed. Earth and water along with more fire and air. It seemed that the flames destroyed their own casings as well as the lights around them, as it got hotter and hotter.

The hallway erupted in bursts of steam and swirls of dirt as more of the reservoirs of energy broke, creating quicksand monsters that whipped in every direction.

I stumbled back, away from the torrent of elements.

Through the filter of the dimensional wall, I heard the pained screams of the Nephilim children, their anguished wails like a million fingernails continuously scraping down a chalkboard.

I heard a yell and looked behind me.

The demons still marched down the hall, pushing past each other despite the liquid flame that gushed from holes in the walls.

I destroyed a few more lights behind me and raced down the hall. There had to be an emergency exit around here somewhere.

I pushed through a door into an office. At least, it was an office in the real world. Here, it seemed to be an entrance hall of some sort. A door stood at the other end. In the real world it looked like a storage closet of some kind. Here, though… well, there was one way to find out.

I opened the door, forcing my wounded muscles to obey my will.

A staircase led down to an endless darkness.

The wails of the Nephilim changed. Now they were no longer dying souls, but living spirits. The Nephilim bodies in the human reality had died, and their souls, like that of The Eyes, now roamed the demon reality. And they were coming this way.

I couldn't go back.

Holding the sword in front of me, I went forward, down the stairs, on and on until I reached a tunnel, and then I followed that for what seemed like miles before coming to what appeared to be a central command station. Demons milled about, some watching monitors, others pressing buttons, and still more doing activities I couldn't begin to comprehend.

One monitor displayed an image of the daycare, almost completely burned down now. Nephilim and demons alike streamed from it, surging toward the perimeter wall to escape the flames. The demons in this room didn't appear to care much what happened on the surface. They must've been the demon equivalent of desk monkeys, only recording and monitoring, not acting.

At the other end of the room was a door. I stood just in the hallway, as yet unnoticed, and plotted my route to the other side carefully.

Catch the first one off guard, smash the fire lights on my way past, run through the other door while the control room was in flames.

Of course, I had no idea where that door led. It could dead-end the way the one in Nevada did. Or, it could branch off in a million directions.

I had no way of knowing if there was an escape that way or if I'd have to find a place to hide until the flames died down and the demons deserted this outpost, or if I'd run into a barracks of some sort and be overwhelmed.

My arms throbbed. Blood soaked my dress, the dress Bridget picked out to make me happy, even though I would've worn pink taffeta if she'd asked.

Oh, Bridget. I'm so sorry. I should've said something. Should've done something. I should've killed Dionysius, no matter how badly it would've pissed you off. I failed you.

302

The strain of being in this dimension too long pulled at me, despite my accelerated healing. Or maybe because of it. My body wouldn't last much longer. But I had to keep moving.

Down the hallway behind me, I heard the faint shouts of demons coming my way. Dozens, maybe hundreds of them, would be on me in moments. And sometime before that they'd alert the ones in this room and I'd be trapped.

I didn't have a choice.

I took the sword and scraped it against one of the yellow lights, digging a little hole in the covering. A tiny spurt of flame spat out from the hole. Tiny cracks formed out from it.

I didn't know exactly how the system worked, but based on the jet that had erupted upstairs, I hoped there would be enough pressure to create a time bomb of sorts. I did the same thing on a couple more lights, yellow and white, then ran into the control room.

I swung the sword at the demon nearest the door, sliced off his head, then bolted for the other door.

A second demon gave a shout and launched toward me.

Pain stabbed through me I lifted the sword, and I heard something in my arm tear as I thrust the sword into the demon's head.

My left arm burned with a fire as hot as the one I'd started in the daycare. This had to be the worst muscle tear I'd ever gotten. My arm was now virtually useless, which meant my sword arm was equally so. I could barely heft the sword one-handed, let alone use it effectively, despite how I focused on the altered physics.

I cradled the sword's blade in my injured arm for leverage and used my good arm to slam the hilt into the lights. And then I ran. Straight for the door and into the hallway beyond.

I heaved the sword hilt and smashed more lights, one by one, my movements getting slower and slower.

I could only do a few before my arm got too tired. I couldn't use the sword any more.

With one last surge of energy I slipped it back into the scabbard.

The streams of fire filling the hallway separated me from the demons in the control room, but they'd push through despite the pain in a moment.

At least I had time to put some distance between myself and them. I started to limp forward and something bumped my leg.

A piece of metal.

The table leg. It had come loose when I put the sword back and was dangling from my thigh holster. The lightweight, incomprehensible metal was perfect for this job.

I pulled it out and began smashing yellow lights behind me as I staggered down the hall. It wasn't as effective as the sword, but it at least cracked them. That was probably better. It gave me some time to gain some distance between myself and them before they exploded fiery heat.

Before long, I came to a room. I paused and looked inside. There was a table, much like the one I'd found myself on in Nevada.

Lying on it was a man, unconscious. I walked toward him and almost fainted. *Trent?*

SIXTY-TWO

It wasn't possible. Trent was dead.

At second glance, I realized it wasn't him, but the resemblance was more than a little disturbing.

Brandon Harding. The politician. It had to be.

I patted his face a couple times. "Hey. Wake up."

He opened his eyes briefly, stared at me, and then his eyes rolled back in his head, and he was out again.

Shit.

I couldn't leave him here.

My legs wobbled.

No time to think. I had to keep moving.

A quick glance around the room revealed nothing useful for prodding him awake.

No. Of course not. He couldn't be awake here.

Sometimes I wondered if I was going senile as well as crazy.

I opened a portal and started to drag him through, but he was too heavy, especially given that I was doing it one-handed.

I thought for a moment.

That might work.

I stood right next to him and opened a portal, then stood on the other side of the gurney and pressed against it with my legs, pushing it through the portal.

Once on the other side, the metal bent, sending the man toppling onto the floor of the cavern.

He woke with a jolt and sat up. "Where am I? Who are you?"

306

"I'm Jack. I'm—never mind. I don't have time to explain right now. Can you walk?"

He stood, a little shakily, but he nodded. "I think so."

Darkness started to cloud my vision.

No.

I did *not* have time for a coma right now.

I had to get back in the demon dimension. I gave a quick look around the landscape in the human dimension.

"Go out that door and take a left. Just keep walking, no matter what happens. You may not be able to see me, but I'll be right behind you."

He nodded and hobbled out the door.

I went through the portal to the demon dimension, smashed the yellow lights, and a couple white ones just to make sure there was enough oxygen to keep the fire going, then limped after him down the hall, smashing lights and starting fires.

We passed two more rooms. One was empty, and the other contained a pregnant woman.

Apparently she hadn't been affected by whatever triggered the labors of the women on the other side.

I did the same thing with her as with the man and she, too, woke up once she was back in the human dimension.

"Can you help her walk?" I asked the man.

"Yeah. C'mon, Miss. We're getting out of here."

Behind us, I could hear the pained yells of demons. They were getting closer.

I tore a tiny hole in dimensions so the two prisoners could hear me. "Faster. We have to move."

The tunnel started to incline slightly. Could that mean this was an exit heading toward the surface?

I hoped so.

A few moments later, the tunnel forked. Ahead and to the right was a set of stairs, and to the left was a dark, deserted-looking tunnel.

"Go to the right. Up the stairs," I instructed.

I started to follow them and stopped.

Something tickled the back of my neck, starting faintly and growing until it sent a chill shooting through me.

"Get her up the stairs. I'll be there in a minute."

I took a step down the dark hallway. The sensation grew stronger. A presence I hadn't felt in what seemed like ages.

I ran down the hall until I came to a door.

I tried it, but it didn't budge.

I hit it with the table leg a few times, but still nothing.

One option left.

I pulled the sword from its scabbard, wincing, tears streaming down my face as I bit my lip through the pain. Using my good arm to hold it and my injured one for balance, I wedged it between the door and the frame.

It budged.

I pushed harder. Again a budge, but it wouldn't open.

I was too tired, too worn down, too hurt.

I couldn't do this much longer. I had to get out of here before it was too late.

But he'd saved me when I was in a similar position. I couldn't just—

I was such an idiot sometimes.

I opened a portal right over the doorknob, and when the metal folded, pushed the door open.

I stood there panting. A pair of glowing yellow eyes looked me over, and a wash of confused emotions emanated from a nephilim ghost that seemed so weak it could barely move.

"I'm getting out of here. You coming?"

I walked back toward the fork in the tunnel and started up the stairs.

The Eyes followed closely behind.

The man and woman I'd rescued stood at the top of the stairs, unable to get past the demon door. I was almost to the top of the stairs when I wobbled, almost toppling backward.

The Eyes caught me and steadied me. He put his hands to my head, but instead of my strength buffering him as it had last time, his little remaining strength buffered me, keeping me awake long enough to get to the top of the stairs.

I tried the door, and it opened into a storage closet in the real world.

The man stepped through and opened the human door. "A locker room? Where are we?"

I glanced around. There were no more demon walls here, so I could see everything. "We're at the Talking Stick Resort Arena. Keep moving. Find a phone and call 911. They'll take care of you."

The Eyes and I walked through into the locker room in the other dimension. I turned to him. "Go to my apartment. Dionysius can't reach you there. I have to go back to the daycare." I walked through the ethereal walls and toward the road beyond.

The Eyes followed. "You don't have the strength."

"I don't have a choice. That's where Dionysius will be. I need to end this."

Even from here I could see the blaze, both in this dimension and the other, of the daycare burning. I started to jog that direction, and immediately my knees buckled.

No, no, no. Not yet.

Tears stung my eyes. I couldn't stop now. I would never have another chance. I had to end this. Tonight.

I crumpled to my knees, willing my body not to give out on me.

My arm throbbed, dried blood stiffened my clothes, and every muscle in my body burned.

The Eyes touched my head again, supplying me with a trickle of energy.

"Stop," I told him. "You're almost dead. I can feel it."

"If you die, I'm dead anyway, and if Dionysius wins, I will be tortured beyond any pain you humans and your mortal, finite bodies can imagine. At least this way I'm still alive. Go on. You have to kill him."

"Yeah. I really, really do."

SIXTY-THREE

I pushed to my feet and jogged again toward the blaze. The Eyes followed, though more slowly, weakened by helping me.

The rock wall in this dimension had been torn down in many places. It looked like demons had just barreled through in their attempt to escape, effectively removing the "force field" from the other dimension.

The police had cordoned off the area, but the crowd of spectators had grown to a mammoth size. Fire crews worked to put out the inferno, but the fire in this dimension still fed on the demon structure and the charred bodies of the demons and Nephilim whose human forms had died in the real world and spiritual bodies had died here, so the fire on both sides still raged.

I hobbled to the center of the parking lot, which was an empty space in both dimensions, and ripped a hole to the other dimension.

"Dionysius!"

My voice echoed back to me over the over the barren ground. "It's over!"

Heads turned my direction, the stares of people who didn't notice me passing through walls as I traipsed through the other dimension, but could see me through the hole in the air, settling on me in perplexed silence.

Portals gaped open all over the place, presumably where demons had tried to escape the fire by entering the human dimension. The heat of the Phoenix air matched that of the demon dimension.

Duh. Another thing that made perfect sense now, that I had been too blind to see before. The unnatural heat wave in November. Demons had been ripping holes between realities at an exponential rate as they took their victims and spawn back and forth between realities, building their army.

Much like the fire that raged behind me, the climate of the demon dimension bled through the tears in reality to overwhelm the city. Another reason to end this war. The tears in dimensional walls had to heal so the weather could get back to normal.

"Dionysius!" I hollered again.

Onlookers stared at me through the holes, peeking through tears between universes they couldn't see as I yelled.

"Your army is dead. Your base is destroyed. Your plan failed."

Chills ran up my spine, nausea worse than any I'd felt before rushed over me as a wave of fury and hatred hit me.

Dionysius, terrifying in his snarling gargoyle form, stalked toward me from the rubble heap that had been his base. "Do you really think you are any match for me? You're so tired you can barely stand. You're wounded. And even at your best, you're weak here."

"I killed your entire spawn army. I still have enough in me to kill you, too."

"Foolish worm. Do you think those idiots stupid enough to get trapped and a few half-breeds were the extent of my army? I am still the Prince of this region."

"No, you're not. I'm taking it from you. I'm claiming this province. You and yours aren't welcome here any more."

He snarled, fangs dripping saliva. "It's not that simple. You can't banish me from my own land."

"Then I'll kill you, and by right of conquering you, I'll claim it from you."

I mustered every ounce of strength I had left and drew my sword. My arm still throbbed, but the strength the Eyes had fed me bolstered me and sped up my healing.

I forced the sword up. I needed what little strength I had for leverage and balance.

Dionysius and I circled each other like feral beasts.

"I foiled your plot."

"Idiot. You know nothing of my plan. It is only just beginning. The prophesied one will be my tool, my slave."

"That was your plan? You were trying to rule the world by setting that guy up as your puppet? Is that what you were trying to do to Trent?"

Dionysius's eyes narrowed.

"He found out, didn't he? He figured out that you wanted to set him up to be this false savior so you could rule through him. The call he got that night, it wasn't a random tip. You knew he was trying to thwart your plan and you set him up. It was *you* driving the car. You called on your army to kill him, staged the crash so no one would ever know what Trent knew. Well, congrats. You killed your messiah."

"It doesn't matter. There is another. I have already begun preparing him."

"Oh, you mean Brandon Harding? Yeah, he's not yours anymore, either. I found him, in your tunnels. He's on his way home already, and now he knows about you."

"*What?*" Dionysius bellowed.

"Like I said. Your plan? Over."

"I will *kill* you for this."

"Yeah? Let's do it, then."

He lunged for me and I struck at him with the sword, just nicking his leg.

He snarled and grabbed my injured arm, yanking me toward him.

I screamed, the agony almost making me lose my grip on the sword.

I rolled to the ground away from him, yanking my arm from his grasp, and raised the sword again, jabbing it wildly in his direction.

I poked him a couple times, but didn't do any serious damage.

My strength was waning quickly, and pain blurred my vision.

I was going to die. I knew that with absolute clarity.

But I was going to take him with me.

I pushed myself to my knees. Using the sword to support myself, I stood up. He lunged again.

I parried his fist with the sword, succeeding in carving a long slice in his forearm. Again and again, around in a dance, he attacked and I parried, nicking and grazing him a little at a time, not really injuring him, while I grew weaker and weaker.

A smile parted his lips, and he bared his yellowed fangs.

He could see I was almost done.

He crouched, then leapt, throwing his full weight toward me.

I lifted the sword and stumbled back. I fell to the ground, expecting him to impale himself on my sword, like the other demon had, but the sword bent, folding like paper under him.

Dion, the famous basketball player, rolled over the top of me.

We'd fallen through a portal.

I squeezed out from under him and drew my gun, firing as many shots as quickly as I could at him, which wasn't easy one-handed.

Dion screamed and dove back through the portal.

His body would heal almost instantly there. It was now or never.

Grabbing the sword, I called on the last drop of energy in my body and heaved myself through the portal after him.

Dionysius was already starting to recover. He stretched his limbs and tossed his head, as though shaking out a kink in his neck.

And I had no strength left. I couldn't even lift the sword.

Someone grabbed me from behind, holding my head.

I gasped as energy surged through me, one powerful dose of strength.

The Eyes. When had he gotten here?

I could feel him dying. Any moment now, he would cease to exist. He collapsed.

Somehow, I knew, when he died, I would no longer be able to traverse this dimension. My connection here would be severed, and if I were still here, I'd never get out and no one would ever find me.

The Eyes gave everything he had left so I could kill Dionysius.

I raised the sword with both hands, despite the pain.

Dionysius looked at me. He slowly clenched ant unclenched his fists.

He took a step toward me, unfurling his beastly claws.

I stepped back, gauging the distance between us, planning my next move.

He slashed at me. I raised the sword in a defensive posture, succeeding in nicking his arms, but got a slice in my hand in the process.

He lunged again, sending me back, fighting to keep my balance, to keep from being sliced like a salami. I countered with the sword, injuring him about as fast as he healed.

He snarled and crouched, looking like he was preparing to jump.

I braced for the impact.

He leapt several feet into the air, and I lifted the sword straight up.

He crashed into me, tackling me, but with the sword lodged in his gut.

I focused on the strength I had in the fourth dimension and shoved him off of me, rolling away and pushing to my feet.

Dionysius heaved to his knees, the wound in his side slowing him down.

I took a deep breath and raised the sword.

"This is for Bridget, you bastard."

I swung.

Dionysius's gargoyle head toppled from his body, rolling across the ground.

His body fell to the ground and in its place stood his spirit, still hearty and strong, but only able to exist in this dimension.

"And this is for everyone else." I dove into him, reaching out with my good hand as I went, ripping the fabric of the universe, dragging his spirit with me.

I hit the ground in my own dimension with a heavy thud as Dionysius disintegrated beneath me.

***

Sunlight stabbed my eyelids making me wince. I tried to open my eyes and closed them again immediately to protect them from the glare.

"Jack?"

I forced my eyes open. "Chase?"

His face slowly came into focus. He held my hand. "It's me. How are you feeling?"

"I'm not sure yet. How long was I gone this time?"

"Not long. Only two days."

"I feel like I should be in more pain than I am."

He chuckled. "You're on some pretty powerful medication. You've got broken ribs, deep lacerations, and so many torn tendons and muscles and ligaments in your arm that I can't keep track. They did surgery to repair some of the damage. The rest they'll wait to see if they heal on their own, but you may need more surgeries in the future."

I suddenly realized what I'd only noticed in passing when I first woke up. "You're holding my hand."

"Yes. I've wanted to since the day we met, but every time I touched you, I felt like I was getting drowned in an icy lake. I don't know what changed, but ever since you came back the last time you've felt… normal."

"I know. It was the Eyes. The one I was connected to. It was because of him that I could go there. He's dead now. The connection is broken. That's probably why you can touch me. But that also means I can't go back anymore."

"Good." Isaac strode through the door. "I haven't forgiven you for the last two times you nearly killed yourself doing that."

"But you won't have to," Chase said. "Dionysius is dead."

"Yes," I said. "Completely obliterated."

"So it's over," Isaac sighed.

"Not even close. Dionysius was one small piece in a giant global puzzle. There are countless more like him, all trying to grab hold of their little kingdoms before the prophecies are fulfilled. We took Phoenix back. We won this battle, but I fear the war is just beginning."

Chase nodded, his face solemn. "Then we'll fight."

"No," Isaac said.

Chase and I both looked at him.

"What do you mean? We can't *not* fight," Chase said.

"You feel free," Isaac told him. "But, Jack, you need to sit this one out. I have something to tell you. Something they found when they ran your blood work. You're pregnant."

I gawked at him.

"It's human. I made sure." Isaac smiled at me. "You're almost three months along."

I lay back on the pillows and closed my eyes.

Pregnant?

I was having Trent's baby. I didn't know what would happen in the future, but now I would always have a part of Trent with me.

Whatever came, whatever wars I had to fight, I had something to fight for.

Someone knocked at the door.

"Come in," I called.

It was the captain.

I smiled, until the next person walked in behind him.

Desiree.

I couldn't even wake up from a coma in peace. "Hi, guys. Thanks for stopping by."

"I'm glad to see you're awake," the captain said, reaching out to pat my hand.

"As am I." Desiree smiled her sappy, fake smile. She turned toward Chase. "I'm ready to go whenever you're done visiting your friend."

That explained why she was here at all. Even after everything I'd been through, that petty troll could still get under my skin.

"I brought some of your things," the captain said. "Thought you might want them close." He set my badge on the table, then handed me a cloth-wrapped bundle.

I unwrapped it.

The Hamet Sword.

Desiree reached out to touch it, and the weird, demonic metal bent.

She raised a perfectly sculpted eyebrow. "Why do you have a rubber sword?"

I smiled as sweetly as I could. "It goes with my outfit."

Other Books by Avily Jerome

The Amulet Saga

Acknowledgements

Special thanks to Ben Wolf, who edited this story and helped me fill in a lot of gaps, plot holes, and inconsistencies.

Thank you to Lindsay Franklin, my dear and wonderful friend who tirelessly answers my questions, brainstorms with me, and gives of herself to help me out.

Thanks to Kirk, my amazing cover designer, for bringing Jack to life.

Thank you to my wonderful beta-readers, who eagerly devoured this story and gave me their thoughts for improving it, and to my street team for being excited to share this story with the world.

And, as always, thank you to my husband for giving me the support, time, and encouragement I needed to make this book happen.

About the Author

 Avily Jerome is a writer and freelance editor. She spent five years as the Editor of *Havok Magazine*, an imprint of Splickety Publishing Group. Her short stories have been published in multiple magazines, both print and digital. She has judged several writing contests, both for short stories and novels, and she is a book reviewer for Lorehaven Magazine.

She is also a writing conference teacher and presenter, and she enjoys speaking to local writers' groups and going to SFF cons.

She loves all things SpecFic, and writes across multiple genres. Her writing heroes include Joss Whedon, Robert Jordan, and J.K. Rowling, among others.

She is a wife and the mom of five kids. She loves living in the desert in Phoenix, AZ, and when she's not writing, she loves reading, spending time with friends, and experimenting with different art forms.

www.ingramcontent.com/pod-product-compliance
Lightning Source LLC
Chambersburg PA
CBHW020644030726
47498CB00002B/363